Journey's Lost and Found

Sommerhjem Journeys Series:

Journey's Middle

Journey's Lost and Found

Journey's Lost and Found

B. K. PARENT

iUniverse, Inc.
Bloomington

Journey's Lost and Found

iUniverse books may be ordered through booksellers or by contacting:

iUniverse
1663 Liberty Drive
Bloomington, IN 47403
www.iuniverse.com
1-800-Authors (1-800-288-4677)

ISBN: 978-1-4759-6436-3 (sc)
ISBN: 978-1-4759-6440-0 (hc)
ISBN: 978-1-4759-6438-7 (ebk)

Library of Congress Control Number: 2012922767

Printed in the United States of America

iUniverse rev. date: 03/13/2013

ACKNOWLEDGMENTS

Many thanks to the Chapter of the Week Group who have been my main readers, critics, suppliers of ideas and support, and have kept me on track; to Celeste Klein who encouraged me daily; to my sister Patti Callaway, Flika Gardner, and Joni Amundson who insisted on their chapter every week and let me know if the cliff hanger at the end of the chapter worked; to René Carlberg, Cathy Carlson, Sarah Charleston, Glennis Cohen, Sarah Huelskoetter, Beth and Josh Irish, Vickie Keating, Jenni Meyer, niece Anna Perkins, Connie Stirling, and Robin Villwock for also being members of the Chapter of the Week Group and reading the story.

I would like to thank my niece Kris Storage of the Wild Gate Stable of Oregon, Wisconsin, for her valuable knowledge and insight concerning horses. Thanks also goes to my niece Elizabeth M. Parent for her technical assistance on the Sommerhjem Journeys Series facebook page.

Once again, many thanks to my niece Katherine M. Parent for her cover art. I can only hope the inside of the book is as good as the cover she has designed.

A special thanks goes to Linne Jensen for surviving editing another book with me. I am extremely grateful for her knowledge of grammar, punctuation, and the ability to make sure the stories have consistency. Thanks also to Gale Stone for finding errors we missed.

To my brother Thomas R. Parent, my friend, my fishing partner, and a fellow fan of fantasy stories. I think he might have enjoyed the Sommerhjem Journey's series.

To CEK, always.

INTRODUCTION

Journey's Lost and Found was written originally as a serial. The chapters were each approximately four plus pages long and sent via e-mail to friends and relations once a week. A cliffhanger was written into the end of each chapter in order to build anticipation for the next chapter or, in some cases, merely to irritate the reader. You, as a new reader, have choices. You can read a chapter, walk away, and then later pick the book up and read the next chapter to get the serial experience. Another choice is to just read Journey's Lost and Found as a conventional book and "one more chapter" yourself to three o'clock in the morning on a work or school night. Whichever way you choose, I hope you enjoy the journeys of Greer, Kasa, Meryl, and Tashi.

Prologue

Nissa leaned back in her camp chair and put her feet up on one of the rocks surrounding the fire pit. The fire had burned down to coals. Her hand continued to run over Carz the hunting cat's head, and every once in a while, she pulled gently at his ears. The others who had been sharing the campfire with her had all gone off to their beds. Nissa had chosen to linger for just a while longer to reflect on what had happened this day. Little had she known when she had left home in the dark of night weeks ago that she would end up in the capital, one of the central figures in helping remove the tyrant Regent Cedric Klingflug from power. When her Da had told her to disguise herself and their rover homewagon and take to the road, she had not imagined even in her wildest imaginings where the back trail out of the village of Mumblesey would take her. This day everything had come together at just the right time to make it possible for the transition of rule of the country of Sommerhjem to occur, but not without a great deal of plotting, planning, and a hefty bit of drama.

If Queen Octavia, the previous ruler of Sommerhjem, had not died when her daughter Princess Esmeralda was just a young lass, what had transpired this day might never have happened. There would have been no reason to appoint a regent until Princess Esmeralda came of age, at which time she was to have taken over the rule. Unfortunately, Lord Cedric Klingflug had been appointed regent from the time of Queen Octavia's death until Princess Esmeralda came of age. Over the intervening years, Regent Klingflug had become overly fond of being in power. He had set in motion a variety of plans which continued to keep him in power even after the princess came of age, if she managed to survive that long. First and foremost, he had levied higher and higher taxes and created special licenses, resulting in hardship for many in the land. By his abuse of power, he had acquired more and more land and wealth for himself. His rules and taxes caused a great deal of outrage from both the nobles and the common folk who were loyal to the Crown. In addition, Regent Klingflug had kept Princess Esmeralda isolated so she could not gain any popularity among the folk she would come to rule, and also, so she could not come to know her subjects.

The Regent had been aware that there was one thing that could disrupt all of his well thought out plans and schemes. He had known, while many had forgotten, that the position of king or queen of Sommerhjem had not always been a hereditary position. Only in the last few hundred years had the title been passed down from father or mother to daughter or son. Prior to that time, upon the passing of the old ruler, the new ruler of Sommerhjem was chosen by the Gylden Sirklene challenge. Regent Klingflug had had scholars loyal to him find out as much as they could about the Gylden Sirklene challenge, and then he had tried to find and destroy all of the parts and pieces needed for the challenge to be called and carried out. This day he had failed in his quest to maintain power and to prevent the Gylden Sirklene challenge from being called.

"What an amazing day this has been, eh, Carz," Nissa said to the hunting cat. "A good day for Sommerhjem, to be sure, but also one of endings and changes. When I left home all those weeks ago, I thought I would only be gone a short while. I never thought that I would find that being a rover once again would suit me so well."

Nissa thought again about the events of the day and about the two gold oddly shaped rings with deep scratches on their outer surfaces that she had carried in a golden pine spider silk pouch around her neck for the better part of the summer. How odd that I became the one who had two of the nine pieces of the oppgave ringe, two of the nine rings that are needed for the Gylden Sirklene challenge, Nissa thought to herself. She did not know why she had known to put them in the vesseteboks, the golden box set in the sea wall in the Well of Speaking this day, but it obviously had been the right thing to do.

As Nissa sat staring into the coals, she thought back on what one of the elder rovers had said to her. He had said her journey had just begun. What did that mean? Was she meant to find other pieces of the oppgave ringe and return them to the capital, or was she meant to do something else? Nissa suspected that she was not destined to be the only one who would carry pieces of the oppgave ringe to the capital. Actually, after the journey she had taken this summer, she hoped her life would settle down a bit, and she could just be a rover plying her craft. A little peace and quiet might be nice. Only time would tell, she thought, as she began to douse the remaining coals.

"Come on, Carz, time for bed. Tomorrow is going to come all too soon, and who knows what tomorrow will bring."

PART ONE

Chapter One

Greer had always felt he was lucky, but luck had abandoned him this night as he crept down the alley, slipping from shadow to shadow as quietly as he could. It would not do to have the peacekeepers stop him or be spotted by any of the rough trade that lurked in the dark alleys of Høyhauger at this time of night. That would alert the men who were trying to find him. No, he thought to himself, he needed to keep moving and get to the closest of his bolt holes as fast as he could. Greer tried to calm his breathing to listen, but the pounding of his heart was so loud he could not be sure of what he heard. He hoped he had lost the men who were chasing after him.

Slipping from the shadows in which he was hidden, Greer moved swiftly down the alley staying close to the wall, trying to make as little noise as possible. There were no lanterns marking the back doors in this part of town, which was to his advantage. The merchants and folks who lived here would not waste good coin for such a luxury. The other advantage Greer held was the knowledge of all the back alleys and byways of Høyhauger. He did not think those who were trying to find him knew them as well as he did. Now he could only hope the clouds stayed thick and the moon did not show its face this night.

Greer had lived on the streets of Høyhauger for as long as he could remember. He thought he once had had a family, but that was so long ago he was not sure. Greer was just one of the many street lads who got by as best they could, scrabbling from one odd job to the next and trying to eke out a meager existence in the high hills border town.

Being small for his age, Greer looked much younger than his ten and five years. In addition, one of his legs was shorter than the other, causing folks to view him as a cripple, which he had learned to use to his advantage. No one expected him to be able to move very fast. To supplement his income, Greer had become adept at lifting items that did not belong to him, such as fruit and vegetables from the markets, a small roll from a bakery cart, and occasionally he would lighten a purse or two of some coin. His youthful looks and nimble fingers had kept him alive a number of times during the lean periods when odd jobs were scarce.

During the last month, Greer had not had to rely on stealing to keep food in his belly, for he had stumbled onto a steady job at Milkin's Stable. He was to muck the stalls daily, groom the horses, and be there at night to answer late arrivals. He had thought himself set for the harsh winter months. In return for doing the daily chores at the stable, he had a warm place to stay and one meal a day. All of that was gone now, and he was glad he had not abandoned his bolt holes, for nothing good in his life ever seemed to last.

Greer slipped between two buildings into a space so narrow that even he, with his small size, was hard-pressed to squeeze through. He did not think anyone would have seen him slip within the opening, for even during the daylight hours, this section of the wall was deep in shadow. Greer had found this particular bolt hole quite by accident. He had been rummaging in the trash behind the building when he noticed a mother cat slinking through the shadows carrying a kitten. All of a sudden, the mother cat and kitten had disappeared as though the very building wall had swallowed them up. Greer had stayed still and watched. Shortly, the mother cat had just as suddenly reappeared, as if out of thin air. Just a little while later, she returned carrying another kitten. Again, she disappeared. One moment she was there, and the next moment she was gone. After she reappeared a second time, Greer had taken a closer look and had discovered the place in which he was now hiding. Like many buildings in Høyhauger, this one had been built on the ruins of a previous one. The newer building did not quite fit on the foundation of the older one, leaving a narrow space that was hidden because of an overlap between the two buildings.

For one such as him, having a number of bolt holes was an important survival skill in a town like Høyhauger. The town, southernmost on the border of Bortfjell, is situated at the mouth of the pass to the country of Sommerhjem. Part fortress and part town, it is a place of contrasts. In times of peace, a brisk trade moves through the pass, and the wealth of that trade is reflected in the richness of the merchants' homes. Part of the town is still fortified and houses the barracks of the border guard, representatives of the reigning prince, and the administration overseeing the town. In times of unrest, Høyhauger could still be defended. Like many towns, and most especially border towns, there is an underside where folks, some with and some without the blessing of the current ruler, cater to the seamier wants of either the folk who live here or are just passing through. A border town set to regulate or monitor a pass through the mountains also attracts its share of smugglers, who pass between the two countries by ways other than the main, more well-traveled, pass.

Greer felt safe for the moment, but he could not stay here forever. After what he had witnessed in the stable, the hunt for him would not end this night. Others on the street would be more than happy to sell him out for a few coppers. While being small and assumed to be a cripple was so often to his advantage, it also made him very recognizable should anyone want to find him. It made him stand out from the other street lads. What he had done this night meant he could no longer stay in the only place he knew. Where would he go? He had never been outside the town limits, as far as he knew. How would he survive?

Greer also knew he had another problem. He needed to get back into the stable before he left, and do so without being seen, for he could not leave Kasa behind. He knew he was being foolish and placing himself at more risk. He knew he should cut his losses and leave, but he just could not. Greer had promised, and he knew a man was no better than his word. It was one thing to skirt the edge of the law to survive, but one never did so at the cost of one's honor.

One additional job Greer had had at Milkin's Stable was to look after the stable owner's prize border dog and her litter. She had had eight pups, seven of which would bring a great price. Border dogs are known for their intelligence, fierce loyalty, and guarding instincts. It was the eighth pup that concerned Greer. The runt of the litter, with coloring and markings that were no longer considered desirable. In addition, there was something wrong with one of the pup's forelegs, causing him to have an uneven gait. The stable owner would have summarily gotten rid of the pup, had not Greer asked politely if he might have him. The owner had been in an expansive mood that day and had even joked that Greer should have the pup, for they were a matched pair. Greer had managed to keep the pup he had named Kasa out of sight whenever the owner made an infrequent check on the other pups. He had hoped out of sight was out of mind, and he had not wanted the owner to change his mind. If Greer did not return to the stable and get Kasa, the border dog pup would not survive the owner's next visit. Greer had promised Kasa he would protect him.

Greer needed to think. It would not do to go rushing off half-cocked, for that would not serve either the pup or him well. He was sure the men searching for him had not given up. He knew he could not leave Høyhauger without a plan and without provisions. Greer had learned early there was no one he could trust. He had no friends among the other street lads. Why, oh why, had he not followed the stable owner's instructions and left the stable as he had been told? It did not happen often, but every once in a while, the stable owner used the stable for business he did not want others to know about. When that happened, he would just tell Greer to make himself scarce or send him off on an errand. This night, the stable owner had told Greer to leave and not come back for several hours. Unfortunately, Greer's curiosity had gotten the better of him, and he had hidden behind the hay piles to see what the owner was up to. Greer had learned early on that knowing something he was not supposed to could come in handy.

Shortly after Greer should have left, two men he had seen before slipped into the stable and tucked themselves into an empty stall, out of sight. Greer knew they sometimes worked for the stable owner. They were tough-looking men, the kind one would not want to meet in a dark alley. Soon after they arrived, Greer heard the sound of a single horse and rider approaching the stable. The owner stepped out to greet the rider. The rider, a man by the sound of his voice, asked if there was room to board his horse for the night. He had been directed to Milkin's Stable by the stable lad at the town stable. Seemed the town stable was full up. He had been told Milkin's was a good place to board his horse. Greer wondered about him being directed by a stable lad because, as far as he knew, no lads worked at the town stable. He had tried to find work there himself and had been summarily sent on his way, being told the town stable did not hire lads, only grown men.

The stable owner had said, "Of course, of course. We pride ourselves on our clean and secure stable."

The gentleman, for he looked a gentleman from his clothing and fine horse, had ridden his horse into the stable and dismounted. As the stable owner took the reins, the two men who had been hidden rushed out, and first, knocked the stable owner out, and then knocked the gentleman out. That was when things got odd. First, they checked the gentleman to make sure he was unconscious. Then they tapped the stable owner on the shoulder, and he rolled over and sprang up.

"Quick," he had said to one of the men, "you search his saddlebags while I search him. You," he had said to the other man, "be ready to knock him out again if he comes to before I am finished."

Each man proceeded to do his assigned job. Greer had held his breath, not wanting to make even the slightest sound. He knew if the stable owner knew he was there, he would be in a lot of trouble. The man going through the saddlebags told the stable owner that what they were looking for was not there. The stable owner meanwhile had searched through the gentleman's cloak, pouch, and pockets. He patted him down, and even removed the gentleman's boots and searched in them. Going back over the gentleman one more time, the stable owner reached beneath the collar of the gentleman's shirt and pulled out a small pouch hanging from a cord. Straightening, he had turned to the others with a look of triumph in his eyes.

"This must be it," he had said, as he pulled the cord over the gentleman's head.

The stable owner opened the small pouch and tipped its contents into his hand. There was a flash of light. The stable owner flung the pouch and another object straight over the hay pile Greer was hiding behind. Greer could see the stable owner clutching his hand, as he doubled over in pain, all the while yelling to the others to go and get the pouch. Greer could not explain, even to himself, why he had snatched the pouch up, and then quickly looked at his feet where something had hit. He could not make out what it was, but it caught the light. He quickly scooped it up and put it in the pouch. Greer began to back away from where he had hidden himself. He thought he might have made it out of the stable unnoticed if he had not knocked against the pitchfork leaning against the hay, which teetered and then clattered to the floor. The noise had alerted the men, who almost caught him before he could get out of the stable's back door.

All that had happened earlier, and thinking about it now was not going to keep him safe or help him plan how to get himself out of the mess he now found himself in. He was sure the stable owner would be able to convince the gentleman that both of them had been attacked by thugs, and thus he could not be held accountable for what would appear to be a robbery. He might even be telling him that his stable lad was probably in on the robbery, and they should report him to the local peacekeepers.

He wondered what was so important about what was in the pouch. Taking a chance at being seen, Greer squeezed himself through the opening of the bolt hole. He moved out of the safety of the shadows into the light and tipped the contents of the pouch into his hand. The object looked like a very oddly shaped ring made of gold, which did not seem to be in very good condition due to its deeply scratched surface. The ring certainly was worth something because it was made of gold, but it could not be worth all that much. It would be difficult to get rid of unless it was melted down. It seemed odd to Greer that the stable owner had gone to such a great deal of trouble to get that particular gentleman directed to his stable just so he could rob him of something that was not of great worth. The stable owner had not seemed interested in the gentleman's coin or other possessions, just what was in the pouch. What made this ring so valuable?

But what was done was done, and there was no going back and changing it. Sitting here thinking about it was not going to keep him safe, so Greer reentered his bolt hole. He carefully opened a small iron door that had been built into the wall. At one time, it must have been an ash door, when the building had been a home and this wall part of a fireplace. It had kept what few possessions Greer owned dry and safe from the rats and other vermin that lived in the alleys and sewers of the town. He pulled out a rucksack that contained a change of clothes and the supplies he had collected over the years, just in case he ever needed to leave town. His biggest concern was going to be finding food once he left Høyhauger. While he knew how to scavenge in town, he knew little to nothing about living off the land, and even less about traveling in the mountains. He knew he could not just head out the town gate and calmly walk either north into the unknown or through the pass to Sommerhjem, the country to the south. The town gates would be watched. The pass would be watched. How then would he get away?

But first things first. Greer took tight hold of his pack, squeezed himself through the opening of the bolt hole, and stopped to look and listen. Slipping from shadow to shadow, he moved with great stealth and began to retrace his steps, hoping those looking for him would think he would not return to the stable. He arrived at the stable undetected. Not daring to risk entering either the front or back doors of the stable, Greer moved towards the dog run, hoping the dogs would not give him away. Climbing into the fenced area, Greer quietly moved aside the small door that could be opened to let the dogs out of the stable and into the run. Once Greer had the door open, he gave an almost inaudible whistle. It was met with a small yip and a scrabbling sound. Soon a small wet nose thrust itself into Greer's outstretched hand. Gently, coaxing the pup out, Greer quickly closed the dog door, so the other pups would not follow. He picked his pup up, softly admonishing Kasa to please be very quiet. Either the pup was too tired to do anything other than return to sleep, or he understood. Either way, the first problem had been overcome. Now Greer needed to gather some food and figure out how to get out of Høyhauger. Moving quickly, Greer headed towards the more prosperous side of town, hoping against hope that the search for him had not reached that far. If he were lucky, he just might be able to snatch a loaf of bread or some meat pies off an open window ledge with none the wiser, but then what? Dawn was only a few hours off.

CHAPTER TWO

After successfully liberating Kasa without being caught, Greer began to think his luck might be changing. While he was afraid to put the pup down, he knew he was going to have to soon, for Kasa was getting heavier by the minute. Greer had meant to fashion a collar for him, but had not done it, nor did he have a rope to tie Kasa with. When Greer's duties were done at the stable, he had worked with Kasa, trying to get him to stay with him and not run off. Sometimes he had been successful, and sometimes the pup, being a pup, did not do as asked.

"I need you to listen now," Greer addressed Kasa. "You need to stick close. No running off, for we are both in real trouble." Greer felt a little foolish thinking the pup understood, and so was pleasantly surprised when, after he put Kasa down, the pup just sat quietly next to him.

When Greer began to slip from one shadow to the next, the pup did the same. Greer's luck continued to hold. Slipping into the fancy garden of one of the nicer houses, Greer snagged a small loaf of bread off a kitchen window ledge. Ever since he had had the stable lad's job, he had not needed to pilfer food from the kitchen ledges of the fancy houses, but old habits and skills never really go away when one has lived on the streets all of one's life. He wondered at the cooks, leaving food out for the easy taking by the likes of him. Sometimes he thought they might just do it on purpose. Whatever the reason, the pickings were good this night.

Another piece of luck was chancing on a laundry line where clothes had been hung to air out. The warm days of summer were long past, and there was a nip in the air. Greer was sorry that desperation moved him to take several finely-woven wool shirts, which looked to be a bit big but would do for layering when the weather turned bitter. The pants hung on the line were much too large, so Greer left them. The real prize was a warm woolen cloak. Greer made quick work of stuffing the clothing into the bottom of his rucksack. His old cloak would have to do for this night.

No sense having the pilfered clothing in plain view, should someone raise an alarm. In addition, he filched a wide wool scarf, thinking he might be able to make a sling out of it to carry Kasa, if the pup became too tired and needed to be carried. Just as he was about to move on, he heard low voices coming from the gardener's shed next door. Greer put a cautionary hand on Kasa's shoulder and crept forward.

"Well, that should keep them waterproof. You sure you still have enough of the dark left to get out this night?"

"I will, if you would stop talking and worrying and let me be on my way. In several weeks' time, I'll be in Sommerhjem waiting for our mutual friend to get up and sit down to her breakfast, so I can come a calling and deliver . . . ."

"Sh-h-h!"

"What? Did you hear something?"

"No, but you never know who might be about and chance to overhear. Go swiftly and be safe, my friend."

Greer heard movement and saw a tall man with a large rucksack on his back step into the lane that ran behind the houses. The country that had been mentioned, that the tall man was heading for, was to the south of Bortfjell, yet the man with the rucksack was not heading for the town gate that led to the pass that would take him through the mountains to the south. Was he a smuggler? Could this be a way out, Greer wondered, even as he was fashioning the scarf into a makeshift sling. Having made the decision to follow the tall man, Greer picked Kasa up and settled him into the makeshift sling, and they began to slip in and out of the shadows. Greer knew the streets well and could hang back without losing the man ahead, who was also cautiously sticking to the shadows. Greer found himself admiring how such a tall man managed to make himself seem so small as he slipped from shadow to shadow. Greer almost lost the man when they reached a portion of the old fortress wall, but was close enough to see him disappear around a column of stone.

Edging his way close to where the man had disappeared, at first Greer thought he had lost the man he had been shadowing. Greer continued past the spot where he had lost sight of the man, all the way to where the town wall turned to the left, and could see no movement. Greer then retraced his steps. Just as he was passing the column of stone, he felt a hand clamp over his mouth, and he was jerked off his feet.

"So, my young friend, who has paid you to follow me?"

The man had barely finished whispering his question when a low growl came from the sling in front of Greer. There was a quick movement within the sling, and Greer was abruptly dropped. Scrambling to his feet, he tried to run away. The man, however, was too fast and grabbed Greer by his cloak hood, caught his arm, and spun him around.

"You bit me," the man exclaimed, and then revised his thinking when Kasa's head popped out of the sling and growled another warning. "Would you kindly tell your border dog to quiet down, or we'll both be in trouble here. I have no intention of hurting either of you. Just answer my question, and I'll let you go. Now, who sent you to follow me?"

Since the man had an iron grip on Greer's arm and looked big enough and strong enough to break Greer in two with very little effort, Greer answered his question. "No one, sir. No one sent me to follow you."

"No one sent you, or paid you, to follow me?" the man asked.

"No, sir."

"What, you just decided to take an evening stroll, chanced upon me, and decided to follow me? Did you think you could rob me and live?" the man asked, and Greer could hear the menace in his voice.

"Not exactly, sir."

"You were not exactly out for an evening stroll, or you were not exactly thinking of robbing me?"

"Neither, sir."

"You had best explain quickly, for my time and my patience are growing shorter by the minute."

Greer decided, at that moment, he had nothing to lose by telling the truth, or at least part of the truth. He was well and truly caught, and the man could just dispose of him there by the town wall and walk away. It saddened Greer to think that there was probably no one who would mourn his passing, except the pup.

"I overheard your conversation when you were back at the fancy house, and I followed you, hoping you might lead me to a way out of town that would not go through a town gate. I overheard you say you were going to head to Sommerhjem, and hoped, probably foolishly, I could follow you."

"Now, why is it you need to leave the fine town of Høyhauger in the dead of night?"

"I do odd jobs at a stable in return for a place to sleep and one meal a day. This night the owner of the stable told me to make myself scarce for a few hours. I pretended to leave, but hid behind the hay pile . . . ."

"Much as I can tell you are a born storyteller, could you speed your tale up? Time is passing at a dangerous clip."

"Yes, sir. Two men the owner employs from time to time came and hid in one of the stalls. A lone rider, a gentleman from his dress, approached the stable and asked the stable owner if he could board his horse overnight. The two men rushed out from where they had hidden, knocked the stable owner out, then knocked the gentleman out, but they really didn't knock the stable owner out. He and the others searched the gentleman and his belongings." Greer responded in a low whispered rush. "Unfortunately for me, I knocked over a pitchfork when I tried to take off, and the stable owner sent the two men after me. I don't think they are going to stop looking for me, and so I need to get out of Høyhauger."

Greer took a deep breath and held it. He did not mention the pouch that he had caught, or what it contained, which was now hanging around his neck.

"That story is so tall and unbelievable that I don't think you could make it up. So, did you steal the border dog on your way out of the stable?" the man asked, recognizing him for what he was, a coveted expensive border dog.

"No, sir, he's mine, fair and square. No, I didn't take him on the way out. I had to go back for him."

"Unbelievable. Well, come along then. You can continue to follow me, but know I won't be slowing down for you, or be stopping to rest. If you can't keep up, I'll leave you behind."

With that said, the man turned and began walking back the way they had come. Greer hesitated for only a moment and quickly followed. They climbed up a stair that led up to a path that ran along the edge of the old fortress wall until they came to a small break in the crumbling stone wall.

"This first part is going to be tricky, so you will need both hands and good balance. You might want to let me take the pup."

Greer looked through the break in the wall and in the darkness could see no way to go beyond it. Did the man intend to push him to his death and fling Kasa after him, or did he just want to steal Kasa and leave Greer behind?

The man must have been reading Greer's mind, for he said, "The old fortress wall has crumbled here, and just about five feet down is a ledge. If you are reluctant to let go of the pup slung in front of you, you'll never get down. I intend to go first. You will need to hand the pup down, and then slip yourself over the edge. I'll grab you and bring you down to the ledge. We need to hurry."

Greer thought about it for a few seconds, and then pulled the sling from his shoulder. This man could have disposed of him at any time since he had caught him, but had not. While not willing to trust easily, Greer weighed his options and decided that staying in Høyhauger was even less good for his health than swinging his body over the edge into the unknown.

The man slid over the edge, and Greer heard a soft thump as he landed. Slowly and carefully, Greer lay down on the ground and lowered the sling holding Kasa over the edge, lowering the pup down. He felt the man gather the pup in and then heard the man say it was his turn. Greer had been afraid often in his life, but sheer terror clutched at him now. The idea of swinging his body over the side of the ledge and dangling there, hoping that the man would indeed lift him down, was terrifying. How long he would have stayed frozen in place he would never know, but when he heard voices on the trail behind him, he quickly scooted himself feet first over the edge. Strong hands caught him, lifted him down, held him close, and put a cautionary hand over his mouth. Greer nodded his head that he understood he should be quiet, and the hand was removed.

As soon as the voices became distant, the man spoke. "The ledge you are standing on is about a foot to two feet wide and rough in places. You'll need to hug the wall and move carefully. Once we get past the fortress wall, the path enters a crevasse. The way will get easier there."

After the first loose stone was kicked off the ledge they were traversing, and he did not hear it hit below, Greer was thankful that he could not see where he was. As he moved forward, he was sure a lifetime or two passed before he felt a wall rise up on the side opposite the one he was desperately leaning against. A weak gray light began to filter into the crevasse they were moving through, but time had ceased to matter to Greer. All he knew was that he could not lose sight of the man in front of him, for he was hopelessly turned around. The path they had followed had taken so many twists and turns, and had so many side passages, he did not even know what direction they were now headed. After a while, fatigue set in, and it was all Greer could do to put one stumbling foot in front of the other. He was extremely grateful when the man called a halt for a rest.

Only when Greer sat down on a seat-high boulder and saw the man take off the sling and gently lift Kasa out of it did Greer realize that the man had been carrying Kasa all of this time. Kasa stumbled a little, yawned a huge yawn, and then upon seeing Greer, rushed towards him. In his excitement, Kasa got moving too fast and did a summersault, landing at Greer's feet. This sight brought a tired smile to Greer's face.

"We need to speak very softly," the man cautioned. "Sound carries in the mountains, and we're not out of danger yet. I don't want to have to explain to the border patrol what I'm doing on these back trails. We'll take a short rest here. Do you have a name, lad?"

"Greer, sir. And what should I call you?"

"Zareh will do for now. If you and the pup are thirsty, there's a small spring just beyond that bush to your left. You can fill up your water skin, if you have one. It's important to keep liquids in you at these heights."

Greer rummaged around in his rucksack to locate the water skin he thought was shoved somewhere near the bottom. Once the water skin was located, he got up slowly from his seat and went to find the spring. Kasa came with him, and after Greer filled the water skin, both of them took time to have a long cool drink of the crystal clear water. Greer could not remember ever drinking water that tasted so good.

The rest and refreshing water did not carry Greer for long. He soon slipped back into a haze of fatigue, often stumbling, once falling, but always moving forward. His feet had begun to hurt. The shoes he wore did not fit all that well anymore and had been well worn before this climb had begun. He was grateful that Zareh continued to carry Kasa. They stopped a second time for a short rest and to eat something. Zareh gave both Greer and Kasa generous pieces of jerky, and Greer reluctantly shared part of a small loaf of bread. He knew he was feeling selfish, but survival habits did not go away, even when someone offered to share food. Greer had spent much of his life not knowing where his next meal would come from.

All too soon the rest stop was over, and the trek began again, up and down, over this boulder, around that rock outcrop, until Greer stumbled one more time and collapsed. He struggled to get up, but his meager reserves of strength were gone. He knew Zareh had said that if he could not keep up, he would be left behind. He could only hope that Zareh would look after Kasa.

Chapter Three

Greer came to and found he was trussed up like a goose roasting on a spit, hands and feet tied, and slung over something moving. Every bone and muscle in his body ached.

"You must be getting soft in your old age. Couldn't leave him behind, could you?"

"Yah, well, what would you have done? Left him to the scavengers? Besides, the border dog pup started whining, and I didn't want him to give us away. It was either go back for the lad, or let the pup loose," replied Zareh.

"You're right. Would've been a waste of a good border dog pup," the older man said, with a great deal of sarcasm in his voice.

"Don't know what you're grousing about. You had the cushy job. All you had to do was wait on this side of the border with the pack animals while I carried one small lad, and one small pup, plus my pack, for miles and miles through the mountains," Zareh retorted.

"Oh, my heart bleeds for you," the older man replied, making a show of staggering back and clutching his chest. "So, now what are you going to do with them?"

"Don't know. Don't know why I let him follow me, but something just nagged at me that it was important that I bring him along. He looks like a typical street lad, but there was something in his manner or his speech. Like I said, I don't know. It will work itself out. In the meanwhile, let's get as far away from the Bortfjell border as we can before dark."

Greer did not hear anything else for he had slid into unconsciousness once again. The next time he woke, he found he was lying on the ground wrapped in the warm cloak he had stuffed in his pack. He did not even have the energy to worry that the men he was with had rummaged through his meager belongings. He would worry about that later, but for now, he could smell the smoke of a wood fire promising warmth. The smell of something delicious cooking caused his stomach to growl loudly.

"Good thing we're across the border out of Bortfjell and in safer territory. That stomach rumble of yours would surely give us away to any border patrol or thieving scoundrels within a mile's hearing," said the other voice Greer had heard before he had drifted off again. "Come on, lad, get your body moving before Zareh gets back and eats, and we feed your portion to that pup of yours."

Greer managed to untangle himself from his cloak and finally stood up. It took some doing since every bone in his body ached. He wondered how many bones that was, as he hobbled over to the fire and sat down on a stump next to it, welcoming the warmth. Greer looked across the fire and finally got a good look at the man who had invited him to dinner. He looked incredibly old to Greer. The man was tall like Zareh and in good physical shape. His hair was white, as was his trimmed beard. There were crinkles at the corners of his eyes, from either squinting into the sun a lot or laughing often. Kindness and good humor poured off of him like rain from a roof. The older man handed Greer a bowl of something that looked like hash and smelled like food fit for a prince. It was all Greer could do not to shovel it in as fast as he could, but he did not want to look desperate.

While Greer ate, the older man kept up a running conversation. "Name's Pryderi. You've met my son, Zareh. He's off gathering up some more firewood and taking a gander about. Told me your name is Greer. You have a last name to go with that?"

Greer could not think of a good reason not to reply, so he answered between mouthfuls. "No, sir. No last name. Just Greer."

He had not thought about his name in a long time. He had just always been Greer, or Greer the cripple, or small Greer. Folk who lived on the streets had names that described them. He could not remember any one of the street lads ever going by a first and last name. It may have occurred to him a time or two that other folk had last names, but he had never found that important. Maybe he had had a last name at one time, but he could not remember it if he had.

Pryderi nodded and went on talking, after filling Greer's plate a second time, as if not having a last name was nothing unusual. "That's a good border dog pup you've got there. Very loyal. Hasn't left your side since we set up camp here. Got coloring much prized in Sommerhjem. Ah, you look surprised. Only those snobby rich folks on the north side of the border in Bortfjell want border dogs that are dark and tri-colored. Here we like the old coloring best, and your border dog pup is a fine example. What happened to his leg?"

"Don't rightly know, sir," Greer answered between mouthfuls. "Don't think he was born that way. I'm thinking he was rolled over on by his mum and somehow his leg got twisted. Stable owner I worked for let me keep him 'cause he said he was worthless."

At the raised inquiring eyebrow of the older man, Greer explained that the pup's coloring alone would have been enough for the stable owner to dispose of Kasa, and the bad leg would have clinched the deal, good coloring or no.

"Kasa took to me right away, and well . . . ." Greer did not want to explain to this stranger that the pup was the first living being Greer could ever remember who seemed to like and trust him. He was relieved that he did not have to explain further, for Zareh had returned carrying a load of wood.

"Ah, I see young Greer is back with the living. Did you leave me anything to eat, lad?" Zareh's question did not seem to need an answer, so Greer kept on eating. "I scouted our back trail a ways, and checked our forward trail. Doesn't look like anyone has been this way in a while. Let's get the meal out of the way, clean up, and get a few hours of sleep. Hopefully the weather will hold, and we can be all the way out of these mountains by day after tomorrow. I'll take the first watch."

Out of these mountains, Greer thought to himself. He had hoped after the last grueling upward climb they would now begin to descend out of the mountains, but then he did not even know where they were. He had missed part of the journey while unconscious, draped over the back of a pack animal.

Greer did not know what to think about these two. Were they really as kind as they seemed, or did they have some plan that boded him no good? He kept waiting for the other boot to drop, but so far, it had not. He also found himself very curious about what had brought Zareh to Høyhauger, and what he was carrying that he could not take through the town gates. Maybe it was not so much what he was smuggling out, but who he was. Perhaps he did not want to be seen in Høyhauger. Greer worried that the two men would suddenly decide he was a risk they did not want to continue to take, and it would be easier to just push him off a ledge and be rid of him. He thought about pretending to sleep, only staying awake, and then trying to sneak off on his own. He threw that plan out right away, for what he knew about surviving in the mountains could end his life just as easily as being hurled off a ledge. Greer decided to stick with the two men for now.

Greer had other things to think about as he settled once more to sleep. Why was it, he wondered, that when one chose a spot of ground to lie on, it looked perfectly smooth, free of tree roots and rocks, but the minute one settled in, there were lumps and sharp edges sticking into one's hip and shoulder. While he lay there trying to adjust his body into a more comfortable position, Greer began to think about what had happened back in the stable. Why had the stable owner pretended to be knocked out? What had caused the flash of light when the stable owner had opened the pouch he had taken from the unconscious gentleman? What had caused the stable owner to fling the pouch away? What had caused the stable owner to clutch his hand as if it were hurt? The biggest question, Greer thought, as he shifted away from another sharp rock that was digging into his waist, was why had he grabbed the pouch and the misshapen gold ring from the floor and run? The job at Milkin's Stable was the best one he had ever had, and with winter coming on, the promise of a warm place to sleep and one solid meal a day was not something to be thrown away lightly. It made him no never mind that the stable owner was pulling a trick on the gentleman. He would never have told, but no, he had to go and pick up what had been flung and run as if a pack of crazed hounds were after him. He probably could have returned the pouch in the morning and been back cleaning the stable, back safe in a place he understood, instead of trying to sleep on the rocky ground high in the mountains, depending on two strangers. Why had he chosen to do what he had done?

At the time, Greer had not looked carefully at what he had picked up off the stable floor. Thinking back now, he remembered the ring had felt very warm in his hand, almost hot, but maybe he had just imagined that. He had quickly placed it in the pouch which was attached to a cord, and had put the cord around his neck, stuffing the pouch inside his shirt. Greer knew he would not be able to examine more closely what was in the pouch right now either, no matter how curious he was, because it was too dark to see and sleep was more overpowering than his questions. He soon drifted into sleep, hoping that his mountain guides would still be there in the morning. He would puzzle through the mystery of the pouch and its contents when he had a private moment.

It took two more days of arduous climbing, following narrow animal trails, and walking through short narrow passages, before the downward descent began. The landscape gradually began to change from rock and lichen to tall pines, and the walking became smoother. Greer was always glad when they finally stopped for the night, for while his muscles had begun to toughen up, he was not used to walking long distances, and his shoes were never made for scrambling over hill and dale. His awkward gait was giving him trouble. This day, rain had been falling in a fine mist since midmorning, and the damp and cold had penetrated deep into his body, causing his muscles to grow tight and stiff. What Greer would not have given for a warm hayloft at this moment. He had begun to envy Kasa, who walked beside him some of the time, but also was picked up and placed in a sling on one of the two pack animals and allowed to ride much of the time. Greer was grateful that the two he was following would allow Kasa to ride, for Greer was not sure he could have carried Kasa the whole way.

At noon, they stopped at a spot next to a tall outcrop of stone to rest and have a small meal. It was the first time Greer had really had a chance to look at the changed landscape, for while they were walking, his head was most often down looking at the ground so he would not trip on anything in his path. It was so green here compared to the land he had seen from the walls of Høyhauger. What he had seen beyond the walls of the town was a bleak, rocky land covered with scrub trees and brush. He had heard the land farther north was said to be forested, and that there was good farmland beyond that, but he had never been outside the town walls. As Greer sat there sharing his meager meal with Kasa, he discovered he liked the fresh clean smells surrounding him. He especially liked the smell of pine.

All too soon it was time to begin walking again. Even though the path they were following was strewn with pine needles forming a cushion underneath, Greer was not sure just how much longer he could continue to walk. The soles of his shoes were worn through in places and the blisters, bruises, and cuts on his feet were painful. He did not want to mention it to either Zareh or Pryderi. He did not want them to think he would not be able to keep up, and he did not want to be left behind. Pushing himself slowly to his feet, he gritted his teeth and began to walk, placing one foot in front of the other. By mid-afternoon, the day had become a haze of pain and agony. Greer walked about twenty feet beyond the other two who had stopped, before their voices penetrated the fog in his mind.

"Greer! Stop! Don't move!" Zareh yelled with such command in his voice that Greer stopped. "Don't move," Zareh repeated. "Just to your left and above you, about head high, not more that ten feet ahead of you, is a hunting cat. They are not known to harm humans, but it is best not to do anything to provoke her. She may have kits nearby."

Greer glanced upward with his eyes only, not daring to move his head, and saw the biggest cat he had ever seen in his life looking down at him. He wondered, in an odd moment of panic, if the hunting cat could see his knees shaking. He could not take his eyes off the hunting cat. Everyone stood frozen in place. Suddenly, Greer caught a blur of movement out of the corner of his eye, and saw Kasa race past him to the foot of the outcrop, come to an abrupt halt, and begin to growl. How the pup had managed to get out of his sling and off the pack horse was a mystery Greer did not have time to think about right then. He tried to call to Kasa, but his voice did not seem to work. He did not know what to do. Should he stay still? Should he move? That hunting cat could dispatch Kasa with one swift swipe of her paw. Before he could decide what to do, the hunting cat leapt from her perch, landed lightly on the ground, and snatched Kasa up in her teeth. Greer yelled "No!" as he began to run forward, and his "no" was echoed by the two men behind him.

Chapter Four

"Hold, lad! Don't be foolish. There's nothing you can do," Pryderi yelled, hoping it would penetrate the lad's mind, since both he and Zareh were too far away to grab the lad in his headlong rush to save his pup and get himself injured or killed.

It all seemed to happen in slow motion. The hunting cat turned, holding Kasa between her teeth, just as Greer, in his haste to get to his pup, tripped on a tree root hidden beneath a thin layer of pine needles and stumbled forward, landing on his hands and knees, just a few feet away from the large hunting cat. A soft warning growl came from deep within her throat as she looked past Greer to Zareh and Pryderi, giving them a look that halted them in their tracks.

Greer struggled to his feet and stood as straight and as tall as he could, trying not to look as terrified as he felt. He did not know what to do, but he knew for sure he could not let the hunting cat harm Kasa. Very slowly, he put two imploring hands out in front of him and addressed her.

"Please, don't hurt him. He was only defending me. Could I please have him back?"

Even as the words came out of Greer's mouth, he could not believe he was standing and facing down a hunting cat. The hunting cat looked at him long and hard, and took several steps forward. Greer held his ground. The hunting cat slowly and gently placed Kasa in Greer's outstretched hands, reached out, and touched a paw to Greer's chest. She gave a slight nod of her head, turned, leapt back up on the rocky outcrop and vanished around the next boulder. Greer let his breath out when he realized he had been holding it. He set Kasa down and was examining him when Zareh and Pryderi rushed up.

"Lad, you are either very brave or extremely foolhardy," Pryderi said, shaking his head. "I've never seen anything like it. Never in all my born days."

"Are you alright, lad?" Zareh questioned. "Is the pup alright?"

Greer had to take a moment to catch his breath and gather his wits before answering, all the while running his hands over Kasa, who was wiggling and thumping his tail, enjoying the attention.

"Kasa seems to be fine, if a little damp, and none the worse for wear. I'm not quite sure I'm fine." When Zareh looked at him with concern, Greer explained. "I'm not hurt anywhere, other than a few bruises to my hands, and knees, and pride," Greer said ruefully. "Mostly, I don't understand what just happened. Is it usual for hunting cats to give back their prey?" questioned Greer. Is it usual when a hunting cat touches your chest you feel a warm overflowing of calm, Greer wondered, but he held that thought back.

"It isn't usual for a hunting cat to come anywhere near humans. There are some few exceptions, of course, where a hunting cat and a human have paired up. Then they might share what they caught, but I don't think Kasa was ever going to be a tasty morsel. I think the hunting cat just picked him up to stop him from growling. It almost looked like she just wanted to, I don't know, approach you, or something," Pryderi said, scratching his head in consternation. Slapping his hat on his knee to dislodge any dust it might have accumulated, Pryderi shoved it back on his head and suggested that they move on, that the day was not getting any younger.

As Greer walked along, he would glance up and often found either Zareh or Pryderi looking back at him. Whatever had just happened back there with the hunting cat had them all puzzled. Kasa appeared unaffected by his encounter with the hunting cat and scampered alongside Greer, as if nothing untoward had happened. By the time it was time to halt that evening and set up camp, Greer was extremely grateful. His feet were hurting to the point that they were numb. His neck also had a kink in it from swinging his head down to watch the trail and up to check the rocks and trees above him, in case another hunting cat should appear.

Greer sat down with a groan that he could not prevent escaping his lips, and that attracted the attention of Zareh. Greer sat very still, hoping against hope that Zareh would turn back to what he had been doing, but he continued to fix Greer with his attention. Suddenly, he stalked over to Greer and demanded that Greer show him his feet. Greer froze. He worried that if he showed Zareh his feet, Zareh would realize Greer was not going to be able to keep up much longer. Zareh had said if he could not keep up, he would be left behind.

"Show me your feet, lad," Zareh said, this time in a much gentler, kinder voice.

Reluctantly, Greer did what was asked. He lifted his right foot up and the worn thin sole, or what was left of it, chose that moment to simply flop off from the toe down to the heel, and hang there, held momentarily by a thread. Gravity, however, proved too much for the thread, and the sole landed in the dirt below, exposing the blistered, cut, and bleeding bottom of his foot.

"Ah, lad, why didn't you say something?" Zareh asked, and there was a great deal of compassion in his voice. "Pryderi, can you bring the medicine kit over? We have a problem." Turning back to Greer, Zareh asked again why he had not said anything.

"I didn't want you to leave me behind if I couldn't keep up," Greer stated honestly.

"I guess I should've expected no less from someone who would stand up to a hunting cat. I imagine you have no reason at all to trust that either Pryderi or I wouldn't leave you behind, since I clearly recall saying that to you, but we will not leave you behind. Right now, we need to do something for those feet so they don't get infected. Thanks," Zareh said, as Pryderi set the medicine kit down on the ground next to him. "Do you think you can find something in our supplies that might work as foot coverings to protect his feet once I get done cleaning and wrapping them?"

"I'll see what I can do," Pryderi replied.

Greer thought he did not have any feeling left in his feet, but he was sorely mistaken, for when Zareh poured some liquid over the sole of each foot, it burned like fire. Greer tried very hard not to cry out, but a whimper escaped his lips. Zareh apologized, but explained it was necessary to wash out the cuts and broken blisters. Just when Greer thought he could take no more, Zareh slathered something on the bottom of his feet that was cooling and numbed the pain completely. He then wrapped Greer's feet with some clean cloth. Pryderi handed Zareh a pair of felted slippers, which ordinarily would have been more than several sizes too big, but with the cloth wrapped in a number of layers around his feet, they would protect the wrappings and keep his feet warm. He would not be able to go very far in them.

"Try to walk on those feet as little as you can this night and keep them elevated as much as possible," Zareh directed. "Now drink this. No, lad, it won't harm you. 'Tis just an herbal tea."

Not long after Greer had drunk half the tea down, Zareh lifted the cup out of Greer's lax hands and gently laid him down, wrapping him in his cloak and adding an extra blanket.

"That sleeping draught I mixed in his tea ought to keep him knocked out until morning. Rest would be the best thing for him right now. Doesn't it make you wonder what Greer's life has been like up to this point," Pryderi remarked, "for him to walk on those feet without complaint?"

"More to the point, is that his experience with folks has taught him to trust so little, to expect that we would truly leave him if he couldn't keep up," Zareh replied sadly. "A more immediate question, however, should be just what was that all about with the hunting cat? That was so strange. It was as if something about the lad attracted the hunting cat. Didn't you think so?"

"Everything seemed to happen so fast, but now that I've had some time to reflect on what happened, I think you're right. That hunting cat hasn't gone away either. I've caught glimpses of her, off and on all day, following us."

"So have I, and that's also unusual. A hunting cat can be close, and you would never know. They are rarely spotted, yet this one has offered us glimpses of herself all along the trail but has kept her distance. Odd," remarked Zareh.

"How much farther before we meet up with the others, do you think?" asked Pryderi, changing the subject.

"At least several more days, depending on the weather. We'll need to rearrange the packs in the morning so we can put Greer on one of the pack animals. He shouldn't be on those feet for the next several days. Neither his feet, nor what's left of his shoes, can handle it. We'll have to carry more, and that might slow us down."

"If you're implying that a few more pounds in my pack will slow me down, son, you had best take those words back right now. I can still out walk you any day, and don't you forget it," Pryderi said, throwing Zareh a mock glare.

"Since you're so strong and hardy, then you can take the first watch. I'm going to get some sleep," Zareh said through a yawn, and proceeded to find a somewhat clear and level spot near the fire to settle down on.

Pryderi leaned against the boulder behind him and stretched his feet out to the fire. Half of him was alert to the night around him. He separated out the sounds of the wind in the pines, the skittering noises of small night animals foraging for food, night birds calling, and the occasional soft sound of wings gliding overhead. The other half of him was going back over the last several days. He had been surprised when Zareh had showed up with the lad and the border dog pup in tow. It was unusual for his son, who was cautious to the extreme, to have allowed the lad to follow him. Especially considering how very risky it was for Zareh to be in Høyhauger to begin with, and considering what he had carried out. Zareh was skilled enough to have known the lad was following him through the town streets and alleys, and could easily have eluded him, but he had not. Even odder was the fact that once Zareh had confronted the lad, he could easily have gotten rid of him, by fair means or foul, but instead had brought him along. He had to have weighed the importance of why they had come to Høyhauger in the first place against the risk of allowing the lad to accompany him, and with a pup no less. Even odder was the fact that Pryderi was not even sure his son could adequately explain why he had done what he had done.

Suddenly, Pryderi sat up a little straighter and became alert. Something besides the mystery of the lad's inclusion in their party had entered his consciousness. Something seemed amiss. He listened intently, and then the absence of sound struck him. The small rustling had stopped. The birds had stopped calling. Now there was only the sound of the wind. He questioned whether he should wake Zareh or continue to listen. He decided to continue to listen. Drawing his legs slowly under himself, Pryderi stood and placed his back firmly against the boulder he had been leaning against. The spot they had chosen to settle in for the night was fairly defensible from above, tucked in as they were under a long overhang.

With little haste, Pryderi quietly kicked dirt onto the glowing coals that were all that remained of their cook fire. Once the coals were mostly covered, making their campsite less visible, he walked over and woke Zareh with a voice little above a whisper.

"Something's not quite right. Something, or someone, may be out there. You go move the lad and the pup in next to the wall, and I will bring the pack horses in closer."

Zareh rose silently and swiftly moved to the far side of the now almost extinguished fire. He picked up Greer and carried him to the rock boulder Pryderi had been leaning against, settling him parallel to the wall. Greer did not wake, and the sleepy pup padded alongside of Zareh, flopping down and snuggling into Greer's body as soon as he was settled. Meanwhile,

Pryderi had been busy bringing the pack animals in closer and securing them, so that they could not run away easily.

"It could be a false alarm, but . . . ."

"No, you're right. It's too quiet," Zareh whispered back. "Besides, I would rather lose a little sleep than be caught unaware. We can't discount that someone could have been on our trail, or we may have crossed paths with smugglers. It could be some larger animal out hunting has quieted the other animals and birds."

The two men stood side by side barely breathing, listening to the night, hoping to hear something that would give them a clue as to what had silenced the normal night sounds. Suddenly, one of the pack animals shifted, and in the dying light cast by the last embers of the fire, the two men saw first one, and then another, hunting cat slip silently in under their overhang. The two hunting cats glided swiftly and silently to flank Greer's still sleeping form. Three things struck Zareh immediately. First, both of the hunting cats were smaller and younger than the one they had encountered earlier. Second, neither of the two pack animals had reacted at all to the hunting cats. Third, the pup was now no longer asleep, and was sitting up very alert, directly in front of Greer's body in a clear defensive stance, but not bothered at all by the two flanking hunting cats. In fact, he seemed oblivious to the hunting cats on either side of him, but was instead facing outward.

The night continued to be deathly still. Nothing but the wind seemed to move, and even that had died down a bit. All those under the ledge, except the pack animals, seemed to be straining forward just a bit, as if that would make their hearing better. Seconds ticked by, turning into minutes, before both of the hunting cats' ears pricked forward. Then both men caught the sound of stones skittering across rock. Something or someone had to be on the path about a quarter of a mile back where there was a rocky section. There had been a small rock slide there recently, and there was a lot of loose gravel on the path.

Who would be out there moving along the path at this time of night? Was it someone who had followed me, Zareh wondered. Just as he asked himself that, another thought entered his mind. Could it be the lad who was being followed? Had he jeopardized his task by bringing the lad along? Well, there was nothing he could do about it now. As quietly as possible, he smothered the remaining coals of the fire, moved back to brace his back against the rock, and settled in to wait.

CHAPTER FIVE

Anyone looking in under the ledge from the outside would have seen a strange tableau, if there had been light enough to see, Pryderi thought to himself. Two pack animals tethered and standing docilely, when they should be shifting nervously at the very least, being so close to two hunting cats. Two men standing side by side, alert but very still. The most unusual sight, however, would have been the two hunting cats sitting still as statues, flanking a sleeping lad who was being guarded by a border dog pup. Could the night get any stranger? Just as Pryderi asked himself that question, the clouds that had been thick all night, holding a threat of rain, moved on. The surroundings changed from being blanketed in a thick darkness to being bathed in bright moonlight. So much for the safety that the darkness had provided, though they were still hidden in the deep shadows under the ledge.

Zareh felt his father move towards the pack horses, and when he returned, he handed Zareh his short bow and a quiver of arrows. The ledge they were under had given them shelter. In addition, they could not be approached from above, but they were vulnerable from the front. As they watched, three men emerged from the tree line into the clearing. Simultaneously, an arrow flew and embedded itself into a tree trunk, right next to the head of one of the strangers. Zareh's first thought was that was quite a shot his father had just made, when he realized that his father had not moved. Now there was a troubling thought. Someone had made that shot from above them. Could things get any worse?

A voice called out from across the clearing. "Hold your fire. We mean you no harm. We just want the lad."

"And why would you be wanting the lad?" Pryderi asked.

"His father sent us after him. You know younglings. Got in a fight with his da, and set off to prove him wrong by heading out on an adventure. We've been trailing him these last few days and glad we've finally caught up to you. His father is more than willing to pay you well for your time, and I'm sure, kindness to the lad."

"Not the story the lad told us," Pryderi answered back.

"I'm sure not," the voice in the darkness answered smoothly. "That lad, he's quite a storyteller. Probably told you he was a street lad and gave you some story to convince you he needed to get away from town. He's a lonely lad, not many friends, and though his father has tried to discourage him, he spends entirely too much time at the back gate talking to the street lads. Knows the lingo, so I'm sure he's quite believable. Quite frankly, I'm surprised he was able to keep up."

While he had been talking, the other two men with him had been very slowly and carefully edging themselves away from the speaker. Two more arrows flew out of the darkness, barely missing them, halting their progress.

"I would suggest that you three remain at the head of the path," Pryderi stated firmly, as if he had been the one who had shot the arrows. "If what you are saying is true, why didn't you approach us earlier before dark, or wait until the light of day to approach us rather than sneaking up in the middle of the night? If you're so good at tracking us, then that means you knew where we had stopped to camp."

"Look, we don't care what you were doing in Høyhauger, but we really can make it worth your while to hand the lad over to us, and you can be on your way," the man said, and now there was an oily, wheedling tone to his voice.

Zareh thought that the man probably assumed that he and his father were smugglers, or at the very least on the wrong side of the law, or what passed for law in Høyhauger.

"Not interested," Zareh replied.

The man took a step forward, hands outstretched in front of him, and was about to speak when an arrow flew through the night air and stuck in the ground in front of him, its shaft quivering with force. Backing up quickly he said, "Look, if the lad is so important to you, then you can keep him. I just made up the story about his father. He is just a worthless street lad. No one cares what happens to him, but he has something that doesn't belong to him, and our employer wants it back. He's willing to pay a high price for it."

"Still not interested," Zareh replied.

"You drive a hard bargain," the man at the head of the path replied, and named a price that would have set a man up for a very comfortable winter's stay at a nice inn.

"You have given me two stories about the lad, and no answer to my question as to why you are skulking about this forest in the middle of the night, so I have little reason to believe you, and even less to trust you. I'm not interested in handing the lad, or anything in his possession, over to you," said Zareh.

"Well, that's the only way you're going to make a profit this night. I'm certainly not going to tell you the name of our employer, so you can make your own deal, and we're not going to stop following you. Sooner or later, we'll get what we want, and you'll get nothing."

"Let me rephrase what I just told you. I'm not interested in handing the lad or his possessions over to you at any price. He and what he has are not for sale, so it would seem we are at a standoff."

Or maybe not, Zareh thought, since he knew that the arrows that had been flying had come from neither him nor his father, but from someone who was standing on the ledge above them. He wished he knew if this were a friend or another foe. He also wished he knew why two young hunting cats were guarding this lad who was wanted by the men on the trail. What did this all mean?

Even as Zareh thought these thoughts, the situation swiftly changed. First, the man who was standing to the left of the speaker disappeared into the shadows in the trees. At the same time, the man to the right of the speaker was also swallowed up by the shadows, and before the speaker could utter, "What the . . . ," a large hunting cat glided out of the trees and crouched in front of the speaker, looking ready to spring.

"For your own wellbeing, I would suggest you don't move a muscle," a voice from above Zareh and Pryderi stated mildly, directing his comments toward the speaker, or at least Zareh and Pryderi hoped that was so.

The man who had been speaking and making offers to Zareh and Pryderi did not look so confident now, faced with a hunting cat in front of him coiled to leap, emitting a low growl to add to the menace of her threat. Both Pryderi and Zareh were distracted momentarily by the sound of a body dropping quietly to the ground from the lower edge of the ledge they were standing under. When they turned to face outward again, the man who had been standing at the edge of the glen was no longer there, nor was the hunting cat. She was now standing next to the newcomer.

"Perhaps we could all put our bows down, see if we can get your fire going again, heat up a warm cup of tea, and have a civil conversation," said the stranger mildly. "Those other gentlemen, and I use the term loosely, won't be joining us. They're a little tied up at the moment. I'm sorry, where are my manners? I am Bowen of the forester clan that watches over this area."

Pryderi and Zareh introduced themselves and thanked Bowen for his timely assistance. "What brought us to your attention?" Pryderi asked, hoping that they had not just gone from the kettle into the fire.

"The female hunting cat came and found us earlier this day. It's not often she seeks one of us out. She seemed to indicate we should follow, so we did. I see her two kits are standing guard over your young charge. What's so special about him?"

"I wish I had an answer to that question myself."

Zareh needed to come up with a plausible answer without revealing too much. He had to take a moment to think his answer through. This forester fellow seemed friendly enough, but he also held the upper hand. Zareh had no illusions that other foresters were lurking within the shadows of the woods that surrounded the clearing. He could not afford to be delayed more than he already had been, for what he and his father had come this way for was more important than even one small lad.

"I met this youngster when I discovered he was following me," Zareh continued. "He told me he witnessed the attack of a gentleman by his employer and feared for his life, so he ran. He needed a way out of Høyhauger that was not being watched." Zareh hoped that Bowen would not want to question him further, but that was not to be.

"And your business in Høyhauger?"

This conversation was getting a little uncomfortable for Zareh. This far north he did not know where the forester clans' loyalties lay. "Would it ease your mind if I told you that my father here and I are not smugglers and just passing through?"

"Not in the least."

"Well, um . . . ." Zareh stalled, using taking the pot of tea water off the now blazing fire as an excuse not to answer Bowen's question. Maybe changing the subject would get Bowen off this line of questioning. "Are you assigned to patrol this area by the Crown, or is this where you grew up?"

"Yes and yes. Now please answer my question, for it grows late."

"Truth?"

"Truth would be as refreshing as is this tea."

"I took the back way into Høyhauger on an errand for Lady Celik, a member of the interim ruling council. It was important that no one know I had been there, or who I had seen. As I was heading out, I noticed the lad here was following me. I apprehended him and felt it was to both our advantages to take him along."

"You seem to know the back ways pretty well. I take it this was not your first time slipping into and out of Høyhauger," Bowen said.

"My father and I owe a huge debt to Lady Celik and have often taken on tasks for her. I will tell you that we mean you and yours no harm, nor do we mean to harm the lad. Life has already done a good enough job of that. And I will tell you, he has made it this far on shear grit and determination. I intend to find a better place for him in Sommerhjem than he ever found north of our border." Zareh surprised himself with the vehemence of his answer.

"Having watched you both put yourselves at risk and watched you both be unwilling to give up this lad, who is a relative stranger to you, I'm inclined to believe you. It doesn't hurt that the hunting cats seem to trust him in your care. We'll keep watch for the rest of this night, so you can sleep away what little of it remains. Tomorrow we'll take care of your unwelcome guests and clear your back trail, making it much harder for anyone else to follow you. Some of my folks will accompany you out of the high hills and see you on your way."

"We would be grateful for your continued help."

Bowen got up and dusted off his pants. He left as quietly as he had arrived.

Father and son looked at each other, and their silent communication seemed to suggest that they might as well follow Bowen's instructions, for there was nothing else they could do. Zareh checked on Greer to make sure he was still alright. Both the young hunting cats had settled in next to Greer, and Kasa was tucked in between them. Zareh slowly reached his hand towards Greer's head, and none of the animals moved to stop him. Zareh checked Greer's forehead for a fever, but his skin was cool to the touch, which was a relief.

As Zareh settled into his blanket roll, he had a chance to reflect on what had happened over the last hour or so. He was certainly grateful to the foresters for their timely intervention, for he did not know how the standoff with the three men from Høyhauger would otherwise have come out. He was also relieved to know that their back trail would be cleared, so anyone else who tried to follow them would not be able to pick up their trail. But the looming question in his mind was not that they had been followed. And he wanted to kick himself for not being more careful covering their trail. No, the looming question in his mind was the one the forester had asked. Just what made Greer so special, and what was it that he had that those who had followed him wanted?

CHAPTER SIX

Greer awoke the next morning, feeling all cozy comfy toasty warm, and realized his feet were not screaming in pain. His good feelings abruptly vanished when he tried to get up and could not move. He was pinned to the ground by an unaccustomed weight holding him down. Even worse, his cloak hood was pulled down over his eyes, and he could not see. Not knowing what was going on, Greer made himself go still, but his earlier waking movements must have betrayed him. Adding to his confusion and slight panic was hearing a voice he did not recognize.

"Ah, it would seem your young charge is awake."

Still not knowing what was going on, Greer felt some relief hearing Pryderi's voice.

"Zareh, why don't you see if you can get that pile of fur off the lad so he can get up and have some breakfast? The hunting cats seem to understand you mean him no harm."

What was Pryderi talking about? What hunting cats? Greer tried to move again, but he could not even manage to get an arm out.

"If you all would be so kind as to move so Greer could get up, that would be appreciated," Zareh told the two young hunting cats and the border dog pup.

Slowly the hunting cats stood, and took their time stretching, before gliding out from under the overhang as silently as they had entered. Kasa just snuggled in closer to Greer's stomach, not willing to leave the warm nest he had made. Zareh just lifted him up and set him aside. He then moved back Greer's hood and asked, "How are you feeling this fine morning?"

Greer sat up and stretched, finding his muscles were not as sore this day as they had been the day before. His feet felt considerably better, but then he had not tried to walk miles on them yet. When he looked past Zareh, he saw the source of the voice he had heard. It was a man of middle years dressed all in forest colors, a patchwork of greens and browns. Greer imagined if the man stepped deep into the trees, he would be hard to notice, but then maybe that was the point of his clothing. Too bad, he thought, one could not combine materials and colors to make clothing that would allow one not to be noticed in the shadow of a building. That certainly would have made his life easier in Høyhauger. Shaking these thoughts from his head, he tried to concentrate on what Zareh was saying, finding himself still a little muzzy from sleep.

". . . and then the two young hunting cats came in under the ledge and took up guard positions on either side of you . . ."

Pryderi thrust a bowl of something warm into Greer's hands and handed him a spoon. Expecting the sour mash porridge he was used to, Greer was surprised when he tasted the nutty grain and dried fruit mixture that filled his mouth. The warm food was an added distraction, and Greer almost missed what Zareh said next.

". . . so it would appear that the men who confronted us last night were following you, not me. They seemed to think you had something they wanted," concluded Zareh.

When Greer looked up from his bowl, all the faces sitting around the fire were looking at him. He slowly set his bowl down and looked furtively right and left, assessing whether he might make a break for it, but running would not work here. He did not know the lay of the land. He did not have half a dozen bolt holes in which to hide. More to the point, his feet would not hold up, and he was not wearing shoes. What was he to do? What should he say? Had Kasa been undamaged, he might have been able to get away with telling them he had stolen the border dog pup, but he had already burned that bridge when he had first talked to Pryderi and Zareh. He knew better than that. One of the first painful rules he could remember learning on the streets was never, never give information away. Another rule he had learned was if you are going to lie, keep it as close to the truth as possible. Greer was reluctant to mention the pouch around his neck and its content. He still did not know why he had taken it, and something was compelling him not to mention it now.

"Just answer me one question," Pryderi intervened. "Do you have something that might belong to the three scalawags or someone who might hire them?"

The type of men Pryderi was asking about could be working for the stable owner. The stable was just a convenient legitimate business that the stable owner used to cover up any number of the not so legitimate deals and scams he had going at any one time. It was with some relief that Greer felt he could honestly answer that, no, he was sure he did not have in his possession anything that belonged to the men who had confronted Pryderi and Zareh the night before, nor anything that belonged to their employer. Greer did suspect the stable owner had hired the men, but he could not be sure. If, however, they were to ask about the gentleman who had been in possession of the pouch and its contents prior to being knocked out by the stable owner's thugs, then that was another story. Thankfully, his answer seemed to be enough for the questioners, and he was left to finish his breakfast.

While the campsite was being cleaned up and items were being stowed in packs, Bowen had slipped back into the forest. He had asked that they wait until his return before beginning their trek for the day. Greer had stood up and taken a few tentative steps, testing out his feet, when Pryderi admonished him to sit back down.

"I don't know how you think you're going to walk on those feet. The cloth I've wrapped around them won't last a mile after the felt slippers fall off, which would be almost immediately since they are at least several sizes too big for you, even with your feet wrapped," Pryderi scolded. "No, we're going to figure out a way for you to ride one of the pack animals. Just need to rearrange the load, but we're waiting on Bowen, for he asked us not to load up quite yet. Don't know what he has in mind."

What Bowen had in mind was a small, rugged, shaggy mountain horse that he was leading when he reentered the clearing. Following him were several other foresters leading several horses each.

"I've had my companions bring several more horses so that all of you can ride. Not that we haven't enjoyed this little interlude you've provided, but moving you as quickly as possible out of our forest land seems like a good idea, one that I don't think you'll object to. We will, pardon the pun, attempt to cover your tracks by back walking and riding your back trail. Some of our group will also ride with you. Just because the three we apprehended last night seemed intent on catching up to the lad doesn't mean others might not be coming this way looking for the two of you," Bowen said, looking directly at Pryderi and Zareh.

"We're once again indebted to you," Zareh replied. "When we have a chance, we'll get word to Lady Celik that the foresters of Fjell Skoj are loyal to the Crown."

"As we have always been, even when the Regent moved us out of our beloved hills and sent us to a forest far to the south. If Lady Celik has Lady Esmeralda's ear, please extend our thanks once again for her move to get all of the forester clans back to the woods they were born to."

"I'll do that, for that's the least I can do for you and yours."

With that said, Pryderi lent Greer an arm, and Greer hobbled over to the small horse that was being held for him. While Greer had been around horses working in the stable, he had never actually ridden one, and that was no small cause for concern on his part. Because he had told them he worked in a stable, they probably assumed he knew how to ride. However, his face must have given him away.

"You do know how to ride a horse, don't you, lad?" Pryderi asked.

"Well . . . , I, err, understand how to ride," Greer began.

"Ah," Pryderi commented. "You know how to handle and groom horses, but you have never ridden one, have you?"

Greer felt discombobulated, for he thought he was better at hiding his thoughts and emotions than he seemed to be able to do with Pryderi.

"Not to worry lad. These mountain horses are very sure-footed, and on the narrow trails we'll be traveling, your horse will just follow the horse in front of him. We'll not be galloping but traveling at a slow but steady pace. You'll just need to keep your balance and hold on."

Greer could only hope the horse he would be following would not go over a cliff and his horse would not just docilely follow right after. Pryderi lifted Greer onto the mountain horse and spent some time adjusting the stirrups. Pryderi told Greer he could let his legs dangle on the flat stretches of the trail, but he needed to put his feet in the stirrups when they were going up or down hills.

"Make sure you also grip with your knees," Pryderi said.

Just before they were to leave, Bowen approached Greer and handed him a pair of high laced soft leather . . . . Well, Greer really did not know what to call them, for they were not like any shoes or boots he had ever seen.

"These look to be your size. This night, when they unwrap those feet of yours and put more salve on, have them lightly rewrap them, and then, put these on. The insides are lined with sheepskin and should cushion your feet while keeping them warm. The lacing will help support your ankles. The soles are hardened elk skin and will handle the roughest of trails. Have had mine for a long time now, and they're only a little worse for wear," Bowen said, looking down at his own feet.

"I can't take these, sir," Greer said. "I have no coin to pay you."

It saddened Greer that he could not buy these boots. He guessed he would call them that, for lack of a better word. They looked so comfortable, and he had never in his life had anything that finely made, or new, for that matter.

"I'm sorry, I thought you understood. These are a gift. Anyone who can get the attention of not one but three hunting cats must have some forester blood in him. That practically makes you family. We take care of our own, you know," Bowen said.

Bowen hoped he had given the lad a reason to take the foot coverings without hurting his pride. But maybe "lad" was not quite accurate. Now in the bright morning sunlight, Bowen could see that the lad's small stature may give the impression that he was young, but there was a physical maturity there that suggested otherwise, if one really took a look at him beneath the dust and dirt. Something to think about.

Greer rationalized that he needed the boots for his very survival, since he would not make it to the edge of the clearing in foot rags. The longing to possess something new just once in his life, he had to admit to himself, was also part of the decision. He reached out and took the leather boots into his hands and thought he had never felt anything so soft. After he thanked Bowen, Bowen showed him how to lash his new boots in front of him to the saddle. Then Bowen left to have some last minute conversations with Zareh, Pryderi, and the foresters who were going to travel with them.

Greer, to his relief, found sitting on the horse was not uncomfortable. He was thankful that he was on one of the rugged mountain horses and not one of the taller ones that the rest of the party would be riding. He was a bit anxious about what would happen when the horses actually started moving. Finally, it was time to move out. Zareh had come over and explained to Greer that the foresters would be with them until they got down from the heavily forested high hills.

"We're lucky they came along when they did," Zareh said. "Besides the obvious of taking care of the three who were following us, the forester clans know every rock and tree in the forests they live in and manage. They also know the paths and byways and will get us to the lowland hills quicker. In addition, it'll be nice knowing someone will be covering our back trail, in case there are others who are far too interested in our business than is healthy for us. Now, please do not be as stubborn about your backside as you were about your feet. If you start to hurt, let someone know. We'll take breaks to stop and get the kinks out. No one is going to abandon you in these woods. You can stay with us as long as you choose."

Those were fine words, but a lifetime of scrabbling to survive warred against trusting words of promise from anyone, though Greer had to admit that so far, the man who had led him out of Høyhauger had been both kind and fair. He would just have to wait and see.

The path that led out of the clearing was reasonably level, and the mountain horse had a smooth walk, giving Greer time to adjust to being on top of a horse. Because of his recent work in the stable, he knew his way around horses, but riding one certainly gave him a different perspective from leading or grooming one. Once he felt somewhat comfortable, and did not feel he was in imminent danger of falling off, Greer had a chance to finally look at the countryside they had been passing through. When he had been hiking, trying to keep up and not be left behind, he had mostly looked where he would put the next foot, and by the time they stopped, he was too tired to take in the view. Now he could see they were traveling through a stand of huge pines, the size of which Greer had never seen. The floor of the forest was coated with pine needles, and very little grew under the trees except for a few sparse short plants. The air smelled wonderful, fresh and crisp with an undertone of pine. He thought to himself that if the rest of the trip out of the forest were like this, he might even let himself enjoy the journey.

That thought came crashing to an abrupt halt not more than fifteen minutes later when the party broke through the trees and ahead of them was a panoramic view of a high cliff on the left of the trail and a view over a valley far below on the right. The trail hugged the side of the cliff and made a steep descent into the narrow valley below. They cannot be thinking of taking these horses down that trail, Greer thought, just as the lead horse started downward.

CHAPTER SEVEN

Greer thought to himself, alright, this is it. I'm going to plunge to my doom, but I do not have to watch, He promptly closed his eyes and gripped the mountain horse between his knees so tightly that the inside of his legs went numb before his horse had even started forward. Greer sat there waiting for his horse to move when he was pulled out of his panicking thoughts by Zareh's voice behind him, suggesting he needed to loosen up on the reins or his horse was not going to move at all. That would be just fine with him, Greer thought, but then began to think more rationally, and slowly eased up, allowing his horse to begin to move forward.

"Just give the horse his head," Zareh suggested. "He knows what he's doing and will get you down safely."

Greer felt a well of hysteria bubbling up inside of him, thinking about the idea of giving the horse his head. A mental image began to form of all horses coming with detachable heads and so when one wanted a horse, one went into the tack room or barn and picked out the horse head one wanted, and then went to the stall or pasture and presented the head to the headless body. The trick would be to find the right horse body to go with the head one picked. Greer further began to think about picking a white horse head and placing it on a black horse's body, or picking a small pony head and placing it on a draft horse's body, and . . . . He was jerked out of these rambling thoughts when his horse abruptly tilted downward, and he began to hang on for dear life. He had tried to keep his eyes closed at the beginning of the downward journey, but being in the dark as to where he was going was worse than knowing where he was going.

Greer only made the mistake of looking to his right and downward once. Seeing the sheer drop off made his stomach take a really bad dip, and after that, he looked only straight forward, keeping his eyes on the horizon. He wished he had something to block out sound too. Listening to small rocks and stones being kicked off the path and tumbling forever down was also disconcerting. Greer hoped this path was going to be the only one like it, as the party progressed ever lower from the high hill forest towards the lower lands. Finally the ordeal was over, and Greer was able to pry his hands off the front of the saddle, but was not sure if he would ever have feeling in them again. Once down, the lead forester called a halt. Greer tried to unclench his knees and dismount, but like his hands, his knees did not work very well. When he slid down off the saddle, thankful that the ground was not all that far away, his knees buckled, and he found himself sitting on his rump.

Pryderi came over and gave Greer a hand up. "Now, that wasn't as bad as you thought it would be, now was it, lad?" Pryderi asked, with a twinkle in his eye.

"As compared to what?"

"Ah, I'll have to give that question some serious thought. In the meantime, you might want to try to bend your knees and shake your hands to get the kinks out."

Greer thought about Pryderi's suggestion. Since he did not want to embarrass himself further, he looked around for a small flat rock he could put his foot on to make his legs level, for knee bends were somewhat difficult for him. Fortunately, the ground next to his horse yielded what he was looking for and, holding on to the side of the saddle, Greer tentatively tried to squat down. He was only mildly alarmed when both his knees made popping sounds. The stretching and moving did help, and all too soon, the lead forester was telling them to mount up, for the day was a wasting.

The narrow valley where they were resting, at the bottom of the harrowing trail they had just descended, was not very long. Soon they were climbing again, but there were no more steep trails for the rest of the day. The route they were following at times merged with wider paths, and at times became narrow animal trails taking them ever onward. Greer understood all too well that he was hopelessly lost. If the foresters decided to abandon them at any time, and if Zareh and Pryderi went with them, Greer would not know how to be self-sufficient in the forest. At that moment, he felt a pang of homesickness wash over him for Høyhauger. He did not have much of a place there, but at least he knew how to survive in the streets and alleys. He did not like the feeling of being dependent on others.

Being a realist, Greer understood there was no going back to Høyhauger. He did worry about what would happen to him when they got out of the forest. He realized he did not know much about Sommerhjem. He knew enough to know that not all towns were like the border town he had grown up in. He had heard Pryderi and Zareh talking about meeting others and traveling on to Klippebyen. He had heard Klippebyen was just a village, which was all well and good, but what would he do there? If there were street lads there, they would most likely have their own territories and not welcome a stranger. Living on the streets was all that Greer knew how to do. He did not know a trade or a craft, he knew nothing of farming or fishing, and he had only rudimentary knowledge of reading and writing. Maybe he should have stayed in Høyhauger and taken his chances. Greer was still thinking about his future, or lack of future, when the party halted for the night.

After Greer had taken care of his horse, he began to help with the other horses, for it was something he knew how to do. He supposed he could also have volunteered to gather firewood. The rest of the party should be grateful he had not volunteered to cook, he thought to himself, as he continued the rhythmic brushing of the horse Pryderi had been riding, finding comfort in the repetitive work.

"Does frowning that hard help with the brushing? Is it like sticking your tongue out when you're concentrating?" asked Pryderi in a teasing voice. Seeing that the teasing had missed its mark and failed to lighten whatever heavy thoughts Greer was having, Pryderi changed tactics. "Something seems to be really bothering you this afternoon. Want to talk about it? I'd be happy to lend a listening ear."

What was it this day about detachable body parts? First horse heads and now ears, Greer thought. On a more serious note, what was he to say? Should he tell the truth? He wondered what Pryderi would say if he said, 'Well sir, I really don't know if I can trust any of you and I'm totally lost in this forest and don't know how to survive in the woods much less in this country. I have no skills and I don't know what is going to happen to me when we get to Klippebyen. Oh, and by the way, what is the penalty for thieves and pickpockets in this country if you get caught?' Instead he said, "Just thinking about the journey ahead, sir," which was a truthful answer.

Pryderi had the strong feeling he was not getting the whole answer from Greer but decided to let it go for now. He changed the subject. "Did you check the hooves of my horse? It seemed like she was favoring her right forefoot."

"I checked all of her feet before I started brushing her. Her hooves were clear. I wonder if she strained a muscle?"

"Here, let me get a jar of liniment out of my bag. Better to be safe than sorry, for we have a long way to go before we can get fresh horses. This liniment works on folks too, for sore muscles and sore spots. Feel free to use it yourself. Speaking of sore spots, before you settle in for the night, let me take a look at those feet of yours and put some fresh salve on."

"Yes sir, I will."

"You will what? Use the liniment or let me put some fresh salve on your feet?"

"Ah, both, sir."

"Good. Finish up here, for food is almost ready. We need to talk with our guides, find out where we are, and how far we are from where we are to meet those waiting for us. It's time to begin some planning ahead."

Greer was a bit surprised that Pryderi was going to include him in the planning. Up until now, Greer had just followed along, not really knowing what was going to happen next. He felt some relief knowing he would be privy to a little something of the plans. Once dinner was over, the lead forester cleared away a patch of dirt. In the fading light, he drew a crude map indicating where they were and the route he planned to take to get them to the site where Pryderi and Zareh's associates were waiting. Much to Greer's relief, the route would take only two more days and did not entail any more steep cliff-hugging paths.

Greer learned the forest lands they were traveling through ended along a ridge that bordered a long valley that was farmed by Farmer Yorick O'Gara, who was the youngest son of the O'Gara clan, known for their breeding of fine draft horses. When the Fjell Skoj forest clan was, as they put it, banished from their beloved forest and moved south, they had become acquainted with the O'Gara breed of horses. After the Regent Cedric Klingflug had been deposed, and the Fjell Skoj foresters were allowed to return to their home forest, they had met with Farmer O'Gara and invited his youngest son Yorick to move to the valley and begin a breeding program to produce a new breed of horses that would be larger than the small mountain horses, but as steady and surefooted. The valley they were heading for was ideal for raising horses, and the farm was a joint effort between the foresters of Fjell Skoj and Farmer Yorick O'Gara.

"You know, all this talk about the O'Gara farm just reminded me of something," Pryderi stated. "Besides breeding horses, Farmer Yorick O'Gara has another breeding and training program going on. He has also started to breed border dogs, which makes sense if you think about it. He is going to want to see that border dog pup of yours. Looks like he comes from good bloodlines."

Greer was not sure what impelled him to get up and go dig around in his pack for the slim book he had been puzzling over just before the stable owner had told him to get lost for a while. He had stuck it in his shirt, thinking he could use it to pass the time until he could return to the stable. The stable owner was going to be furious when he discovered it missing, so Greer was twice as glad he was not in Høyhauger. Though Greer had not had any formal teaching where reading and writing were concerned, he had learned enough over the years to puzzle some things out. The slim book he had taken was a record of border dogs the stable owner had bred, and Greer had wanted to find out about Kasa's line.

"I was looking at this before I was asked to leave the stable and never had a chance to give it back," Greer said. "I wanted to know about Kasa, and maybe figure out why he has such a different coloring from his littermates. I had forgotten I had it. Maybe it was what those men who followed us wanted. I would've been happy to give it back, for I truly didn't mean to take it."

Greer also wished he had thought of the slim book earlier when he was being questioned as to what he had that those men had wanted. Maybe it was not too late to plant the idea that the slim book was what they were looking for, so the knowledge of the pouch and its contents would be safer.

"Let's take a look at what you have there," said Pryderi, holding out a hand. After he had taken a moment to flip through the pages, he admitted he could not make heads or tails out of it. "Hold on to that book for a while. When we get to the O'Gara farm, you can show it to Farmer Yorick O'Gara. He'll be better at making sense of it and also might find it very interesting. Once he has a chance to look at it, if it is as important as you say to return it to the stable owner, he will arrange a way."

Greer felt this would be a good solution. While he had taken things in order to survive, he did not think of himself as a thief, for he never stole things to fence or just for the sake of stealing. He might have lived on the streets and been among the lowest of the lowest classes, but he had his pride and his own code of what was right and wrong. It surprised him that Pryderi had not commented negatively about how he had come to have the book or that he had kept it. So far Greer had to admit to himself that the two he had been traveling with had treated him well. Yet he still was not ready to put his full trust in either of them, for old habits die hard.

The next day's journey went well. The trees had begun to change from the tall hill pines to new growth forest. The forester who was in charge told Greer during the noon rest that a fire had swept through this area and the forest was just now beginning to look recovered. The forest was denser here, but the trail they were following was more defined. They were now following ridges for long periods of time before they descended down to the next ridge. Greer had begun to enjoy riding, now that he was not so sore every night and his feet had had a chance to heal.

Once the party had stopped for the night and set up camp, Greer was asked to fetch some water from a stream that was a short way away from the camp down a steep bank. He was cautioned to take care near the stream, for the rocks could be slippery. With due care, he had made his way down the embankment to the stream, had filled several water skins, and only needed to fill the last one before carrying them up the hill. Maneuvering the last water skin, which was the biggest, into the swiftly running stream was more difficult than the smaller water skins had been. As Greer leaned forward to press the water skin further into the stream, his foot slipped, and he tumbled forward into the cold water, hit his head, and was swept downstream.

Chapter Eight

"Are you alright? Are you alright?" said an unfamiliar voice.

"No, I am not alright. I have an aching head. What just happened here?"

"I am so sorry, sir. We have both been knocked unconscious by two very unsavory men."

"How could this have happened? I was told this was a safe part of town and you had a reputable stable. You are the stable owner, are you not?"

The stable owner was prepared for this question, and without a moment's hesitation he said, "That young rascal, that street lad Greer who I thought was more trustworthy, who out of the kindness of my heart I gave a job to, a place to stay, and one square meal a day, has betrayed me. He must have had a deal with the men who knocked us out, let them in, and showed them where to hide. Fortunately for us, some friends of mine who were stopping by chased the men off and that . . ."

". . . is a lie," stated an extremely tall woman, who strode into the stable as if she owned it.

"No, m'lady, 'tis the truth, I swear it. They knocked the gentleman and me out, and when my friends appeared, they ran off. My friends chased them."

"So, we will wait then for your friends to return to make a report, or perhaps we should call the peacekeepers and ask for their help," the imposing woman said, looking straight at the stable owner, who in turn was unable to return her look and had begun to sweat profusely.

"Well, I don't know when exactly they will be back. It might be a long wait. You don't need to stick around. Just tell me where you're staying and I'll send word."

The stable owner at this point stopped wringing his hands and pulled a grubby square of cloth from his pocket to wipe his forehead. Turning to the gentleman who had been rendered unconscious in his stable, the owner was particularly fawning when he assured him he would stable his horse at no cost for as long as the gentleman wanted. He hoped that would make up for the gentleman having been attacked. He just could not imagine what had gotten into that stable lad of his.

"You lie really well, but what is coming out of your mouth are still lies, with the exception of the offer to stable the horse for free," the tall woman suggested. "I was following this gentleman here and was delayed by a street beggar just down the lane. I had a clear view up towards the stable, and no one came up the lane to the stable or down the lane from the stable. I would conclude that your stable lad and those who attempted to rob this gentleman here left out the back way. If your friends arrived just in the nick of time to chase after the robbers, they would have run into them on their way out. That would certainly have caused a commotion and attracted attention, yet I heard only one shout from here. Your story has more holes in it than a rusty bucket. Let us try again."

The gentleman who had been knocked out listened to the exchange but remained silent as he studied the tall woman. Her height alone would have made her stand out, but it was more her air of command and intelligence that showed through, giving him some idea of who, or rather what, she was. The staff she carried was even more telling. The woman who was so skillfully handling the lying stable owner was a seeker, one of those individuals whose life's purpose was to gather and hold the old knowledge and find that which had been lost. The question was, why was she following him?

While the gentleman was thinking these thoughts, the stable owner had a number of thoughts running through his mind also. He, too, had recognized what the woman standing before him was and was sorting out what he had heard about seekers. A seeker was not a common sight in Høyhauger, but not unknown. So many rumors swirled around them. It was well known that no matter where they went, it was forbidden to harm them. It was known that awful things happened to those who did. Some rumors hinted that they held knowledge long lost and because of it could read minds or had special ways of determining the truth. What was he to do? What could he tell her to get himself out of the spot he was in and yet not betray those who had hired him, for to do so would make his life worthless. He knew he needed to get them out of the stable, for what would happen if the two he had hired came back? They could give everything away with a slip of the tongue.

"Let us start again then. The gentleman here was directed to your stable by a stable lad at the town stable, is that correct? Remember, I will know if you are lying."

That statement was mostly a bluff, but Seeker Zita hoped the stable owner would not know that. She looked at him with as much intensity as she could muster, considering the hour and the urgency. She needed to get this matter taken care of so she could get on with what she really wanted to do this night, and that was to have a serious chat with the gentleman who was standing so quietly next to his horse.

"Uh, yes, I believe that is so."

"How odd, for when I stopped by the town stable just a short while ago, one of the men there had a street lad by the scruff of the neck. He was trying to shake information out of him as to why he was posing as a town stable lad, waylaying late arrivals, and directing them to other stables. Let us try again. The street lad said he had been paid by several private stable owners to send business their way."

"Now you can't fault a fellow for being enterprising. Just a little healthy competition, yah know." That statement was followed by a very nervous laugh.

"A dubious business practice at best, but I had the opportunity to talk to the street lad. Since he knew it would be useless to lie to me, he informed me he was instructed to route this particular gentleman to this particular stable. Care to explain that?"

Another bluff, for Seeker Zita had not wanted to get the street lad into any more trouble than he was already in by letting this unethical stable owner know the lad had given up the information not out of fear, but for the price of a silver coin.

"Well, ah, he must have mistaken what I said. I paid him a little extra to send the richer looking customers my way," the stable owner replied, which was close to the truth and he hoped it would suffice. The longer they stood here and talked, the greater the chance that the two men he hired would return. He needed to get these two on their way.

"About your stable lad," said the gentleman, who had been unusually quiet up to this point, "You say this lad was involved in the attack on me, and I suggest you don't lie in front of the seeker here."

"I might have misspoke about the lad, now that I think about it. He probably just ran off when he saw the men attacking. He's just a little lad. I'm sure he'll be back in the morning. Yah see, I gave him a border dog pup, and he'd never leave him." The stable owner thought if he told about the border dog pup, he would show these two that he was a good sort.

"You gave a street lad a border dog pup?" the gentleman said incredulously.

"Well, sir, the pup was not a prize border dog pup by any means. Coloring was all wrong and well, to be truthful, had a bad leg too. Would have put it down, but the lad seemed to have a soft spot for it, so I didn't see the harm."

"Shall we check and see if he has returned?" the gentleman suggested. "Perhaps he can tell us something."

The stable owner was glad to be out of the intense scrutiny of the seeker as he led the way to the ladder to the hayloft where the street lad had a pallet to sleep on. He hoped Greer had not returned to the stable, for he suspected the lad had seen too much and would tell the seeker what, in truth, had taken place.

"Greer, you up there? Come down now, lad!" There was no response. "He doesn't seem to be here right now." Turning to look at the two who had followed him, he hoped they would go now, but that was not to be.

"Show me where his pup is," the gentleman demanded.

"Of course, sir. Just this way." The stable owner led the pair through the tack room to a side door that opened into a snug room housing the mother border dog and her pups.

"And which one of these pups belongs to the lad?" the gentleman asked.

The stable owner moved towards the pile of pups and began lifting and moving them, searching in vain for Greer's pup.

"Well?"

"The pup is gone. Maybe the lad took him out for a walk," said the stable owner, but his tone of voice was not very convincing.

"I think, sir," said the seeker, "that we are not going to get either the whole truth out of this dubious fellow here, nor is the street lad likely to return anytime soon, so we will have no opportunity to question him. We can check back in the morning. I would suggest we have gotten as much information here this night as we are likely to get. I don't think those who attacked you are likely to return."

"I imagine you are right," the gentleman replied and felt immensely tired. His head ached, but his heart ached even more. He had been so close, and now he was right back to the beginning again. He was roused out of his musing by the seeker's next question.

"Have you arranged lodging for the night?"

"No, I was going to stable my horse and then proceed to find a place to stay. Now I will need to start over. Find a new place to stable my horse, for I will not leave him here, and then find a place to stay."

"If you would allow me, I can suggest a place that will meet both of your needs."

"I would be most grateful. Lead on."

The gentleman turned and gave the stable owner a look that left him feeling less relieved than he had hoped with the imminent departure of the two.

As the pair exited the stable, the seeker suggested they postpone formal introductions and conversation until they got to the inn she had in mind. "This place isn't fancy but it's clean and secure, which I am beginning to believe is a very rare virtue in this town."

The two walked side by side, the gentleman leading his horse. Both were alert to the environment around them, which was becoming more obscure as time passed, due to a rising ground fog. After about fifteen minutes, the seeker directed the gentleman and his horse to turn down a side lane and then suggested he continue while she waited just inside the opening of the lane.

"I think we are being followed," the seeker whispered. "I would like to find out if that is so, and by whom. Should you not be leading a horse, we could probably lose whoever is following us, but . . . ." She really did not have to finish her sentence.

The gentleman followed the seeker's request and led his horse down the narrow lane. The seeker meanwhile had slipped into the shadows next to a building and waited. She did not have to wait long before a street lad, who had been following them, cautiously slipped around the corner into the lane. Unaware of the seeker hiding in the shadows, the street lad began to follow the gentleman and his horse. When the seeker stepped in front of him, and before the lad could bolt, she gained a very strong grip on his arm.

"So, lad, you could try to convince me that you were just out for an evening stroll, but know that I would not believe you."

"I've gots some information for the gentleman you're with, if he makes it worth me while," the street lad said slyly. "I cans tell him where the street lad he's looking for is."

"Well then, we had best get a move on, and you can negotiate with him as to how much this information is worth."

Perhaps more than you think, she thought to herself. Upon reflection of their time at Milkin's Stable, it seemed to her the gentleman she now found herself walking with had more interest in the street lad who was working at the stable than the attempted mugging warranted. While he had tried to cover up his emotions, the gentleman had seemed almost defeated when it looked like the lad had taken his pup and was not going to return anytime soon. He seemed more concerned about the lad's whereabouts than the fact that he had just survived an attempted robbery. The seeker found that very interesting indeed.

It turned out that the information the street lad had was not worth the copper the gentleman paid for it. The street lad told him the lad he was looking for, who he described as a small cripple lad, worked at Milkin's Stable.

The gentleman was gracious, but informed the street lad that that was old news, flipped him a copper for his effort, and turned to continue down the lane. The lad slipped away into the thickening fog. It did not take much longer for the pair to reach the inn the seeker had suggested, and she was greeted warmly by the innkeeper. It was obvious to the gentleman she was known here. Soon the pair was settled in by the fire with a warm drink and the promise of food.

"Now that we are settled, it might be a good time to introduce ourselves. I am Seeker Zita, and you are?"

"Lord Avital of Dugghus, at your service. I am grateful for your timely arrival at the stable and your assistance."

"What brought you to Høyhauger, if I might ask?"

"It is a long story, but in light of the hour, I will give you the shortened version. My wife passed away several months ago . . . ."

"My condolences."

"Thank you. As I was saying, my wife passed away a few months ago after a long illness. In her dying days, she felt it necessary to get something off her conscience. When we were first married, she became with child, and I was very excited for our first born to arrive. Unfortunately, business had me away when the long anticipated event happened. When I arrived home, I was greeted with the news that our son had been born but lived only a few short hours. We had several children after that, but not until my wife was in her dying hours did she reveal that our first born did not die. He was born with one leg shorter than the other. My wife was so insecure in my feelings towards her that she thought I would not love her if she presented me with what she thought of as a damaged child, so she sent him away. There was a couple who worked for us at that time who had recently lost a newborn child. My wife gave our son to them along with a good deal of coin. They left immediately and settled in Høyhauger, where they set up a small shop. Seems he was from here and still had relatives here. After my wife died, it took a while to put my affairs in order so I could be absent from home for as long as it took to try to find my son, if he were still alive."

Lord Avital paused to take a sip of his warm drink. "Upon arriving in Høyhauger, I located where the couple my wife had given our son to had lived. Unfortunately, about ten years or so back, an epidemic swept through Høyhauger and neither of the two had survived, nor apparently had their relations. When I inquired about their child, folks vaguely remembered him, but no one could remember what had happened to him. I chanced upon a merchant who heard I was looking for a lad who was, as he described it, a cripple. He told me about a street lad named Greer who had one leg shorter than the other. His coloring was right, but perhaps not his age. So far I have had no luck locating him and had inquired of some street lads to help me find him."

"So either by chance or design you were directed to Milkin's Stable this night."

"So it would seem. Regretfully, if the street lad who was working at the stable is my son Tal, he is now gone, and I am back to the start of my quest once again," Lord Avital said sadly.

CHAPTER NINE

"Yer pardon, sir, ma'am, but there's a street lad at the door, and he's insistent on seeing you, sir. I tried to encourage him to come back in the morning, but he will not go away," said the innkeeper.

Lord Avital followed the innkeeper to the door and stepped outside. Standing on the lower step of the front stoop was an underfed youngster clothed in a mismatched collection of clothing and rags. Lord Avital could only wonder if this was what the lad Greer looked like and how he lived. Even now it was incomprehensible to him how his late wife could have thought he would not love a child, no matter what, and would wish a life such as this lad lived on their son. To be fair to his wife, she could not have known their child would end up on the streets.

"You the bloke givin' out coin for information on Greer the gimp?" the street lad asked, pulling Lord Avital out of his thoughts of the past and dragging him back to the present.

"If you are here to sell me the information this Greer lad works at Milkin's Stable, you are too late."

"Aye, he worked there, he did, but he's run off, and I can put youse on his trail."

Lord Avital felt his heart begin to speed up, but his mind was telling him to take care, for this street lad could just be telling him a tale in order to get some coin out of him. Lord Avital became aware at that moment that Seeker Zita had stepped through the open doorway and was peering down at the lad at the bottom of the steps. She certainly presented an imposing figure. He noticed she had grabbed her staff before she had come outside, and he could have sworn it glowed in the light from the lantern hung to the left of the door.

In a voice that was deceptively soft, Seeker Zita asked the lad how he might have acquired such information, and why the two of them should believe him. After all, it had been a street lad who had directed the gentleman into harm's way once already this night.

"I gots me reasons for talkin' wit' yah, but coulds we do it some place not so open?"

Lord Avital looked to Seeker Zita for direction, for he did not know what was custom here, and she knew the innkeeper. She gave a nod of her head, turned, and walked back inside. Lord Avital followed, and the street lad brought up the rear. Instead of stopping in the great room and resettling themselves by the fire, Seeker Zita led them to a dimly lit side room, ushered them in, and closed the door. The room held only a table, and the rest of the floor space was empty. Hung along the walls were chairs. Seeker Zita lifted one down and handed it to the street lad. Taking one for herself, she settled in at the table, leaving Lord Avital to reach up and take down a chair for himself. As Lord Avital pulled himself up to the table, he noticed Seeker Zita had placed her staff across the table. He saw the street lad was looking at it and appeared much less cocky.

"Now, lad," Lord Avital began, "this should be private enough. The hour grows late, so you had best get on with your tale."

"What abouts me coin? How much yah willin' to pay for knowin' abouts the gimp? Wents to a bits of trouble ta find yah, I dids."

"How much will depend on how quickly you get on with your tale, and if it tells us anything new," Lord Avital replied. Seeker Zita remained silent and let Lord Avital negotiate.

"Word went out that the Milkin's Stable owner was offerin' a reward to anyone who would give him the whereabouts of the gimp see, the same one youse was askin' about earlier. Seems he gots somethin' the stable owner wants. The ways I figures it, youse might pay more than the stable owner for the information, youse bein' a gentleman and all. Yah see, I gots me this bunch of younger lads as looks up to me, and so I sent out the word I needed to find the whereabouts of the gimp. One of me lads was liberatin' a meat pie from the bake house up in the posh area and spotted the gimp. He was doin' some liberatin' too, if'n youse knows what I mean."

"Go on," Lord Avital encouraged.

"Me lad see, he's almost a better climber than a squirrel, and he tooks it upon his self to follow the gimp, since the gimp was poachin' on our territory, so's to speak. Lost him for a while, but when he spots him again, he's with this tall bloke, a foreigner he was by his dress, and they was slippin' outa town down the old smugglers way."

"Do you know what he is talking about?" Lord Avital asked Seeker Zita.

"I do."

"Does this lad's tale telling have any truth in it, or is he just blowing smoke?"

"I have a question for you," Seeker Zita stated. "Was the lad alone before he met up with the tall bloke?"

"Well, he weren't travelin' with no other street lad, if'n that's what yer askin'." Then the street lad seemed to recall something, so continued. "Me lad says the gimp had a pup followin' him for a time. When he caught up with the gimp later, he was carryin' somethin' in a sling. Couldn't make it out. The pup was no longer hangin' around him. Musta found somethin' to hunt."

"I suggest you pay the lad, so he can be on his way. You will not be selling this information to anyone else this night, now will you?" asked Seeker Zita, as she reached for her staff, lifting it off the table and knocking the end sharply on the floor. A subtle move, but hopefully effective.

"No, no, I'll not be sellin' the information to anyone else this night," the street lad answered, as he was pocketing the coin Lord Avital had handed him.

No, he would not be selling the information this night, Seeker Zita thought, but he had not said he would not sell it in the morning. Seeker Zita escorted him to the door. He fled down the steps and was swallowed up by the fog.

Settled once again in the great room by the fire, Lord Avital asked Seeker Zita her opinion on what the street lad had just told them.

"There are many ways in and out of Høyhauger, but very few ways through the mountains to the south. My feeling about the stable owner is he is not just a simple merchant but someone who has his fingers in a lot of pies in this town. If what the street lad said is true, that this lad Greer has something the stable owner wants, the stable owner probably called in a number of favors, and all of the regular routes out of town are now being watched. The old smugglers way is little known, there being easier and better traveled routes protected by what one could almost call a smugglers guild, which by the way, exists due to the ruling prince of this province. He makes a nice profit off of them."

Lord Avital moved to get up out of his chair when Seeker Zita's voice stopped him. "I can understand that you might want to rush off to follow this tip, but I have a suggestion." Lord Avital sat back down. "I know the old smugglers way. Traveling on foot in the dark, if you have never taken that way before, is highly dangerous. Also, you disappearing from town abruptly without your horse is going to cause notice."

"What would you suggest I do? My reason for coming to this town, for all appearances, is now gone."

"What I would suggest is we leave in the morning, go out the town gate, and take the pass back to Sommerhjem. No, wait. I am not suggesting you give up your search. Hold on, I'll be right back."

Seeker Zita stood up and left the great room to climb the stair to the sleeping room she had rented for the night. Going to one of her travel bags, she opened the front flap, pulled out a thin leather bound folder, and went back down stairs. Motioning Lord Avital to join her at a table near the fire, Seeker Zita lifted a lamp off the mantle and lit it, placing it on the table. Upon opening the leather folder, she carefully removed a very thin folded piece of parchment and opened it up.

"This map was done by another seeker who spent an extensive amount of time in these mountains. Here is Høyhauger. Here you can see the pass gate, and the pass through the mountains. These other lines here represent other more discrete ways of leaving town and traveling south through the mountains."

"Why are the lines different colors?"

"The key to the colors is here," Seeker Zita said, pointing to the lower left hand corner of the map. "Those lines in brown show the normal routes in and out of the mountains and the town. See, here is the main town gate leading to the pass. You probably came in that way."

Lord Avital nodded that Seeker Zita's supposition was correct. "Go on."

"These trails in blue are the trails the smugglers control, and these trails in red are the ones traveled most frequently by the border patrols. The dotted ones are the border patrols of Bortfjell and the solid ones indicate the border patrols of Sommerhjem. As you move into Sommerhjem, you will see green lines. Those are the major trails that go through the Fjell Skoj forest and are looked after by the forester clan who lives there."

"Where is the trail that the street lad told us about?"

"You see this very faint line here?" Seeker Zita indicated, pointing to a line so faint that it was hard to see in the lamp light.

"Yes."

"This is an old, old smugglers' route and little traveled these days. It was always a very difficult trail to traverse, and for the first several days, has to be traveled on foot. If our street lad was not making up a story just to earn a little coin, it would seem Greer went this way. My guess is he was not traveling alone."

"Why would you suspect that?"

"If he is like other street lads I have encountered, they most often have never left the village or town they have grown up in. They have great survival skills within the town confines but very little knowledge of how to survive outside the town. This Greer must have had a powerful incentive to cause him to leave the town. To do so, he would most likely have needed help. I traveled this way for a time with a tall bloke and his father. I know he was headed to Høyhauger, and he was the one who showed me the old smugglers way. Of course, the description the street lad gave us could fit a lot of folks."

"Since this is the only information we have about where Greer might be, if you will show me where this trail begins here in town, I will head out at first light."

"There will be no need for that. Leave at first light certainly, but leave on horseback through the town gates and through the pass. No, I am not discouraging you from looking for Greer, but here, look at this map again. See here where the old smugglers way ends?" Lord Avital nodded. "It ends in the Fjell Skoj forest and nothing passes through the forest without the forester clan knowing about it. What we should do is take this trail here after the pass and head into the forest."

"You wish to come with me?"

"Yes, of course. I did not come all this way to find you just to have you wander off. At any rate, I know the Fjell Skoj foresters, and we can ask for their help."

It took a few moments for Seeker Zita's words to penetrate, and then Lord Avital realized this was the second time this evening Seeker Zita had mentioned that she had been looking for him. Sitting back down, Lord Avital crossed his arms, looked at the seeker, and suggested she explain.

"You are aware of what happened in the capital at the summer fair, are you not?"

"I am aware that the former regent has stepped down, and there is an interim ruling council, but when all of that was happening, my wife was dying, and my attention was elsewhere."

"That is a lovely way to put the Regent's abrupt departure from the capital, but needless to say, it was in many folks' opinions long overdue. The Lady Esmeralda called the Gylden Sirklene challenge, which mandates an interim ruling council for one year. At the end of that time, any who wish to take the challenge to become the next king or queen can."

"What would that have to do with me? I have no wish to rule Sommerhjem."

"What happened in the capital that third day of the fair is a long story in the telling, but because it is late, I will cut to the end and tell you the important part that concerns you. After the challenge was called, a box set in the sea wall of the Well of Speaking was opened. According to the Book of Rules, the box is designed to hold the nine pieces of the oppgave ringe. All nine pieces need to be returned to the box in order for the next part of the Gylden Sirklene challenge to commence. Two of the pieces have already been placed in the box. A call has gone out for the seven remaining pieces of the oppgave ringe."

"I repeat, what does this have to do with me?"

"It is believed that your family has been the guardian of one of the pieces. It is a small oddly shaped gold ring with what looks like random scratches on the outer surface."

Lord Avital's hand went swiftly to his collar. He reached inside his shirt and felt for the pouch he had worn for years, ever since his father had entrusted him with it. The pouch was gone.

Chapter Ten

As dreams went, this was a really good one, Greer thought to himself. He was dreaming he was snuggled down in a warm soft bed. I'll just stay in this dream a little longer, he thought. It was better than waking, picking the hay out of his hair, and trying to shake the dust out of his cloak before climbing down the ladder from the hayloft of the stable. As he lay there with his eyes tightly closed, trying to hold onto the last tattered remnants of the dream, he became aware of a delicious, tantalizing smell. He could not recall ever having something smell in a dream.

"Ack, I think our young friend is awake."

"Good, good. I was beginning to worry, for he has slept too long."

"Well, you might sleep the day and night out too if you had taken an unexpected journey down the Raskalt, especially if you had tumbled through rapids and over falls. He is certainly a very lucky fellow to have survived the journey at all."

What journey, what falls, Greer thought to himself. When he tried to sit up, he abruptly laid back down. He hurt all over. It was then that the memory of the past few days came rushing back.

"Here, let me help you, lad. You lift up slowly, and I'll put a few pillows behind you. We'll take it slow."

Greer opened his eyes once again and took a good look at the woman who was speaking. She was quite elderly in his opinion, with wispy white hair sticking up in a wild array around her head. Her face, etched with a myriad of fine lines, held the most strikingly blue eyes he had ever seen. She was not a tall woman by anyone's standards and was dressed all in various shades of green. He winced as she helped him sit up and rearranged the pillows behind him. Being upright gave him a new perspective of the room he was lying in. For one, it was one of the most beautiful rooms he had ever seen. Everywhere he looked from floor to ceiling was wood, polished wood carved in a way he had never seen before. Walls made out of wood, cupboards, shelves, tables, all carved wood.

"Where am I, and how did I get here?" Greer asked, once he was settled sitting up.

"Well, if we lived by the ocean, I could claim you came floating in with the tide, but since we are in the high hills nowhere near the ocean, that just won't do as an explanation. You are in the Fjell Skoj forest in my home, which my young friend, you should know is located about twenty feet up in a very large tree. I hope you are not prone to walking in your sleep. As to how you got here, you came by water. Floated in you did, on a pile of branches. Seems you are a very popular fellow, for a great number of folks have been searching for you. I suspect you are probably hungry, so you just rest right there while I go fetch you a nice bowl of soup."

Once the woman had left the room, Greer took the time to really look at the room he was in. Out of habit, he first checked entrances and exits. There was the door the woman had left out of and a very small window that Greer would be hard-pressed to squeeze himself through, small as he was. And what had the woman said about being twenty feet up? Was her cottage built on the side of a cliff? No, she had said they were in a tree. A more pressing question was, who were all these folks who were searching for him? Without conscious thought, his hand crept to his neck, and he felt for the cord that held the pouch he had grabbed up at the stable. The cord was still there, as was the pouch and its contents. He quickly made sure the pouch was tucked back in under his shirt when he heard footsteps approaching.

"Now then, once you get some food in you, have a bit more of a rest, it will be best for you to try to get up and get those sore muscles moving. Your ride down the Raskalt did not break anything that we could tell, but it did toss you around quite a bit. You certainly are black and blue all over."

Greer had a moment of panic when he realized he was wearing only what appeared to be a long shirt with the sleeves rolled up. He felt trapped. He was in a room where the only way out was through the woman in the doorway holding a tray, and then he was certainly not dressed for an escape through the Fjell Skoj forest. All of these thoughts were swirling around in his head when one more thought entered. Kasa! What would become of Kasa? How would he ever find him? Would Zareh or Pryderi look after him? He had to get out of here. He had to find Kasa. Greer flung the covers back and was trying to get out of bed when he heard the woman call out a name, and a man of similar age and dress entered the room.

"Now, lad, if you didn't want the soup, all you had to do was say so," the man stated, winking at Greer, while gently pushing him back into the pillows and drawing the covers back up. Seeing the look on Greer's face, that look he had seen in trapped animals, the man took on a more sober demeanor. "It's alright, lad, there's nothing to fear here. You are safe. No harm will come to you here in the Fjell Skoj forest, not while you are under the protection of the Fjell Skoj foresters."

It was then that Greer finally really took a look at the two who were looking back at him. He worried that he was losing his edge, for usually he was much more observant than he had been these last few minutes. These two were dressed in a variation of the dress that Bowen and his men had been dressed in. As his panic began to subside, Greer began to remember what had happened to him. He remembered he had been down by the stream, filling the water skins, and had slipped. What happened after that was a blur. He remembered hitting his head, and he thought he had blanked out for a while. After that he had drifted in and out of wakefulness. He seemed to recall the feeling of fur under his hands, but that could not be right.

"Ellwood is right. You are safe here. I'm sorry if you thought otherwise. Now sit up a little more, so I can put this tray on your lap. You need to eat to get back on your feet."

"Thank you, mistress," Greer replied, as a tray containing a bowl of thick rich soup and a large slice of crusty dark bread was placed on his lap.

"Oh, pish posh! None of that mistress this and mistress that here. I have reached an age where I can be called what I want. You call me Aldona."

"Aldona," Greer said, trying the name out, "just exactly what is the Raskalt, and where exactly is here?"

"Why the Raskalt is the swift stream you came floating in on, and had you not gotten yourself on that raft of branches and twigs, I swear we would have been picking you up in battered pieces. The Raskalt tumbles down through these hills in a series of rapids and small falls. You must have Neebing luck, lad, that's all I can say. Now as to where you are, you are in our home, which is located about twenty feet up in a very old quirrelit tree. There are about twelve families who have their homes here in various trees surrounding an open area. We have lived here almost all of our married life, with the exception of the few years when that terrible Regent made us all move to a southern forest. We cherish living here now more than ever. Never again will we take this forest or this way of life for granted."

Aldona turned, but not before Greer had seen the beginning of tears in her eyes. He did not quite understand her deep loyalty to a place. He had never felt connected to Høyhauger, and that thought surprised him. He had lived in Høyhauger as long as he could remember, but leaving it had not been overly hard. Nothing and no one held him there or beckoned him to return. The only living creature that mattered to him was Kasa.

"Now Aldona, there, there," Ellwood crooned as he patted her hand. "'Tis over now. We're home to stay. Never again will foresters willingly leave our homes or our forests. All of the forest clans have decided that. With the calling of the challenge, the old ways are returning to Sommerhjem. No more fretting now."

Greer wished he knew what they were talking about. What in the world was a Neebing and what challenge? He had more pressing issues at the moment, however. "Who was looking for me?" Greer was a little afraid of the answer, hoping against hope it was not someone the stable owner had sent after him.

"Why all of the Fjell Skoj foresters of course," stated Ellwood, as if this answer should be obvious to Greer. When he noticed the slight confusion on the lad's face, he said, "We take such a dim view at losing someone who is under our care. Once it was noticed that you were missing, Bowen was alerted, and he sent out messenger birds to all corners of the forest calling for a search. He also included in his message a caution about strangers traveling off the regular paths and lanes through the forest. You washed up on our bank yesterday evening and are about a two day's ride from where you went into the Raskalt. We sent off a messenger to let Bowen know you were here and safe, if somewhat less than sound. He got in touch with your party, and we expect them here sometime early tomorrow."

Aldona sat with Greer while he finished his soup and kept up a lively chatter about the life in the small community she and Ellwood lived in. Her ventures into knowing more about Greer were met with one word or short answers and told her very little about the lad. It was not long after Greer had soaked up the last of his soup with the heel of the bread when his eyes drifted closed. Aldona removed the tray resting on his lap and pulled the covers up. When she left the room, she left the door slightly ajar so she could hear Greer if he were to wake. Aldona then went in search of Ellwood.

"Pretty closed mouth, that one," Aldona suggested to Ellwood. "He comes from the border town of Høyhauger and, from the looks of things, is both underfed and overly cautious. The clothes he was wearing were cobbled together by less than skilled hands and certainly mismatched. He doesn't seem to have any family."

"Makes you wonder why he is being looked for by other than the clan, now doesn't it?"

"Did you get more news?"

"Bowen sent another messenger bird which arrived when you were in with the lad. Seems besides the three they intercepted earlier this week, two more strangers are in the forest, the seeker Zita and a gentleman who is traveling with her. They too are looking for Greer. I was surprised Seeker Zita has returned to our forest so soon. She was here not so long ago, and from my conversation with her, she had not anticipated returning back this way so soon. Anyway, Bowen suggests we call in the others from their various duties in the area to make sure the lad is well protected. Seems the hunting cats have shown an interest in him also."

"How odd," remarked Aldona. "Such an unassuming folk to generate so much interest."

"I wonder if it has something to do with the pouch woven of golden pine spider silk he wears around his neck?"

"You haven't been snooping now, have you old man?"

"No, old woman, I have not. It was just when we first got him here and got him out of those sopping wet rags he was wearing and into the nightshirt, I noticed the cord around his neck and looked at it. The finely woven pouch was such a contrast to the rest of the lad's attire that it struck me as odd. I did not look inside, for I know better than to go poking around in anything made of golden pine spider silk as well as you do. We understand the old ways."

"I missed seeing the pouch."

"You were busy taking the lad's boots off and thinking of tossing them out," suggested Ellwood.

"Well, even forester-made footwear can only stand up to so much abuse. A tumble down the Raskalt might have been more than they could take."

"Ah, ye of little faith. While they may not be as good as new, they are now dry and have come out only a little the worse for wear. Actually, they may be in better shape than our youngster. When he wakes, I'll make sure he gets a fresh coat of liniment on those bruises and more salve on his feet."

"That would be good. Now that the lad's awake, he will be better able to tell you where it really hurts. I noticed the lad has one leg longer than the other. The boots he was wearing were obviously of forester origin, so I guess they were given to him by Bowen or one of his party. They certainly will protect his feet and keep them warm, but they do nothing for his balance and gait. Do you think you can figure something out?"

"Not an original thought, my dear. I went to sleep thinking about it, and this morning I took them over to Brogan. Always handy to have the best leatherworker in the Fjell Skoj forest living just two trees away. He is going to make a new pair of boots for the lad and build up the sole of the left boot so that when wearing the boots the lad will stand even."

"Why not just add additional sole to the boots the lad already has, since you said they are still good?"

"Brogan was worried the lad would be more off balance in the built-up boot than he is now, since he probably has adjusted to his uneven gait. If the built-up boot is not to the lad's liking, he will still have a good pair of boots."

"That makes sense. What does not make sense, however, is the fact that a hunting cat just looked in the front window."

CHAPTER ELEVEN

"Let's go over what happened at the Milkin's Stable one more time," Seeker Zita said calmly, with more patience that she felt. She had been so close to accomplishing her goal only to have it snatched away. Lord Avital may have lost a chance of possibly connecting with his long lost son, and that was tragic in a very personal way, but she had been moments away from finding someone who either had known, or might know, where to find one of the seven missing pieces of the oppgave ringe. Now that moment had been stolen away.

"I arrived, dismounted, and was talking to the stable owner. Suddenly two men rushed out of a nearby stall, and I saw one of them knock the stable owner down. Then the second one hit me with something, and I remember little after that. I am afraid I am no help."

"You are certain that you had the, well, the pouch and its contents on your body when you arrived in Høyhauger, and more importantly, when you dismounted at the stable?"

"I have worn that pouch for a great many years. My father entrusted it to me when I married and told me I was to always keep it close. He said it was a sacred trust that our family had held since time out of mind. I was to guard it with my life. I was to pass it down to one of my children; the one I felt would best be able to guard it when the time came. When I asked him about what it was and what the significance of it was, he could not tell me, only that it was extremely important. I actually never took much stock in his ramblings, for he was quite old and ill when he gave the pouch into my keeping. I would have just thrown it in a drawer if he had not made me swear on my honor that I would keep it with me. Now you tell me that my family has been charged with guarding this piece of the, what did you call it?"

"The oppgave ringe."

"Right, the oppgave ringe, which was last seen over several centuries ago."

"Correct. I appreciate that the hour is late and the tale is, I am sure to your mind, fanciful, but the oppgave ringe is very real and extremely important to our country. The rulers of our land had been chosen by the Gylden Sirklene challenge from the time we came to Sommerhjem up until several hundred years ago. That all changed after the extremely long reign of King Griswold. As he crept up in years, his daughter began to take over the day to day ruling of our country, and when King Griswold finally died, she just assumed the reign. She also lived quite some time, and by then it just seemed natural that her son take over the reign. He did not live quite as long as his mother, but his daughter then became Queen. She was the mother of Lady Esmeralda. The Queen's untimely death led, as you know, to the naming of a regent and all that happened after that. Over the years, the Regent acquired more land and more power. He tried to prevent the royal heir, the Lady Esmeralda, from assuming the throne."

"So, just like our country had forgotten how rulers were supposed to be chosen, we as a family had also forgotten, over the long years, why the object in the pouch was important. We only knew that it needed to be protected for some reason."

"That would seem to be the case for your part of the oppgave ringe. Once the challenge is over and a new ruler is chosen, the nine parts of the oppgave ringe are placed in the safe keeping of various families until they are needed again. Because of the length of time between the last calling of the Gylden Sirklene challenge and now, who has those pieces has been lost. There are hints and clues here and there, and the seekers and others have been charged with tracking down the remaining pieces. So many of the trails are cold or lost in obscurity. The royal librarian stumbled across a clue in an old letter from your great grandfather to a previous royal librarian that led me to you."

"She must have told someone else, unless you did, for how would anyone know what I carried when I did not even know?"

"I am sure I did not tell anyone, nor was I followed, but there are those everywhere who are still loyal to the Regent. Any one of them could have been doing their own research or inquiry. The royal library is open to all and has been for as long as anyone can remember. The former regent, Lord Cedric Klingflug, had a number of members of his court who regularly used the library. The royal librarian certainly could not keep track of all that they looked up. Lord Klingflug could have anticipated that someone might call the challenge and been searching for what constituted it. We may never know. What is almost certain is the fact that I was not the only one looking for you, and you led all of us on a merry chase, since you were on a quest of your own."

"It makes sense that the piece of the oppgave ringe, or more accurately the ring in the pouch, was what the stable owner was after. I think we can safely assume he did not get it, and maybe, just maybe, the lad named Greer left with the pouch and its contents. It would be a satisfying irony if that were so. The ring that has been entrusted to my family, ironically, might still be in the safekeeping of my family, if Greer is indeed my son," Lord Avital said, looking bemused.

"We can only hope that is what happened. It also means we need to be extra vigilant when we leave in the morning, for I do not trust the street lad who gave us the information about Greer. Oh, he may keep his promise this night not to sell the information as to when and where Greer left the town, but I would not put it past him to sell the information to someone first thing in the morning. These street lads have an odd sense of honor. They follow the old 'a man is only as good as his word' ideal, but they also have a highly honed sense of cunning. 'No, no, I'll not be sellin' the information to anyone else this night'," Seeker Zita said in an extremely good imitation of the street lad. "Notice he did not tell us he would not be selling the information to anyone ever. Just he would not sell it to anyone before morning. We had best try to get some sleep during what is left of this night and leave at first light. I will inform the innkeeper to have food packed for the journey."

Lord Avital stood and bid Seeker Zita a good night along with his thanks. His steps were slow and heavy as he climbed up the stairs to his sleeping room. So much had happened this last year, the loss of his beloved wife, the discovery of the secret she had kept for the past fifteen years, and now two more losses. Was Greer really his son, or did he desperately want him to be, so this quest would end? Then there was the loss of the pouch and its content. He was not prepared for adventure, for traveling all over hill and dale, for intrigue. Dugghus was a small holding, known mostly for its fine wool coveted by weavers both in Sommerhjem and abroad. He should be home now overseeing the estate instead of gallivanting around the countryside. Now it seemed his quest had just taken another twist. Had he known what it was he wore around his neck all these years, would he have done anything differently? He just did not know, and the hour was too late, his heart too sore, and his mind too tired to try to figure it out.

Once Seeker Zita had talked to the innkeeper, she too headed up to her sleeping room. After taking some time to rearrange her travel satchels and write out several messages on very small pieces of paper, Seeker Zita quietly opened her door a crack, checking to see if anyone was about. The hall was empty, dimly lit, and nothing stirred. Slipping through the door, Seeker Zita walked the length of the hall to the backstairs, pulling her cloak tightly around her. She made her way down the stairs and into the kitchen, which was lit only by the glow of the dying cook fire. Thinking she had made it this far undetected, she was startled when a voice whispered out of the darkness.

"I ask your pardon for startling you. I was on my way to find you. I would have arrived sooner, but the streets have been a bit busy this night, and the rooftops are not quiet either. I am a friend of your tall friend from across the border and have a message for you."

The man who spoke remained in the shadows, which gave Seeker Zita pause. "And you are?"

"It would be best if we kept names and faces unknown, for these are dangerous times, and the less you know, the less you can tell others. I have made my way across the town at some peril to myself, for your friend felt it was important for you to get this message. You can do with it what you wish. He asked me to tell you he found the book you were looking for and would leave it with and I quote, 'the young farmer'. I have no idea what that means, but he assured me that you would."

"Yes, thank you for both the information and the risk you took coming here."

When the brief exchange was over, the man left by the backdoor to the kitchen. Before he had left the shadows, the man had pulled the hood of his cloak over his head so Seeker Zita did not get a look at his face. She gave him time to be some distance away from the inn before she too left by the back door of the inn and headed to the inn's stable. Her luck at being undetected continued to be bad. The youngster who cared for the inn's stable slept there and must have been a very light sleeper. Seeker Zita had no more than taken two steps through the stable door when the lad was climbing down out of the loft, asking if he could help her.

"No, lad, it's alright. Go back to sleep. I've just come to check on the messenger birds."

"I've been real good lookin' after 'em. I fed 'em just like you said and ah, um, well sees, I was aworryin' about 'em gettin' cold so I, um, well, um, I took 'em up ta the loft wit' me this night. Glad I was I did 'cause there was this woman come into the stable askin' if'n we had messenger birds. Heard we did. Never have that I can remember. Glad I was I'da put 'em messenger birds up in the loft and covered 'em so as she was none the wiser. I did right?"

What the lad had just disclosed was worrisome. Why would someone come looking for messenger birds at this particular inn at this particular time? Were they trying to get their hands on her messenger birds?

"You did very right, and thank you for both your quick thinking and for caring for the messenger birds. Mind if I come up to your loft?"

The lad was disconcerted for a moment, for no one had ever thought to ask permission to come up to the loft where he stayed. That this important woman, this seeker, would ask made him feel more important than he had ever felt in his life. Feeling a little foolish he doffed his hat and made a short bow saying, "If'n you would step this way, m'lady," like he was some fancy footman inviting her into a grand manor house.

"Why, thank you kindly, my good man," Seeker Zita said, going along with the lad's play acting and climbing the ladder into the loft.

There was a little light coming in the hayloft door, which was open to the cool night air. The lad led the way to the back corner of the loft where he had hollowed out a space in the hay. After he lit a well-contained candle, she was able to see his living area more clearly. A clever design, Seeker Zita thought to herself. He had cobbled together a room by building two walls with old broken wooden boxes and barrels that he had packed with hay to keep out the drafts. He had also set his bed up over the horse stalls so in the winter, with the loft doors closed and the stable doors closed, the heat from the animals below would keep the nest he had made for himself somewhat warm. On a crude table rested the small cage that held her messenger birds.

Seeker Zita pulled the cover off the small bird cage and looked inside at the messenger birds. There was nothing remarkable in their looks, just plain brown birds, small in size. They had few markings and were fairly indistinguishable from a number of other small brown birds, except for their exceptionally wide wingspans and long forked tails. These messenger birds were swift and strong. They had the uncanny ability to ride the up and down drafts, and soar long distances on the winds. In addition, none could fault their intelligence and homing instincts. Once released, no matter where they were, they seemed to always find their way home to their birth roosts.

Seeker Zita had carefully thought out what she wanted to say and then had translated her words into a code few could read. It was important to get her messages out, but she could not afford to have the information fall into the wrong hands. It was always a risk to send a message by messenger bird because they were such small fragile creatures traveling vast distances. Wind, harsh weather, and birds of prey were just a few of the dangers they faced. She could only place her message in the tube attached to the messenger bird's leg, release the messenger bird, and hope for the best.

Once the two messenger birds Seeker Zita released had flown out of sight, which was fairly quickly given the time of night and scarce moonlight, she thanked the stable lad, slipped him some coin for his care of her messenger birds, and climbed back down the ladder. In a few scant hours she would be back here to pick up the cage holding her few remaining messenger birds, load up her pack animal, and leave Høyhauger with Lord Avital. It remained to be seen if their departure would attract notice.

Chapter Twelve

Pryderi decided, while he might not be having the time of his life and sleeping on the ground had been much more comfortable when he was much younger, being on this trip with his son was far more interesting than sitting in the village square talking about the good old days with his cronies. The day had certainly begun to look up now that they had heard that the lad Greer had been found and was alive. The message the forester had received suggested Greer was a bit worse for wear, but basically alright. No major damage, which was pretty amazing considering he had taken an unexpected trip down the Raskalt. The dilemma facing him and his son now was what to do next? Did they go several days out of their way to pick the lad up, or did they continue on course, meet with their companions, and get on with their task? They were torn.

"I realize how important it is to get going, but I can't help feeling responsible for the lad," Zareh stated. "It is all well and good that some kindly forester couple is looking after him right now, but you know as well as I do that the forest is an extremely strange place to Greer. Can you see him settling in here? I don't doubt the foresters would look after him, but I also don't think Greer would tolerate living on the charity of others. I think what might be best would be to send word on to our companions and tell them to head home. While we would probably not be much missed back home, the absence of the others would be noticeable. You and I will take the time to pick Greer up before we head to Farmer Yorick O'Gara's farm. It will certainly put us more at risk after we leave O'Gara's farm because we will be more vulnerable as a smaller group, but I think we will just have to chance it."

"I agree. I was going to have difficulty leaving the lad behind if that is what you felt was best. I should have known you would not be able to do so. There is just something about the lad . . . ."

Pryderi's speech was interrupted by one of the forester guides suggesting that time was a wasting and it was time to hit the trail. She just wanted to know what trail they wanted to follow. They told her they wanted to head towards the village Greer was in. The trail to pick Greer up brought them out of the high hills and down through a series of long narrow valleys, always following the Raskalt. When they stopped for a noon meal, Zareh found his father standing on the bank of the Raskalt, just shaking his head over and over.

"How the lad survived a ride down this stream is beyond me," Pryderi stated. Looking to his right upstream he pointed out the short falls, and then he indicated a series of swift rapids downstream. "Who knows how much longer those rapids go beyond that bend in the stream. I guess we'll find out when we travel farther on. That lad must have some kind of luck to have survived that stretch."

The rest of the day the group rode in relative silence. The foresters were a quiet lot by nature, and Pryderi and Zareh kept to their own thoughts. The night passed uneventfully and early morning found the group beginning the ascent out of a deep valley. The trail they followed was more established than many of the ones they had traveled over the last few days. They had followed the Raskalt up to this point, but it left this valley through a deep cut, tumbling and churning its way down between high rock walls through a series of rapids and small falls. After climbing for several hours, the lead forester called a halt at the top of the valley at the beginning of a narrow cut through the hills.

"This would be a good place to dismount, rest the horses, and stretch our legs. We have several more hours to ride before we reach the settlement of Trelandsby, and it's all downhill from here. Do not wander too far off because I'm sure we are being watched. Our clan members are not as trusting these days as we once were," the forester stated.

"Well, you can hardly blame them for not trusting strangers, now can you, all things considered," said Pryderi in an aside to Zareh after both had dismounted and walked a little way away from the foresters. "It will be a long time before the memory, or the ordeal, of being ripped out of their home forests and moved by orders of the Regent fades. This is just one of the many painful legacies the Regent's rule has left in our land. How close we came to having Sommerhjem split and torn by various factions is more than frightening, and that threat has not ended."

"While I don't think we will see the rise up of the folk like happened the week of the capital fair, that doesn't mean things are all rosy either. Just because the Regent has been booted out doesn't mean he has lost all of his influence. Like the foresters, there are other factions that were affected by the Regent's rule and dictates. They are now much less trustful of the rule from the capital," suggested Zareh.

"All too true I'm afraid, son. Unfortunately, there are always those who would take advantage of others during times of uncertainty. I'm also concerned that if we don't look like a united land, those countries that border us might think we are too weak to maintain our own borders."

"I don't envy the interim ruling council, and I'm glad I'm not on it."

"I'm in wholehearted agreement with that sentiment. Even worse would be to sit on the bench of the courts and try to straighten out all of the claims brought before it by those who rightfully felt they had lost land or livelihood due to the Regent's arbitrary rulings, unreasonable license fees, or taxes. That alone is going to take a long time and continues to feed the uncertainty and unrest."

"Even more unsettling to most is the Gylden Sirklene challenge. No one living can remember the events of the last one. Even the elders have only family stories handed down concerning it, which are of very little help and often conflicting. The challenge seems more the stuff of tall tales than something that is real. So many folks distrust the whole idea. It smacks too much of old granny tales to be real, and yet there is enough residual memory to give credence to the whole idea. The two things keeping folks sticking with the new way of things are one, the Regent is no longer in power and two, the stories that came out of the capital about what happened in the Well of Speaking certainly have given a lot of us pause. Very trustworthy folks witnessed the arcs of light that shot out of the golden box that was set into the front wall of the Well of Speaking."

"I heard it described as a column of light that rose up out of the box in a steady stream and carried all of the colors of a rainbow. They said it rose and rose until it almost touched the clouds and then arced out in all directions until it formed a canopy in the sky. The light pulsed out of the box for several minutes, and as abruptly as it had started, it just stopped," said Pryderi. "Folk from all corners of Sommerhjem swear they saw the light in the sky that day. Those who lived right on the borders said it came down and touched the ground just at the edge of their land. Ah, our guide is motioning that it is time to continue our ride."

The group mounted up and rode the short distance through the narrow cut in the hills. The site that greeted them was awe-inspiring. In the center of the long valley spread out below them were three rings of trees scattered on the valley floor that dwarfed the trees on the valley hills above them. The ring of trees in the middle of the valley closest to the Raskalt held the largest of the large trees.

Zareh pulled his horse up next to his father's and remarked, "Those are the largest quirrelit trees I have ever seen."

"I've seen a few individual quirrelit trees that were larger, but never a grove this large. A memory-making sight to be sure. That must be Trelandsby."

One of the foresters, who had pulled up next to the two, confirmed it was indeed Trelandsby. The group made its slow way down into the valley and was greeted graciously when they arrived in the village. Pryderi and Zareh were told that one of the villagers would take care of their horses and pack animals. They were then invited to go to Ellwood and Aldona's home so they could see for themselves that Greer was indeed alright.

Greer had tried to stay awake, but his body had another idea. He was napping when Pryderi and Zareh stepped onto Ellwood and Aldona's porch. Aldona held a finger to her lips and motioned the two men to sit.

"The lad is napping again, and I have let him sleep, but he was anxious about your arrival. I had best go wake him. I'll have him come out onto the porch, for the fresh air will do him good." As an afterthought, Aldona said they of course were welcome to come inside and sit a spell, not wanting them to think they were not welcome in her house.

"We thank you kindly for the invitation, mistress. The porch suits us just fine," commented Pryderi.

With a nod of her head, Aldona turned and entered her home, heading to the kitchen to put together a tray of some bread, cheese, and fresh cider along with some sturdy earthenware mugs. Once she had finished arranging the tray to her liking, she went to fetch Greer. Standing in the doorway of the small bedroom where Greer lay napping, she called softly to the lad and he was immediately awake. Aldona had noticed that Greer seemed to sleep almost with one eye open and wondered what kind of life he had led to have developed such a trait.

"Your two friends have arrived and are on the porch. Are you up to seeing them?"

Greer did not know the answer to that question. Would they be mad at him for leaving the group so abruptly even though he had not planned on his journey down the Raskalt? Would they be angry at him because he had caused them to delay their trip out of the forest? Were they just stopping in to check on him but then were going to move on without him, or would they ask him to continue to travel with them? What if they did not? Where would he go? He knew the forest, while beautiful, would never feel safe or like home to him.

"Are you coming or not, lad?" Aldona asked.

"I'm coming. Just let me get my boots on and I'll be right out."

"We'll be on the porch then," Aldona said, as she turned and walked away.

Greer took his time lacing up his boots. He then went to the wash basin and splashed cold water on his face to help him wake up and shake off the bone-weary tiredness he felt despite the nap. Besides being worried about what would transpire in the next few minutes, he was also worried that Aldona had only mentioned that two men were waiting on the porch. He hoped against hope that she had just not thought to mention Kasa. Was the pup still with them? Was he alright? Had he been just too much of a burden so they had disposed of him? Stalling was not going to get the answers he needed and stalling was not going to change them either. It was better to head out to the porch to face the two men and his immediate future than to hide in the bedroom like a coward. Straightening himself up as best he could, Greer took a deep breath, ran his fingers through his hair to try to tame it a bit, straightened his shoulders, and walked out the bedroom door.

As he entered the great room, Aldona chided him. "Don't dawdle, lad, your friends are waiting and they've ridden hard to get here."

Nodding acquiescence, for Greer was worried his voice might quaver, so high was his concern about what was going to happen next, he walked to the front door and stepped out onto the porch, only to be pushed back through the doorway by a small lunging body of fur. Once Greer regained his balance, he hunkered down and greeted his pup with the same amount of enthusiasm, ruffling Kasa's fur, scratching behind his ears, and just hugging him so hard that the pup began to squirm almost as hard as his tail was wagging. It finally occurred to Greer to wonder if dogs were allowed in Ellwood and Aldona's house, and so he straightened up, ready to apologize.

"I'm sorry . . . ." he began.

"For what? Being excited to see your dog?" Aldona remarked. "Does a body good to see a lad and his dog together. Now you two scoot on out. I'll be there in a moment with something to drink."

Greer picked up Kasa, who seemed to have grown in the few days they had been apart, and stepped out the door. Pryderi and Zareh rose to greet the two and told Greer that they had been worried about him, that they were glad he was alright. Aldona came out carrying the tray holding the refreshments, and the men rose again to help her. Once all were settled, they caught each other up on what had transpired since Greer had slipped into the Raskalt and ended up in the village of Trelandsby.

"So, what do you think of living in a tree?" Zareh asked.

Greer was not quite sure how to answer Zareh's question. If he indicated that he had enjoyed living in the tree house with its warm and comfortable bed and three meals a day, would Zareh think he wanted to stay here? If he said he did not like living in the tree house, would he insult Ellwood and Aldona?

That decision was taken out of his hands when Ellwood, who had joined the group, said "Now don't go putting the lad on the spot. Of course living in a home built in and around a tree would be a joy for anyone for a while, but might never feel like home to someone who was not born and raised here."

Greer wondered what it would be like to live in the same home for years and years, to have a safe place to sleep each night, to know and trust your neighbors. Greer realized that Pryderi had addressed him and he had not heard the question.

"Pardon?"

"I said, lad, what's next for you? Ellwood and Aldona have said you could stay here, or you can continue on with us. It's your choice."

When Greer thought about staying in the forest and living with the elderly couple, he did not immediately dismiss the idea. The pair had been extremely kind to him, but something did not feel quite right. Something was urging him to travel on even though he did not know where that choice might lead.

"So, lad, what will it be? The life of a forester or something else?" asked Pryderi.

"Something else," Greer answered, "so long as it is not a river rafter!"

Chapter Thirteen

"Halt, who travels the Fjell Skoj forest ways?" asked a forester who stepped out onto the forest path, bow and arrow at the ready.

"I am Seeker Zita, and the gentleman who travels with me is Lord Avital of Dugghus. We offer no harm to the Fjell Skoj forest and only wish to travel through. We are trying to locate a man and a lad who may have passed this way recently."

"And what is your business with those you seek?"

How odd, Seeker Zita thought to herself. I have traveled this forest several times before and I have been greeted, but never stopped with questions about my business. If anyone asked a seeker their business, which was unusual in and of itself, it was usually to offer aid. More often than not one would say "what is it you seek and how might I be of assistance?" This inquiry by the forester was both pointed and sounded protective. In addition, Seeker Zita was not sure what the right answer to the question was. Did they reveal to this stranger that the lad might be Lord Avital's son? No, she thought not. Did she let on that she was looking for Zareh this close to Høyhauger and have word somehow get back that he had been in the vicinity, which likely would not be good for him? She could draw herself up to her full height and take on a haughty air and hope that the forester would let them pass, but she thought the old "you would question the right of a seeker to safe passage" attitude would not foster goodwill. Maybe part of the truth would work.

"We became separated from them in Høyhauger and hoped they had come this way," Seeker Zita responded, trying to keep the irritation out of her voice, but she must not have been completely successful.

"Your pardon, Seeker. No disrespect was meant with my question, but we have had several groups of strangers in the forest these past few days also trying to find a man and a lad, plus one confrontation that could have turned ugly."

Seeker Zita could feel Lord Avital go very still next to her upon hearing the forester's words. "The man and the lad are well though?" she asked.

"The last I heard, the man you are looking for and the lad are well and safe. I can direct you towards them if you choose. Do you know if you were followed on your way to the Fjell Skoj forest?"

"I have no doubt that our journey from Høyhauger was noted. The pass was well traveled the day we left, so it would have been easy for someone to follow us. While we have not seen anyone behind us, nor have we been interfered with, I have had an uneasy feeling lingering just at the edge of my consciousness that there has been someone behind us. It is quite urgent that we catch up with the pair we hopefully are following before anyone else does."

Seeker Zita did not catch any movement or signal from the forester who was still blocking their path, but suddenly two more foresters slipped out of the foliage lining the path.

"These two will escort you and others will watch your back trail."

With that said, the forester stepped aside, allowing the two to pass single file. Their escorts motioned them to take a side path they came upon a short while later. This side path led to a small clearing where their escorts' horses were tethered.

"May I inquire as to where we are heading?" Seeker Zita asked of the forester who was riding next to her.

"Our last word on your friends indicated they were in the village of Trelandsby. The way I heard it, the young lad has had himself quite an adventure. He became separated from the group and rode the Raskalt into the village, rather than the horse he had been lent."

"The Raskalt?" Lord Avital inquired.

"A rather swift, rough and tumble river which is great for fishing but not so good for swimming or rafting," the forester replied. Then, seeing a look of anxiousness on Lord Avital's face, he reassured him the lad was fine. "Why he was in as good a condition as he was no one has quite figured out, but he appears fine, if a little stiff and bruised."

"How long will it take us to get to the village of Trelandsby?" Lord Avital asked.

"Normally it would take several days, but there's a storm brewing north of us, and it feels like it's going to be a nasty one, so it might take a little longer."

The group found out just how prophetic the forester's words were several hours later when the ever darkening skies opened up and a deluge followed, accompanied by lightning, thunder, and howling winds. Tree branches cracked and fell in the forest around them. The ground beneath the horses' hooves became a slippery mix of mud and pine needles that caused even the sure-footed mountain horses trouble. Finally, the forester in the lead signaled the group should dismount.

"There is a very narrow side valley about a quarter of an hour walk from here that might provide some shelter where we could wait out this storm. We'll need to lead the horses, and the way will not be an easy one."

By the time the party arrived in the narrow valley, they were cold, soaked, and miserable. There was some shelter from the rain under the branches of several huge pines that grew close to the sheer vertical wall of the valley. By snuggling up close to the valley's high wall, at least the cold penetrating wind was considerably less. All of them knew there would be no riding on in a storm of this intensity, so they all set about making themselves as comfortable as possible under the conditions. Seeker Zita and Lord Avital took charge of the horses and quickly removed saddles and saddle bags. They unloaded the pack horses and piled everything under waterproof tarps. While they were taking care of the horses, the foresters rigged up a shelter made from a combination of pine boughs and waterproof tarps.

All were happy to be out of the rain. While not exactly snug and warm, the shelter was a slight bit better than being out in the elements. The storm continued to swirl around them, the thunder being so loud and continuous it was hard to carry on a conversation. By the time the storm settled down into a steady drizzle, night had fallen and it was too dark to continue.

⌘⌘⌘

Even though Ellwood and Aldona had reassured Greer that the tree home had endured storms far worse than the one that had come up suddenly that afternoon, he was not convinced. It was disconcerting to feel the floors vibrate and move under him, but he tried not to show that he was just a tiny bit terrified. Kasa was huddled close to Greer as he sat on the floor with his back to the wall. He hoped his excuse for being on

79

the floor had been accepted, that Kasa was very nervous about being in a shaking house, for he did not want to look the coward in front of the adults.

"This old tree has survived storms and winds much worse than this," Ellwood said with some pride in his voice. "These quirrelit trees are both strong and flexible, not to mention highly fire resistant. Couldn't ask for a better place to be on a dark stormy night, all snug and warm. I pity the clan members who are out on patrol this night. The forest can be a dangerous place when the wind whips through it like it is doing right now. The storm should be over by morning, or at least the worst of it, and you can be on your way. We'll miss the company though."

"We thank you for your hospitality and most doubly thank you for the shelter from this storm. Glad I am that it is going to blow over soon. I think that unless you have lived in a tree all of your life, this swaying and creaking could make a body a mite nervous from time to time," said Pryderi, placing a warm and solid hand on Greer's shoulder as he settled himself on the floor next to Greer. "I suppose you get used to the movement of your house like sailors get used to the movement of their ship. For myself though, I would prefer a solid stone cottage floor under my bed, if it is all the same to you. No offense."

"And none taken," laughed Ellwood.

"Since you all are hopeful of leaving at the break of dawn, it's best that you try to get as much sleep as you can. The gentle swaying of the tree might just lull you into a good night's sleep," Aldona suggested with a twinkle in her eye. "Ellwood, why don't you take the pup out one last time while I get these gentlemen settled. Would Ellwood taking your Kasa out be alright with you, lad?"

While Greer did not want to look afraid in front of the others, he also did not want to venture out on the swaying catwalks, ramps, and ladders which provided ways of moving in and out of the trees and connected the houses of Trelandsby together.

Aldona must have seen the indecision in Greer's face, for she said, "Ah, let the old man take the pup out, lad. He's been itchy as a bug on a squirrel wanting to get outside and check on things. This gives him a polite excuse to abandon his company and host duties. Go on with you now, so as I can get these men settled without your interference," she told Ellwood, making shooing motions with her hands. "Okay with you, Greer?" Aldona turned, but not before giving Pryderi a wink which Greer did not see.

Greer was happy to agree and gratefully followed Aldona down the short hall to the bedroom he had been staying in. Even though he was very tired, sleep did not immediately follow once his head hit the pillow. Worry kept him awake, and not just the worry about whether it was really very wise to sleep in a house built in a swaying, creaking tree, but rather also the worry about what was ahead. He was certainly relieved that Pryderi and Zareh had come after him, but how long would they put up with someone who was so inept in the countryside? It had occurred to him, as he had lain convalescing from his trip down the Raskalt that he knew very little about the two men he was traveling with. He thought he knew they were of Sommerhjem. He knew they were father and son, but beyond that he knew very little else. Did they live in a town or in the country? What did they do when they were not traveling? How long would they want him around, and what was to happen to him? Greer had been so independent all of his short life, he was really very uncomfortable having to depend on others and did not quite trust the kindness that had been shown him so far.

❦

The night was a long, wet, miserable one for the party gathered in the narrow valley, despite the shelter the foresters had rigged. Water in the form of rain coming down steadily accompanied by the strong wind had a way of finding any hole or opening in their tarps. Warm woolen cloaks, while good at holding in warmth even when wet, could not hold off the chill by the time morning came.

"It will be slow going this day I am afraid," the lead forester told Seeker Zita. "The soggy, muddy trail ahead, which takes us through long stand of pines, will be slippery with its thick covering of pine needles. Also, we will need to remove any downed trees that lie across the trail, and that too will take time."

Seeker Zita glanced at Lord Avital and saw a look of consternation flash across his face. She knew how anxious he was to catch up with the lad he thought might be his son, but she also knew the foresters had an obligation to tend their forest. Lord Avital's urgent need would not change that. They certainly could thank their guides and try to find Trelandsby by themselves, but Seeker Zita did not think that would be acceptable to the foresters, and she wanted to maintain their goodwill.

Turning to Lord Avital she said, "They understand your need but also have obligations to the forest they are charged with maintaining. I am sure they will get us to Trelandsby as swiftly as they can under the circumstances."

"Am I that easy to read then?" Lord Avital said ruefully.

"Not so much, but I too am anxious to be on my way. If we are lucky, any large trees that fell had the common courtesy to fall away from the paths, trails, or lanes we hope to travel over the next few days."

Unfortunately for the party, a very large inconsiderate tree had fallen across the narrow path at the mouth of the narrow valley where they had spent the night. It took everyone cutting and hauling branches to clear enough of the tree away to give access to the large trunk, and then it took another good hour before that could be dragged to the side. By the time the path was once again passable, all of the folks were hot and sweating, but at least they were no longer chilled.

Lord Avital fervently hoped there would be no more delays for he was now, with this delay, even more anxious to get to Trelandsby. He hoped the lad and his traveling companions would still be there by the time he and Seeker Zita arrived.

CHAPTER FOURTEEN

The shaking woke Greer, and at first he feared the tree house he was sleeping in was becoming uprooted. Then he realized that Zareh was calling his name and shaking his shoulder.

"Come on, lad, 'tis time to rise and shine. Dawn is here and there is just enough time to grab a bite to eat before we head out."

It worried Greer that he had not heard Zareh's approach and that the man had had to shake him awake. That never would have happened in Høyhauger. He was getting too comfortable and that, he knew, could lead to disaster. He had always needed to be on the alert and now was not the time to stop that practice. Mentally beating himself over the head was not going to fix anything, Greer knew, so he quickly washed up and gathered his meager belongings together before he headed out of his sleeping quarters. It was with some regret and longing that he looked back through the doorway to what had been his room, if ever so briefly. It was the first place he could ever remember sleeping in that was snug, warm, and held a bed piled high with blankets.

The journey out of the valley that held Trelandsby was easy, and Greer enjoyed the horseback ride on the fairly wide trail that wound its way through the forest. One of the younger foresters, who was accompanying them, took to riding next to Greer. The morning passed quickly with her pointing out trees of interest and explaining how the foresters lived off the bounty of the forest, which provided for most of their needs. She also explained that they had good relations with the farmers who tilled the lands that bordered the forest, and through barter provided what the forest could not.

Though Greer had gotten somewhat used to riding, he was glad when the party stopped for a midday meal. Zareh had assured him that by the time they reached Farmer Yorick O'Gara's farm in three days, barring bad weather, he would feel like he had been on horseback all his life. Greer hoped that Zareh meant that he would feel comfortable and confident rather than feel a lifetime of soreness. He was also a little worried about what was going to happen once they got to O'Gara's farm.

The weather held, and as the party moved out of the forest, the travel became even easier. Most of the foresters turned back at the edge of the trees, but several continued on with Zareh, Pryderi, and Greer. The land spread out before them in gentle rolling hills covered with tall waving grass. Groves of trees were scattered here and there, dotting the landscape.

The openness of the sky was a little disconcerting to Greer, after growing up in a walled town in the mountains. Here one could see for a long way and see if anyone was about, but at the same time, they could see you, thought Greer. The open space of the surrounding land gave no place to hide.

That evening around the cook fire, Zareh expressed some of the same thoughts. "We are fairly safe during the day, unless met with a large band of folk who have ill intent, but that would be unlikely here. This area is under the protection of Lady Xantara, and she has little tolerance for shenanigans. However, be that as it may, darkness can cover up a host of activities, so I think it's best that we post a sentry just in case."

The night passed uneventfully, as did the next two, and the group arrived at Farmer Yorick O'Gara's farm shortly before noon. Greer did not know what he had expected, but he found the look of the farm inexplicably welcoming. The main house and all of the outbuildings were made of native stone. The exposed beams and wood on the outsides of the buildings were intricately carved. Unlike so many of the buildings in Høyhauger, which had been built of gray blocks of stone, these buildings were made of stones in a variety of colors and seemed more like they had grown out of the earth rather than been placed upon it.

As they approached the main building, a number of border dogs raced in from all directions and formed a line fronting the house. While they merely stood there, in no way appearing menacing, neither growling nor barking, they gave the clear impression that the party should proceed no further.

"Hallo the house," called out one of the foresters.

The front door swung open and two men stepped out. Greer watched in surprise as the border dogs broke ranks and, as quickly as they had come, were gone. He had not heard either of the men on the porch say anything nor had he noticed either of them give any kind of signal. All he knew for certain was that he wanted to know how that had happened.

"Sorry about the reception, but these days it's better to be safe than sorry," the older of the two men on the porch stated, as he moved towards the group, who were still mounted. "Be welcome. I am Farmer Yorick O'Gara, and this young lad here is Journeyman Evan of the Glassmakers Guild. Journeyman Evan, why don't you escort our guests to the stables to get their horses settled? I'll go alert cook that we have seven more for the midday meal. You'll be staying, won't you?" Farmer Yorick O'Gara asked, directing his question towards Zareh.

"For at least the night," Zareh replied.

Before Farmer Yorick O'Gara could direct the same question to the foresters, the lead forester told him they would stay for the midday meal, for they were very fond of Cook's cooking, but then they needed to get back to their regular duties.

Turning back to Journeyman Evan, Farmer Yorick O'Gara asked if he could prevail upon him again. "After taking the party to the stables, would you please show the guests where they can bunk down for the night? Oh, and why don't you put the young lad there in with you?"

As Greer rode his horse following Journeyman Evan to the stables, he had a chance to observe him. He did not look like any guild member Greer had ever seen. His clothes were not fancy and looked more like what a stable lad would wear than one of the nose-in-the-air guild members. All the guild members Greer had ever interacted with in Høyhauger would never have taken a request from a mere farmer and would certainly not have complied as cheerfully.

Once the horses were settled, Journeyman Evan led the group to a long low building, which he explained was where the farm workers and visitors stayed. The building struck Greer as funny, for it somewhat resembled the stable with a low overhanging roof and a number of doors along the front. Sort of a stable for folks, he thought. Journeyman Evan pointed to a door, and told Zareh and his father that they could put their gear in there and settle in. He then beckoned Greer to follow him.

Upon opening the door, Journeyman Evan gestured for Greer to enter and said, "It's not much, but it's clean, warm, and dry."

The door opened into a stone-walled room that held a bunk bed along the left wall and shelving to hold gear and personal possessions under the small window on the back wall. A small fireplace on the right wall was fronted by two benches. There were pegs on the wall on either side of the fireplace for hanging clothes and cloaks, and there was a rag rug between the benches and the bed. The space was simple, but adequate.

Greer was feeling uncomfortable, for he had never shared a room with anyone, mostly because he had never had a room. He was unclear as to whether this Journeyman Evan fellow lived here, and if so, how he felt about someone moving into his room. He would have felt more comfortable wrapped in his cloak sleeping in a hayloft and did not know what to do.

Journeyman Evan must have sensed his unease for he said, "Like I said, it isn't much, but it's pretty nice for guest quarters, I can tell you. I've stayed in some where sleeping in the barn or a cave would have been nicer. Not here at O'Gara's. This farm is fairly new, and when they were building it, they knew there would be frequent visitors, since this horse breeding program is a joint effort between the foresters and the O'Gara clan." When Journeyman Evan saw that Greer was still holding back, he added, "The pup is welcome here, too. You can put your gear on one of the shelves on the far wall. No one will touch it. I've been here a few days, so pardon the mess. If you want the top bunk, I can move my things out. Just tell that pup of yours not to chew on my boots while we're sleeping."

"The bottom bunk will be fine, but you might want to sleep in your boots. I can't guarantee what Kasa might do."

Once the words were out of his mouth, Greer felt surprised at himself. Normally he was reluctant to carry on conversations with strangers, but there was something about this Journeyman Evan fellow that put him more at ease than he had felt since leaving Høyhauger. He found himself curious about this journeyman who neither dressed nor acted like any guild member he had ever come across. Even the apprentices in Bortfjell paraded around in their guild finery and put on airs. Before he could reflect further, he heard the ringing of a bell, and Journeyman Evan told him that it was the call to the midday meal. With some reluctance, Greer left his pack in the room. It contained all his worldly possessions, which he knew were pitifully few. He was even more reluctant to leave Kasa in a pen with a litter of border dog pups about his age, but Kasa, without a backward glance, rushed forward to join the tussle between pups over a large knotted rope.

The room the meal was served in was a medium-sized one holding several long tables with benches. There was a fireplace at each end. The fare was simple but filling and served family style. Greer was surprised to see Farmer O'Gara seated at one of the tables along with the foresters, what appeared to be farm workers, and several children.

"Pull up a bench, and get yourself some vittles. We don't stand on ceremony here," Farmer O'Gara said.

Both Greer and Journeyman Evan did as directed. When the meal was finished, Pryderi asked Greer to join him. Farmer O'Gara called Journeyman Evan over just as the lad was about to leave the room. Once the room was clear of everyone but Farmer O'Gara, Pryderi, Zareh, Greer, and Journeyman Evan, Farmer O'Gara addressed those gathered there.

"Your companions left several days ago. I was sending a number of horses back to my father's farm, so they went with the riders taking the horses. I suspect that should provide some safety in numbers, and also, since they were dressed as farm workers, create some misdirection."

"That's good to know," replied Zareh. "I'll be less worried about their return home now."

"Well, that was the good news. The news to be concerned with is that two separate parties have been here looking for a lost lad. One story has it that this lad is a thief and stole something of great value from a noble of Høyhauger. The other party suggested that this lad is a long lost heir to a great noble family. Didn't say what family nor where this family lived. I didn't put much credence in either story. However, the urgency and persistence of both parties did strike me. The description of the lad they were looking for fits closely to Greer here."

Zareh quickly filled Farmer Yorick O'Gara and Journeyman Evan in on what had transpired on their journey to the farm. Greer was beginning to feel very uncomfortable, for all eyes were looking at him as if he would be able to explain why so many were interested in his whereabouts. He continued, for some unexplained reason, not to want to tell them about the pouch that hung around his neck.

"I find the part about the hunting cats fascinating. It certainly is not unheard of for hunting cats to interact with folk. I have a friend Nissa, a rover, who travels with a hunting cat named Carz, but he has been with her since he was a small kit. I wonder why the hunting cats were so interested in you?" Journeyman Evan asked, directing his question toward Greer. "Maybe it's because you defended your pup, and they respected that. Maybe they were not there for you, but for Kasa," Journeyman Evan said, and all could hear the mischief in his voice. His statement certainly lowered the tension in the room.

"Do you have any idea why a lad who fits Greer's description is being sought after?" Farmer Yorick O'Gara asked.

"Why don't you show Farmer Yorick the slim book you didn't have a chance to return to the owner of Milkin's Stable? He might be able to understand it better than we can. Do you have it on you?" Zareh asked Greer.

When Greer had left his pack back in Journeyman Evan's room, he had slipped the slim book out of its side pocket and brought it with him. He had had very little of worth in his life, but years of surviving on the street had taught him to always secure anything he might have that others might want. He reached inside his shirt and pulled out the book. His interest in what was written inside outweighed his reluctance to give the book up. He handed the book to Farmer O'Gara.

"Before I look at this, tell me about your border dog pup and the litter he came from."

"There were eight pups in all. Kasa was the only one of his coloring and markings. The other pups were dark black to the point that they had only a little of the copper or cream markings. Their heads appeared broader and squarer than Kasa's, and they looked like they would have a heavier chest. Also, only a few were blue-eyed. I noticed your border dogs have more variety in their markings and coloring but, again, none look quite like Kasa."

Again, Greer did not know why he felt so comfortable talking, but maybe because the attention had steered away from him and onto a safer topic.

"Your Kasa has both the coloring and the markings of fine border dogs who not only show remarkable intelligence, fierce loyalty, and guarding instincts, but are also instinctive herders. My Da would certainly like to get his hands on your border dog pup." Upon seeing the look that crossed Greer's face, Farmer Yorick O'Gara said, "No, no, lad, not to take him away from you, but to breed him with his border dogs. The only breeder that we know of who has border dogs similar to yours is Lord Avital, and he is most reluctant to part with any prize border dog pups. What you said about the direction your former employer is taking in breeding border dogs is worrisome. Let me take a look at what you have here."

88

While Farmer Yorick O'Gara looked at the slim book, Pryderi got up and poured another round of tea for everyone. Once Farmer Yorick O'Gara worked his way through the book, he began to flip back to back pages and then flip forward again. He looked up after he closed the book and said, "This is not good!"

CHAPTER FIFTEEN

"This is not good at all," Farmer Yorick O'Gara exclaimed, shaking his head.

"What is not good?" Zareh asked.

"From what I can tell from this very interesting book Greer accidentally walked off with, his former employer is trying to breed back into his border dogs what it has taken a long time to breed out. Do you know the history of border dogs?"

"Only vaguely," Pryderi and Zareh said at once, while Greer and Journeyman Evan shook their heads no.

"No one really knows the origin of the breed. It has been suggested that long ago there might have been wild dogs that roamed the high hills and mountain regions. Tales suggest that when our folk moved into this land, they brought with them herding dogs to manage their livestock. Those herding dogs interbred with the wild dogs, and the new dogs were fiercer than the herding dogs. This was not a bad thing when Sommerhjem was new, untamed, and grazing and settling land was in dispute. As the land became tamer, the shepherds and herders began to breed dogs that combined the best traits from both breeds. They bred for great herding instincts, intelligence, loyalty, and guarding instincts. What they tried to breed out was the extreme viciousness. What your former employer seems to be doing, however, is attempting to reverse the breed back to the more vicious variety. It is no wonder he was not all that anxious to keep your Kasa."

"Why not?" inquired Greer.

"Of the eight pups, yours is most like the original herding dogs in coloring, markings, and temperament, whereas the others sound like they are more like the fiercer wild ancestors. Often when you are breeding for one specific trait, you get a throwback which embodies the traits you are trying to eliminate. We have seen that in our horse breeding program here, which is not all bad, since my father and I are trying to improve two different lines of horses needed for two different tasks. How your pup is going to turn out does not worry me so much as to why anyone in Bortfjell would be deliberately breeding a loyal, intelligent, but unpredictable very fierce guard dog, a type of dog more suited to conflict than peace."

"It would seem this book and this information needs to get to the capital," stated Zareh. "Father and I are heading that way anyway, for we have other information we need to get to Lady Celik. Knowing now what this book represents, I can begin to understand why folks are looking for Greer. I am beginning to worry that there are too many folks looking for a man and a lad, or two men and a lad of Greer's description. Somehow we need to throw them off track, but how?"

"I don't mean to be rude, but is it his physical description or his gait that is used to describe him?" Journeyman Evan asked.

"Well," Farmer Yorick O'Gara started thoughtfully, "the two groups that came by here were looking for a lad who has one leg shorter than the other and walks with a funny gait. They gave no more description than that. Not whether he was short, tall, or of medium height. Same for weight. They did not describe his hair or eye color. Just said he was a lad and limped."

"But he's not a lad," Journeyman Evan exclaimed. "Maybe he is just short like the Günnary are short. Maybe his folk get their growth late, or he just comes from short folk. They are looking for a lad who, and again I ask your pardon, Greer, who has a rag tag appearance and a distinctive walk. We can change your looks just by changing your clothes and giving you a haircut. The gait is another issue."

"Maybe not," Greer said quietly, but not so quietly that the others had not heard. All of them turned and looked at him questioningly. "When I was fished out of the Raskalt, my new boots that Bowen gave me were very wet, but Ellwood worked on them until they were almost as good as new. He, however, had noticed that one of my legs was longer than the other and had a leatherworker named Brogan make me another pair of boots. From the outside they look the same, but he built up the inside to make my legs even. I haven't had a chance to try them, and I don't know if I can walk in them. If I can, no one will know my legs aren't the same length."

"Even with the change in clothes, hair, and those boots, those who are out there seeking Greer are still going to be looking for a man and a lad, or two men and a lad, traveling from this direction. While the risk is less high, the risk is still there, and it jeopardizes your other tasks," suggested Farmer Yorick O'Gara, looking at Zareh.

"They might not think to look too closely at a journeyman and his apprentice however," Journeyman Evan proposed.

"Ah, now, Journeyman Evan, lad . . ." started Farmer Yorick O'Gara.

"Wait. Hear me out. Greer, you said you had worked in a stable as a stable lad. Is that correct?"

"Yes."

"So you know your way around horses and can handle the everyday care? I am the journeyman to the master of the horse for the Glassmakers Guild, who is also the master of the horse for the Woodcrafters Guild, the Potters Guild, and several other smaller craft guilds whose main guildhalls are in the capital. None of the guilds I mentioned really has need of a full time master of the horse and so have joined together. As we head into the winter season when fewer of our guild members will be traveling, it is a good time for Master Cynfarch and me to go out and visit with various breeders to look at their stock, and in some cases, return mares for breeding. That is why I am here looking at this new stock Farmer O'Gara has, to see if a horse or two of his might meet some of our needs. After my stay here, I am heading on to other farms, including my family's, and wending my way back to the capital. It would not be unusual for an apprentice to be traveling with me, that is, if that would suit you, Greer. Mind, I can't make you an official apprentice, but once we get to the capital, I think I could talk Master Cynfarch into at least giving you a job. It will not be an easy journey, and you will certainly have to work along the way. This is not going to be a free ride, no pun intended."

Greer thought about what was being suggested. He felt somewhat comfortable with Zareh and Pryderi. They had been kind to him, but he also suspected that they held much back from him. They had secrets and tasks he was now beginning to realize his staying with them jeopardized. Also, he really did not know where they were headed eventually and what would be there for him once they reached their destination. Zareh had taken him along at first because it was the easiest thing for him to do, short of killing him. Why he had not left him on the trail, or why he and Pryderi had come after him after he had been swept down the Raskalt, was still a mystery to Greer. Since he did not want to repay kindness with continuing to be an added burden, he needed to give serious thought to what Journeyman Evan was proposing. While he was thinking it through, the discussion continued to go on around him.

"Your proposal has a lot of merit to it, Journeyman Evan, but I can also see a number of pitfalls. Clothing for one," suggested Zareh.

"Actually that is less of a problem than you might think. I had all of my gear packed to head out with Master Cynfarch, thinking I would be journeying with him this winter. The morning we were to leave, he called me into his study and told me I had been made a journeyman. He then handed me a bag containing my journeyman's cloak and several changes of clothes. Because he still wanted to leave right away, he gave me no time to do anything other than change. I stuffed the old cloak and clothes in a pack and tied them onto the pack horse along with a pack containing the new clothes Master Cynfarch had given me. I still have the apprentice clothes with me, and if there is someone here who could alter them, they should do. You really do not want me to do the mending or sewing," Journeyman Evan said, an infectious grin forming on his face. Sobering quickly, he stated that while he could provide clothing, gear was another matter. "Then there is just that pesky problem of a horse for Greer, since the one Greer rode in on belongs to the foresters."

"None of that is insurmountable. I expect we can cobble together the gear. I've an old gelding that I was going to put out to pasture this winter that might have one long journey left in him. I think we are forgetting a major obstacle," Farmer Yorick O'Gara stated.

There was a chorus of questions from the others.

"Greer is from Bortfjell."

It took a moment for the import of that simple statement to sink in.

"Ah, well, every great plan always has some little hiccup in it," Journeyman Evan said with a shrug.

"Greer knowing very little about Sommerhjem, its folk and customs, not to mention he has never been to the capital, seems rather more than a little hiccup," Pryderi stated wryly.

Greer made a throat clearing noise, which caused the rest of the group to center their attention on him. "S-s-s-sir, I, I, I, um, be, be, beggin' yur par-par-pardon . . . ." Greer's voice trailed off. He looked down at the table top, a picture of abject misery, seeming even smaller than he was, flinching a little as if expecting a cuff at any moment.

"Oh you sly boots," laughed Zareh. "I forgot how highly skilled you might need to be to survive the streets of Høyhauger as long as you have. Maybe we should get him an apprenticeship with the royal players."

"Ah, I can see my new apprentice is a lot more skilled talking to horses than he is to folk. My master discovered him in a scuffle one day on a back street of the capital trying to stop this huge hulking brute from beating a cart pony to death for some infraction. Near as to killed the lad. Master Cynfarch brought him back to our stable and put him to work. He has proved his worth, so made him an apprentice."

Journeyman Evan told the tale with such ease that Zareh was moved to laughter once again and remarked that maybe there were two sly boots in the room.

"Well, lad, what do you think you might like to do? Under other circumstances, I could offer you a place here, since you know your way around horses and don't appear to be afraid of hard work, but I'm not sure as to how safe that would be for you. We are still way too close to Bortfjell to make sleeping peacefully each night likely," said Farmer O'Gara.

"You know you can continue on with us," Zareh said, and Greer could hear the sincerity in the offer.

He felt torn, not only because everyone was willing to take a risk on his behalf, but because they might be taking that risk for the wrong reason. Sure, the slim breeding record book he had that belonged to the Milkin's Stable owner was apparently more significant and important than he had realized, but in truth, it was minor to what he wore about his neck. Yet something kept him once again from speaking of it, even though this was an opportune moment to say something. As Greer had done as long as he could remember, he weighed his options. He made a mental image in his head of a spice merchant's scales. He would put what was good about each offer on the right side of the scale and what was risky or bad on the left side of the scale to see which side tipped downward. He found that the idea of harm coming to any of the parties offering a place with them weighed heavily in his decision. In the end, he decided that Journeyman Evan's idea offered the least amount of risk and the most to gain. Something else was tugging at him to accept Journeyman Evan's offer to ride with him, but Greer could not put his finger on just what that was. Almost an urging coming at him from somewhere outside of himself, but he quickly discounted it.

"I think my best choice would be to go with Journeyman Evan," Greer stated, with as much conviction as he could muster.

Even knowing it was probably for the best, Zareh was surprised he felt a loss. He was still trying to figure out why this lad brought out such a protective nature in him, and he was finding it difficult to let him go. He knew he and his father really did not need the added risk of what was following Greer, since they still had to get to the capital with what he had brought with him out of Bortfjell. The added knowledge that border dogs were being breed for conflict once again was also of concern. Still there was just something about the lad that pulled at him. His reverie was interrupted by Farmer Yorick O'Gara asking Journeyman Evan if he still intended to leave in the morning.

"I would like to. I've just thought of something else though. Did any of the folks stopping by here mention Kasa when they were describing who they were looking for?"

"You know, now that I think about it, one of the men might have mentioned the pup," said Farmer Yorick O'Gara.

"He is somewhat distinctive," suggested Journeyman Evan.

"I'll not leave him behind," Greer said, feeling panicked.

"No, no, I'm not suggesting that. It is just a problem we need to solve before we leave."

"Let's have a talk with my wife. She has a long day ahead of her since she is our only good seamstress and is a right good hand at haircutting. I suspect she might know how to change the color of a pup too. As a matter of fact, you could do me a favor. I have a female border dog I've been wanting to get to my father. Maybe you could take her along, and then folk might think Kasa is her pup. Wouldn't hurt to have a good herding border dog along to keep the horses in line, not to mention Kasa."

The rest of the day went by in a blur for Greer. Once told what was needed, Mistress O'Gara took charge, and there was just no way of saying no to her. She gave everyone orders. Journeyman Evan and Farmer Yorick O'Gara were sent off to gather the gear Greer would need. She sent one of their sons off to get the old gelding and give it a good brushing. After taking Greer's measurements and taking a look at the clothes Journeyman Evan brought to her, she ordered Greer out to the nearest horse trough with a towel and a chunk of soap. She suggested he might want to wash that hair of his several times and then try to get the tangles out before the evening meal.

By the time the meal bell peeled out, Greer had gotten as many of the tangles out as he could, had been introduced to the gelding, cleaned and waterproofed the old tack for the horse, and gathered his gear to be packed. After the meal and a haircut, Mistress O'Gara had ordered him to the bathhouse, because she said she was not going to put clothes she had sewn her fingers to the bone for on a trail-dusty body.

"Neither a ride down a river nor rain count as a bath in my mind," she had told Greer, handing him a stack of neatly folded clothes. "Journeyman Evan, take him off to the bathhouse. I had the larger basin filled with hot water before the meal. It should still be warm. There are towels there."

Greer had used public bathhouses in Høyhauger when he had been flush with coin but had never been in a private one. The warm water felt good on his still sore body, and it was not until he felt the pouch he wore bump against his chest as he settled himself that he realized he had not taken it off. He covered it quickly with his hand and slid lower into the water. He hoped Journeyman Evan would not notice it or ask about it.

Journeyman Evan caught the flash of movement out of the corner of his eye and saw the pouch just as Greer slipped lower into the water. The sight of the pouch made of what he was sure was golden pine spider silk brought a flash of memory of another golden pine spider silk pouch, what had been in it, and what had happened in an unforgettable moment in the Well of Speaking this summer. He wondered what Greer carried in his pouch and then wondered what a street lad was doing with a pouch made of golden pine spider silk.

Chapter Sixteen

Not knowing Greer well enough to ask him about the pouch of golden pine spider silk, Journeyman Evan tucked the knowledge away. His rover friend Nissa had told him about the special properties of golden pine spider silk. Cloth woven from it had the ability to properly shield an object of power and keep it from being recognized by those who might be able to read it if it were not properly shielded. Was the pouch Greer wore masking some object of power, or was it just holding a small ordinary item that was important to Greer?

"We had best get out of the water before we look like the last apple in the barrel in the root cellar come spring," Journeyman Evan remarked. "We still have a lot to do before we can get some sleep. I would like to leave at dawn, if possible."

Greer reluctantly pulled himself out of the bathing basin and toweled dry. Next came putting on the clothes Mistress O'Gara had altered to fit him. As he stood there wrapped in a towel, he fingered the fine weave of the cloth and knew he had never worn clothes either as soft or undamaged as these, or as new. After he had dressed, he glanced in the highly polished metal mirror that hung on the dressing room wall, and a stranger looked back at him. He looked more his age, he thought, with the short haircut and the more adult cut of his clothes. Because of his short stature, when he had lived on the streets and only had his own poor sewing skills to tailor clothes to fit him, he had scrounged the rag pickers' barrels for clothes that fit his size, which were most often clothes for a much younger lad. What he wore had added to the illusion that he was younger than he, in truth, was. After leaving the bathhouse, Journeyman Evan directed him to the stables.

"Now if I were a really puffed up new journeyman, I would make you do all the work, and I would just sit back with a cup of tea and watch you toil, but the guild I belong to frowns on journeymen and journeywomen taking on airs. Besides, one of the things masters and journeymen and journeywomen are supposed to do is to teach apprentices, so, apprentice, think of this as your first lesson."

Spreading out a tarp over fresh hay in one of the stalls, Journeyman Evan brought in several packs and said, "Since we have but one pack horse between the two of us, we will need to repack these packs to distribute our gear and supplies. Pack your personal gear and items you want close at hand in these saddle bags. Make a roll out of your rain cloak and tie that on the back of the saddle. Whatever does not fit in your saddle bags, you can pack in the packs the pack horse will carry. Let's spread everything out here and then repack. That way we will both know where everything is."

Working with someone like Journeyman Evan was an unusual experience for Greer. He was not used to folk who had patience. If Greer had made a mistake when the owner of Milkin's Stable had showed him what to do, he would know not by words, but because he had been cuffed soundly and berated. Idiot and dunderhead were names he had often been called because he had not moved swiftly enough or fast enough to suit whoever was directing the task. Journeyman Evan on the other hand, had not only told him what to do but also showed him if he did not do it quite right. Journeyman Evan also explained the whys of what he was asking.

"Well now, you could stuff the extra clothes in the pack that way, but if you fold them like this and roll them, they take up less space and are not as wrinkled when you want to wear them. Personally, I don't never mind if I go around wrinkled, but it has been drilled into my head that when I am traveling for the Glassmakers Guild, I represent them, so I should not look like an unmade bed. Since you are now going about as my apprentice, it would not do for me to let you get by looking slovenly," Journeyman Evan had told Greer.

Working together, the packs were done to Journeyman Evan's satisfaction in short order. They were just heading out of the stables when a pack of border dogs came racing around the side of the building, and a small pup came barreling into Greer.

"Hey there, little one, best you slow down a bit," Greer said, holding the pup off as it frantically tried to lick his face. It was not until he had put the pup out at arm's length and really looked at the wiggling bundle of fur he held that he realized he was holding a very changed Kasa. Instead of the dappled gray, cream and copper colored coat, Kasa was now two tones of brown and would no longer be taken for a border dog. He now looked more like a mixed breed mutt.

"Looks like Mistress O'Gara is good with all kinds of alterations. Clothes, folks, pups," Journeyman Evan stated wryly. "Neither of you would match your descriptions at this point, which is a good thing, I'm thinking." Noticing that Greer was looking a little disconcerted, Journeyman Evan quickly changed the subject. "So have you tried the new boots yet?"

When Greer shook his head in a negative, Journeyman Evan suggested Greer might want to try them out and mentioned he was going to go and make himself acquainted with the other border dog that was going to travel with them. Journeyman Evan suspected that Greer might need a little time alone to adjust to all of the changes that had occurred to him in the last few hours, though it was hard to tell, for Greer was not an easy one to read.

Greer walked slowly back to the room he and Journeyman Evan were sharing with Kasa running forward and then back to him, demanding his attention, and then hurrying off again. In Høyhauger he had known who he was, and where he stood. Though he knew he was at the very bottom of society, he knew the rules of how he was to act, what was expected of him, and what to expect. Now he was at a loss as to who that stranger was who had looked out at him from the dressing room mirror.

His feeling of strangeness did not end when he tried on the boots Brogan had made for him, and for the first time, stood up and found himself not leaning to the left. It was an odd sensation and very disorienting. Greer took a step, and then a second, but miscalculated where his foot was in relation to the floor and stumbled, just catching himself before he fell. This walking business in the built-up boot was going to take some getting used to. Greer knew he needed to get used to it quickly, for it was imperative that he not look like he limped or had an uneven gait. If he did not, all the changes of clothes and haircuts were not going to be that good of a disguise.

Greer spent the next little while taking careful steps around the sleeping room while Kasa very wisely curled up under the bunk bed out of the way. By the time Journeyman Evan arrived, Greer felt steadier, but that was on an even floor. The uneven ground outside might prove to be another matter.

"So, how are the new boots?" Journeyman Evan inquired.

"Strange, but manageable on the flat floor. I'm a little concerned about trying to walk or run on uneven ground," Greer admitted.

"Maybe we should look for a good stout walking stick for you. I often walk while traveling because I get too stiff and sore staying mounted on horseback all day. A tall walking stick is a great friend on a rocky trail. Let's take the time to look through the brush pile next to the wood lot and see what we can come up with. We'll peel the bark off and maybe beg some leather out of Mistress O'Gara to wrap around it to give your hand a firmer grip."

Greer sat down on one of the benches next to the fireplace and took off the boots. Brogan had cautioned him to break them in slowly to prevent blisters. Pulling on his other boots quickly, Greer stood and followed Journeyman Evan out the door. Kasa scrambled up and was out the door before him. Once they reached the brush pile, they spent their time looking for good walking sticks and tossing sticks for Kasa. Anyone looking at them at that moment would think they were just a pair of carefree farm lads goofing off when they should probably have been chopping or hauling wood. This picture of normalcy continued after the evening meal. The two lads sat on the farmhouse porch, each whittling the bark off of his walking stick, dogs asleep at their feet.

"My friend Nissa is a woodworker," Journeyman Evan remarked casually. "She'd have a right good laugh at me attempting to make a walking stick look like anything other than a barkless tree branch. I have no talent for carving. Like as not, if I were a woodworker, I would spend more time bandaging up cuts than actually carving. Nissa is a rover, the one who travels with a hunting cat. You ever met any rovers?"

"Nope."

"Many rovers pass through Høyhauger?"

"Never paid much mind as to who was passing through."

The two worked for a while longer, each lost in his own thoughts. Journeyman Evan showed Greer how to wrap and tie the leather bits he had begged off of Mistress O'Gara.

When the walking sticks were done, Journeyman Evan said, "There is one more thing we need to do. These walking sticks look like they were just made, and the story we have put together is that you and I have been traveling for a while, so follow me."

Journeyman Evan led Greer into the house and proceeded to put the end of his walking stick into the cook fire in the kitchen hearth. Not for long, but just long enough to put a nice brown on the end of the wood. He then scooped up some ash and rubbed it up and down the length of the walking stick, being careful to avoid the leather. After Greer had done the same, he led Greer to the tack room of the stable where they both oiled the leather on the walking sticks. Journeyman Evan encouraged Greer to let some of the oil dribble down the stick and then mix it with the ash.

"Almost done," Journeyman Evan remarked, as he took his walking stick out, laid it on the ground and rolled it in the dirt with his foot. When he was done, he took a cloth, soaked it in the watering trough and gave the stick a good rub down. When the task was done, the walking stick looked well-used. "Not bad. A few days of travel, and a good soaking out in a rain, and this walking stick will look like a long-held friend. Nice job. We had best hit the hay, for dawn comes early."

That night as Greer lay in bed, sleep did not come quickly because his mind refused to shut down. What a strange day it had been. Certainly like no other he could remember. What he really could not figure out was why all of these folk were helping him. Back in Høyhauger, any number of folk would have sold him out faster than one could blink an eye. All the whys that had been gathering in his head kept circling and circling as he tossed and turned. Greer began to be worried that he would wake Journeyman Evan with his restlessness. He had even thought of getting up, when the pouch of golden pine spider silk began to warm, and something soft gently touched his cheek for a brief moment. Suddenly, Greer felt calmer, and the whys did not seem to matter quite so much as he slipped into a deep, restful, dreamless sleep.

The next morning was one of leave-taking. Zareh and Pryderi headed out first, but before they left, Zareh pulled Greer aside. "I just want you to know that my father and I feel badly about leaving you to find your own way, but from what Farmer O'Gara has told me, you can trust Journeyman Evan. He's a clever young fellow. After we take care of business at the capital, I will leave a message at the Glassmakers Guildhall as to where you can find Father and me. Remember, you will always be welcome with us."

With that said, Zareh took his leave. Pryderi, who had been standing next to him reached out and clasped Greer's hand. "You take care now, lad, and you mind that young pup of yours. Safe journey."

Pryderi turned abruptly and mounted his horse. With a wave, the two rode off. After they left, Greer opened his hand to find that Pryderi had slipped him some coin. Greer had never felt richer, and it was not because of the gift of coin.

Greer and Journeyman Evan took their leave shortly after Zareh and Pryderi, heading straight south, following the foothills of the mountain range that formed the easternmost border of Sommerhjem. Zareh and Pryderi had headed southwest in order to pick up the royal road that bisected the country, for they intended to travel much more swiftly to the capital.

As they rode, Journeyman Evan explained to Greer that since he was going to be in the north country on business for Master Cynfarch, he had been given permission to visit his family's farm.

"The foothills of the Ryggrad Mountains are good for raising horses, and my family raises good riding horses, much in demand."

Greer's curiosity got the better of him, so he asked why Journeyman Evan was not raising horses on the family farm.

"Ah, I think it's time for me to give you a quick course on how things work here in Sommerhjem. The vast majority of the folk who came here first were farmers or fishers by trade, for the soil was rich for growing and the sea was rich for harvesting. Still are to this day. Once Sommerhjem became settled, the need for crafts folk, merchants, traders, and others arose, not to mention a place for art, music, and plays. It either was a tradition the folk brought with them or the tradition developed, but somehow folk figured out that just because you were a child of a blacksmith, it did not necessarily mean you had the talent or the want to be a blacksmith, so guilds were formed to teach crafts, trades, and arts. An apprentice, journeyman, master system was formed within the guilds at that time." Journeyman Evan looked at Greer to see if he was following him so far. Greer nodded that he understood.

"Of course, there is an exception to every rule, and in the case of Sommerhjem, it's the rovers," Journeyman Evan continued. "There are folks who are fiercely independent and also have trouble staying too long in one place. The rovers are like that. They are a pretty closed clan, so not just anybody can become a rover. Most are born into the clan, though there are some exceptions. Rover youngsters are encouraged to follow their inclinations as to a craft or trade. Some have a natural talent or calling. It might reflect what one of their parents do, and so they learn from that parent, or they might find someone to teach them a craft or a trade outside of the guildhalls. They serve a useful purpose in our land, for guild members are most often are found in the larger towns, and rovers take their trade to the outermost reaches of Sommerhjem. They fulfill a need that is sometimes not met by those of the guilds. They often earn their living during the fair season and with commissions. Anyway, nowadays, guild folk who are in a trade or craft are always on the lookout for youngsters who show an interest in or a talent for that craft or trade. While my sister showed great interest in the breeding, raising, and training of horses, my head was often elsewhere. A journeyman glassmaker spent time at our farm installing a window my mother had commissioned, and I got interested in what he was doing. When he left, I went with him. I found, however, that while I was a good mechanic at making glass, I was not really an artist at making beautiful glass items. When Master Rollag discovered I had more talent with horses than glass, he suggested I might want to apprentice under Master Cynfarch. It has been the best of both worlds. I still dabble in glass, so my training there has not been wasted."

Journeyman Evan spent much of the morning's ride continuing to fill Greer in on how the society of Sommerhjem worked. It was shortly before noon when Journeyman Evan pulled his horse a little closer to Greer's, and in a quiet voice said, "I think we are being followed. Not sure though, because the dogs haven't sounded any alarm. No, don't turn around."

Chapter Seventeen

"The woods we are traveling through thin out a little way beyond that bend up ahead, and we should pick up a wider road there that will travel level and straight for several miles. If there is someone following us, we should either be able to spot them, or they will have to stay quite a way back. There is a small crossroads inn about an hour's ride down this road, and I suggest we stop there for the midday meal. Stopping there will accomplish two things. Most small inns like this one will be the center of local gossip, so we might pick up some indication whether or not the search for you has come this far. Also, when we leave, we will have a better idea if we are being followed. Alright with you?"

Greer nodded his agreement with Journeyman Evan's suggestion. "I would like to stop up ahead once we are out of the woods. Kasa is looking pretty tired, especially considering he has traveled twice as far as we have this last half an hour."

"It was a brilliant idea for us to bring an older border dog with us, for Louve is great at letting Kasa explore within limits, but you are right, both of them could use a rest. Stopping will also give us a chance to look at our back trail without being too obvious."

Greer settled himself more comfortably in his saddle and damped down the urge to look over his shoulder. He, too, had felt like they were being watched, but since he had left the border town of Høyhauger, he was not as confident in his instincts. In the town, his survival skills had been honed to a razor's edge, but here in the country he was not familiar with the everyday pattern of sounds. He did not know when he heard a branch snap whether that indicated something dangerous, or just a squirrel dashing through the trees. He knew Journeyman Evan was savvier about traveling in the country, but it was disconcerting to have to rely on someone other than himself.

Though on alert, the next hour passed quickly. Kasa had settled into the makeshift carrier on the pack horse and was deeply asleep. Louve ranged ahead of the horses, but not very far, and Journeyman Evan kept up his, at times humorous, monologue concerning the history and customs of Sommerhjem. The first real test as to how Greer's new look was going to work lay ahead. By now he was convinced that Journeyman Evan was certainly glib enough to do the talking for the two of them, so he did not have any worries about that. He had practiced enough in the new boots that he felt confident he could get from his horse into the inn and back out without falling flat on his face. As the crossroads inn came into sight, Greer pulled his horse to a sudden stop.

"Journeyman Evan," Greer called out just loud enough to get Journeyman Evan's attention. "Hold up a minute, would you?"

"What is it?"

"My name."

"Your name?"

"Yes, my name. Those who are looking for me might know my name. Though often addressed as 'hey you' or 'lad' or 'gimp,' I do have a name, and some folks in town knew it. All the differences we have made in my looks and walk could be meaningless if whoever is looking for me asks if they have seen a lad named Greer. Is it so common a name in Sommerhjem that it won't matter?"

"No. You're right, not so common a name. Good thing you thought of that. Why didn't we think of that before? Okay, we can figure this out. How about Kort? Kort and Kasa. Has a nice ring to it," Journeyman Evan said, and there was a hint of mischief in his voice. "To avoid confusion when we get to the inn, I will just address you as apprentice. If anyone asks your name, I will tell them it is Kort. That work for you?"

Greer slowly nodded. He thought there might be a joke in the name that Journeyman Evan had picked as an alias for him, but he did not know. Teasing for fun was not something he had experience with. Mean teasing he knew all too well. He was not used to someone like Journeyman Evan, who one moment seemed very adult, and the next was filled with mirth and mischief. Journeyman Evan had such an easy way about him that Greer thought folks would often underestimate him. It probably served him well when horse trading.

The inn they approached was a low stone building built into the hillside. Attached to it was a stable. The land west of the lane they were traveling showed the remnants of a large garden and harvested fields of grain and hay. Beyond the stable, there was a series of small cottages which Journeyman Evan explained probably housed the innkeeper's extended family, most of whom worked at the inn or on the adjoining farm. Journeyman Evan told Greer that this crossroad was quite a ride from the pass into Bortfjell at Høyhauger, and it led to one of the major routes south. Many travelers stopped here for the night, for the inn had both sleeping rooms to rent and camping, for a small fee, in the grove just to the south beyond the cottages. It was also known for its food, plain fare but hearty. More important, it was a fairly safe place to stop. No one would mess with their horses or pack animal.

"How can you be so sure of that? This place doesn't look very secure."

"Ah, you haven't met the innkeeper's family yet. The stories go that the innkeeper was once a smuggler who no one messed with, for he is a big brute of a man. He got tired of the smuggler's life and settled here. His offspring take after him in both size and fierceness. There is often a rough and tumble crowd of trappers and traders here, but no one causes trouble. It would be a good place to spend the night, but we need to put in some distance this day, so alas, we will need to move on after the midday meal." Having said that, Journeyman Evan gave a huge sigh. "Cook here makes the best berry tarts outside of the capital."

When Greer and Journeyman Evan reached the inn, a very tall muscular lad about their age stood up from where he had been sitting next to the inn's front door. "Will you be staying?" he asked.

"No, just stopping for a bite to eat and a chance to rest the horses."

"Just tie the horses over there to the left. I'll water them and watch over them. Nice border dog. What's her name?"

"Louve, and that pup sleeping in the basket on the pack horse will probably not move. He is a bit tuckered out, but if he does need to get down, just tell Louve to contain him."

"Ah, hadn't noticed him. Fine looking little pup. Mixed breed?"

"Ayup. Got some border dog in him, but who knows what else."

"I'll look after them."

"Thanks," Journeyman Evan said, as he headed towards the inn door and motioned that Greer should follow him.

All the while Journeyman Evan had been talking to the inn lad, Greer had been unobtrusively looking about. There were a number of other horses hitched where their horses were to go. In addition, there were two wagons with horses still hitched to them. Greer noted that several of the horses may have carried riders from Bortfjell. He could tell by the saddle blankets and bags. He touched Journeyman Evan's arm and in a very quiet voice told him what he had noticed. Thus warned, the two stepped through the door and entered the inn.

Unlike some of the inns Journeyman Evan had had the occasion to stop at, this one had a higher than usual ceiling. A huge fireplace took up one wall, and the large wooden beams in the ceiling were darkened with the smoke from years of fires. There were tables scattered about the room with benches on the long sides. Several tables were filled with groups. One small table held two rough-looking men.

Journeyman Evan led Greer to a small table next to the wall closest to the front door and positioned himself with his back to the wall. He gestured to Greer to sit next to him. "Easier to talk this way," Journeyman Evan said in a voice just loud enough to be heard by those in the inn, but not so loud as to draw attention to themselves. Shortly after they sat down, a tall woman of middle years came bustling out of the kitchen door, wiping her hands on her apron.

"Sorry, young gents, hopes youse haven't been waitin' too long. What can I gets youse this day? We've gots a nice barley soup with a bit of old rooster thrown in," she said with a wink, "or there's some venison stew. Bread's fresh this mornin'. A good hearty dark rye."

"I'll take the soup if you can throw in a hunk of cheese with that bread. What about you, apprentice?"

As the woman looked on expectantly, Greer looked down at the table top, trying to look just a bit bashful, and said, "S-s-sou-soup, if, if, ah, p-p-pl-please."

"Bread and cheese for you too?"

Greer nodded his head, still keeping his head down.

"Gots yourself a bit of a shy one there in youse's apprentice, don't youse, Journeyman?" the woman said good naturedly.

"Doesn't need words when he works with the horses and dogs. They seem to have no trouble understanding him," Journeyman Evan stated, and as he did so, he realized that what he had said was very true. Greer was good with the animals. He also realized that Greer rarely talked unless he was asked a question or needed to impart information. All during the morning ride, Journeyman Evan had been doing the talking. He began to realize that he knew very little about Greer.

"Be back in a shake with your food. Would you be wantin' some ale?"

"Just water, please," Journeyman Evan replied.

While they waited for the woman to return with their meal, Greer, without seeming to, checked out the entrances and exits from the room and paid close attention to the folks who were dining. Habits die hard, he thought. Never be far from an exit, always know other ways out of a building or situation, and check out the others in the room. He did not concern himself so much with most of the others gathered, for they seemed like farmers or travelers like themselves. He kept a wary eye on the two rough-looking men he suspected were from Bortfjell.

After the woman plopped down their meals, she was beckoned over by one of the two Bortfjell men Greer had been surreptitiously watching.

"You, Cook, we're looking for a man . . . ."

"Well sir, I've been looking for one, too," the cook said with a teasing laugh, looking over her shoulder to direct a wink at the folks behind her.

"Look," the man started again, "We're looking for a lad . . . ."

"I thought youse said youse were looking for a man," the cook retorted.

Greer and Journeyman Evan could hear quiet chuckles from the others in the room. They also noticed the man who was asking the questions was turning a bit red in the face.

"We're looking for a particular man and a particular lad, or two men and a lad." The man held up his hand before the cook could interrupt again. "We're willing to pay good coin for some information."

"Now what would be so special about these folk youse are looking for that youse would be willing to part with some coin for information? Who are youse looking for?"

"We're looking for a man or two men, who are traveling with a lad, and probably coming from the north."

"We've had a number of folks who would fit that description pass through here this year."

The man who was talking was now beginning to grow purple in the face. He looked like he was going to leap out of his chair and throttle the cook, when the other man sitting with him put a restraining hand on his companion's arm.

"Your pardon, mistress. Let me try to clear this up. The young lad was a street lad and a small time thief in Høyhauger. He stole something of importance from our employer. We think he was either kidnapped or ran off with smugglers. Another searching pair encountered them in the Fjell Skoj forest, but they slipped away. It was reported that one of the men was of middle years and one was white-haired. The lad is around ten to twelve years, short, and walks with an uneven gait, having one leg shorter than the other. Now, has anyone here seen the likes?"

The folks in the inn all looked at each other and at the men making the inquiry, but no one offered any information. Folks shook their heads or shrugged their shoulders. Not getting any information, the men threw some coin on the table and left. The cook quickly cleared their table, remarking to the group gathered that she was more than happy to see the last of those two. She came back over to Journeyman Evan and Greer's table and asked if they needed anything more just as Greer was wiping up the last of his soup with the heel of the bread.

"Ah, that's whats I likes. Young fellas with healthy appetites. Another bowl of soup and more bread for the two of youse?"

When Journeyman Evan looked regretfully like he was about to turn down her offer, the cook informed him that she was not charging by the bowlful. By the time she returned with more soup and bread, many of the other diners had left. She was followed out of the kitchen by a younger woman who helped her clear the tables and wipe them down.

"Youse know, there're either a lot of gimpy lads missing from Høyhauger, or there's somethin' strange goin' on," the cook said to the younger woman. "That's the third group that's stopped by here in the last few days lookin' for a man, or two men, and a lad with a limp. First ones says the lad's some sort of missin' heir, second ones says he took him a valuable border dog, and now these two tells me he's stole somethin' of importance from their employer. What's a body to believe? Personally, even if I had any information about the poor gimpy lad, I'm not sure I would gives it to the likes of thems as has come lookin'."

Both Greer and Journeyman Evan had finished their meal by the time the two women had finished clearing the tables. Journeyman Evan stood up, walked up to the cook to pay for their meal and ask if there were any fruit tarts available.

"Be happy to pack youse a few to take with you. Wait right here."

In a few minutes she returned and handed Journeyman Evan a paper wrapped bundle and asked, "So's where's the two of youse headin'?"

"I've got family a ways southwest of here, so we're heading there. Thank you kindly for a delicious meal."

"Youse are right welcome. If youse are back this way, stop again."

Journeyman Evan took his leave and signaled Greer to accompany him. After thanking the man outside the inn for watching their horses, dogs, and gear, the two mounted up and headed out. After they had gone a short distance, Journeyman Evan pulled alongside Greer and suggested that he had that feeling of being watched again, but he had not spotted anyone following them from the inn.

Chapter Eighteen

The afternoon wore on with little change in the monotony of rolling grassy hills covered with trees at the top. They passed few folks on the road, and while Journeyman Evan could not shake the feeling they were being watched, neither he nor Greer spotted anyone or anything behind them. To relieve the stiffness of riding, they occasionally dismounted and walked a bit. Greer was thankful for his walking stick, for he was still not very confident walking in his new boots. If they saw someone approaching while walking, they would quickly mount up, for they were safer on horseback.

By the time it was time to find a place to camp for the night, Greer was more than ready to get down off his horse and onto solid ground once again. He had learned a few things about camping during his journey so far and so volunteered to take care of the horses, gather firewood, and haul water. Journeyman Evan pitched the lean-to and, after the fire was going, began to fix the evening meal. Greer did not think he should subject Journeyman Evan to his cooking, since he knew how to cook very little.

Once they had eaten and cleaned up, Journeyman Evan put a bit more wood on the fire and settled back. He thought it was time to gather a little more information about his traveling companion. The setting was relaxing, a small grassy knoll overlooking a fair size pond. The night sky was filled with stars, and there was not a hint of rain. The night would grow quite cool later, but for now, close to the fire, it was pretty comfortable.

"It's hard to imagine that so many folks have been sent to find you just because of a book containing border dog bloodlines. I suspect there's more to this story," said Journeyman Evan, hoping Greer would respond.

"Maybe because I witnessed the owner of Milkin's Stable trying to rob the gentleman. May have been a new scheme on his part, this making it look like he had been hurt, too. Maybe he had pulled that before, but I think I would have heard whispers of it on the streets. I have thought on it and have wondered if the gentleman was a specific target. I don't know what happened to him after I ran. Strange though, I have felt pushed to move on ever since that day." Greer gave a quick start, realizing he had said the last sentence out loud. What had compelled him to do that?

"Look, I know you don't know me, and I suspect you don't trust folks very much, but at some point you are going to have to trust someone. Much as you would like not to be, you have to be dependent on me, since you do not know this land or its ways. To be brutally honest, you do not have the survival skills needed to live off the land, no offense meant."

"None taken."

Journeyman Evan acknowledged Greer and went on. "You have no real destination, no plan, and yet something seems to be driving you willy-nilly onward, falling in with companions who for some unquestioning reason seem to be carrying you along in their wake and . . ."

What Journeyman Evan would have said to finish his statement was cut short when a low-throated growl came from just beyond the firelight. Kasa did not stir, but Louve jumped up and took up a position just north of where they were sitting. Strangely enough, while Louve was on alert, she did not make a sound. Both Greer and Journeyman Evan quickly stood. They grabbed their walking sticks and were holding them ready to defend themselves. Each stood quietly listening, to see if he could distinguish what was out there. Greer caught movement out of the corner of his eye just in time to see Kasa stand up and stretch.

"Kasa, stay. Louve, contain," Greer said in a command voice just above a whisper.

Neither border dog responded, and Kasa suddenly scrambled forward dashing past the trio who stood at alert. Greer made a motion to move after him, but Journeyman Evan reached out and gently grabbed his arm.

"Hold on."

"But Kasa . . . ."

"Seems to be bringing a friend to join us," Journeyman Evan said, as calmly as he could manage. Even though he was acquainted with one hunting cat, it was more than disconcerting to have three walk into the light of the fire. It was hard to be overwhelmingly frightened as he watched Kasa trying to herd the three towards them.

Finally, the largest of the three hunting cats reached out and placed a large but gentle paw on Kasa's back and pressed downward. Kasa stopped what he was doing immediately and lay down. Greer found himself thinking that he wished he could get Kasa to mind that fast.

The two smaller hunting cats swiftly began pulling out lean-to stakes, and when Journeyman Evan made a move to go to stop them, the largest of the hunting cats gave a warning growl.

"I take it you want us to leave," Journeyman Evan said. "Not a problem. Why don't you let me get our gear out of the tent before your companions collapse it? That alright with you?"

The large hunting cat nodded.

"I'll get the horses saddled," Greer said in a voice that was much calmer than he felt. None of the hunting cats made a move to stop him.

Since they had unpacked only their cooking and sleeping gear and the lean-to, the breaking down of camp and reloading the pack horse took very little time. While Journeyman Evan quickly made sure the fire was doused and completely out, Greer made a sling out of a blanket and tucked Kasa in. He did not know what was going to happen next, but he did not want the pup left behind or lost in the dark. Both mounted up and their horses were immediately flanked on both sides by the two younger hunting cats. The largest of the hunting cats took the lead and Louve took up a protective position in the rear. The pace the lead hunting cat took was steady but not frantic. She led them down the lane past the pond and then turned abruptly, leading them east towards the foothills. The land was rockier here, and the large hunting cat led them across a flat rock shelf down into a swiftly running shallow stream.

Greer wondered why they were walking the horses along a stream bed, but felt it would be best not to break the silence. With the dark and his growing tiredness, Greer began to lose track of time, and may even have nodded off, when he was jerked abruptly awake as his horse lurched out of the stream onto another rock shelf. Kasa gave a little yip, having been squished between Greer and the saddle when Greer's body had been thrown forward.

"Everything alright back there?" Journeyman Evan asked.

Greer checked on Kasa before he answered. "Sorry. I must have dozed off. We're fine back here."

"Greer, look behind you."

Greer turned in his saddle, and at first, he did not know what Journeyman Evan was talking about. During the ride following the hunting cat, they had climbed steadily higher off the rolling prairie they had been camping on and now had a fairly clear view of their back trail. Greer could see it was growing lighter, but then he became confused. Did the sun not rise in the east? Just as that thought passed through his mind, he caught a faint hint of smoke on the wind.

"Prairie fire. Not uncommon out here this time of year. We would have had ourselves quite a scramble trying to outrun it, depending on how close it started to us and how hard and from what direction the wind was blowing. There are plenty of streams that come out of the hills here, so often the fires just burn a section between streams if there isn't a strong wind. Wonder what started it. Folks around here are very careful with fires, especially this time of year when it's so dry."

"Won't this be bad for the farms that depend on the prairie for their livestock?"

"No, as odd as it might sound, the fires are a good thing. After a burn, the prairie renews itself."

"Another question?"

"Yes."

"Was the fire the reason the hunting cat led us up the stream for so long? The fire is still quite far away."

"I don't think so. I once met an old trapper who said the most difficult place to track game was on rocky ground or in running water, and our friend ahead of us there has taken us across or through both. If anyone has been trying to follow us, our trail is now pretty obscure."

"How would someone be able to follow us without our being able to see them?"

"Maybe by scent or, well, I have an idea, but I will need brighter light to check it out. If it is by scent, the water would have taken care of that. Our guide seems to be getting impatient, so we had best get moving again."

Maybe a better question would be how would someone know to follow them, unless they had somehow let something slip at the inn or someone at the O'Gara farm was not as loyal as Farmer Yorick O'Gara thought. Thinking about it more was not going to solve the puzzle, so Greer turned his attention towards staying on his horse. The large hunting cat turned the party south, and soon they were following a trail along the bottom of a ridge. They traveled for several more hours, but to Greer it seemed like days before the hunting cat stopped. Just to the left of the trail was a small spring. The hunting cat stuck her muzzle into the clear water and drank.

The two smaller hunting cats joined her, and then all three walked a little way farther up the trail and settled down.

"Looks as if we have come to the end of our ride," Journeyman Evan suggested, as he swung down and walked over to Greer's horse. "Hand the pup down to me. At the very least we need to water the horses and give them a rest."

Greer was so stiff and sore, he was not sure he was going to be able to move out of his saddle. Between riding and then trying to walk in the new boots, his body creaked and groaned more than the leather saddle when he finally swung his leg over and slid to the ground. After leading his horse to the spring for water, Greer tied him to a nearby tree and slowly sank down to sit on a boulder near the spring. Journeyman Evan stood leaning against a tree.

"What is it with you and hunting cats?" Journeyman Evan wondered out loud.

"Honestly? I have no idea."

"I don't know about you, but right now whatever else they are, they are more intelligent than we are."

Greer just quirked an eyebrow at Journeyman Evan.

"They are napping in a warm sunspot, and we are not. I'll take first watch."

The sun was high in the sky when Greer woke slowly. He found himself lying on his side. Kasa was curled up next to his stomach and the largest of the hunting cats had her paw raised over his shoulder. Greer looked deep into the hunting cat's eyes, but could see nothing that caused him to fear her. She jerked her head over her shoulder, and Greer saw Journeyman Evan was sound asleep leaning against a tree trunk. So much for waking him for second watch, he thought. The hunting cat turned, walked over to the middle of the trail, and sat down facing Greer. She was joined by her two smaller companions.

"Ah, Kasa, I think it might be time to go. I'll go wake Journeyman Evan."

Once Journeyman Evan got over being embarrassed about falling asleep on watch, and muttering that if a Master Clarisse ever heard about it she would surely have a good laugh, he did a quick scout around where they had rested. He suddenly called Greer over.

"Come take a look at this," Journeyman Evan stated, pointing at the ground.

Hunkering down, Greer looked where Journeyman Evan pointed. He found himself looking at their horses' hoof prints. "It is clear that we are looking at the hoof prints of only two horses, probably ours."

"Well, that is the good news part of what we are looking at. It would seem that this is probably a little used trail and there have not been horses along it recently, or at least not since the last rain."

"I hear a bad news part of this."

"When you look at the two sets of prints, what do you see?"

"Two sets of hoof prints."

"Look closer."

Greer looked at the hoof prints again. They were horse hoof prints. He did not know what Journeyman Evan wanted him to see, and then he looked closer. One of the hoof prints was very distinguishable. Where the others were uniformly U shaped, one of them had a bar across the closed end of the U.

"You see it, don't you?" Greer nodded. Journeyman Evan got up and walked over to where the horses were tied. "You check your horse, and I'll check mine."

"Here," Greer called. "Left rear and the shoe is very new."

Journeyman Evan took a look. "Not a bad fit, but not the best. He won't go lame, but we might as well have been leaving sign posts with arrows pointing where we were traveling."

"Do you think our trip up the stream would throw someone off our trail?"

"Most probably. It would take a really excellent tracker to follow that trail. A bigger question would be, did your horse already have that shoe on? More to the point, if not, who on Farmer Yorick O'Gara's farm put that shoe on your horse?" said Journeyman Evan.

"Maybe the most important question to ask is how did the hunting cat know to lead us here in such a way as to hide our trail?" suggested Greer.

CHAPTER NINETEEN

"Another important question is why did the hunting cat lead us here?" questioned Journeyman Evan. "Our guide, however, is looking impatient, so we had best follow. Not following is most likely not an option."

"I suspect you're right. There is nothing we can do at the moment about the horseshoe. We can only hope our ride up the stream will confuse anyone who might be following. Do you know where we are?"

"Yup. We are in the foothills of the Ryggrad Mountains in northern Sommerhjem."

"Let me rephrase my question," Greer said, as he swung himself up onto his horse. "Do you know exactly where we are in the foothills of the Ryggrad Mountains in northern Sommerhjem?"

"Exactly?"

"Exactly!"

"Well . . . ."

"Alright then. Do you know in general where we are, but," Greer held up a hand before Journeyman Evan could speak, "a more specific in general than the last time?"

Journeyman Evan, by this time, had also swung himself into the saddle. "To be honest, all I can tell you is I know we are east of where we were yesterday, and I think slightly farther south. Am I lost? Not exactly, for if we follow the Ryggrad Mountains south we will eventually reach some type of settlement or farm, but I cannot guarantee that it will be before our food runs out. I'm not really sure exactly where we are, and I've never traveled in this area before."

Journeyman Evan's answer did nothing to reassure Greer, but at this point there was not anything he could do about it. The large hunting cat had stood and moved slightly down the trail, looking over her shoulder to see if she were being followed. Greer urged his mount to move forward, and Journeyman Evan followed, leading the pack horse. Louve took up the rear guard position with Kasa at her side, and the two smaller hunting cats slipped into the tall grass that grew on either side of the trail. Though each of the two lads had their separate misgivings about blindly following the hunting cat, at the moment there did not seem to be a better plan. So far the large hunting cat had moved them out of the way of a prairie fire and had helped them blur their back trail.

⁓⁓⁓

Lord Avital had been greatly disappointed when they had missed the street lad, Greer, in Trelandsby and wondered if he were on a wild goose chase. Maybe he should just head home. He missed the comfort of his own bed and the high sheep-dotted hills. He missed having the evening meal with his children. While he knew the estate was being well looked after by his sister and her husband, and his three other children were probably having the time of their lives with their cousins, this last disappointment was making him question why he had ever left Dugghus. He knew that grief over the loss of his beloved wife had something to do with it, and when he had left, he had not been thinking clearly. He needed to decide what to do by morning. Should he go on with the seeker, or should he just head home?

In the morning, Lord Avital was no closer to an answer than he had been the night before. He was drinking a hot cup of tea, sitting on the porch of Ellwood and Aldona's tree home where he had stayed the night, when he saw Seeker Zita approaching.

"Good morning. Did you sleep well?" Seeker Zita asked.

"Good morning to you, and I slept fair."

"I had a chance to speak with the foresters this morning, especially to Ellwood and Aldona. They said that the one of the two men the lad is traveling with is who I suspected he was, and so I can reassure you the lad's in good hands. You said your son would be about fifteen years old now?"

"Yes."

"Aldona suggested that the lad she took care of was not a young lad. His size and clothing gave the suggestion that he was a young lad, but once he was cleaned up, and she had a chance to take a good look at him while he was sleeping, she noted he was older. That certainly gives more credence that this Greer fellow might be your son, for his physical description and age seem to fit." Seeing that Lord Avital was taking in what she was saying, Seeker Zita continued. "There's more."

"Go on," Lord Avital said and held very still, waiting for what Seeker Zita would say next.

Seeker Zita looked around to see if anyone were within listening range, and seeing no one, continued. "When Greer was first brought to Ellwood and Aldona for caretaking, Ellwood had the task of getting the lad out of his wet clothes and into a dry nightshirt. Once he had the lad stripped down, he noticed Greer was wearing a small pouch around his neck. It looked, Ellwood told me, to be of a very fine weave and made of golden pine spider silk. When he went to take it off, thinking it was also soaked, he was surprised to find it was dry and a little warm to the touch, so he just left it on and tucked it in. Never mentioned it to anyone else, except to his wife. Had forgotten about it until I asked this morning. He has promised not to reveal this information to anyone else."

"Did he mention the color of the pouch?" Lord Avital asked, trying not to get his hopes up.

"Yes. Ellwood said that is what had surprised him the most. Considering the state of the lad's clothes and the amount of dirt still ingrained in the lad's skin, even after being tumbled down the Raskalt, the pouch was cream in color and not a bit worn or dirty. The cord holding the pouch was a washed-out blue."

"I am sure there are other small cream colored pouches made of golden pine spider silk with faded blue cords, but the description fits the one I have worn all my life. Do you know where they were heading?"

"Yes. They were heading to Farmer Yorick O'Gara's farm, where I had intended to head later in my journey, but I think I will head there sooner. Something I need to pick up is waiting for me there. It is not too far out of the way and keeps both of us heading south. I have felt you have been torn as to where to go from here. If the lad is your son, an extra day on the way home might be worth the detour. If he is not your son, or is not there, you can then decide what to do next, but at least you will be headed in the right direction if you choose to return home."

"You are right. Both in your suggestion as to where to head next and that I have been torn. I was just wondering if I am chasing about because I was having difficulty being home without my wife. I have other children, you know, and I have left them to go wandering off."

"What little I know of you, I would suspect you left them and your estate in good hands."

"I did that, and while this journey so far has been very disappointing, I have learned much about myself and Sommerhjem, which will not be wasted when I return home. During the Regent's reign, I and mine tried to stay as little noticed as possible so as not to attract attention. In doing so, we survived better than most, but on the other hand, we did nothing to help those in need or be a voice at the court. I wonder how many others did as we did and thus contributed to the Regent's ability to gain power and commit nefarious deeds."

"I think you did what many did. You tried to protect your own, especially in the last few years. I also suspect that whoever becomes ruler next is going to find that the nobles and the common folk alike will no longer be as compliant or as quiet, and will demand a stronger voice in ruling Sommerhjem. I suspect that is as it should be. The way the present interim ruling council was set up by those who came before us suggests that the rule was not just held by the large landholders in the past. Well, we could carry on a discussion of the future of Sommerhjem all morning, but that is not going to get us to the O'Gara farm. I suggest we head out."

The two thanked Ellwood and Aldona and took their leave. The ride to the O'Gara farm was without incident, and Lord Avital used the times he and Seeker Zita could ride side by side to ask her more about her observations of the places she had traveled. He found her an interesting traveling companion and enjoyed her company. His comfortable mood did not last much beyond the entrance to the O'Gara's farmhouse where he learned he had missed Greer once again. Even more disturbing was the news Farmer Yorick O'Gara gave them over dinner.

"It was determined that the lad traveling with two adults was drawing too much interest, so Zareh and Pryderi traveled on to the southwest and Greer left with the Glassmakers Guild Journeyman Evan. We all decided that the two young fellows traveling together would be better, especially because Greer is disguised as Journeyman Evan's apprentice." Farmer Yorick O'Gara went on to tell the visitors about Greer's and Kasa's disguises and how the boots had evened out his gait. "That's the good news."

With great trepidation, Lord Avital asked, "What is the bad news?"

"About half a day after they had left, one of my hands happened to be in the pasture and noticed an odd horseshoe print. It would appear that someone replaced a shoe on the horse Greer is riding, making the print quite recognizable. I think I know who did the switch, but I can't prove it. I have sent him off with another of my hands and several foresters to check out places in the forest that would be good winter homes for a few of the horses we are mutually raising. It will keep him from gathering any more information and passing it along, but I'm afraid that the horseshoe print makes the lads' trail very easy to follow."

"Did you send anyone after them to warn them?" Seeker Zita asked.

"I did, but a prairie fire swept through the area where they were traveling and that obscured any trace. My folk rode the edges of the area that had been burned but did not discover any tracks. I have great confidence that they were not trapped by the fire. Journeyman Evan is very savvy about the land and prairie fires, so I can't imagine he was caught unawares. Plus the lads had two border dogs with them and they, not to mention the horses, would have raised an alarm. I'm sorry I don't have better news."

"Do you know where they were heading?" Lord Avital asked.

"Journeyman Evan had mentioned he was going to stop at a few more farms farther south that breed horses, and then he was going to go home to visit his family. The best bet would probably be to head to his family's farm. I sent a rider on ahead to give them some warning that Journeyman Evan might be being followed and about the distinctive horseshoe. His family lives a good five day ride from here. Come, I will show you where on the map I have in the tack room."

"Would not the folk who changed the horse's shoe also have known where the lads were heading?" Lord Avital asked.

"We all knew that Journeyman Evan was going to swing by his family's home, but he was very closed-mouth about what other farms he intended to visit on the guilds' business. That lad is a born horse trader."

"So, no one knew where he was heading right away, but someone may have let others know he was heading to his family's farm at some point," stated Lord Avital.

"As far as I can tell, that is correct."

"So, in a nutshell, their tracks can be followed because of the horseshoe, their disguises are not so good because someone here might have let someone not from here but interested in Greer know what to look for, and it is general knowledge that Journeyman Evan is heading for his family's farm. Is that about right?" inquired Seeker Zita.

"In addition, there seems to be no way of tracking the lads, and we will only call attention to them if we wander the countryside asking after a Glassmakers Guild journeyman and his apprentice that fit the descriptions of Journeyman Evan and Greer," suggested Lord Avital. "So, now what?"

"I would suggest we head towards Journeyman Evan's family's farm. It is in the direction that both of us want to go, and we will obviously not be leading anyone there who does not already know that is Journeyman Evan's eventual destination. If they are not there when we get there, you can then figure out what you want to do next. We can leave information with Journeyman Evan's parents how to contact you if the lads show up there," said Seeker Zita.

"I agree. We will leave in the morning then?" Lord Avital replied.

⚹

Greer and Journeyman Evan followed the large hunting cat through the afternoon. For the last several hours, they had been traveling higher into the foothills of the Ryggrad Mountains and were now riding on a narrow trail at the base of a tall cliff, hemmed in on the downhill side by tall dense pines. As the afternoon wore on, the gloomier and cooler it became, until they felt like they were riding at twilight. Soon the tree branches overhanging the trail were so dense and low that riding under them became difficult, so Greer and Journeyman Evan dismounted and began to walk, leading the horses. Greer was thankful that both the border dogs stayed close, for if Kasa decided to run off at this point, they would be hard-pressed to find him in the dense foliage.

Just when it seemed like the true night would find them still walking cautiously along the narrow path, they came through a particularly dense mass of branches and emerged into a clearing filled with sunlight and flowers. In the middle was a large vine-covered mound where the vines kept shifting and moving, even though there was very little wind in the clearing. Oddly enough, there was a chimney stack sticking out of the mound. The largest hunting cat headed straight for the mound, and seemingly out of the vines, was greeted by a booming voice that said, "Well Vadoma, who have you brought to visit me?"

122

Chapter Twenty

As Journeyman Evan and Greer looked more closely at the ivy-covered mound, they could make out the shape of a cottage under the jumble of vines. The vines slowly shifted to reveal a porch and the owner of the booming voice. When he stood, he rose up and up and up and was one of the oddest looking men either of the lads had ever seen. Tall and rail thin with long shaggy hair and skin the color of pine bark, the man more resembled the trees surrounding his cottage than the folk he faced. As Greer rode closer, he realized he had been mistaken about the man's clothing. He had thought the man had been dressed in the same type of green and brown clothes typically worn by the foresters that allowed them to blend in with their surroundings.

Journeyman Evan interrupted his questioning thoughts by expressing quietly to him, "Is that man covered in leaves, or am I seeing things?"

Journeyman Evan was not seeing things, for the man who had greeted the hunting cat was indeed draped in leaves, or to be more accurate, twined in vines which started out of the tops of his boots and extended upward until they threaded through his beard and hair.

"Well, lads, don't be shy now. If'n Vadoma brought you, I'll trust her instincts that you're not here to do me grave harm."

As if our chances to do grave harm were all that good, thought Greer as he dismounted. We are three and a bit, facing a very tall man flanked by three hunting cats. The odds are very much in their favor and not ours.

"Might I invite you to stay the night? The day grows late and both of you look like you could use a good meal. Just take your horses down that path to the left. There's good grazing in the clearing there. Not to worry about them wandering off. You can put your gear in the hut at the edge of the clearing. Water and varmint proof. When you have the horses settled, come back here."

While he had been talking, Louve had been creeping closer and closer to the tall man. "Well, come here, lass. Let's take a look at you." With that said, Louve bounded up the steps and sat at the man's feet, tail wagging.

Greer led his horse and the pack horse down the path the man had indicated, entering the clearing first. He heard a gasp from Journeyman Evan behind him, and when he turned, he saw a look of astonishment on Journeyman Evan's face.

"Will you look at that grass!" Journeyman Evan exclaimed, and Greer could hear the envy coloring his voice.

Greer could not think of a reason why he would want to look at grass, much less feel envious about a large clearing filled with a lush, brilliant green carpet of grass. The streets where he had grown up boasted very little in the way of vegetation.

"Is there something special about the grass?"

"I've never seen a clearing or field like this in all my travels. There is nothing here but grass. No weeds or other plants. What many a farmer who raises livestock would give for a pasture like this. It's no wonder that the man said we would not have to worry about the horses wandering off. What horse would want to leave this place? If you want to unload the pack horse, I'll take care of the other two and turn them out."

Greer nodded his agreement and turned his horse over to Journeyman Evan. He then set about his task. First, he gently lifted the still sleeping Kasa down, who yawned, stretched, and then abruptly sat down to scratch an itch behind his left ear. After the horses had been rubbed down and the gear safely stored in the small hut, the three headed back to the cottage.

"What do you think of our host?" Journeyman Evan asked.

"I've never seen the like. It's your land. Are men like him common among your folk?"

"I don't think a giant of a man covered in vines would be common in any country," Journeyman Evan remarked. "Ah, I see our escort has come to check on us."

Greer looked up and saw that Vadoma, the largest of the three hunting cats, sat with an air of impatience ahead of them on the path. Kasa, who had been exploring the brush along the side of the path, upon seeing Vadoma, rushed forth to greet her as if she were a long lost friend. Upon seeing that Greer and Journeyman Evan were following Kasa, the hunting cat stood up, turned, and led the trio back towards the cottage. When

Vadoma reached the cottage steps, she padded right up to the strange looking man, and Kasa followed, tail high and wagging.

"Come along, lads. Any friends of Vadoma and this young pup are welcome here."

The voice was so welcoming and kind that Greer immediately became suspicious. He had heard both men and women use kind words in that tone of voice in Høyhauger to entice street children into carriages and dwellings, and the children were never seen or heard from again. Some said they were sold to be servants or laborers on large estates in Bortfjell while others said they were sent to work in the mines. Some of the tales told of what happened to the children were best not repeated and would give anyone nightmares.

"Journeyman Evan, we need to get Kasa and Louve and go. This could be a trap." Greer looked over his shoulder and saw the way back to the horses was blocked, for the two smaller hunting cats had taken up the rear and were following close behind. At the moment, Greer knew he had few options, but he also knew he had not survived on the streets as long as he had by trusting too easily. Reluctantly, Greer moved forward.

"Come on up and sit a spell. Seems like introductions are in order. I be Ealdred Haines, and you are?"

"I am Journeyman Evan of the Glassmakers Guild, and this is my apprentice, Kort."

"Are you also of the storytellers or bards guild, Journeyman Evan?" Ealdred inquired, causing Journeyman Evan to start.

"Why, why, no, sir. I do serve other guilds under the master of the horse at the Glassmakers Guild, but serve neither of the two you mentioned."

At this point the three hunting cats had taken up positions that ringed both Journeyman Evan and Greer. The vines that had moved aside to allow sunlight onto the porch had moved again and formed a green cage across the front of the porch.

"I can see by the scars on your hands and forearms that you have worked with glass. From the calluses on your hands you have mucked a few stalls in your day, but your friend here has never handled a piece of hot molten glass in his life."

"Ah, well, you see, sir, he is not apprenticed as a glassmaker but rather under the master of the horse for the Glassmakers Guild," replied Journeyman Evan.

"And you, Kort, so you're an apprentice to this journeyman here are you?"

"Yeh, yeh, yes s-s-sir," Greer stuttered in a quiet voice with his head down.

"And these two fine border dogs. Do they belong to you?" Ealdred asked Greer.

"The female Louve belongs to Farmer O'Gara the elder, and we are taking her to him from his son. The young pup belongs to Gr, er, Kort," said Journeyman Evan.

"Do you always answer for your apprentice?"

"No, sir. It's just that he is shy and has a little trouble speaking sometimes and . . . ." Journeyman Evan's voice trailed off under the intense scrutiny of Ealdred.

"The pup has a limp. Tell me about it," Ealdred said in a voice that commanded.

"Well, sir . . . ." Journeyman Evan started.

"Not you. Kort. Was he born that way?"

"I, I, I, don't th-th-think so," Greer replied, still keeping his head down and holding back the overpowering urge to grab Kasa and run, as he watched Ealdred pick Kasa up and run his hands over him.

"Hum-m-m. No breaks that I can detect. Dislocated, I think. Let's see if that can be fixed."

With that said, Ealdred briskly rubbed his two large hands together, and to Greer's eye, Ealdred's hands turned a deep red. He thought he could feel heat emanating from them even from where he stood. Ealdred then placed his hands over and under Kasa's leg and just held them there for several minutes. Kasa went limp, and Greer started forward, but Journeyman Evan caught him by the arm.

"Wait," Journeyman Evan urged.

Ealdred did something swift with his hands, and Kasa gave out a tiny whimper. When Greer would have broken the hold Journeyman Evan had on his arm, Ealdred held up a hand and said, "Give the pup a minute or two to recover, and then he'll be as right as rain. I did not harm him, lad, just put the bones and muscles back in their right places. He'll be a little sore, but you know pups, nothing keeps them down for long."

True to his word, in a few moments Kasa was squirming in Ealdred's hands, trying to get down. When he did, his walk was even and steady. Greer wondered if Ealdred could fix his leg so easily, but dismissed the idea as quickly as it had come. He could not help feeling both envious and a bit jealous of Kasa.

"Now, lads, why don't you tell me why this pup has been made a different color? Am I looking at a pair of thieves then?"

"No sir, he's mine fair and proper!" Greer blurted out and could not take the words back. Arrugh, he thought to himself. Not a fortnight out of Høyhauger and away from the streets, and I cannot even keep in character for several hours, much less for days. No wonder he had always been a loner. If one were alone, no one cared about who could betray whom, and one could not get anyone else hurt. Now his slip out of character could put Journeyman Evan in jeopardy, who, Greer suddenly realized, had become as close to a friend as he had ever had.

"Ah, it would seem the pup is not the only one whose colors have been changed recently, but my mother always told me that weighty discussions should never be had on an empty stomach. Come along, lads, let's see what we can rustle up for dinner."

Stooping, Ealdred turned and entered the cottage. Vadoma went next, with both the border dogs following behind. Greer felt a not-so-gentle nudge on his backside propelling him reluctantly forward and knew it was not Journeyman Evan who was urging him onward. As he stepped across the threshold, he was amazed at the amount of light that came streaming through windows he had not seen from the outside. Then it struck him that the vines that had covered the windows had pulled back. Who or what was this tall thin giant of a man who commanded the vines? He was at once scary, and yet Greer could not dismiss the gentleness with which he had handled Kasa.

"Hope you don't mind simple fare. Good hearty bread, cheese, apples, honey if you like, and fresh cider. I've got some cold rabbit the dogs can share."

The meal was a quiet one. Greer had trouble working up a good appetite due to anticipating the conversation that was sure to take place once the meal was over. Once the dishes and cups had been cleared away, Ealdred leaned back, steepled his fingers on his chest, and looked at both lads.

"So, Journeyman Evan, I'm thinking you are who you say you are. You are a journeyman with the Glassmakers Guild. You work with horses, and I can understand why you might be in this area due to the farms that breed horses in the region, though you are pretty far off that beaten track. Your apprentice, Kort, here is another matter. Either of you care to explain? I would not be asking, but Vadoma rarely brings anyone to my door, so I must admit you are a puzzle I would most like to solve."

Both of the lads remained silent, each trying to think of what to say, or if to say anything for that matter. How much information should they give away, and how safe was it to talk to this man?

Greer knew that he had often avoided answering questions by turning the conversation and questions back on the questioner, so he decided to try that approach.

"Your pardon, sir, but just what is it you did to Kasa?" Greer asked. He had decided to drop the stuttering, for it was clear that Ealdred had seen through that ruse.

"I warmed up his shoulder joint and got the muscles to relax enough to slip the leg bone back into its socket. I have a bit of the healing touch and so hopefully everything is back where it belongs. If you are careful with him, he should be fine. Now then, how long have you lived in Bortfjell?"

It was with great effort that Greer kept his facial expression neutral. "Why would you think that, sir?"

"Because I have not always lived here and have spent much of my life studying languages. Used to be able to pinpoint where folks were from just from the way they talked. I would guess you have spent most of your life in or around Høyhauger, but there is just a touch of southern Sommerhjem in there also."

That cannot be right, thought Greer. Maybe he had picked up some of Journeyman Evan's speech patterns, but that idea was quickly extinguished when Ealdred pinpointed where Journeyman Evan was from, and it was not southern Sommerhjem.

"What I find even more intriguing is how someone from Bortfjell came to be Neebing blessed."

Chapter Twenty-One

Greer looked to Journeyman Evan for an explanation, but he just shrugged his shoulders, indicating he had no more idea as to what Ealdred was talking about than Greer did.

"So, lad, I think you need to tell me the true story as to why you are here."

Greer remained silent, quickly assessing his options. There were doors leading off the main room of the cottage they were presently in, but he did not know where they led and if the doors led to another way out of the cottage. The front door was now blocked by the two younger hunting cats. Vadoma had gotten up and was now lying down next to Kasa. The vines had moved across the windows, resembling bars. The sudden loss of light in the room due to clouds covering the sun added to Greer's feeling of being trapped. With no way out and an affirmative nod from Journeyman Evan, Greer gave a brief summary of how he had ended up in Sommerhjem. He left out the part about the pouch he carried around his neck, which he was more than aware of, since it had begun to grow very warm.

"So, you think all those folks looking for you are after you because of a lineage book, do you?" Ealdred questioned.

"That must be it, sir," Greer stated, trying to put as much sincerity into his voice as possible.

Ealdred just looked at him, and the silence in the cottage grew and grew while the pouch around Greer's neck became warmer and warmer. The pouch then began to become increasingly hot to the point of moving from uncomfortable to almost unbearable. Ealdred continued to stare at Greer, and Greer remained silent. Journeyman Evan watched them both, knowing something important was happening, but not really understanding the standoff between the two. How long the silence would have gone on was anyone's guess, if Vadoma had not broken the frozen scene by getting up and walking up to Greer. She sat in front of him and raised her paw. Journeyman Evan shifted to stand up, concerned about his friend, but the look Vadoma gave him caused him to abruptly settle back into his chair. Turning her attention back to Greer, Vadoma lifted her paw up to Greer's chest and placed it directly on the pouch. Immediately the heat that Greer had been feeling cooled, and comforting warmth spread through him. Along with the comforting warmth came a feeling of calmness and peace. With a slight nod of her head, Vadoma stepped back and lay down at Greer's feet. Kasa came over and snuggled up next to the big hunting cat.

"Greer?" Journeyman Evan said, looking at him.

"Well, now, that's a good start. Am I to presume that I am addressing a young man named Greer and not a lad called Kort?"

Seeing as there seemed little need to dissemble about his name, Greer acknowledged it.

"Got a last name to go with the first?"

"Not that I know of," Greer answered.

"Obviously there is more going on here than what you have said so far. Care to elaborate? I can be a very good listener."

When Greer continued to hesitate, Vadoma sat up and placed a huge paw on Greer's leg. Again Greer felt the warmth and reassurance flow from the big hunting cat to him. Taking that as a sign, and also recognizing that not talking was going to get him nowhere, Greer cleared his throat and described what had really happened in Milkin's Stable what seemed now a lifetime ago.

"I really can't tell you why I didn't just go back to the stable and return the pouch to the stable owner. Something, some feeling I had, just screamed at me that if I had gone back to the stable owner, my life was not going to be worth much, even if I returned the pouch. I could not stick around to return it to the gentleman it belonged to. I'm sorry, Journeyman Evan, that I didn't say anything sooner, but something always seemed to hold me back from mentioning the pouch to anyone."

"As well it should, if what you carry is what I suspect," commented Ealdred. "If you would, lad, let's see what it is you carry that has attracted the protection of not one but three hunting cats."

Greer did not know what to do. The dimly lit room with the vine bars on the windows and door made him feel trapped, as did Ealdred's words. On the other hand, the hunting cat Vadoma seemed to be reassuring him he was safe. Seeing his hesitation, Ealdred made a slight gesture with his head, and several things happened at once. The vines withdrew from the windows and door. The two younger hunting cats came and curled up next to the hearth, resting their heads on their paws as if they had not a care in the world and were just settling down for a nap. The sun chose that moment to come out from behind the clouds, but Greer did not think Ealdred was responsible for that.

"I'm sorry, lad. My theatrics with the vines most probably have been a little intimidating and less than hospitable. These are unsettled times we live in, and I was being cautious. What you need to understand is that Vadoma would tear my throat out if I meant you even the slightest bit of harm. She brought you to me because she thinks I might be of some help."

Reflecting back over the last few days, Greer could see that the hunting cat's actions could be taken two different ways. First would be the assumption that he and Journeyman Evan had taken, that the hunting cats were in a sense herding them towards Ealdred for some nefarious purpose. The actions taken by both the hunting cats and the tall man since they had arrived had added to the growing sense of menace and constraint. Now Ealdred was suggesting that Vadoma and her two companions had brought Journeyman Evan and him here to gain some assistance from Ealdred. Greer weighed what Ealdred said carefully before he spoke.

"I only glanced at what is in the pouch briefly before I left Bortfjell. Since then I have not a lot of opportunity to look at it closely. I have been rather busy with just trying to survive and have always been surrounded by folks. What I do know is that, in the brief glimpse I got of what the stable owner flung my way, that the object was round and glinted of gold. It looked like a misshapen gold ring with deep scratches. Something hurt the stable owner's hand when he took it out of the pouch, but when I picked it up, it just felt warm to me."

When Greer finished talking, he looked at Journeyman Evan and saw a shocked look on Journeyman Evan's face.

"What?" Greer asked, directing his question to Journeyman Evan.

"Oh my!"

"'Oh my' is not a very helpful answer," Greer quipped, beginning to feel irritated. As he had so often in the past few days, he felt adrift in this strange place. He knew too little to feel safe. Here he was, running from who knows whom, for who knows what reason or reasons, and instead of things becoming easier or clearer, everything just became more muddled. What he needed were answers, and he needed them now. Reaching into his shirt he pulled the pouch out and pulled the cord over his head. Carefully opening the pouch, he tipped the gold ring into his hand.

When Evan reached out to touch the ring, Ealdred admonished, "Careful, lad. Best not to touch an object such as that unless you are meant to." Journeyman Evan quickly withdrew his hand but did lean in to get a closer look, as did Ealdred.

"Ever seen the like, either of you?" Eldred questioned.

Greer shook his head no, but Journeyman Evan said, "I have. I've seen two enough like it as to be made by the same hand."

"Well, what is it, and why is it important?" Greer asked, for he had grown impatient.

"It would appear what you picked up off the Milkin's Stable floor is only one of the seven most sought after items in Sommerhjem," Journeyman Evan replied, shaking his head in wonder.

"But, what is it?"

"It is part of the oppgave ringe," Ealdred said, taking pity on Greer. Between the two of them, they explained just what it was Greer held, and why it was important. "I'd put it back in its pouch if I were you, lad. Best not have it out of its protective covering. Your having that ring explains much, but not all."

"It certainly explains why so many have made such an effort to find you," said Journeyman Evan, stating the obvious.

"It also explains the hunting cats," said Ealdred.

"I understand why those in Høyhauger were after me, but why the hunting cats?"

"I am not sure I can explain fully, because what I will tell you is only speculation on my part. You may not know that Sommerhjem, Bortfjell, and the country to the south of us are very old, old lands that we are just recently come to. When our folk arrived here, Sommerhjem was empty and had been so for a very long time, but there are ancient places here that indicate that we are not the first to occupy this land. Very little is known about those who came before us, or why they left. Records indicate some of the animals we know these days were here before we came. Hunting cats, griff falcons, and a few others are scarce now and do not usually spend much time with folks. They have always seemed more intelligent than most give them credit for. They seem more attuned to the land.

Sometimes I think there are things at work here that we folk neither know about nor understand. Even more mysterious is whether we brought some of that mystery with us or discovered it here when we first arrived. So much knowledge is lost from one generation to the next, but that is not what concerns us at this moment. You, Greer, need to get to the capital as quickly and as safely as possible, for what you carry around your neck is vital to Sommerhjem. Know there is nothing about this situation that is going to be easy or without danger. You are not even of Sommerhjem and its folk, yet this land needs you to carry the contents of that pouch south. I suspect that for some reason, no one else will do. You can choose to believe this or not, but I think you were meant to be in that stable at that hour so you would end up with the pouch."

Greer could only look at him as if Ealdred had lost his mind. "No, no, that doesn't make sense. I was in the stable at that moment in time because I let my curiosity override my good sense. I picked up the pouch in a moment of sheer recklessness and panic."

"Believe what you will, but know that however, and for whatever reason, you came into possession of the pouch and its contents, and you are meant to follow this adventure, quest, whatever you want to call it, to the end."

"Why can't I just give the ring to you, or to Journeyman Evan, or to the next passing rabbit, and be done with it?" Greer asked.

"Maybe I can answer that," said Journeyman Evan quietly. "After the commotion at the Well of Speaking this summer, I had a chance to talk with the royal historian, who is probably the folk most knowledgeable about the oppgave ringe. He seemed to think that there were only certain folks who could actually handle the rings before the challenge, and others did so at their peril. The mistake the stable owner made was to take the ring out of its pouch. Had he left it in the pouch, he might have gotten away with the theft."

"So, I could just give it to a trusted someone, and they could take it to the capital?" Greer asked.

"That might be possible, but it is the second part of the charge of having a part of the oppgave ringe that might not work for you. See, getting it to the capital is just the first part of the task," answered Journeyman Evan.

"And the second part?"

"The piece you carry must be placed in the box that is set into a low wall in the Well of Speaking to join the others. It sounds like you are the one to do that, for you can handle the ring. Some passing rabbit, even if it were intelligent and lucky enough to make it to the capital, would not be able to do that."

Lucky rabbit, Greer thought to himself. Oh why, oh why, did I not simply leave the stable for a few hours? If I had, none of this strangeness would have happen. "So, now what?"

The answer to that question was not immediately forthcoming, for a great ruckus created by the call of many birds interrupted the conversation inside Ealdred's cottage. Suddenly the vines shifted completely, blocking the windows and doors, and the sounds of branches moving and scraping on the roof filled the inside the cottage. The hunting cats swiftly flanked Greer and faced the door.

"Quiet, someone's coming."

CHAPTER TWENTY-TWO

"Hallo, Ealdred, you home? I have that glass you ordered for the green houses and can help you install it."

"I suspect that is Master Opeline from your guild, Journeyman Evan. I have been expecting her. Wouldn't that be a bit of irony, or maybe, a bit of good luck? I want to make sure she is by herself, so wait here," Ealdred cautioned both Journeyman Evan and Greer. Ealdred left by the front door through a narrow opening of parted vines.

"Do you know her?" whispered Greer.

"I have met her only once, for she doesn't reside at the guildhall in the capital, but rather lives and works at the glassworks here in the north. She is what is known as a practical glassmaker. She makes everyday glass rather than artistic glass and has a reputation as a hard worker and skilled installer."

In a few minutes, Ealdred returned, followed by a slender woman who would be distinctive wherever she went, for like the glass she made, her skin was translucent in appearance and her hair was the color of frosted glass. When she spotted Journeyman Evan and Greer, she smiled.

"Looks like this installation job just got easier. Journeyman Evan, isn't it?" she said, nodding at Journeyman Evan. "I don't think I recognize your apprentice, but then I don't get to the capital all that often."

"What is it you are set to do here?" Journeyman Evan asked quickly, to try to give himself some time to think.

If Master Opeline commandeered both of them to help her with some project involving glass, she would surely catch on quite quickly that Greer had absolutely no experience handling glass. That would give him away to her more quickly than anything else. Even the explanation that he was new and was apprenticed to the master of the horse would be no excuse. All who work with the guild are taught from the start how to handle glass no matter what their assigned duties. He did not know the master well enough to know if he could trust her with Greer's secret, which he himself was just coming to grips with.

Sensing Journeyman Evan's dilemma, Ealdred intervened. "I have several small greenhouses set into the hillside to take advantage of the hot springs that supply my bathhouse with warm water. The greenhouses are small, and I have diverted some of the hot water from the springs through the greenhouses, creating a steamy warm interior. I can grow a kitchen garden year 'round in them. Just think of fresh beans and lettuce even in the cold months. Master Opeline created some frosted glass for the roof panes and some nice clear glass for the sides. Unfortunately, several of the side panes were broken because of birds flying into them, and an errant tree branch cracked a roof pane. Those all need to be replaced. Have you come up with a solution to the birds, so they don't continue to fly into the clear side panes?"

Distracted by Ealdred's question, Master Opeline began to describe how she had brought glass panes with the shadow of a hawk embedded in the glass and thought it would give smaller birds pause before they headed towards the greenhouse panes.

"I would like to take credit for the creation of the bird shadow glass pane technique, but alas, I need to give credit where credit is due. Master Clarisse figured out the solution to the problem."

"You know Master Clarisse?" Journeyman Evan asked.

"Yes, we go way back. Grew up together in fact. Learned to read and write under the same teacher. She is actually the one who encouraged me to apprentice with the Glassmakers Guild." Looking straight at Journeyman Evan she said, "We of the Høyttaier clan tend to help each other. And warn one another of rascals we might want to be wary of," Master Opeline said, and there was a slight trace of humor in her voice.

Master Opeline mentioning the Høyttaier clan took Journeyman Evan aback, and he had to pause a moment to think his response through. The Høyttaiers were important because they carried the knowledge of how to read the old language, and Master Clarisse had been able to read the Book of Rules governing the Gylden Sirklene challenge. The Book of Rules was written in the old language, and if no one had been able to read it at the Well of Speaking when the first two rings of the oppgave ringe had been placed, the Regent might not have been forced to step down. Regent Klingflug, during his reign, had tried to systematically dispose of members of the Høyttaier clan.

So far as Evan had heard, no one other than Master Clarisse had stepped up and declared themselves to be a member of the Høyttaier clan since that summer day at the Well of Speaking. Why was Master Opeline telling him she is a Høyttaier? Had Ealdred said something to Master Opeline when he was outside, but then, what would he have said?

Once again, Ealdred anticipated Journeyman Evan's confusion and questions. "I bet you are wondering how I can get the very best practical glassmaker, and a master glassmaker to boot, to come all the way up here not only bring to the glass, but also to install it. Helps when she's your sister."

"Oh my," Journeyman Evan said, and abruptly sat down.

Greer thought to himself that Journeyman Evan seemed to have a very limited vocabulary lately. Journeyman Evan's "oh mys" had not boded well so far. Life, though hard, had seemed much less complicated when he lived in Høyhauger. He had never paid much attention to who ruled, or if the ruler was a good one or not. He really did not know, nor had he cared, how rulers came into power. Finding a safe place to spend the night, or scrounging for his next meal, had been what he had focused on. Now he found himself in a new land where he held something of great importance to a great many folks that could help determine who would rule Sommerhjem.

"It now seems that we each have reasons we need to trust each other," Ealdred suggested. "We of the Høyttaier clan rarely let others outside of the clan know of us, and you two hold a secret even greater than we do. Ah, Greer, you are looking puzzled, and I can't say I blame you. Let me try to explain."

All four settled in and Ealdred spoke about the history of Sommerhjem. Greer felt that if his days continued like they had over the last few weeks, he might just know more than most about Sommerhjem's past. When Ealdred was done, he then filled his sister in on what had transpired earlier, so that now she, too, was aware of what Greer carried.

"Once you leave here, your journey will become more dangerous, for I can't imagine that those loyal to the Regent aren't aware of you by now. We need to misdirect them somehow. Tell me everything that has happened so far, since you left Høyhauger," requested Master Opeline.

Though Greer was not sure he wanted to repeat again what had happened to him over the last several weeks, it seemed that since Master

Opeline knew the most important secret, telling her the rest was not a big deal. When he was done, she had a thoughtful look on her face.

"It would seem to me that if word got out at O'Gara's farm that Greer was traveling with you disguised as your apprentice, and Greer's horse was marked, then those folks who might be trying to find you need to be thrown off track once again. I would suspect that there are those loyal to the Regent looking for either you two or that horse. Hum-m-m," Master Opeline remarked, and then looked at Journeyman Evan. "You have what, two riding horses and a pack horse?"

"Yes'm."

"You have experience driving a team of horses, I am sure."

"Yes'm."

"I have an idea. Why don't we switch means of travel? I will take your horse and Greer's, plus put my gear on your pack horse, and you will take my horse and wagon. That way, those who are following you might end up following me. There is no doubt that I don't resemble either of you two, so that should confuse those who are seeking you out."

"That's too dangerous," Ealdred said, with a great deal of concern in his voice.

"That's where you come in. You can ride Greer's horse and between the two of us, I don't think anyone will cause us too much trouble. Besides, you need to get out of these hills every once in a while and stretch your legs."

"Humph, stretch my legs indeed. You just want me to come to your northern guildhall and work with the plants in your greenhouse. I suppose you have killed off anything remotely green by now."

"Well, there is that, and . . . ."

"Excuse me," Journeyman Evan broke in. "Is your wagon empty then?"

"Ah, smart lad. Good question, and no, the wagon is not empty. I have several crates of bird shadow panes that I was going to drop off at the guildhall in Tverdal. I imagine someone from there could return the wagon to my guildhall. You could just tell them that I got held up and asked you to do a favor for me. Don't imagine you will have much trouble getting transportation out of Tverdal."

"No, I am sure I can wrangle something for us, but there is the matter of Greer's horse. Farmer O'Gara was going to put him out to pasture when he gave him to us to use . . . ."

"No matter, lad, I'll bring him back here, and he can keep the grass down in that pasture he is in now. Of course, that will be after I have his shoes changed."

"So, now that that's settled, we had best get to work. Journeyman, I think you had best instruct your apprentice how to handle glass. Always a useful skill," Master Opeline remarked.

The four worked until it was too dark to see that day, and then worked through the morning of the next day, before all of the panes of glass were installed. They spent the afternoon airing out the contents of their packs, repacking, and getting ready to depart early the next morning. The plan was that Greer and Journeyman Evan would leave first and follow the lane out on which Master Opeline had driven in. Master Opeline and Ealdred would take a back way out following a deer trail, and sweep their back trail for a while, before they gained a more traveled way. Hopefully, that would keep those who were looking for Greer and Journeyman Evan based on the horse's shoe print from finding where the horse had been and would not lead the searchers back to Ealdred's home.

While Greer thought that changing from two lads riding horses followed by a pack horse to two lads driving a wagon might confuse some, there was still the issue that they were two lads traveling with two border dogs. He was surprised the next morning when Kasa was followed into the meadow by a strange black dog, and it took him a moment to realize that the black dog was Louve. With the full black coloring, she looked a lot less like a border dog. Well, now we have three out of the four of us looking different, but is that going to really make any difference? Journeyman Evan was still Journeyman Evan, and if others knew he had left in Journeyman Evan's company as his apprentice, once they arrived in Tverdal, would not the word get out? Greer guessed he would just have to take one day at a time.

There was one more thing Greer felt he should do before he left, so he went in search of Vadoma. He was not really sure if the large hunting cat would even understand, but he felt he owed her thanks for helping and leading them here. He found her sitting on the porch. He stepped towards Vadoma carefully, not knowing what else to do, and squatted down until he was at eye level with her. Glancing around to see if anyone else was within ear shot and listening to hear if anyone was in the cottage, Greer cleared his voice before he spoke. "Ah, I wanted to thank you for all you did." Greer felt more than a little embarrassed. Looking down, he would have missed Vadoma's response if she had not raised her paw and placed it gently on his knee. He looked up in time to see her nod her head once. Soon after his private meeting with Vadoma on the porch, both parties were ready to leave.

Ealdred gave last minute instructions. "If you follow the lane west for several hours, you will come to a place where the lane forks. Take the fork to the left, and the lane will wander southwest. There is a good camping spot by an old quarry. Assuming you do not run into trouble, you should reach the old quarry in time for the evening meal. If you continue on the same lane the next day, you should reach the royal road midday."

After farewells were said, Greer and Journeyman Evan started off. Greer had had little occasion to ride in a wagon, and he was not finding his first experience very comfortable. Because of his height, he found his feet neither touched the floor nor could he brace them against the front of the wagon. The lane was not a smooth one, and after an hour of bouncing around, he wondered if he would even survive the wagon ride. Journeyman Evan took pity on him and stopped the wagon long enough for Greer to crawl inside and curl up on some packs with both the dogs joining him. As he drifted into an uneasy sleep, he wondered what was going to happen to him next.

Chapter Twenty-Three

As the sun grew higher in the sky, the air inside the wagon became uncomfortably hot, so Greer decided that bouncing around was going to be better than lying there roasting. He was sure, from the heavy panting coming from both border dogs that they needed to get out from under the canvas covering also. Banging on the side of the wagon to signal Journeyman Evan to stop, Greer was relieved that the wagon slowed almost immediately and then stopped. Both Greer and Journeyman Evan climbed down out of the wagon, as did the two border dogs. After stretching their legs, Journeyman Evan pulled a small empty crate out of the wagon and wedged it between the bench seat of the wagon and the front of the wagon.

"This might help," Journeyman Evan said, pointing to the crate, and indeed it did.

When Greer climbed up and sat next to Journeyman Evan, his feet rested comfortably on the crate. If the wagon swayed or bounced, he now had some leverage to keep himself upright. Kasa settled on the seat between Journeyman Evan and Greer, and Louve walked alongside the wagon, having become tired of riding. The woods they had been traveling through had thinned, and the hills had become more rolling, with scattered grassy areas beginning to appear. The rest of the day was uneventful, the quarry landmark was easy to find, and they set up camp there for the night. It surprised both Greer and Journeyman Evan when Vadoma and the two younger hunting cats showed up just as the last rays of sunlight slipped behind the far hills.

The way to Journeyman Evan's family farm had not been a difficult one, and Lord Avital continued to find Seeker Zita a knowledgeable and skilled traveling companion. He found with each passing day, however, his longing for home and hearth grew, and his hope for finding his long lost son diminished. He had had high hopes when they had reached Trelandsby, only to find they had missed the lad called Greer. When they had reached Farmer Yorick O'Gara's farm, in addition to missing Greer, they learned that his trail had been lost due to a prairie fire. They also learned someone in Farmer O'Gara's employ had marked Greer's horse and probably passed on his new description. Lord Avital's last hope had been to find that Greer and the lad Journeyman Evan had safely arrived at Journeyman Evan's family farm, but they had had no word from their son. After hearing the news that Greer was not at Journeyman Evan's family farm, and having no other leads to follow, other than the faint hope that Greer would somehow make it to the capital, Lord Avital reluctantly decided it was time to head home. He could go on to the capital and wait, but Seeker Zita had told him she was traveling that way and would get a message to the Glassmakers Guild, to a Master Rollag or a Master Clarisse, who would both want to know what had happened to Journeyman Evan. In addition, she would pass on the information about Greer's suspected connection with Lord Avital.

"I am so torn, but I really think I should go home. Going to the capital and not finding the lad called Greer there is more than I think I can handle," said Lord Avital wearily. "I am comforted to know that you will be heading there, know folks who will follow up on what has happened to Journeyman Evan, and will be able to counsel Greer concerning his possible connection to me. I hope both the lads are well and safe. If something should happen to the lad I hope is my son, I will feel responsible."

"Now that's just disappointment talking, and you are not making sense. The lad Greer is a survivor. That he survived the streets of Høyhauger for ten years suggests he is intelligent, clever, and resilient. He is also old enough to make choices, and so far it seems like he has made some fairly good, or lucky, ones. From how both the foresters and Farmer Yorick O'Gara have described him, he is not a talker, but he is always listening and alert. Those two traits will take him far. As soon as anyone knows anything, a message will be sent to you. You are right to go home, for this journey wears on you. Waiting around the capital hoping that, at the very least, Journeyman Evan will show up so you can find out what happened to Greer will not serve any purpose other than adding to the heavy burden you have placed upon yourself. If you are going to worry day in and day out as to the fate of both the lads, you might as well do it at home where you are comfortable, busy, and surrounded by family and friends."

The two traveled all morning together, but when they reached the fork in the road that would take Lord Avital home and Seeker Zita towards the capital, they parted ways.

⤜⟀⟐⟀⤛

"I know that Master Opeline said we should head to Tverdal, but I'm very well known there, and I think that could create some problems," suggested Journeyman Evan. "I'm thinking we should bypass Tverdal and stop at a farm I know. I'm thinking that for us to get to the capital as quickly as we can, and with as little fuss and danger, we might as well do it in style."

"What do you have in mind?"

"I think we should stop at the Deaver's farm. Besides being incredible cheese makers, they are very loyal to the Crown and could help with confusing our back trail, if there is anyone who might have even a remote idea of where we are. Once we get to their farm, I'm hoping they will help us get to Glendalen undetected, where I have friends in high places."

"So you think there might still be folks on our trail after all this?"

"There are eyes and ears everywhere. I'm sure that the word is out to look for two lads, who are probably connected to the Glassmakers Guild, and at least one dog. As we get closer to the capital, there are more towns, villages and farms. We will come in contact with more folks on the road and wherever we choose to stop for the nights. I think we had best change our look once again, or at least our means of transportation."

As they continued to travel that day, Greer took the time to reflect on what had happened over the last few weeks. Every once in a while, a traveling storyteller would come to Høyhauger and entertain in the town square during the day. The tales were often fanciful and stretched one's imagination, but what would folks think if a storyteller told what had happened to Greer as a tale? No one would believe it could actually be a true story. The poor storyteller would probably be pelted with rotten vegetables for telling such an outrageous tale.

In spite of the improbable adventure Greer had been on, if he measured where he was now compared to where he had been, even with the trip down the river and the very real danger they were in, he realized he was inexplicably happy. If anyone were to ask him why, he was not sure he would be able to tell them. He knew that knowing there would be a next meal because they had packed enough supplies to last them for several weeks was part of it. He knew that having a clean sleeping roll which would keep him warm on cool nights was part of it, but that certainly was not all. Having Kasa certainly contributed to his good feelings too. In reflecting on this unexpected feeling, Greer realized that Journeyman Evan was a major contributor to how he felt. So, this is what having a friend feels like, he thought. Over the last few days he had grown to trust someone, something he had never done before.

Each night when they stopped and made camp, Vadoma and the two younger hunting cats would join them, often bring a contribution for dinner. By morning, the hunting cats would be gone, and even though Journeyman Evan and Greer tried to spot them during the day, they rarely did. Journeyman Evan produced a map one evening and showed it to Greer. He told Greer the royal mapmaker had made it for Master Cynfarch and several others, knowing they would be traveling to lesser traveled areas of the country, and had requested they note any changes or new paths.

"See, here is where we are now," Journeyman Evan said, pointing to a spot on the map. "If we keep following this road, we will meet up with the central royal road, and if we follow it, we will come to Tverdal. What I am suggesting is that we follow this lane here and bypass Tverdal. If we travel, then, down this lane, it will take us to the Deaver's farm. We are actually going to go past the farm and then double back on a back lane. The way I figure it, we can pull off the lane close to the farm, and I'll walk in to talk to Farmer Deaver and make arrangements. I don't want to arrive at the farm directly in case there are others than the family there. The fewer folk who know we are in the area the better."

It was just dusk when Journeyman Evan pulled the wagon over into a small clearing near the Deaver's farm. All of them were more than ready to step down and stretch their legs. They had decided Journeyman Evan would wait until full dark before he headed out. They had just sat down to eat a cold meal when Greer remarked that it felt strange that Vadoma and company had not shown up yet.

"Do you think it's getting too close to a town for the hunting cats?" Greer asked.

"I don't know. I have been surprised they have traveled this far with us as it is."

Just as Journeyman Evan finished speaking, they heard the sound of soft footfalls coming down the lane. Greer looked up to see a striking woman with long dark hair holding a long thin stick and approaching them flanked by the two young hunting cats. She was preceded into the clearing by Vadoma.

"I am afraid the hunting cats being late is my fault. I am not as familiar with this lane as I am with others around the farm. It is good to hear you again, Journeyman Evan," said Siri. "These hunting cats with you?"

"More like we are with them," quipped Journeyman Evan.

"Why didn't you come all the way into the farmstead?"

"It's a long story, but we wanted to make sure there is only family at the farm."

"Well then, let us start with first things first. Who are your friends?"

"I'm sorry. Let me get you a seat, and I'll do the introductions, although I can see that Kasa and Louve are not going to wait on formality." The border dogs had already joined the hunting cats.

As Journeyman Evan turned to grab an empty wooden box out of the wagon, he noticed Greer had anticipated the need. When Greer set the box next to Siri, she reached out and lightly touched his shoulder. When he would have moved away, she told him to wait, and there was such command in her voice that he did not even think of moving away.

"Place your hands in mine, please," Siri asked, and without even stopping to think or question, Greer did so. Siri held them briefly, and then let them go.

"So, Journeyman Evan, I think introductions are in order, but we had best keep our voices very low, even though the hunting cats will give us fair warning if anyone comes too close."

After Journeyman Evan made introductions, all three sat down, and Journeyman Evan explained much of what had happened over the last several days and on their journey. Siri listened intently without interruption. While he was talking, Greer's thoughts were on the odd sensation he had felt when Siri had held both of his hands. They had certainly been warm, and Greer was sure he had felt a warm tingling feeling passing between their hands, but maybe that was just his imagination at work. Something had passed between them, however, of that he was sure.

When Journeyman Evan wound down the telling of their adventures, Siri told him that she felt he had made a wise decision to avoid Tverdal. "You are right in presuming the fewer who know you are in the area the better. So, if I get the gist of what you are thinking of doing now, you need to find alternative transportation into Glendalen, and you need the horses and wagon you are now currently traveling in to get to Tverdal, but not tomorrow, or even the next few days. Have I got that correct?"

"Yes," answered Journeyman Evan.

"You are in luck, for tomorrow we have a number of deliveries of cheese to several shops and inns in Glendalen. I have a few errands I need to run, and so, we had intended to take the larger wagon. I suspect we can slip you into town without anyone noticing. I am sure Farmer Deaver would be happy to hold onto your wagon for several days before he has one of his children drive it into Tverdal. They will need a plausible excuse as to why they have a wagon and horses belonging to the guild."

Greer, who had been silent during the exchange up to this point, spoke up. "It is often better to stick close to the truth than to tell and then try to remember a lie. Why not just tell them that one of you found the wagon and horses in a small side glen off the back lane bordering the Deaver's farm? You could say that whoever had driven it there appeared to have abandoned it."

"It will cause some worry for a while," said Journeyman Evan thoughtfully, "but once we get to the capital, we can send messages to my folks and to Master Opeline."

Siri was silent for quite some time before she spoke up. "A credible idea. Now then, grab your personal gear and let us abandon your horse and wagon. I must say, Journeyman Evan, you arrive with the most interesting traveling companions. What is it with you and the Neebing blessed?"

CHAPTER TWENTY-FOUR

The early morning hours found Greer and Journeyman Evan, their gear, and the two border dogs hunkered down behind two crates in the Deaver's cheese delivery wagon, heading for Glendalen, and what Journeyman Evan hoped was safety. They had met the night before with Farmer Deaver and his wife, two of his sons, and Siri to solidify the plans for the next day. One of Farmer Deaver's sons was going to pick up the abandoned wagon and horses and tuck them away on the farm. When several days had passed, he would "discover" them and drive the wagon into Tverdal to the Glassmakers Guildhall. There he would talk to Master Meriter and fill him in on the truth of why a Glassmakers Guild's wagon had been left at their farm. Journeyman Evan had assured them that Master Meriter was very trustworthy and would know what to do with the wagon.

Journeyman Evan and another of Farmer Deaver's sons, Cal, spent some time pouring over a map of Glendalen. Journeyman Evan needed to locate on the map just where he had once exited the underground tunnels that would, he hoped, lead him into Glendalen Keep unobserved. He knew they had exited the town sewer system somewhere between the second and third town walls, had walked several blocks down a lane, and then turned into an alley to take refuge in a small home. As he talked about the area, Journeyman Evan remembered that just after they had exited the sewer, he had noticed a particularly funny-looking gargoyle perched on the wall opposite the place they had come out. He remembered it because once his eyes had adjusted to the light in the lane, he had been startled by the gargoyle, thinking it was someone perched on the wall spying on them. He could laugh at himself now, but he had to admit his nerves had been stretched a bit taunt then. Journeyman Evan explained to Cal that once he located the gargoyle, he would be able to find the small house he needed to find. He did not tell Cal about the tunnel entrance, for concerning that, he had been sworn to secrecy.

"Oh, aye, I know the one. Tip my hat to him as I pass on my delivery rounds. He's such a silly looking fellow that . . . ." Farmer Deaver's son's face reddened, and he cleared his throat. "Well, you know . . . now then, that is here on the map, and folk are used to me going that way. The delivery wagon has side panels that open so we can get at items in the middle and towards the back. I could pull up opposite the gargoyle and get down to check a horse's hoof. I'll let you know we are at the right place by knocking twice on the side of the wagon. When the way is clear, I'll rap four times quickly, and you all can disembark. You can be ambling down the lane before I move on, with no one the wiser."

After all the planning was done, Mistress Deaver found them some hand-me-down clothes they could wear and sent them off to the bathhouse to get cleaned up. Following a hot, relaxing soak, they settled down to catch a few hours of sleep.

Now that the wagon had stopped its jolting on the rutted farm lane, the ride smoothed out, and Greer settled in to reflect on what had happened in the predawn light. Kasa had been so restless that Greer had taken him outside, thinking he needed to relieve himself. As soon as they had stepped outside, Kasa had settled at his feet. Out of the deep shadows, Vadoma and the two smaller hunting cats had emerged. Vadoma had walked straight up to Greer, had touched noses with Kasa, and then placed a paw on Greer's chest, sending a warmth and calm throughout his body. That touch had lasted only briefly, and then Vadoma had stepped back, nodded her head, turned, and slipped back into the shadows with her two companions. Greer had felt then, as he did now, that Vadoma had been saying farewell. He hoped she had heard him when he had whispered his thanks.

Even though he had lived in a town all of his life, Greer found himself strangely reluctant to enter one again. He did not know if it was just the idea of entering a town where he did not know all of the ins and outs or whether he had grown to appreciate the space and freedom of the countryside he had been traveling through. It also occurred to him that he was drawing closer and closer to the capital with each passing day. Once there, he was unsure what was to happen to him after he did whatever it was he was supposed to do with the piece of the oppgave ringe he was carrying. Life was carrying him along willy-nilly much as the Raskalt had. He just had to hope he survived the ride.

All too soon Greer could hear the hollow sound of wagon's wheels passing over a bridge, and then the ride took on a new rhythm of the wagon's wheels on cobblestones. The wagon stopped and started as Cal made his deliveries. Greer was glad they were traveling in the cool of the morning, for the smell of cheese was already heady. He could not imagine what it would be like to be inside the wagon once the sun began to beat down on the roof.

The wagon stopped again and both the lads heard two distinct knocks on the side of the wagon. Both grabbed their packs and got ready to move. Moments later they heard four sharp raps, and Journeyman Evan, being closest to the side door, cautiously opened it. Seeing the way was clear, he quickly jumped down, turned, and pulled his pack out. Then he reached in, holding out his arms to take Kasa. Louve jumped down and stood by Journeyman Evan on alert. Greer jumped down, grabbed his pack, and then closed and fastened the side door. Meanwhile, Journeyman Evan located the opening to the sewer, which was very cleverly hidden. Instead of slipping inside, he motioned Greer to follow him and walked away from Cal and the wagon. Once the wagon was out of sight, the two doubled back. Journeyman Evan, after checking to make sure no one was about, slipped into the opening. Greer followed him inside.

In a whisper, Journeyman Evan explained his actions. "I did not want to give away the location of the entrance to Cal, or anyone for that matter. I should not even be revealing it to you, but that cannot be helped. I hope Lord and Lady Hadrack will forgive me."

There was very little light seeping in from the outside, and Greer wondered how they would find their way. That question was quickly answered when Journeyman Evan reached up and unhooked a lantern that was hanging several feet beyond the entrance. Once lit, it provided enough light to show them the path that ran next to the wall and just a foot above the sluggish water that ran down the middle of the tunnel. Anticipating the narrow paths and sometimes difficult passages ahead, Greer had once again rigged a sling to carry Kasa, and the pup seemed to know that now was not the time to scamper about. Greer thought he would not be able to carry Kasa around for much longer, for the pup was growing and becoming heavier with each passing day.

Journeyman Evan fervently hoped he remembered what he had observed the first time he had traversed these tunnels. When he had been in Glendalen attending the summer fair, he and others had been asked by

Lord Hadrack to gather information after an important meeting held in the Keep. At that time he had noticed Captain Gwen, the head of Lord Hadrack's guard, who had led them through the tunnels, had often looked up and to her right when they came to a cross tunnel or branch. She did not make an obvious show of looking, but once Journeyman Evan had caught on, he had noted that there were very faint symbols etched into the stone, and he had tried to memorize the symbols as they went along.

Journeyman Evan walked at a steady pace, taking turn after turn as if he knew where he was going. At least they were going upward instead of down, he thought to himself. The only part of this plan that was a little iffy was what to do once they got to the actual Keep. He was not quite sure how to get out of the tunnels, but he would deal with that when he got that far.

Soon they were out of the sewer system and into the passageways that ran through the Keep. Enough light came from the cleverly disguised openings along the way to allow Journeyman Evan to douse the lantern.

From then on they moved in fits and starts, looking through spy holes to check where they might be. Journeyman Evan knew he was taking extra care to move quietly, but compared to Greer, he thought he must sound like a great herd of horses stampeding through a canyon. He could only admire how Greer was able to move so silently and thought this was a skill he would have to ask Greer to teach him. Greer, however, was getting weary from climbing uneven stairs, for he was still not quite comfortable in his new boots that evened out his gait. The strain of moving so cautiously was beginning to wear on him. He hoped they found a way out of the passageways soon, for Kasa seemed to be gaining weight by the minute and becoming restless. Finally, Journeyman Evan signaled for them to stop.

"Did you hear that?" Journeyman Evan whispered so softly that Greer almost did not catch what he said.

Greer gave him a negative shrug and tried to focus on what Journeyman Evan might have heard, but it was difficult to concentrate over the sound of his heart pounding and Kasa wiggling to be let down. Finally, Greer hunkered down, took Kasa out of the sling, and attached a leash onto the collar Cal had fashioned for him. Greer had not heard anything, but Kasa was straining at his leash, scrabbling for purchase on the well-worn stone steps. Greer quickly picked him up, quietly admonishing him to settle down, when a bright light suddenly appeared on the landing above them.

"I would stand very still and not attempt to run if I were you," stated a commanding voice from the bottom of the stairs. "Lord Hadrack is going to want to know who dares skulk around the hidden passageways of Glendalen Keep."

"The Lady Hadrack is most curious too as to why you could not just come in the front door, Journeyman Evan. It's alright," Lady Hadrack remarked from the top of the stairs to the guard standing at the bottom of the stairs. "I know this young rascal."

"Begging your Ladyship's pardon, but you can't be too careful these days, especially with Lord Hadrack being at the capital and all. Maybe it would be best if I call for more help," stated the guard Minka.

"It is in Sommerhjem's best interest that no one knows we are here, which is exactly why we did not ride up to your front gate and ask to be announced. I ask on behalf of my friend here that we have a private audience with you, Lady Hadrack. Your guard is one more folk than I want to know that we are here."

"M'lady, again, I must caution you . . . ."

"Thank you, Minka. I know you are only here to look after my safety and the wellbeing of the Keep, but I assure you, I know Journeyman Evan here. Also it does not look like his friend is any threat either, other than perhaps tumbling down the stairs being dragged by that small pup. Come, all five of you, follow me." With that said, Lady Hadrack turned swiftly, and the rest were hard-pressed to keep up with her.

After a few minutes they turned into what appeared to be a dead end to Greer. Lady Hadrack did something which Greer could not see, and suddenly the blank stone wall in front of them silently pivoted, providing a narrow opening which she slipped through. Kasa lunged after her, so Greer had little choice but to follow. He found himself inside a small cedar-lined wardrobe with shelves holding sweaters and other cold weather clothing.

"Is Beezle here?" Greer heard Journeyman Evan ask.

"No, he is back at his own estate right now. His mother needed his help. When word of your earlier adventures got back to her, I suspect she just needed to see that he was fine and in one piece. We expect we will see him back soon. Minka, please find Captain Gwen and return with her. You are to speak to no one, absolutely no one. Do you understand?"

"Yes, Lady Hadrack."

"Do not run. Walk casually through the halls until you find her. If she is busy, respectfully wait until you can speak to her privately. Once you have her attention, both of you are to return here without attracting any attention to yourselves. Do you understand?"

"Yes, Lady Hadrack."

"Good. I know I can trust you and trust that you will get the job done." With that, Minka turned and left the room.

"You are sure you can trust her?" Journeyman Evan asked.

"With our lives. There are only a handful who know how to navigate the tunnels and passageways of the Keep. It would not do to entrust that knowledge to just anyone. If we did, it would be like leaving the backdoor open to those whom might wish to harm us, even though we think we are safe since we have locked the front door."

"Was it just luck that Minka chanced upon us, or do you have guards patrolling the passageways? For that matter, how did you find us?"

"I would answer that question, but then I would not be able to let you leave this room," Lady Hadrack answered with a smile, but both the lads were aware that her answer was a serious one, despite the smile. "Now, Journeyman Evan, perhaps you could introduce me to your friends here."

"I beg your pardon. Where are my manners? Lady Hadrack, this is my friend Greer, the young pup is Kasa, and the other border dog is Louve."

"I am pleased to meet you, Greer," Lady Hadrack stated.

Greer felt panic rising up. He had no experience to draw on as to what to do in the presence of a noble. Did he bow? Journeyman Evan had not. And now Kasa had just stood on his hind legs and placed his dirty paws on the skirt of Lady Hadrack's fine gown. He gathered himself, ready for the blows that were sure to come for not controlling his dog.

"I, I, I'm so sorry," Greer stammered, stepping forward to grab Kasa. Before Greer could cross the small room to reach Kasa, Lady Hadrack scooped Kasa up and was holding him away from her, just as a knock came at the door.

"Check and see who that is, will you, Journeyman Evan?" Lady Hadrack requested.

Journeyman Evan opened the door a crack, and Greer stood frozen to the floor. What if Lady Hadrack was so offended by her gown being dirtied by Kasa that she ordered him killed? He did not know what he should do.

The door swung open, and Minka and a guard captain entered. Lady Hadrack addressed Minka. "Here take this pup, would you, and . . . ."

CHAPTER TWENTY-FIVE

"Your pardon, m'lady, but Kasa meant no harm," Greer managed to say, but his voice sounded abnormally high to his ears.

Seeing the look of panic on Greer's face, Lady Hadrack said, "No harm done, but I thought Minka, who is good with animals, might convince Kasa that he would be more comfortable if his paws were washed off. I take it Kasa is yours."

"Yes, m'lady," Greer managed to reply, and his heart that had somehow moved to his throat moved back down into his chest. "I'm sorry I didn't have better control of him. If you wish to punish someone for the dirt on your gown, I stand ready."

Lady Hadrack looked carefully at the lad who stood before her. Here was not a lad, as she had first thought, but a young man ready to take responsibility for the dirtying of her gown, even though anyone who had ever owned a pup knew that the unexpected often happened with them. It would seem Journeyman Evan picked his friends well, she thought.

"Pish posh, gowns can be cleaned, and pups will be pups. Now that that is settled, this is the captain of the Keep's guard, Captain Gwen. Captain, I am sure you remember Journeyman Evan, and this is his friend, Greer. They have come calling by the back way. We were just getting around to hearing why Journeyman Evan felt he needed not to be seen. Let us all take a seat."

Greer looked around at the sitting room they were in and worried about sitting on any of the furniture. While he knew his clothes were clean, and he was also reasonably so, this room was the most elegant of any he had ever been in. He thought he might just stand, but when he noticed all of the others had taken a seat, he reluctantly sat down.

"Now then, Journeyman Evan, if you would be so kind as to enlighten us," Lady Hadrack suggested.

"I'll be brief and to the point. My friend, Greer, came into possession of what I believe is one of the pieces of the oppgave ringe, which others wanted and tried to steal. Since Greer took possession of the ring, he has been sought by folks who probably don't want the ring so they can bring it to the capital and place it in the box in the Well of Speaking."

"You are sure it is one of the rings?" Lady Hadrack asked.

"It certainly fits the description that Nissa gave of the two she placed in the box, and what I observed. A gold band that looks as if it had been all bent out of shape, but it had been made that way. The rings I saw had deep scratches along the band, which did not look like a regular pattern, but looked like they had been carved into the band rather than put there by hard wear. The ring Greer carries looks the same. We need your help. We are certain that even though we have changed appearances and traveling companions several times, those seeking Greer probably know he is traveling with me. The closer we get to the capital, the more likely it is that I might run into someone I know, and word will get out that I am in the area. Word might get back to the Glassmakers Guild and to Master Cynfarch, who will then have folk trying to find me so he can take a piece out of my hide for not doing my assigned tasks."

Just as Journeyman Evan finished saying his piece, he noted that Greer had started briefly. It took him only a moment to realize that Greer had taken what he had said literally and thought that Master Cynfarch might actually beat him.

"Now, you all know that Master Cynfarch is the most mild-mannered of men and more importantly, since he made me a journeyman, he trusts my judgment, so he would never actually beat me. Probably just mildly inquire as to why it has taken me so long to get Greer to the capital, and if I had written my mother to let her know why I was delayed visiting home. Anyway, we need to travel from here to the capital in a way that no one takes too much notice of us, and which involves as few folk as possible. The more folks involved, the more chances there are for someone to give us away, intentionally or not."

"Why not just send the ring to the capital with someone we trust? I could get word to Beezle," Lady Hadrack suggested.

"I think that would be a great solution, but not one that would work. I think not just anyone can carry parts of the oppgave ringe. Greer, tell them what happened when the stable owner you used to work for touched the ring."

All eyes turned to Greer, who became even less comfortable than he had been. He realized it was time he took part in the discussion, since it was about him. "When the stable owner took the ring out of the golden pine spider silk pouch, I saw a flare of light, and then he threw the ring away from himself and clutched his hand as if it hurt greatly. When I picked it up, it just felt warm to the touch. Also, if truth be told, I am reluctant to let the ring leave my possession. It is as if I feel responsible for it, strange as that may sound." Now that he had put his feelings into words, Greer felt there was truth in what he had just stated.

"Well, we will need some type of plan to get you to the capital. Why don't we just dress them up as Glendalen guards, and they could travel with me to the capital? Who would look twice at us riding down the royal road with so many traveling back and forth?" Captain Gwen inquired.

"Do they all dress like you and Minka?" Greer asked.

"Yes, we are wearing the standard uniform," Captain Gwen answered. "Why?"

"Are those shiny boots you are wearing also standard, even when you are traveling?"

"Yes, and again, why?"

Journeyman Evan started to speak, but Greer gave him a look that said he would handle the question. "One of the reasons I'm recognizable, besides being short," he said with a rueful smile, "is that one of my legs is shorter than the other. The boots I am now wearing disguise that fact, but if you put me in a Glendalen guard uniform, these boots I'm wearing would be very different from what you are wearing, and I would stand out, if anyone looked at us with a discriminating eye."

"If only Shueller were here," said Journeyman Evan with a sigh.

"I was just thinking the same thing, but I have not seen or heard of him since summer," commented Lady Hadrack. When she noticed Greer sending a questioning look toward her and Journeyman Evan, she explained that Shueller was a rover shoemaker that they both knew.

Sommerhjem was certainly a different land from Bortfjell, Greer thought to himself. Here this noble chatted quite casually with a journeymen and was well acquainted with a rover shoemaker. Lady Hadrack seemed to treat her guards more like friends than servants and did not appear to be snobbish or stuck up at all. Kasa had certainly taken to her, for he was now sleeping peacefully on her lap, lying on his back with his tummy being rubbed gently. He wondered if all the nobles in Sommerhjem were like this. It took a moment for Greer to drag himself out of his thoughts and pay attention to what was being said around him.

"No matter how careful and how sworn to secrecy another shoemaker might be, word could leak out and that might give away that Journeyman Evan and Greer were in Glendalen," Captain Gwen remarked. "So, anything that requires a uniform like a guard, footman, or household servant is out. Having them travel as tradesmen only works if they know the trade, should someone ask for their assistance."

"We could always dress them as ladies-in-waiting," Lady Hadrack said to lighten the mood. Seeing the appalled look on both Journeyman Evan's and Greer's faces, she amended, "but those boots of Greer's would not go with any traveling dress I know of. I suggest that you lads take advantage of this suite and rest for a while, while the rest of us go about our daily routines. We will be back in several hours with food and hopefully some ideas of how to get you secretly out of Glendalen and to the capital. Do not answer the door without looking through the peephole. Do not open the door unless you see one of us, and we say the words 'drizzle cakes', either alone or in a sentence. Now lock up after we leave."

"Begging your pardon, Lady Hadrack, but with my known weakness for drizzle cakes, I would probably open the door without thinking," Journeyman Evan said. There was a distinct hint of mischief in his voice.

After Lady Hadrack and the two guards left, Journeyman Evan locked the door, crossed the room, and flung himself into a chair. Feeling uncomfortable with what he thought was Journeyman Evan's anger, Greer suggested that maybe it might be better if he tried to get to the capital on his own, for he did not want to create problems for anyone.

Journeyman Evan's response to Greer's suggestion was pithy to put it mildly, and he explained to Greer that he was just frustrated. Getting into Glendalen had been easy, but getting back out was proving to be harder than he had expected. Journeyman Evan suggested that they might as well get comfortable and catch some sleep, for who knew what to expect next. Several hours later, they heard a soft knock at the door. Journeyman Evan rose, looked through the peephole, and listened cautiously at the door for the password. Upon hearing "drizzle cakes", he opened the door a crack and then opened it wider. Lady Hadrack and Captain Gwen entered. Journeyman Evan hoped they had been more successful coming up with a plan to discreetly and safely leave Glendalen than either Greer or he had.

Once everyone was settled, Lady Hadrack began the discussion. "I have thought and rejected more plans over the last few hours than there are berries in those berry tarts you are so fond of, Journeyman Evan."

There was good humor in her voice, and Greer was surprised once again how comfortable Lady Hadrack was to be with.

"While sitting in an obligatory, but extremely boring, meeting, I had the thought that maybe we are going about getting you to the capital unnoticed the wrong way. Now, mind you, this solution might be anticlimactic considering the twisty, winding, convoluted, and sometimes dangerous ways you have traveled up to now, but it has a high probability of working." The other three looked at her expectantly. "Instead of trying to dress you up as something or someone you are not, it makes more sense for you to just go as yourselves. Wait, before you raise all sorts of objections, hear me out. I need to go to the capital and will be riding on the royal road by carriage, with a small contingent of guards. Lady Esmeralda and the interim ruling council have increased the number of royal guards patrolling of the royal road, and so far, all parties have held to the ideal that no harm comes to those who travel it."

"When you say go as ourselves, does that mean that you will let others know that Greer carries part of the oppgave ringe?" asked Journeyman Evan.

"Yes."

Greer astonished himself by speaking up. "I would not wish to put you in danger, m'lady. Our going with you might attract the wrong type of attention, and at some point each day we will have to leave the road to stop for the night."

"That is one of the advantages of being part of the nobility. We only camp when we choose," Lady Hadrack snootily stated with her nose in the air. "When we do choose to camp, it is in sturdy camping caravans with fine linen sheets and blankets of the softest wool. We, of course, bring our cook and baker and . . . ." She really could not keep it up and burst into laughter, relieving the tension in the room.

"Actually, Greer, stopping for the night will not be a high risk, for there will be a safe place to lodge each night with friends who are loyal to the Crown. Lord Hadrack and I were aware we might need to travel back and forth to the capital over the next year at the request of the interim ruling council. Because of opposition to the Regent, early on we made arrangements that would keep us safe on the road. I have made this trip a number of times over the last few months, and always in safety. I would risk none of us, and especially, would not risk what Greer carries. I think this plan might work. It is more unexpected than you changing costumes, horses, and means of transportation, one more time."

Everyone was quiet for a long moment, thinking over what Lady Hadrack had suggested. The more each of them thought about the new plan, the more it began to make sense. Soon they were into a discussion as to what needed to be done before they left in two days' time.

"We need to get all of us presentable for the journey," Lady Hadrack suggested. "That means Greer, we need to get you to the tailor, who will probably have my head on a platter when I ask him to whip up a traveling wardrobe for you in less than twenty-four hours. Captain Gwen, can you get the boot maker here to take a look at Greer's boots and cobble up some more formal ones, the kind that will go with the clothing he will need at court?"

Greer, who had been drifting along daydreaming while the discussion of clothes and things swirled around him, jerked his head up. "M-m-me, at the royal court?" he stammered.

CHAPTER TWENTY-SIX

Lady Hadrack found Greer in the late afternoon sitting in a small walled garden tossing a ball for Kasa and wondered if this young man had known very many carefree moments. She hated to disturb him, but she had felt a growing concern about Greer over the course of the day. On the outside, he had handled the poking and prodding of the tailor, the boot maker, the barber, and others with an outward calm, but she had sensed he was very uneasy. Journeyman Evan had filled her in on Greer's background, at least what he knew, or suspected, about it. Lady Hadrack had begun to worry about Greer, much as she would worry about any of her own children if they found themselves in a strange and unfamiliar place.

"That's quite a pup you have there," Lady Hadrack said, to break the silence of the garden. She had noticed that the pup Kasa was very important to Greer and felt if she got him talking about the pup, it might make Greer more comfortable with her. "Journeyman Evan tells me that this two-tone brown color is not his real color."

"No, m'lady, he is a tricolor, dappled gray, cream and copper. I'm told his markings are much like the border dogs of old. He should turn out to be quite a handsome fellow when he is full grown. His hair will be long and silky with a warm undercoat for the colder weather."

"Lord Avital will be green with envy when he hears about that border dog pup of yours. He is the only one in Sommerhjem who has been successful in breeding border dogs with that coloring. So," said Lady Hadrack, trying to ease into a new subject now that she felt Greer begin to relax a little, "when you get to the capital and place the ring in its proper place, what do you see yourself doing after that?"

"I don't know. I have no trade and little schooling. I don't think many of the skills I gained on the streets of Høyhauger would be much appreciated in the capital. I've never had the luxury to think much beyond the next meal or the next day. Journeyman Evan said he would talk to the master of the horse at his guild and see if he could get me a job there. I'm not sure I want to be in a town anymore, though I don't know what I would do in the country. I'm worried about what will come next." Greer could not believe he was telling this noble his concerns, but there was something about Lady Hadrack that felt comfortable.

"You might be surprised by the number of offers of employment you will get after you place the ring. I would caution you that while some offers will be legitimate, other folks will want you only for the prestige they think associating with you will bring. If you would wish guidance on what to do, please do not hesitate to come to either me or my husband. If you would choose to return to Glendalen, you would be welcome here, and we would work with you to find a place to your liking."

Greer was silent a long time, and Lady Hadrack could see he was sorting through all she had said. "It is almost a relief to hear that there are those in Sommerhjem who would take advantage of others," Greer said ruefully. "So far, everyone I have met has been helpful and kind, and I had begun to wonder if I had fallen into a dream. I thank you for your generous offer, and I will consider it."

"I hate to break up your quiet time with your pup, but we need to get together and finalize our travel plans. Word has spread that we will be traveling to the capital, and others have come forth requesting to join our party. There is still great uneasiness in Sommerhjem, and so folk tend to travel in larger groups. Several merchants will be traveling with us, as well as the young woman who delivers and trains our messenger birds. While those who choose to travel with us will know your real situation and reason for traveling south with us, as long as you are traveling in my party, I am not concerned that any of them would do you harm or try to prevent you from reaching the capital. Bring Kasa and follow me, if you would."

The rest of the time passed quickly at Glendalen. Greer felt as if he had been scrubbed within an inch of his life, what with bathing every day. His hair had been trimmed again, and he had endured what seemed like hours of fittings with the tailor. How different the last few days were compared to what his life had been in Høyhauger. In just a few short weeks he had gone from living as a street lad, just trying to survive, to sitting at a noblewoman's table dressed in fine clothing.

In the morning he was going to be riding in a comfortable coach heading towards the capital and had been informed that he would most probably be meeting with the interim ruling council and Lady Esmeralda, formerly a royal princess and former heir to the throne. All because I am a thief, Greer thought to himself. I stole something that was being stolen from an unsuspecting nobleman. It is he who should be carrying this ring to the capital and getting any recognition or credit, not me. With those thoughts in mind, Greer asked Lady Hadrack if he might speak with her privately after dinner. She invited him into a small sitting room and closed the door.

"You look troubled. What is on your mind?"

"I don't think I should be the one to go to the capital. The ring isn't mine. I'm a thief. I'm sure Journeyman Evan has told you the whole story. The ring is not mine to keep or give away."

"Let me tell you a little about the oppgave ringe. My husband and I have spent considerable time trying to learn as much as we can about the Gylden Sirklene challenge and about the rings. In the last several months, we have been helped in that pursuit by the royal historian, the royal librarian, and Master Clarisse of the Glassmakers Guild. There is surprisingly little information about either the challenge or the rings, but what we have found out is the rings always disappear, in a sense, after the challenge and just as mysteriously reappear when they are needed. As odd as it might sound, the rings seem to choose their carriers. If you are in possession of part of the oppgave ringe, you are meant to be so. Whoever the gentleman was who had the ring may have been meant to carry it to the point he lost it, but you are the one who is meant to handle it now. That would seem to count for a lot."

"But rings can't pick and choose whom they want to have them," Greer protested.

"Ordinarily I would agree with you, but not in this case. Ask yourself, why was the stable owner not able to hold onto the ring, and yet you can?"

Greer had no answer. The night before, when he had been alone in his room, he had opened the pouch and tipped the ring out onto his hand. It had been warm in his hand, but not overly so. Nothing that could not be explained away as holding warmth from his body. No flash of light had appeared when the ring had left the pouch, and the ring had certainly not hurt him. He did not have an answer for Lady Hadrack.

"My feeling, Greer, is that you are meant to take that ring to the capital. After you have put it in its proper place at the Well of Speaking, then, if you wish, we can send inquires out and try to find out who the gentleman is who was robbed in Høyhauger."

After talking with Lady Hadrack, Greer felt that there was really no other choice but to let things run their course. He was heading to the capital and to not head to the capital was not really an option. Where else would he go, and what would he do anyway? While he was uneasy traveling so openly, he did understand that this plan really had the possibility of working. It would seem Lord and Lady Hadrack were both very well-known and very well liked in Sommerhjem. Anyone attacking them, or those under their care, did so at great risk.

The early dawn light found Greer and Journeyman Evan climbing aboard Lady Hadrack's carriage. His possessions were now packed in a soft leather pack and a small trunk. Kasa had on a fancy leather collar and leash. He had been very patient with being bathed and groomed so his coat now shone brightly, showing his true colors. As Greer settled himself on the soft, cushioned seat of the carriage, he wondered if any of the street lads who had roamed the streets of Høyhauger would even recognize him now. Most likely, all they would see would be a mark ripe for the pickings. At least that was one thing he did not have to worry about. Pickpockets would get little from him, for although he was dressed well, he was just as poor in coin as he had ever been. Greer laughed a little to himself, for even if he had coin to be taken, it is hard to pick the pocket or pluck the purse from someone who is also a skilled pickpocket. Greer did not think he had lost his edge in that area.

When they stopped for the noon meal, Greer was surprised to see how many their group included. Besides Lady Hadrack's carriage, there were two more carriages, several wagons, and a number of individual riders in addition to Lady Hadrack's guard. Greer was really curious about the small wagon in their midst that held a number of cages stacked up at the back and along the sides.

"What do you suppose is carried in those cages?" Greer asked Journeyman Evan.

"I would guess messenger birds," Journeyman Evan replied over his shoulder, as he was trying to retrieve something out of his pack.

Why would anyone need that many messenger birds, Greer thought to himself, but did not want to show his ignorance by asking that question. Journeyman Evan must have see Greer's puzzled look, so informed him that messenger birds were a good swift way to send messages because they always returned to their home roosts. However, they needed to be taken from their home roosts to other places in order to be useful. Also, as messenger birds are lost due to weather, prey, or age, they needed to be replaced. For these reasons folk were needed who were skilled at transporting and settling messenger birds into roosts not their own.

"They also bring breeding pairs to those who want to increase their flocks, if they have become diminished. Lady Hadrack told me that the woman driving the messenger bird wagon is named Meryl, and she is heading back to her home just outside of the capital."

While Journeyman Evan and Greer had been talking, the cook and the proprietor of the small wayside inn they had stopped at had laid out a meal on a table set up in the shade of the overhanging eave. Folks in their group were lining up to fill their dishes with the noon meal. Tables and benches were set outside, and the weather was mild enough to eat at them. Greer found himself seated at a table with several of the Glendalen guards, Meryl the messenger bird woman, one of the merchants, and Journeyman Evan.

"Is it true then," the merchant asked Greer, "that you've one of the pieces of the oppgave ringe?"

"Yes, sir."

"So, lad, how did you come to have it?"

Greer and the others had talked about just this situation coming up. Once folks knew he had one of the rings, they were going to be curious about both it and him. All of them had agreed that the truth of how he had come to be in possession of the ring was really nobody's business. They had decided that the simplest explanation was the best, even if it were not quite true. They had thought of saying it had been in the possession of Greer's family for generations, and they just did not know what they had, but that had seemed too farfetched. Besides, that would have led to a conversation about who Greer's family was, and where in Sommerhjem he had grown up. So, instead Greer told the man he had found the ring in the ashes of an old fire pit when he had been camping in the Ryggrad Mountains.

"Got caught out in the rain and found shelter under an overhang. Place didn't seem to be a regular camping spot. I think the ring must have been there for quite a long, long time."

His answer seemed to satisfy the merchant, who got up to get himself a second helping. Greer tried to make himself as unapproachable as possible by looking down with great concentration at his food. He felt someone looking at him and glanced up to see the messenger bird woman watching him.

Interesting story this Greer lad tells, Meryl thought to herself, but it does not ring quite true. She wondered what the real story was, and if riding with someone carrying one of the pieces of the oppgave ringe was going to be as safe a ride as she had thought it would be.

The days passed quickly by as Greer, Journeyman Evan, Lady Hadrack, and the others made steady progress towards the capital. Each night the parts of the group that traveled together went their separate ways, some stopping and not rejoining, and others joining what had become a caravan. Each morning as they climbed aboard the carriage, Greer would check to see who was still with the group from the day before, who had left, and who had joined.

The guard, Minka, who was in charge of making sure Lady Hadrack and her party continued to be safe, declared that she would be bald by the time they reached the capital. Trying to guard them was making her pull her hair out. She had suggested strongly to Lady Hadrack that letting just anyone join their group was causing her nightmares. Lady Hadrack was insistent that traveling along as if they had nothing to worry about was still the right choice.

"Greer, Journeyman Evan, the pup Kasa, the border dog Louve, and I are really all you have to guard. Just be vigilant. If there is someone who joins the group with the intent to harm Greer or steal the ring, you can prevent that. The folks who we started with seem fairly trustworthy, and you can keep the new ones under observation. We are not so big a group that that is too difficult, and besides, I have faith in you and your patrol," Lady Hadrack had told the guard Minka.

For Greer, the ride had been part sightseeing and part education. Between Lady Hadrack and Journeyman Evan, Greer had learned more about Sommerhjem than most of its citizens knew. Lady Hadrack had divided her time between telling him what she knew about the Gylden Sirklene challenge and the oppgave ringe and instructing him on how to act before the Lady Esmeralda and the interim ruling council. Greer had concluded that Sommerhjem was a much more lush and fruitful land than what he knew of Bortfjell. While the ride seemed idyllic, just a jaunt through the countryside, Greer was also aware of increasing tension as they neared the capital. After being pursued since leaving Høyhauger, Greer could only hope the chase was over, and those trying to find him had slunk back into the shadows.

Chapter Twenty-Seven

In the end, Lady Hadrack's idea of traveling in plain sight proved to be brilliant. No one interrupted their journey from Glendalen to the capital, and they arrived without incident at the townhouse kept by the Glendalen Keep nobles. Lord Hadrack was there to greet them and made both Greer and Journeyman Evan feel welcome.

"I have sent word around to the Glassmakers Guild, and Master Rollag, Master Cynfarch, and Master Clarisse will be here shortly. Why don't you folks get settled, take some time to freshen up from the road, and we will meet in the back garden in an hour's time," Lord Hadrack told the group. "I will take the dogs out to the walled garden and give them a chance to stretch their legs while you lads wash up." Upon seeing the look of concern on Greer's face, Lord Hadrack assured him that the dogs would be both safe and well cared for with him.

Greer just did not know what to make of Lord Hadrack. No noble in Bortfjell that he had ever crossed paths with would so casually take it upon himself to watch over a pair of dogs not his own. Lord Hadrack had just scooped Kasa up, getting his face washed in the process, and led Louve down the hall, presumably to the garden, leaving Greer rooted to the spot, not knowing what to do next.

"Come on, Greer, we had best do what Lord Hadrack suggested if we are going to be presentable. Get your feet moving. Lady Hadrack's housekeeper is looking just a might impatient," Journeyman Evan quipped.

Greer had not realized he was standing there stock-still, until Journeyman Evan had spoken. What next, he wondered. What were the guild masters going to be like? He hustled along after the housekeeper and Journeyman Evan, and soon found himself in a sitting, sleeping room that the housekeeper informed him would be his for his stay. His bags had already been brought up, and did the young gentleman want her to unpack for him? He thanked her, but told her he would take care of his things. Unpack for him indeed, Greer thought to himself, realizing he actually had possessions to unpack. More clothes than he had had in his entire lifetime so far. Just as Greer finished washing up, Journeyman Evan knocked at his door and suggested they go down to the garden and wait.

When they arrived in the garden, Greer found Kasa running up and down the bricked walk, vigorously shaking in the air what appeared to be a knotted up sock, and thoroughly enjoying himself. Greer and Journeyman Evan took their seats at a table that was set under an awning. They had hardly sat down before a house servant came bustling up with a tray laden with food and drink.

"Ah, I could get used to this," Journeyman Evan said with a sigh. "Lovely carriage rides, servants bringing food and drink. Alas, it is back to mucking out stalls for me tomorrow."

"As if you ever did a lick of work, you rascal," said a woman dressed in Glassmakers Guild master's clothing. Journeyman Evan leapt to his feet and was caught up in huge hug, and then, a rather brief shaking. "You had us all a wee bit worried, Journeyman Evan."

"My apologies, Master Clarisse. May I introduce you to one of the reasons for my slight disappearing act? Master Clarisse, this is my friend Greer. Greer, Master Clarisse."

Master Clarisse and Greer had just finished exchanging pleasantries when Lord and Lady Hadrack entered the garden accompanied by two older men. Master Rollag and Master Cynfarch were introduced, and each in turn gave Journeyman Evan a bad time, but Greer could see the genuine affection that the three masters held for Journeyman Evan. He wondered what it would be like to be treated like that. They obviously truly liked Journeyman Evan and also valued him. It took Greer a moment to realize that Lord Hadrack had addressed him.

"Begging your pardon, sir, would you repeat what you just said?"

"Lady Hadrack filled us in on your adventures. You two have had quite a journey, but it is not over yet. So, Greer, are you feeling up to meeting with the interim ruling council tomorrow morning, or do you need more time?"

Greer could not believe that he was even being asked his wishes. "I will probably never feel like meeting such an august body as Sommerhjem's interim ruling council, but tomorrow morning will be fine."

"Some members of the interim ruling council thought you should appear before them in the council chambers, and then there should be a big procession to the Well of Speaking. Others suggested that this could all be a fraud, and all the falderal and whatnot over a false ring would only bring embarrassment to them. I suggested we just meet at the Well of Speaking, and if the ring is truly one of the nine pieces of the oppgave ringe, I suspect we will know," stated Master Rollag. "When it is all said and done, I'd like to talk to you, young man, if that is alright with you."

"That would be fine, sir," Greer answered and wondered what a master of the Glassmakers Guild would want to talk to him about.

"Good, that's settled then. Now, how about some supper? I know of a fine inn where . . . ."

"Ah, Master Rollag, I hate to deprive you of a meal at your favorite inn, but I asked Cook if she would prepare a dinner for all of us," suggested Lady Hadrack, her eyes twinkling with good humor because she knew Master Rollag had a weakness for her cook's cooking.

"I will just have to suffer through."

"I wouldn't let Cook hear you say that."

"Before we head into dinner, I would like a word or two with my journeyman, if all of you would not mind. Journeyman Evan, with me," Master Cynfarch commanded, as he rose and headed out of the room.

The look on Journeyman Evan's face was so woebegone that Greer started to get up, thinking this talk was going to be bad for Journeyman Evan.

"I see traveling has not diminished your acting skills any. Are you sure you are in the right guild?" said Master Clarisse.

Journeyman Evan just smiled slightly as he left the room, and Greer settled again, feeling less worried for his friend.

The three guild masters did not stay long after dinner. The plan was set and, early the next morning, they would return to escort Greer to the Well of Speaking. While the others in the household gathered in the sitting room, Greer excused himself, pleading tiredness, and headed up to the room he had been assigned. What was to happen the next day was not weighing on him as heavily as what would happen after that. He knew he could never return to Høyhauger and the life he had led there, but he also did not know what the future held for him in Sommerhjem. He knew now that he had had a taste of a better life, he did not want to go back to being a street lad ever again. He could return to Trelandsby and live with the foresters. He could work for Farmer Yorick O'Gara. He could take Lady Hadrack up on her kind offer to find him a position at Glendalen. Then, there was Journeyman Evan's assurance that Master Cynfarch would hire him, but he really did not know what he wanted to do.

Just as Greer had decided he was no closer to a solution about his future and had settled down to sleep, he heard the floorboards creak just outside his door. In the bright moonlight coming in the open window, he could just make out the handle of his door being slowly turned. Greer swiftly slipped from his bed, silently dashed across the room, and flattened himself against the wall next to the door. The door slowly opened a crack, and Journeyman Evan peeked his head in. Greer grabbed him by the sleeve and pulled him the rest of the way into the room.

"Wha-a-a . . ." Journeyman Evan managed to say before Greer asked him what he thought he was doing.

"I was concerned about you since you headed up so early, but I didn't want to wake you if you were asleep. I'm sorry if I caused you any alarm."

Noticing Journeyman Evan was rubbing his arm where he had grabbed him, Greer said apologetically, "I'm sorry if I hurt you pulling you into the room."

"No matter. So, are you alright?"

"Yes. Just wanted some quiet to think things through. A lot has happened since I left Høyhauger. Tomorrow will bring an end to this part of the journey, and I wanted to think about what will happen after that. Lady Hadrack warned me that my turning up with a piece of the oppgave ringe is going to cause a stir, and for a little while, I will be someone of great interest, but that will soon fade. I cannot continue to live on the kindness and charity of others. I will need to decide what to do next. She suggested that there may be offers of various opportunities, but I need to be wary. Also," Greer held up his hand to stop Journeyman Evan from speaking, "also, I am sorry, in a way, to see this adventure end, for it means everything changes, and, well . . . ."

Greer was silent for a moment, and Journeyman Evan, sensing that Greer was struggling with something important, for once held his tongue.

Finally, Greer looked up. "You see, I can't ever recall having a friend, and now that we are at the capital, things are bound to change, and, well, um . . . ."

"Sure, time and distance make maintaining a friendship a bit harder, but it doesn't stop it, Greer. If you stay in the capital, we'll have more opportunity to get together, but if you choose to go somewhere else, that doesn't mean we stop being friends. Besides, I haven't taught you all you need to know about Sommerhjem," Journeyman Evan stated seriously, though the hint of mischief in his eye did more to lighten the mood than his words. "Now then, we had best get some sleep, for tomorrow is the big day."

"You don't need to remind me, and thanks."

"No matter."

In the morning, Greer rose early and made his way to take a bath. When he returned to his room, he found his clothes laid out, and his boots cleaned and polished. Shortly after he had dressed, a valet discreetly knocked on his door and came in with a clothes brush. When he was done, Greer felt lint, dust, and anything else would not dare to settle on his clothes, for the valet would be there with his brush to attack it. He had visions of walking to the Well of Speaking followed by the valet taking swipes at him along the whole walk. Greer was quietly chuckling to himself over that image when Journeyman Evan knocked on his door.

"Ready?"

"I'm about as buffed and polished as I will ever be. I think the idea I had last night just before I went to sleep was a good one that I should have followed."

"And that was?"

"I thought I should just have gotten up, dressed, walked to the Well of Speaking, dropped off the ring, and returned back here."

"What stopped you?"

"Other than not knowing where here is in relation to the Well of Speaking, and where the Well of Speaking is in relation to here?"

"Yah, other than that."

Greer did not have a chance to answer, for at that moment, Lord Hadrack appeared at Greer's door and suggested both the lads needed to get a move on, or they would miss breakfast. All too soon it was time to proceed to the Well of Speaking. The carriage set off, surrounded by a small group of the Glendalen guard, and traveled without incident to the Well of Speaking. Greer tried not to gawk and look like a total rube as they passed by one building more magnificent than the next, finally entering the beautifully landscaped grounds surrounding the Well of Speaking.

Standing at the entrance was a group of folks all finely dressed and looking important. Lord and Lady Hadrack climbed out of the carriage, followed by Greer and Journeyman Evan. Greer was then introduced to the members of the interim ruling council, including the Lady Esmeralda. He was thankful that Lady Hadrack had coached him on what to do. After the introductions, Greer was surrounded by a contingent of the royal guard and had a moment of panic. Sensing his distress, Lady Hadrack leaned in and had a quick conversation with Lady Esmeralda.

"Wait just a moment, if you would please," Lady Esmeralda requested. Turning to look at Greer, she said, "Would you like someone to walk with you?"

Greer was torn. He discovered he really did not want to walk into the Well of Speaking alone, but on the other hand, if something went wrong, he did not want to get anyone else in trouble. Before he could decide what to do, Journeyman Evan spoke up.

"I would be honored if you would allow me to walk beside you, my friend. Seems we have been on this journey together, so we might as well end it together."

"We would be honored to walk with you, also," came a voice Greer had not expected to hear again. He felt unexpected warmth as Zareh and Pryderi stepped out of the crowd that had gathered behind the members of the interim ruling council.

Greer found himself speechless and could only nod his head. With the Journeyman Evan at his side and Zareh and Pryderi behind him, Greer started forward on the long walk down the steps to the sea wall at the bottom of the Well of Speaking. It surprised Greer that there was a very large crowd sitting on the seats of the amphitheater. He had not expected to see so many folks, and he felt doubly glad that he had been joined by those he knew.

The group came to a halt at the bottom of the steps, where they were joined by Master Clarisse, who Greer had learned was the official interpreter of the Book of Rules governing the Gylden Sirklene challenge. She beckoned Greer forward. Journeyman Evan gave him quiet words of encouragement, and Zareh and Pryderi offered him quiet words of support. Despite the backing of his friends, Greer's shaking legs refused to move his feet, which felt stuck to the ground.

Master Clarisse, sensing his fear, came to stand beside him and said in a firm, but quiet voice, "Let us just take one step at a time. There is really nothing that I know of to worry about. We will just walk up to the box, or more correctly the vessteboks, open the lid, and you can place the ring inside. Easy peasy."

Greer had to smile at Master Clarisse's use of the phrase "easy peasy" and found it relaxed him just a little. Just enough it seemed to get his reluctant feet moving. Once he got to the wall, he was surprised at the smallness and beauty of the box set into the wall and marveled that some enterprising thief had not stolen it. Master Clarisse seemed to sense what he was thinking and assured him that the box had its own safeguards.

"Go ahead, Greer, just lift the lid and place the ring in the box."

Greer pulled the pouch out from under his tunic, opened it, and tipped the ring out onto his hand. He reached out with his other hand to open the lid of the vessteboks and noticed to his surprise that his hand was shaking. Steeling himself for he knew not what, as his hand touched the box, he felt a surge of warmth and calm flow through him. At that moment, he felt a rightness in what he was doing. With more confidence than he had ever felt in his life, he placed the ring in the vessteboks. What happened next amazed even the most skeptical among crowd.

Chapter Twenty-Eight

When Greer placed the ring into the vessteboks, a beautiful light rose high out of the box, shooting skyward, and arcing out, spreading out until it enveloped Greer, shimmering around him in all the colors of the rainbow. There it pulsed for a long moment and then slowly faded. The crowd, which had been holding its collective breath, let out a great sigh. Afterward, when asked, Greer could never adequately describe what it was like to be surrounded by the light, nor did he want to. It was something he just wanted to hold to himself.

The placing of the third piece of the oppgave ringe was a reason to celebrate for the folks gathered, and the rest of the day was a whirlwind of activity for Greer. He met with and was congratulated by Lady Esmeralda and the interim ruling council. There was a reception at the palace and an impromptu fair on the fairgrounds. For the most part, it was reasonably enjoyable, but the senses Greer had honed on the streets of Høyhauger caused him to be aware that not all of the folks he met that day were pleased with the ring having been placed in the box.

It was late in the evening by the time Greer returned to Lord and Lady Hadrack's townhouse. Even though everyone else had gone to bed and was probably asleep, Greer found himself sitting up, staring into the coals of the small fire that had been built in the fireplace in his sitting room. What now, he thought. After all the hoopla of the day, the reality he faced now was that he did not know what the next day would bring. Kasa, sensing his confusion and distress, put his paws on Greer's legs and tried to scramble up onto his lap.

"You are almost getting too big to be a lap dog. You know that, don't you, Kasa?" Greer said, but he did not push the pup away. Rather, he drew him closer and buried his face in Kasa's fur. Earlier that evening, just as he was about to climb into the Glendalen Keep carriage, Master Rollag had pulled him aside and asked him, again, if he might speak to him in the morning. He did not tell Greer what he wanted to speak to him about, but suggested it was important. Greer agreed to meet with him. Master Rollag was such a huge, imposing, and important man that Greer could not for the life of him think what Master Rollag would have to talk to him about. If he wanted to talk to him about a job, Greer did not really know what his answer would be. Too many changes in his young life too fast had left him feeling adrift. He did not want to make decisions too soon, yet he realized he could not stay on where he was, for he had never been one to accept the charity of others easily.

Since he had no new answers to the questions that were going in circles in his head, Greer gently set Kasa down, gave him one last scritch between his ears, banked the fire, and crawled into bed. He did not object when Kasa jumped on the bed and snuggled against his back. Kasa's warm comforting weight helped him let go of his worries and drift into a dreamless sleep. Morning would come no matter if he stayed up for it or slept, he thought, as he snuggled deeper under the covers.

After breakfast, Journeyman Evan asked Greer to meet him at the front door, saying he would be there in a moment. Greer headed to the front door and, hearing someone on the central stairs, looked up to find Journeyman Evan coming down the stairs, carrying his pack. The realization that Journeyman Evan was leaving struck Greer hard. He knew the time would come when Journeyman Evan would need to get back to his life as a journeyman for the Glassmakers Guild, but he did not realize it would be so soon. Journeyman Evan was the first real friend he had ever had, and it hurt far worse than he had expected knowing that his day to day contact with Journeyman Evan might be coming to an end.

"Master Rollag sent word that he would like you to come by the guildhall this morning, so why don't you walk over there with me? After you talk to him, you could drop by the stables, and we could talk to Master Cynfarch," Journeyman Evan said. "Lady Hadrack said you should just leave your stuff here. You're welcome to stay as long as you like. Go get Kasa, and we'll be off."

Kasa is certainly more excited about this walk than either Journeyman Evan or I, Greer thought to himself. Though he knew they were walking through a more affluent part of the capital, still Greer was surprised at the cleanliness of the streets and the beauty of the buildings and surrounding park areas. He knew there must be a seedier side of town and asked Journeyman Evan about it.

"There are certainly poorer sections in the capital, but since the Regent has been pushed out of power, a great deal has been done to clean up the more dangerous areas."

The two continued to walk but spoke little after that, both wrapped up in their own thoughts. After a while they came to the entrance of the park-like fairgrounds where the Glassmakers Guildhall was located. Greer saw little of its beauty, and his footsteps began to slow, for he was feeling rather reluctant to reach their destination.

"Come on, slowpoke, or Kasa and I will just leave you behind," Journeyman Evan jested.

Since there was no delaying the inevitable, Greer picked up his pace and caught up to Journeyman Evan. The guildhall was certainly a good example of its craft, with colorful stained glass windows across the front. When he entered, he had to stop for a moment, finding himself within a dancing rainbow of color from sunlight streaming in through both the windows and the glass dome in the ceiling.

"Gawk later," Journeyman Evan said. "It's not good to keep Master Rollag waiting."

Pulling Kasa closer and shortening his leash, Greer followed Journeyman Evan out of the central hall, down a side corridor, and into a room that was part sitting room, part display room, and part office. Master Rollag rose up from behind his desk.

"Welcome, Greer, Journeyman Evan. I am glad you could make it. Journeyman Evan, Master Cynfarch awaits. When Greer and I are finished with our talk, I will send him out to the stables to see you."

Master Rollag's greeting was both a welcome and, at the same time, a dismissal of Journeyman Evan, with a built-in reassurance to Greer that he would see Journeyman Evan again. Once Journeyman Evan had left, closing the door behind him, Master Rollag invited Greer to sit down.

"Can I offer you some tea?"

"No, sir. Thank you, sir."

"Despite what you may have heard, I rarely have young fellows for lunch, so you might as well relax. Your pup is a good example for you to follow."

Greer looked down and found that Kasa had certainly made himself comfortable, for he was sprawled on his back, his paws in the air, twitching.

"Well, perhaps not quite as relaxed as the pup," Master Rollag said with a smile. "Now then, I have some information to pass along to you of some importance, but it really is not my story to tell. I am expecting someone else shortly, but first I have a few questions for you. I realize you don't know me, and really have no reason to trust me, but I would like to ask you some personal questions. Know that you do not have to answer, but also know I have an important reason for asking them."

"Journeyman Evan seems to put great stock in you, sir, so I'll trust his judgment."

"I know before you came to Sommerhjem you were living on the streets of Høyhauger. Do you have any memory of having a family?"

"Sometimes I think I remember living in a home with others, but then mostly I think I just made that up. I'm not sure if my memories are real."

"I have been told you have one leg shorter than the other. Has this always been true, or did you have some sort of accident, perhaps a broken leg that might not have healed well?"

"I don't recall ever having a broken leg. I think I must have been born this way." Greer was beginning to get just a little uncomfortable with Master Rollag's questions.

"Were you always called Greer?"

"As long as I can remember, I've always said my name was Greer."

"Is that a common name in Bortfjell?"

"I don't think so. I have never met another. At some point, someone said I was a greer, which meant I was watchful, and the name stuck."

"A variation of the word in the old text also means guardian," said Master Clarisse, as she walked into the room. "Sorry, I did not mean to eavesdrop. It would seem you are well named, for you guarded the ring well. I can see you are having a serious conversation, so I can come back later. I just wanted to let you know Seeker Zita is here."

"Give us about five more minutes and then invite her back. Feel free to join us at that time," Master Rollag told Master Clarisse. "Are you familiar with seekers, Greer?"

"Only slightly. Only seen a few over the years. Heard a lot of tales about them, some of them hard to believe."

"Yes, well, as you know, seekers are individuals who are information gatherers. They travel about trying to gather knowledge about our past and the old ways. They are a special type of wanderer, and highly respected. They have been asked by the interim ruling council to seek out information concerning the oppgave ringe. One of them was following a lead that led her to Bortfjell, where she almost crossed your path."

Greer had a somewhat concerned look on his face, for he wondered if the seeker had been looking for him.

Seeming to understand Greer's concern, Master Rollag continued. "The seeker was not looking for you at first. She was trying to catch up with a gentleman from Sommerhjem, a one Lord Avital. It would seem that you caught up with him, so to speak, before she did. He was the gentleman who was waylaid at the stable where you were working. She suspected he, or someone in his family, either had, or knew the location of, a piece of the oppgave ringe. You can imagine her disappointment when she found out how close she had come. She found Lord Avital, but not the ring."

"And on a merry chase you have led Lord Avital and me, young man. It would seem you have become important to him," stated the tall woman who entered the room. She wore an air of command like others wore a cloak. Intelligence shown out from her eyes, and she carried an intricately carved staff, which Greer might have envied if she had not made him so nervous.

Maybe he would not have to make any decisions about what his future held, for this woman obviously knew he was a thief, and stealing from a noble was a punishable offense in Bortfjell. No matter what the circumstance or the kindness of those he had met along the way, how much weight this lord carried in Sommerhjem would determine what happened next. How ironic, Greer thought. I lived on the streets all of my life and did things that were against the law to survive and was never caught. I grab a pouch and a ring, get chased halfway across a country I do not know, become a minor hero for less than a day, and now I could end up in a dark dungeon, never again to see the light of day. Greer gave a surreptitious glance around to see if there were any way he could make it out of the room, but all exits were blocked. His heart sank. No place to run, no bolt holes, no place to hide, and worse than that, he would probably lose the only friend he had ever had. And what would happen to Kasa?

With his head bowed in defeat, Greer looked at Kasa longingly and then straightened himself up. "I know it was wrong of me to steal the gentleman's pouch, and I have no excuse for my actions. A request before

I am led off to wherever you put thieves, if you will. Could you please ask Journeyman Evan to look after Kasa? I don't want the pup to suffer for my actions, or Journeyman Evan either, for that matter."

Three pairs of eyes looked at Greer, and he could see a mixture of emotions in them. Surprise, concern, and in Master Rollag's eyes, a flash of merriment.

It was the seeker who spoke up. "Ah, lad, I am sorry if my statement caused you to think you were in trouble. And besides, I don't think you can steal something that probably chose you in the first place."

At first, Greer was so relieved that he was not going to spend the rest of his days in a dreary dark dungeon that he did not quite understand what the seeker had said. What did she mean that the ring had chosen him?

"I don't understand."

"First, let us be clear that you are not in trouble," Master Rollag stated. "By virtue of the fact that you brought the third piece of the oppgave ringe to the capital and put it in its rightful place, no matter how you acquired it, you are cleared of any wrongdoing on your part, so you had best just sit down and relax. No one is going to charge you with theft, and hopefully Journeyman Evan will get over his disappointment of not acquiring a really fine border dog. I'm sure I have added to your anxiousness by not telling you why I wanted to meet with you this morning. I apologize, Greer, but it is not my story to tell. Maybe we should start over with introductions, settle in with a nice cup of tea, or if you prefer, a tall cool glass of apple cider, and try to straighten this all out. Is that alright with you, Greer? Master Clarisse," who had entered the room behind Seeker Zita, "could I impose upon you to get us some refreshments?"

With affirmative nods from both Greer and Master Clarisse, Master Rollag continued. "Greer, this is Seeker Zita, who I understand along with other seekers, was asked to find information about the pieces of the oppgave ringe and follow wherever that information took them. Ah, thank you, Master Clarisse. We don't much stand on ceremony here, so help yourselves, and when we are all settled, I will give the floor over to Seeker Zita."

Now that being thrown in the dungeon no longer threatened, Greer was more than happy to grab a mug of cider and several pastries. Everyone settled in, and Seeker Zita began to speak.

"I found a reference that suggested that Lord Avital's family might be the keeper of one of the parts of the oppgave ringe, and so I set off to find out if that were true. Unfortunately, I arrived a few days after Lord Avital had left his estate, leaving it and his family in the capable hands of his sister and her husband. I was told none of the family had any inkling about holding a piece of the oppgave ringe. It is not unusual that something like a piece of the oppgave ringe, which holds such mystery and is so important, is held in secret from even family members. I was somewhat discouraged, but still felt like I needed to talk to Lord Avital himself. I asked where Lord Avital was heading and was told he was heading to Høyhauger in search of you."

Chapter Twenty-Nine

Could life get any stranger, Greer thought to himself. He could understand why Lord Avital might be among those looking for him after he had run off with the pouch. That made a great deal of sense, but why would a nobleman from Sommerhjem have come all the way to Høyhauger looking for him? What the seeker was saying did not make any sense.

Noting Greer's look of confusion, Seeker Zita went on. "Let me tell you what Lord Avital told me. It seems his wife died recently after being sick for quite some time. When she realized she was dying, she confessed to Lord Avital that he had a son he did not know about. She was young when they married and very in love with her husband. He was away when their first child was born. It was a lad who had one leg shorter than the other. Lady Avital thought that Lord Avital would not love her anymore if she presented him with a less than perfect child, so she gave the newborn to a couple who were working on the estate at the time. The husband was from Bortfjell, and Lady Avital gave them enough coin to return to the country of his birth, taking the baby with them. How anyone can give up a child, I don't know, but Lady Avital did. She told her husband that their first child had died shortly after he was born. He never knew what she had done until just before her death."

"So, if Greer is their long lost son, he might, at one point, have had a family in Bortfjell? What happened to them? Did they just take Lady Avital's coin and then abandon the baby?" Master Clarisse asked.

"From what Lord Avital could track down when he was in Høyhauger, the family kept Greer and were raising him as their own, but died in some type of epidemic that swept the town when Greer was about five, leaving him alone. Apparently no one stepped forward to care for him after their deaths. If the family who was raising him had any relatives in Høyhauger, either none of them survived the epidemic or none stepped forward to take care of Greer. What amazes me is that you survived at all."

"I sort of remember some old lady giving me a place to sleep when I was younger, but that memory is pretty hazy. Mostly, I just tried to keep out of the way of the bigger lads and lasses, who would take anything one had of value."

"At any rate, after Lord Avital discovered the family that his son had been given to was dead, he began making inquiries about a lad around fifteen years of age who walked with a limp or had legs that were uneven. He heard about you and was going to try to locate you the next day. However, before he had a chance to find you, he had that encounter with the owner of Milkin's Stable and lost his opportunity, for you had disappeared. We then set out, trying to discover where you had gone."

"Just because this lord was looking for a child with one leg shorter than the other who had been taken to Høyhauger and discovered the family caring for him no longer existed, that doesn't mean that child is me."

"You are correct, but the odds of two lads of your coloring and age both having one leg shorter than the other and living in a town as small as Høyhauger are slim. I know Lord Avital would like a chance to meet you and determine for himself if you could possibly be his son, Tal."

"How would he even know if I were his son?" Greer asked. And wouldn't it be a bit of irony if it turned out that I was, Greer thought to himself, but he was not going to get his hopes up.

"I don't know," Seeker Zita replied, "but I can tell you that you have his coloring, and I can certainly see some family resemblance. Lord Avital said he would be able to tell, but would not explain further."

"Does he have other children?" Master Rollag inquired.

"Yes, several."

"Is that going to be a problem for Greer? If he is indeed Lord Avital's son, Tal, he would be the first born."

"Apparently not. In the case of Dugghus, the holding is passed onto the child, male or female, who is best suited to lead it, and that is determined by the current Lord or Lady. Each child is encouraged to follow his or her particular talents, and often that will take him or her away from the holding. Each child is provided for, and Lord Avital suggested none of his children have declared that they want to follow in his footsteps. They are young yet. I think, if Greer is indeed Lord Avital's son, he would be given a great many opportunities and choices."

While the others continued to talk, Greer sat back, lost in thought. What stood out for him was not that he might be part of the nobility, or that he would be given opportunities and choices, but that he might have a family and a place to belong. Was that too much to hope for? He was shaken out of his reverie by a question from Seeker Zita.

"So, Greer, do you think you might like to travel to Dugghus and see if the folk there are your family?"

Of course he would like to find out if he had a family, but Greer hesitated answering, for suddenly swirling through his head were all of the difficulties he might face getting to Dugghus. He had no coin, he had some prospects for employment, but that would delay his going to Dugghus. Even if he had some coin, he did not know his way around Sommerhjem and did not know how far Dugghus was from the capital. Greer had gotten the impression from something Seeker Zita had said that Dugghus was quite far away from the capital, and to the south and east. Maybe he could walk and try to pick up odd jobs along the way. It might take some time, but he was a survivor.

"Greer?"

"Ah, yes, sorry," answered Greer. "Yes, I would like to find out if I'm related to Lord Avital. I was just trying to figure out how I might work my way there. I don't even know where Dugghus is in relation to the capital. It might take me some time to get there."

"Now it is my turn to apologize," Seeker Zita stated. "I haven't finished my tale. After reaching Journeyman Evan's family's farm and not finding you, Lord Avital gave in to his feelings of homesickness and discouragement and returned to Dugghus. He asked me to get his information to the Glassmakers Guild because he knew you were traveling with Journeyman Evan. Both of us hoped you would eventually show up here, or Journeyman Evan would, and he would lead us to you. I was charged with leaving some coin with Master Rollag or Master Clarisse to be used by you to travel to Dugghus. There should be enough for you to purchase a horse, a pack animal, and supplies, with enough left over for meals and lodging. As to getting you there, well, I think between the three of us here, we can come up with a plan."

This Lord Avital was either very trusting or a fool, thought Greer. He had left what amounted to a fortune to a street lad just to provide transportation and a means to get to his holding. There did not seem to be anything that would prevent Greer from accepting his generosity and then turning around and heading back north. He knew other street lads, if they found themselves in his boots, would keep the boots and sell off the horse and supplies for profit. Just as he finished thinking these thoughts, another thought struck him which he voiced out loud.

"If I'm not his son, what then?" And even if I am his son, what if I do not fit in or am somehow unacceptable to the family, Greer thought. He would be riding a good distance from the capital to a more remote region of Sommerhjem, to a place unfamiliar to him. If Lord Avital and his family did not want him, what then? Was it worth the risk?

"Lord Avital told me he would provide for you to return to the capital should you not be his son. Think of it this way, you get to see more of Sommerhjem before you have to decide what to do next in your life. It really is a very low risk offer," Seeker Zita said.

Master Clarisse, who had been silent during this exchange, had been watching Greer closely. While she suspected Greer was well schooled in keeping his thoughts and feelings from showing on his face, she had seen a quick flash of hope and longing when Seeker Zita was talking and realized that this journey was going to be highly risky for Greer. Here was someone who did not belong anywhere. His old life was gone, and he could not return. He had yet to decide what to do with his new life. He was a stranger to Sommerhjem, and his one friend, Journeyman Evan, would no longer be a day to day companion. He had no family that he knew of, and if Lord Avital turned out not to be his father, his hope for home and family would be crushed. No, this was not a low risk offer as Seeker Zita had so casually suggested.

"Well, Greer, what do you wish to do?" asked Master Rollag, "Or would you like some time to think about it?"

"I think I had best go to Dugghus, sir, and find out for sure. If I didn't go, I would always wonder."

"I think that is a wise choice," Master Rollag said gently, for he, too, was well aware of the possible outcomes of the journey. "Why don't you go find Journeyman Evan and invite him to return here with you? When you go out the door, take a left and follow the corridor all the way to the end. Take the stairs down, and they will take you to the outside door. You can see the stables from there."

Once Greer had left, Master Rollag turned to the others. "I suspect Greer is trying not to get his hopes up, but I certainly hope we are not sending him on a wild goose chase. We need to think hard as to how we can best serve him if it turns out Lord Avital is not his father. After all, Sommerhjem owes him a debt for returning the ring to its rightful place. But that is a problem to be worked out later. Right now we need to discuss how to get Greer to Dugghus. Since you came to me, Seeker Zita, with the information about Greer, I have done a great deal of thinking about it. I talked to Master Cynfarch, and we have come to the conclusion that Journeyman Evan should accompany Greer to Dugghus."

"That seems fair," stated Master Clarisse. "After all this, he really should have a chance to see how Greer's story plays out."

While the three waited for Greer and Journeyman Evan to return, they discussed what they could do to help Greer if it turned out he was not Lord Avital's son. Not long after they had finished their discussion, the two lads entered the room, followed by Master Cynfarch.

"I gave Greer time to tell Journeyman Evan his news, but I have not discussed anything with either of them," Master Cynfarch told the three assembled in Master Rollag's office.

"Now would be the time, then," Master Rollag retorted.

"It would seem I have been persuaded to let you slack your duties once again to go scurrying off on another adventure," Master Cynfarch dryly informed Journeyman Evan. "However," he held up his hand to stop Journeyman Evan from speaking, "you will be doing the guild's business on the way back. I have prepared a list."

Journeyman Evan rolled his eyes at the mention of the list, but inside he was doing a nimble quick-stepping jig. He was delighted he would get to accompany Greer on his journey south and fervently hoped that Greer would find a warm and welcoming family waiting for him. In addition, Journeyman Evan was looking forward to the chance to travel to a part of Sommerhjem he had never seen.

The rest of the day went by in a whirlwind of activity. Much to Greer's surprise, Master Cynfarch went with him and Journeyman Evan to the horse merchants. Greer found himself amused watching the master and the journeyman haggle with each other and the horse trader over a number of horses before a beautiful small gray horse was purchased for riding and a dun colored one was purchased as a pack horse. Greer suspected that Master Cynfarch and Journeyman Evan had worked together before when purchasing horses and probably had just worn the merchants down.

Either horse could be ridden, Master Cynfarch had explained, and had also suggested that Greer need not be put off by their smaller size.

This type of horse had been bred as a working horse, able to travel long distances, and were good herding and cutting horses. They would be well-suited to the high hills that surrounded Dugghus.

After walking the horses back to the Glassmakers Guildhall, the two lads made the rounds of other merchants, along with Seeker Zita, to gather the rest of the supplies Greer would need. Greer noted that there was some light-hearted haggling at each place they stopped, but more often than not, the price seemed to him to start out lower than he would have expected and sell for less than he would have thought. Either items were much less expensive in Sommerhjem, or there was something about a seeker doing the purchasing. Merchants seemed eager to sell them new equipment, but Seeker Zita more often than not chose items that were used. She had an uncanny knack of finding just the right thing. When they were looking for a saddle, she slowly wandered through several saddle shops, muttering that she would know it when she saw it. While digging through a pile of saddles dumped in the back of one shop, she pulled out a very dusty saddle, declaring it would do. Greer had been dubious until later that day when he put a rag soaked in leather cleaner to the saddle. Beneath the dirt and grime was a beautiful hand-tooled saddle that showed very little wear.

That evening Lady Hadrack, having been informed of what had transpired earlier in the day, invited the three Glassmakers Guild masters, the seeker, Journeyman Evan, and a few others to a farewell dinner for Greer. Both she and Lord Hadrack had informed him that he was always welcome at Glendalen Keep, and if Lord Avital turned out not to be family, then he was to come to them. They would help him get established. It was a comforting thought when he lay in bed that night, wondering what the next few weeks would bring.

Chapter Thirty

The journey took too long, and was not long enough, in Greer's mind. The traveling was easy, the weather good, and Kasa spent more and more time walking alongside rather than riding on the pack horse. Louve was still with them as well. Seems Farmer O'Gara the Younger had gotten a message to Farmer O'Gara the Elder concerning the border dog. Farmer O'Gara the Elder had sent word on to the Glassmakers Guildhall that either of the lads was welcome to keep Louve. Kasa certainly seemed glad for her company and was learning from her faster than from either Greer or Journeyman Evan. They would decide who was to keep her after they knew the situation in Dugghus.

Journeyman Evan continued to fill Greer in on the history of Sommerhjem. Greer suggested Journeyman Evan was obviously with the wrong guild, that he should have apprenticed with the royal historian instead. Journeyman Evan had laughed at that idea and just continued to fill the hours with stories and tales. Sometimes the two traveled in silence, but Greer found it was a comfortable silence. Each evening when they halted from their travels and set up camp, Greer almost expected Vadoma and her two traveling companions to show up, but they never did.

One day as they topped a rise, Journeyman Evan pointed out the hazy high hills in the far distance. "According to the map, that's where we're heading. The valleys between the high hills are good for crops such as wheat, barley, and hay, and the hills are good for grazing. You are about to enter sheep country. Most of the really fine wool comes from this area. I asked around, and Dugghus wool is considered to be some of the finest in the land. Also, some very famous weavers have come from here, one of whom is Lord Avital's sister. Maybe you have a talent for weaving. You never know."

Greer guessed he would cross that bridge when he came to it. First, he needed to find out if he even belonged here. Surprisingly, the closer they drew to Dugghus, the less anxious Greer became. He was hard-pressed to understand why, but as they moved into the hills, he felt like he was coming home. He did not know if it was because he was back in hill country, but he dismissed that notion because these hills were not at all like the hills and mountains surrounding Høyhauger. He wondered if he felt like he was coming home because he so wished that this truly was home, or if this truly was his home and thus he felt welcome here.

As they crested a rather high hill, Greer got his first look at the land Lord Avital oversaw. The valley that stretched out before them was a very large one with a broad stream running through the middle. In the middle of the valley, on the west side of the stream was a small village. Perched on a small knoll, on the east side of the stream, was a large, but not overly grand, manor house. Beyond the village, along the stream, were what looked to be a series of well-constructed low buildings. Farther down the valley, on the east side of the stream, were barns and sheds. White, brown, and black dots could be seen on the far hills, and Greer realized he was looking at sheep.

"It's a fair looking estate, I'd say," suggested Journeyman Evan. "Certainly looks well maintained."

"What are those low buildings east of the village?" Greer asked.

"My best guess is they are weaving sheds and storage buildings for wool."

"I wish I could enter the village as if we were just traveling through to get a feel for the place, and . . . ."

"And what?" Journeyman Evan questioned.

"You're right. And what, indeed. I don't know what I was thinking. Maybe I am just trying to delay meeting Lord Avital. I'm half afraid I won't be his son and half afraid I will. Does that make any sense to you?"

"Of course. Having come this far, you don't want to be disappointed, and yet on the other hand, if you are his son you face an even greater unknown. Will his family accept you? Will you fit in? Is being a sheep herder what you really want to do with your life? Will you know which fork to use at the first large feast? Will . . . ."

"Enough," Greer said, though he was trying not to laugh. "That did it. We are turning around immediately and heading back to the capital. I can't face the humiliation of picking the wrong fork."

Surprisingly, Greer found the tension he had been feeling when they had topped the rise was now less. Whatever the outcome of the meeting with Lord Avital, Greer knew he had to know, one way or the other, if this man was his father. Taking a deep breath, Greer urged his horse forward at a walk and began the descent into the valley.

As the two came closer and closer to the village, Greer was struck by how neat and tidy the fields, gardens, and cottages were along the lane. When they entered the small village, he noticed the front stoops of the few small shops had been swept clean, and flowers were abundant in the window boxes. The main street was not all that long, and too soon it was time to turn and head over the bridge across the wide stream and up to the manor house.

Greer and Journeyman Evan's arrival would not be a surprise because a messenger bird had been sent to Lord Avital stating that Greer had arrived in the capital and would be coming to Dugghus. Greer knew he appeared the proper young man, for he was dressed well. They had stayed at an inn the night before so he could get cleaned up from travel. Greer also knew his good clothes did not really change who he was, or what he had been, and that worried him. Even if he were Lord Avital's son, what did he know about being the son of a noble?

The two dismounted when they reached the manor house, and Greer called the dogs, telling them to stay with the horses. Journeyman Evan held the horses and watched as Greer mounted the steps and pulled the bell cord. Quite quickly the door was opened, and Greer asked to see Lord Avital.

"He's down at the barn up to his elbows in border dog pups at the moment," the young lass who answered the door said. Behind her a mature woman's voice called out, inquiring who was at the door. "Some young man looking for Father," she replied over her shoulder. Turning back to Greer, she said, "Just go back down the drive and follow the cart track to the second barn. You'll find him there."

Greer thanked her politely, realizing that he was looking at someone who could be his sister. She was short and definitely younger than he was. Her hair was the same color as his, but that did not really make her his sister. She had seemed rather friendly. If she were his sister, he was surprised she had answered the door and not some servant. Going back out to where Journeyman Evan stood, Greer took the reins of his horse and told Journeyman Evan that they were to go down the cart path to the second barn. In a way he was relieved he would not be meeting Lord Avital in some formal parlor in the manor house.

Upon arriving at the barn, a young man who was pushing a wheelbarrow full of muck from the barn asked if he could help them. When Greer said he was looking for Lord Avital, the young man pointed over his shoulder and informed them Lord Avital was in the last stall on the left.

"Just tie your horses up over there," the young man stated, indicating a hitching post to the right of the barn door. "Your horses will be alright there. I'll fetch a bucket of water for each of them after I get rid of this load. Might want to keep the dogs out here, so as not to disturb the young mother."

Greer and Journeyman Evan tied their horses up, told both of the dogs to stay, and headed into the barn. The stall gate was open when they arrived, giving them a clear view of the back of a man sitting in the straw, gently brushing his hand over the head of a border dog and talking to it softly.

"There now, little mother, you're almost done. Feels like it's but one more to go. Just one more and you can rest. That's it now, lass . . . ." Her body gave a long shudder, and a pup was delivered. The female border dog made no move to clean the pup up. "Would one of you lads hand me that clean rag that's hanging to the left of the opening you are standing in?"

Greer reached up and grabbed the rag, handing it over. Three things struck him in that moment. One was that the rag he was handing over was of a finer weave of cloth than even the clothes he was wearing. Second was that the man was even aware that they were there, and finally that the man seated on the stable stall floor was a man with the same coloring as himself. He could not tell the man's height since he was sitting down, but he looked to be of average height, certainly not tall like Master Rollag.

Both Greer and Journeyman Evan stood and watched as Lord Avital gently cleaned the last pup and placed it close to its mother so it could begin to nurse. In all there were six pups, and Greer noted that the mother and four of the pups had the same coloring as Kasa, dappled gray with copper and cream markings. The other two were black, with cream, and copper color markings, but were not the very dark variety that was being bred in Høyhauger. These pups were more like the border dogs that Greer had seen at the O'Gara farm.

Once Lord Avital was satisfied that the whelping was done and all of the pups were alright, he pushed himself to his feet, brushing hay from his pants, turned, and took his first good look at the two standing in the opening. Lord Avital just stood there taking a hard look at Greer, and Greer was taking a long look back. Journeyman Evan's quiet "oh my" broke the spell.

"Oh my, indeed," exclaimed Lord Avital, when he found his voice, for he was looking at his own much younger self. There was no doubt in his mind that the young man standing before him was his long lost son, Tal, but there was certainly one way to prove it. "My wife told me that besides the shortness of one leg compared to the other, my son had a rather large brown, well, she called it a splotch of brown, on the top of his right forearm. Do you have such a mark?"

Greer had not thought of that mark in years. When he had lived on the streets of Høyhauger, his whole body was often the color of the splotch, due to the ingrained dirt that came from living on the streets. It was not until his recent good fortune of being able to bathe more frequently that he had once again become aware of it. Greer pushed up his sleeve to reveal the brown mark. When he looked up, he saw tears in Lord Avital's eyes.

"Welcome home, son." With that said, Lord Avital quickly wiped his eyes, cleared his throat several times, and suggested that they head on up to the manor house, for there were others who were anxious to meet Greer. "Now, where are my manners? Please introduce me to your friend." Greer did so.

When the three of them exited the barn, both the dogs rose, and Kasa rushed forward to greet Greer, as if he had been gone for days rather than a few minutes. Greer then introduced Lord Avital to the two border dogs.

"Well, if I hadn't been convinced that you were my son before this, I would be now. Dugghus folk know border dogs, and you certainly have two fine ones here, especially that pup. Now, tell me all about them." And so, from the barn to the manor, Greer did so, finding Lord Avital very easy to talk to.

Journeyman Evan, watching the exchange, realized how very clever Lord Avital was being by engaging Greer in a discussion about Kasa and Louve to pass the time before they reached the manor house. Journeyman Evan had not missed the reference that Lord Avital had given about others being anxious to meet Greer. Even though Seeker Zita had explained that who would be the next head of Dugghus was not always the first born child, that did not mean that Lord Avital's other children might not see Greer as a threat to both the estate and their father's affections.

Even before they reached the door, it was flung open, and the same lass who had answered Greer's knock rushed out. "Is one of them him, papa?

Is one of them my brother? I didn't even think of that when I answered the door. Ooh, and look at that gorgeous pup." All this was said without taking a breath or waiting for an answer.

"Would you like an answer to any of your questions, or would you just like to keep on asking them?" Lord Avital replied, but he was smiling broadly at the lass. "This young gentleman standing next to me is your long lost brother, Tal, but he goes by the name of Greer, and the other young gentleman is Journeyman Evan of the Glassmakers Guild." Turning to Greer, Lord Avital said, "You do not need to make a decision right this minute on what you want to be called. I know you were called Greer in Høyhauger. Speaking of names, this young lady is Dova. You also have another sister and a brother, plus an aunt, my sister, an uncle, and three cousins. Ours has always been a small family in more ways than one. We do not run to any height either, and it comes late. You most likely will eventually reach my height, but probably not much taller. Your mother, may she rest in peace, did not come from a family of tall folks either. Your brother Ersa, who is just a year younger than you, will try to gloat, for he is just a bit taller than you now, but don't let that bother you. Come, let us go in. Bring the dogs. We don't stand much on ceremony here. Dova, run down to the weaving sheds and let your aunt and your brother know that Greer has arrived. I'll let Cook know that there will be two more for dinner."

Journeyman Evan took in his surroundings when he entered the manor house. As houses of nobles went, it was quite modest and looked well lived in. The furnishings were of good quality, but certainly not new or of the latest fashion, like he had seen in the capital. The manor house was obviously well maintained and well cared for, but not overly ornate. The manor house struck Journeyman Evan as one that was a home. He had also noticed that the barns and outbuildings were well maintained and cared for. This was an estate that put its effort and coin back into the estate, unlike others he had visited where the ruling noble only put a minimum of the profits back into the estate and spent the earnings on fripperies and pretensions.

An older woman came down the main hall, wiping her hands on her apron. Lord Avital addressed her as Mistress Malfreda, the housekeeper, and asked if the rooms were ready. She assured him they were, and she would send a lad down to bring the young gentlemen's possessions up.

"Now mind you, young man, I lost the battle long ago about having dogs in the house, but know that there are always rags at the door to wipe their feet. I will not tolerate paw prints on my clean floors. Is that clear?"

"Yes ma'am," Greer answered.

Lord Avital had leaned over and whispered to them that her bark was worse than her bite, and she had retorted that she had heard what he said. It was a friendly byplay that Journeyman Evan thought had been done a number of times before.

Another lass came rushing down the central stairs, admonishing her father the whole way. "You said you would call me when the pups started coming. Tutor would have let me out of my studies."

"Tutor would have had my head if I pulled you away during your appointed study time for even so important an event as the birth of pups, which you have already seen more than once. Now mind your manners and come meet your brother. Greer, this is your sister Talsia, although you may not want to claim her. She can be a pest," Lord Avital declared as he hugged his daughter.

Talsia made protesting sounds, but Greer could see there was a great deal of affection between the two. Watching the interaction between his father and his sister, Greer wondered if he would fit in here, if he would ever be that comfortable around his new found relatives. His thoughts were interrupted when a woman, who was just a bit younger than Lord Avital, entered the manor house, followed closely by a young man not much younger than Greer.

The woman approached Greer and took both of his hands. "Let me take a look at you. There is no doubt in my mind that you are my nephew. If there were any in yours, you have to but look at your brother Ersa."

Greer looked over the woman's shoulder and was struck silent, for standing behind her was a young man who bore a striking resemblance to Greer.

The words out of Ersa's mouth shocked Greer. "Thank goodness, you are here. Now you can take over learning all the boring bookkeeping stuff and selling and trading, and I can get on with the business of becoming a better and more renowned weaver than my aunt here. You don't have aspirations to learn to weave, do you?"

"I have no idea."

"There is no rush to choose a life path at this very moment," Lord Avital chuckled. "Let's give Greer time to find out if he even likes sheep and all that goes into the wool business. First things first, Ersa. Why don't you take your brother upstairs to his room and get him settled? Also show Journeyman Evan the guest room. Dinner will be in about an hour, so make sure you are at least washed up. I need to meet with your uncle for a little while, so you all will have to excuse me."

Greer discovered that his aunt was still holding his hands. "It's good that you would come. No one would blame you if you did not want to come here after hearing your mother gave you away. Do not think too poorly of her. She was a good woman. I hope you will stay. It would mean so much to your father, who has been so adrift this past year. I am sure you must be a bit overwhelmed, but give us time. We will grow on you."

Greer could only nod. Here this woman was worried he would not stay, and he was worried that they would not want him. She then dropped his hands and gathered him in a hug, which brought a lump to his throat. She quickly released him and suggested that he better scoot, if he wanted to get settled in before dinner.

The next few days flew by, filled with activity. Lord Avital seemed determined to show Greer and Journeyman Evan every square inch of the estate and introduce them to everyone who lived in the valley. Each night Greer had crawled into bed too exhausted to do anything other than drop his clothes on the floor, get into his night shirt, and literally fall into bed.

After Greer and Journeyman Evan had been in Dugghus for a little under a week, Journeyman Evan announced at dinner that he would be leaving the morning after next, for much as he was enjoying being there, he needed to be on his way to attend to Glassmaker Guild business. He wondered if he might spend some time alone with Greer before he departed. No one had objected, so the next day Greer and Journeyman Evan rode off into the hills, followed closely by the two border dogs. Once they were far enough away from the manor house at the top of a high hill that overlooked the valley, Journeyman Evan called a halt and dismounted. Greer followed.

"This looks like a good spot to stop and sit awhile," Journeyman Evan told Greer. The two settled on the grass, and the border dogs lay down at their feet. "First things first. I think Louve should stay with you and Kasa. She seems suited to this place, as do you."

"Do you think so?" questioned Greer, and Journeyman Evan knew he was not talking about the border dog.

"This family was ready to welcome you before you arrived, and I have seen no change of heart in the week we have been here. You will fit in here as much as you let yourself fit in. Your sisters have already begun teasing you, which is a good sign that they consider you to be part of the family. Your brother whistles his way out the door on the way to the weaving sheds. I think you may have a knack for the selling and trading part of the family business. Those skills you honed in Høyhauger could give you an edge in that area. You read folks well, and certainly know a bit about scams and underhanded trading practices, which will steer you clear of unscrupulous folk. How are you feeling?"

"Honestly?"

"Honestly."

"Pretty overwhelmed, but oddly enough content. I feel welcomed here, like maybe I belong, and I have never felt I belonged anywhere before. If nothing else, they will keep me around because they really want Kasa to stay."

"Yah, right. Just going to keep you around because of the border dog," Journeyman Evan said, giving his friend a playful punch in the arm.

The two spent the rest of the afternoon sitting on the hill, sometimes talking and sometimes in comfortable silence. All too soon, they headed back down. The next morning Greer said a reluctant farewell to his friend, who promised to write. He stood on the steps of the manor house, watching Journeyman Evan go until he could no longer see him, and then turned and headed back inside.

Greer's father was there at the door when he entered and placed a comforting hand on his shoulder. Lord Avital did not say anything for a moment, and then said, "Son, I think we had best get down to the barn and check on those pups, don't you? Better alert your sister, the pest, or she will complain to anyone who will listen that she was not included.

193

PART TWO

CHAPTER THIRTY-ONE

Sometimes Meryl felt like a character out of a children's tale, the one where the mother marries the wicked stepfather, and then the mother dies. The lass is then left tending the house for the wicked stepfather and his two nose picking, belching, farting, oafish sons, except Meryl was tending the family business while those three just raked in the profits and did little of the work. Now, truth be told, while, sadly, her mother had passed away after a brief illness, her stepfather was a kind man, and his two sons were only mildly oafish and only belched, farted, and picked their noses occasionally. At least she got to get away from them for weeks at a time, which was a relief.

No, the problem was not with her stepfather or her two stepbrothers. No, the problem was with Fordon, their cousin, who had come to live with them six months ago. His parents had died in a farm accident, and after all was said and done, it turned out that there was nothing left but debts on their farm. Fordon was an only child, and his uncle, Meryl's stepfather, had kindly offered to take him in. Fordon was a little bandy rooster of a young man, who was all charming and smiles when anyone was around, but Meryl had seen him flash a look of loathing towards her stepfather when Fordon had not known she was watching. In addition, she had seen him being cruel towards the messenger bird roost cats, who kept the vermin out of the bird seed, and had seen him deliberately drop eggs and smash them underfoot, all the while protesting it had been an accident.

Meryl could maybe dismiss his actions towards the cats as being those of someone who was genuinely afraid of, or just did not like, cats, but destroying eggs on purpose was not something she could dismiss so easily. Those eggs were what paid the bills.

Meryl's family was in the messenger bird business. They raised, transported, and cared for messenger birds all over Sommerhjem. No matter where in Sommerhjem one released a messenger bird, it immediately flew to its home roost, the roost where it had hatched. The only drawback was once a messenger bird was released and flew to its home roost, it had to be transported back to the folk who had sent the message.

Meryl's family business had regular routes to return messenger birds to their home roosts and to supply new nesting pairs to roosts that had become depleted. Quick communication was often needed between outlying areas and the capital, and messenger birds were still the fastest way of getting information about the country, especially for the more isolated estates, or for someone who was traveling. Certainly for more massive missives, the royal post worked, but for quick communication, the messenger birds were the most efficient.

Because Meryl seemed to be especially adept at settling new breeding pairs into roosts, she often traveled and had recently returned from Glendalen Keep. When she had joined Lady Hadrack of Glendalen Keep's caravan to travel back to the capital, little had she known that she would be traveling in the company of someone who was carrying a piece of the oppgave ringe. He had seemed like such an unpretentious, even shy, young man. Meryl had made sure she had been at the Well of Speaking when he had placed the ring in the box embedded in the sea wall. She was glad she had gone, for seeing that beautiful light rise high out of the box, spreading out until it enveloped the young man, was a sight she would not soon forget. She had wondered what it would be like to be the center of attention of so many folks. Once the hoopla had died down, Meryl had not heard anything more about the ring bearer. A brief flash of fame and then back to obscurity, she had thought to herself.

This day she had other things on her mind. While she had been away, the rest of the family was to have been looking after the messenger bird roost and taking care of the messenger birds. Her two stepbrothers had made a half-hearted attempt to take care of the messenger birds, but in her mind, the place was in shambles. When she had complained to her stepfather, he had seemed surprised and had tried to suggest she was over reacting. She finally convinced him to accompany her to the roost, where he had to admit she had a point.

"Look at the mess. They didn't change the bedding, they only partially swept up the spillage, and they didn't scrub down the perches. The water dishes probably haven't been cleaned since I last did them, and one of the grain bins has moldy grain. Any, or all, of these things can cause the messenger birds to become sick, and then where would we be?" Meryl had asked, exasperation clear in her voice. "In addition, several of the messenger birds were not in their cages but were flying around in the rafters. Someone either didn't open the cages properly or didn't close them properly. Fortunately, the messenger birds know me and allowed me to put them back."

Meryl's stepfather looked about and had the good grace to look abashed. "I apologize. I should have kept a closer eye on the lads. I'll have a talk with them."

"Maybe we should hire and train someone to do the work when I'm away. Someone who might actually want to care for the messenger birds. Mistress Moncha's third daughter Theary has always been interested in the messenger birds, and I know they could use a little extra income. She is already half trained, for she spends time here with me helping when she is not needed at home."

"Ah, well, now, I don't know as we need to go that far."

"Either the lads need to step up and take good care of the messenger birds, or you need to hire someone to do it, because if this keeps up, we will not have a family business. Anyone coming here to see if they want our messenger birds, who has even a speck of knowledge about messenger birds and their care, would turn right around and walk right out after seeing our roost. Of course, I'm assuming the messenger birds haven't already picked up some illness due to my stepbrothers' neglect."

Meryl's stepfather had rejected her suggestion to get and train a helper. Instead he had suggested that she should train Fordon into her away-from-home duties, and then she could stay home and tend to the messenger birds at the home roost herself. That had been a month ago, which is why she now found herself traveling with Fordon and trying to teach him what to do when they delivered messenger birds. He just did not seem to understand why they could not just drop the messenger birds off and move on, no matter how many times she tried to explain it. She could not get it into his head that, besides returning the messenger birds, they also needed to make sure the messenger birds in the roost they were visiting were in good health, talk to the keeper of the messenger birds to make sure there were not any problems, and help settle in a new pair, if that is what they had brought. They also needed to discuss breeding needs and collect records.

It had quickly become clear to Meryl that her stepfather's solution to the problems back home were not going to be solved by her being there. Fordon was not working out. Her stepfather had known she was not thrilled with his solution, so he would be hard to convince that her reasons why Fordon was not suited for the job were not just excuses for her to keep it herself. At least this journey was almost at an end. Just one more stop, which they should reach in the late afternoon, and then they would be heading back to the capital.

The area they were traveling through was one of Meryl's favorites. The possibility that she might have a chance to spot a griff falcon soaring above the high rocky bluffs made it doubly so. Griff falcons were very rare birds which were almost never seen outside of the high hills or mountain forests, but a lone griff falcon had been spotted in the area for the last year.

When Meryl and Fordon had stopped to have lunch, Fordon had taken out his long bow and checked the straightness of an arrow. It was a disturbing sight for Meryl because Fordon often would shoot at some bird or animal just for the fun of it, as opposed to only shooting at living creatures who would provide food. Killing just for the sport of it was something Meryl was very against.

"Why don't you put that away? We certainly don't need any game to fill our pot, for we'll be eating at Klippedal this night. They always send me off well provisioned when I leave."

"Why don't you just shut your yap? Always nattering on about stupid birds or animals. I'll hunt me what I want. You want to try to stop me?"

Meryl did not know why she had even brought the subject up, for she would get further talking to a rock than talking to Fordon. Could this trip be any more of a disaster than it had already been? Fordon was helpful at their stops only when there was someone else around. When no one was looking on, he would insolently lean against a wall, cleaning his fingernails with his knife. No amount of urging would get him to help, unless of course someone came into where they were working. He had also expected her to wait on him hand and foot when they were stopped for the noon meal. She had disabused him of that notion early on in their trip by making herself something to eat and suggesting that, unless he wanted to skip the noon meal, he might as well get up and make himself something. She was glad that she had insisted that they stay at the small country inns along the way instead of camping, for she had visions of him standing against a tree cleaning his nails while she set up camp and did all the cooking. One thing that could be said for Fordon was he had very clean nails.

As Meryl bent over to take something out of her pack, the locket, the only thing she had left of her mother's, slipped out of her shirt and glinted in the sun. Fordon was standing only a few feet away from her. He quickly crossed over to her and grabbed the locket, breaking the chain when she abruptly straightened up.

"Now look what you've done! Give it back to me."

Fordon thought it was great fun to tease Meryl, so he hopped up on a tall rock and dangled the locket just out of reach, swinging it back and forth. His cruel laughter filled the small clearing. Suddenly, there was the sound of wings, and a tyvfugl bird swooped in and snatched the locket right out of Fordon's hand.

Meryl just sank to the earth and tried not to cry. The locket was well and truly gone now, for tyvfugl birds were thieves and especially attracted to shiny objects. Her locket would end up somewhere in the high bluffs above them in a cache with other objects that particular tyvfugl bird had filched.

"Ah, it weren't worth much anyway. I'll probably have to get you a new one 'cause you're going to whine to Uncle, aren't you?" Feeling like he had taken care of the matter, Fordon turned his attention to rummaging in the food pack for something to eat for the noon meal.

Meryl just sat where she was, entertaining thoughts of boiling Fordon in oil, or wishing dragons were real and she could offer him up to one for lunch. Maybe . . . but no, she would do none of those things. The idea of staying home to tend to the roost and sending Fordon off where he might be set upon by bandits, or pressed into service as a cabin lad and lost at sea, was beginning to have some appeal. Sitting there wishing was not accomplishing anything, including making her feel better. Abandoning her job to go off and climb the cliffs trying to find the tyvfugl's hidey-hole would be like trying to find a needle in a haystack. No, there was nothing to be done but to check on the messenger birds, make sure they had some feed and water, and then try to eat something before they took to the road again. Could this day get any worse, Meryl thought to herself.

Standing up and bending to brush off the seat of her pants, Meryl saw a large shadow pass across the clearing. Looking up, she saw a griff falcon slowly circle overhead. The sorrow over the loss of her mother's locket was diminished somewhat upon seeing the beauty of the magnificent bird.

Folks could only wish to see even one in a lifetime. Not only was she having a chance to see the sun glisten off the gold of the griff falcon's wings and the brilliant red of her tail feathers, but she was gliding so low that Meryl could see the startling green of her eyes. She looked to be a young one, not yet grown to her mature size. Meryl was so caught up in the awe of seeing a griff falcon that she was not aware of what Fordon was doing.

Fordon did not see a beautiful rare bird in flight. He did not feel awe, but greed. He knew what the feathers, beak, and talons of a griff falcon would bring in some places. Always looking for a way to make a fast bit of coin, he silently backed over to their wagon, where he had leaned his bow. Stealthily taking an arrow from his quiver, he notched his bow, and raised it.

Something in his actions alerted Meryl, for she turned just as Fordon was drawing back his bow string. Rushing across the clearing, Meryl knocked into Fordon just as he released the arrow. Meryl looked up in horror and watched the arrow fly through the tip of the griff falcon's wing. The bird faltered momentarily, screamed, and then plunged into the trees surrounding the clearing.

"Are yah crazy?" Fordon yelled at Meryl. "Whatcha do that for? I could've had her. Now who knows where she is."

"Am I crazy? That was a griff falcon!" Meryl yelled back in disgust, so angry she felt like hitting someone. So she did just that and hit Fordon several times on his chest.

Fordon batted away her flailing hands and gave her an angry shove, sending Meryl stumbling backward. The force of Fordon's shove, combined with tripping over his pack, caused her to fall. Unable to break her fall, Meryl hit the ground hard, and her head struck a large rock.

The clearing was filled only with the sound of Fordon's harsh breathing as he looked at Meryl lying so still and unmoving. It was when he saw a trickle of blood slowly slipping down the rock Meryl's head lay on that he began to panic. He quickly threw his bow and quiver into the wagon and grabbed the food pack. He was about to put it in the wagon too, but then thought better of it. After all, there were several others in the wagon.

A plan began to form in Fordon's mind. He would make it look like Meryl had camped here. He could tell Uncle that Meryl had taken off on her own, and if anyone found this site, they would think she had tripped, fallen, and hit her head. That is, if anyone found her before the scavenger animals did. It was an accident, he told himself, just a tragic accident.

Uncle and the lads might be a little sad that she was gone, but not for long. Besides, it served her right, making him miss the griff falcon.

Putting his plan in motion, Fordon concluded it would look better if she had a food pack and her gear. As quickly as he could, he constructed a lean-to, dug a fire ring, and stacked some wood in it so it looked like it was ready to light. Fordon set Meryl's gear in the lean-to and stepped back to survey the scene. Now, all he had left to do was relieve her of her coin pouch and he could be on his way.

CHAPTER THIRTY-TWO

It was close to dusk when the griff falcon noticed a stirring in the lass, who had lain so still all afternoon. The griff falcon had been hard-pressed to keep the scavenger birds away. A soft groan came from the lass, and her hand moved from her side to her head.

Meryl touched her head and felt stickiness in her hair. She also felt the huge lump underneath. She knew for sure that her head hurt like the dickens, but for the life of her, she could not remember what a dickens was. Meryl knew her name was Meryl, but she could not remember much else. Everything was very hazy. Something about a golden locket and a tyvfugl bird. Something about a griff falcon. Nothing about who she was, or where she was.

Well, I cannot continue to lie on the ground, she thought to herself, and managed to get herself up on her hands and knees, pausing in that position to let the dizziness pass. Meryl raised her head and looked into a pair of bright green eyes. It took her a minute to focus, and when she did, she found herself looking at a griff falcon. They just stared at each other for a few seconds, and then the griff falcon launched herself upward, somewhat awkwardly, and landed on the roof of a small lean-to. Meryl tried to follow the griff falcon's flight, but turning her head was very painful.

Since standing up did not seem to be a really good option, Meryl crawled towards the lean-to, sensing shelter might be a good idea. As she crawled, she slowly took in her surroundings. Small clearing. Fire pit dug and firewood laid. Lean-to with bags within. I must have set up camp here, she thought to herself. I wonder if I am alone? How did I get this lump on my head? The effort it took to get herself to the lean-to took every ounce of energy Meryl had, and once there, she passed out again.

When she awoke, it was to the scream of the griff falcon and the sound of several pairs of wings beating in hasty retreat. The scream hurt her head, which she grabbed with both hands. It had grown darker since Meryl had reached the lean-to, and while other things might be hazy, knowing how to survive on the road was not one of them. She needed to get a fire going, and while she did not feel hungry, it seemed she should eat.

Rummaging in her pack, Meryl found her fire starter and soon had a small blaze going. In the light of the fire, she took stock of what was in the lean-to. Her pack was of medium size and held several changes of clothes, a warm cloak, all of which were on the bottom of the pack. The top of the pack held all types of items having to do with the care of birds. Meryl did not know why she knew that, but she did. In addition to her pack, there was a blanket roll and a small food pack. Fortunately, animals had not gotten into the food pack while she had been unconscious. In the food pack were several small pots, a cup, and some utensils. Unfortunately, there was not a great deal of food, which was worrisome. Going back to her pack, Meryl looked through the bundle that held herbs and salves, hoping to find something to cut through the pounding headache. Finding nothing in her pack, she searched through the food pack and found a packet of soothing tea. Now, why do I know that and not know where I am, or how I got here, she asked herself.

Fortunately, in the back dark corner of the lean-to, Meryl spotted a water bag. There was not much in it, but enough to make a cup of tea. Meryl did not feel as if she had the strength to go crawling around looking for a water source, but she knew she would need to find one the next day. Moving very cautiously, Meryl straightened her body until she was kneeling and shuffled over on her knees to place the small pot on the coals. As she did so, she saw something move out of the corner of her eye and was surprised that it was the griff falcon. How unusual, she thought to herself. Why had she not flown off? Why was she still here? When she looked more closely at the griff falcon, she realized her right wing did not look quite right. A number of the feathers had been sheared off. No wonder the griff falcon had flown strangely. While the damage to the feathers would not keep the griff falcon from flying, it would impede soaring on the updrafts. It would also limit the griff falcon's hunting ability, for they were known to silently soar overhead and then drop, plunging straight down, drawing up at the last minute to grab their prey with their talons.

"Well, we make a fine pair, don't we?" stated Meryl. "Both of us banged up." Meryl was surprised that the griff falcon did not take off at the sound of her voice. "I should offer you some dinner, would only be polite, but all I have is some bread and cheese. Oh, and some deer jerky."

Meryl tentatively held out a small bit of jerky she had snapped off, and the griff falcon gently took it from her outstretched hand. Meryl rocked back slowly onto her heels, awed.

For some reason it seemed important to Meryl that she should try to find a name for the griff falcon. The name Tashi floated through her mind and seemed to fit. When Meryl addressed the griff falcon as Tashi, Meryl could have sworn that the griff falcon nodded her head, as if that were her name. That could not be, Meryl thought to herself. This bump on my head is causing me to see things that are not there.

Meryl tried to eat a little, but she was plumb out of energy. She finished her tea, banked the fire, crawled back into the lean-to, and curled up in her blanket roll. The last thing she remembered before falling into a restless sleep was the griff falcon coming into the lean-to and perching on her pack.

The call of nature woke Meryl in the early morning. When she tried to stand up, she had to grab the lean-to, almost pulling it down. Once she got her feet under her, she took a few tentative steps and found that while her head hurt, the dizziness had passed.

Once back at the campsite, Meryl had a chance to take stock of where she was. She was in a small clearing that bordered on a narrow lane. She did not know where the lane led, but some sense of danger made her reluctant to follow the lane in either direction. The one memory that stuck clearly in her head was that of a golden locket. It was important, that much she knew. But how was she to find it? A tyvfugl bird had it, and she had to get it back. Looking around, Meryl could see the bluffs above the trees and convinced herself that that is where she would find the locket. That she was in no shape to try climbing cliffs never entered into her muzzy thinking.

<hr/>

Fordon was having second thoughts about what to do next. He had taken the messenger birds to Klippedal and could now head back to the capital, but he needed to make sure Meryl was well and truly dead. He should have checked before he had abandoned her in that clearing, but he had panicked. If she were not dead, he could be in a great deal of trouble.

Besides, maybe he should not have been so hasty. After all, he thought to himself, he had not gone through her pack or checked if she had had any other valuables on her besides the locket. With those thoughts in mind, he made the half day's journey back to the place where he and Meryl had stopped for the noon meal, only to find it empty, except for the lean-to and the cold remains of a fire in the fire pit.

This is not good, Fordon thought. This is not good at all. Had someone come along and found Meryl, buried her and her belongings, or buried her and taken her belongings? Was there anything in her belongings that would tell who they belonged to? Fordon frantically searched the surrounding area for a grave but could find none. He could find no indication that the scavenger birds and animals had disposed of Meryl, either. The only conclusion he could come to was that Meryl was not dead. He had to find her, and either finish the job or convince her somehow that he had not meant to harm her and had gone for help. Part of that was true, anyway.

Fordon searched the clearing one more time, trying to figure out which way she had gone. He had not seen her on the way back to the clearing from Klippedal, so unless she had hidden somewhere while he rode by, he did not think she had gone that way. He did not think that was likely, for once past this stretch of bluffs, the land was pretty open. He could see no indication that she had taken the lane, no footprints appeared in the soft dirt, nor could he see where she might have left the glen. If it had been him, he thought, he would have headed down the lane. Whether or not she had, he needed to, for he either had to catch up with her or get to the capital before she did with a plausible story for his uncle. If she did not show up after several weeks, Fordon knew a good tracker he could hire to pick up her trail and, for a little extra, make sure Meryl did not show up back home.

⁂

It had not taken Meryl long to pack her meager belongings and consolidate the food pack into her personal pack. She had tied her blanket roll on the top of the pack and slung the nearly empty water bag strap across her chest. After making sure the fire was cold, Meryl just stood in the clearing, trying to get her bearings in the early morning light. She was snapped out of her reverie by the sound of wings and looked over to see the griff falcon she had named Tashi making the short flight from the top of the lean-to to the top of a medium size rock halfway across the clearing. Tashi landed facing the bluffs, turned and looked over her shoulder, swung her head twice towards the bluffs, and then flew the short distance to a tree at the edge of the clearing, where she landed and waited.

Since Meryl had come to from hitting her head on the rock, the one constant had been the griff falcon. The only other companion had been confusion. Meryl knew her name. She knew how to take care of herself, but beyond that Meryl knew nothing else, except for the constant feeling that she was in danger. To stay here was not likely to be a good choice. Tashi seemed to be waiting. For what, Meryl wondered. Tashi moved her head back towards Meryl and then forward, twice again, and Meryl felt the griff falcon was indicating that they should go towards the bluffs. With no better plan in mind, and with the image of the golden locket still one of the few memories Meryl could hold on to, she decided to follow Tashi. Meryl still had enough wits about her to step carefully, so as to not leave a trail. Once Tashi saw that Meryl was coming her way, she flew a little deeper into the woods.

And so, as the morning wore on, Meryl would almost catch up with Tashi, and then Tashi would fly a short distance ahead, always remaining in sight. The two followed the base of the bluff for several hours before they came upon a natural spring welling up and flowing into a small basin at the foot of the bluff. Meryl halted, and using her hands, scooped up the ice cold water, and took a long drink. Once she had slaked her thirst, she filled her water bag. When she stood up, Meryl noticed Tashi was perched on a low branch not far from the spring. Meryl stood back, and the griff falcon glided down and took her time drinking from the spring.

Meryl broke the silence by quietly talking to the griff falcon. "So, Tashi, were you as thirsty as I was? Do you think we could stop for a little while? My head is beginning to throb, and I'm a bit hungry." To Meryl's surprise, Tashi nodded her head. "That would be a 'yes' then?" Tashi nodded her head again.

Meryl sat down on the closest rock. Somewhere in the fog that was her mind she thought she remembered that griff falcons were considered highly intelligent. Now where had that thought come from, she wondered. All morning it had been like that. Just snatches of memory here and there, but nothing she could string together.

Meryl looked over the meager amount of food she had in her pack and tore off a small amount of bread. After unwrapping the cheese, she only took a small slice. She gave Tashi several narrow strips of jerky. While she was chewing slowly, Meryl took time to really look at the griff falcon's wing that had been damaged. An image came to her of an arrow going through the tip of the wing, but when she tried to remember more, the thought was lost back into the fog.

"Would you let me look at your wing?" Meryl asked Tashi, as she approached the griff falcon slowly.

Much to Meryl's surprise, Tashi held out her wing. Very gently, Meryl ran her hands over the wing. No bones were broken, and the arrow had not gone through the flesh of the wing, so there was not a wound to contend with. The only problem seemed to be the feathers that had been sheared off, and only the growth of new feathers would eliminate that problem.

"Trimming the broken feathers would help. Would you allow me to do that?"

The griff falcon remained where she was while Meryl turned and walked back to her pack. She opened it and pulled out a leather-wrapped package, untied the ties, and rolled the package open. Taking out a very finely crafted and very sharp scissors, Meryl turned and headed back towards Tashi. The griff falcon spread the damaged wing out towards Meryl and held it there. Had there been anyone nearby who had caught sight of the two, they would have been astonished to see a young griff falcon allowing a young woman to trim her feathers.

Meryl could only wonder if she were still unconscious or dreaming. Somehow she did not think what she was doing at the moment was something commonplace, or something she did every day. On the other hand, how did she know that what she was doing was the correct thing to do for the griff falcon? How could she know how to do this, and not know who she was?

Chapter Thirty-Three

By the middle of the afternoon, Meryl was not sure she would be able to take one more step. The rocky path they had been following along the edge of the bluff had been steadily climbing upward through the thick trees. Her headache had shifted from a dull throb to a constant pounding. *There must be a wee, small, very enthusiastic Günnary miner inside my head with a giant pickax hammering away,* she thought to herself.

"Tashi, I need to stop. I need to rest."

The griff falcon, who had landed on a low branch just ahead of Meryl, rose up, stretched her wings out, and fanned them twice in an agitated manner. Then she turned and launched herself off the branch and flew farther up the trail.

"Tashi, please, my head is killing me. I need to stop."

The griff falcon answered Meryl's plea with a scream, which shot like an arrow through Meryl's already aching head. Tashi then turned and flew another few feet up the trail and screamed again. Meryl was not sure which was worse. Her pounding head and growing fatigue, or her pounding head, growing fatigue, and the piercing ache caused by Tashi's screams. She needed to stop the screaming, so Meryl began to walk again. The rest of the afternoon crawled slowly by in a haze alternating between sheer misery and shooting pain.

It was very late afternoon when Meryl tripped over the threshold of the doorway of a forester's shelter and had just enough wits about her to put out her hands to break her fall. Landing hard on the wooden floor jarred her shoulders and neck and sent her spiraling downward into unconsciousness. It was there, near dawn, that Finn found her.

"Oh, well. Oh dear, dear, dear. Oh, well, yes, it's a good thing you came and found me," Finn said, addressing the griff falcon. "Oh dear, yes indeed. My, my, my. What to do? What to do? Best get her up off the floor, me thinks. Yes, that's a good idea. Get her up off the floor, oh yes indeed. Get her warm and snug, snug and warm. That's what I'll do first."

Meryl woke slowly, aware that not only did her head throb, but her knees and hands did too. She was also aware of a nutty porridge smell and decided she was dreaming. She could not recall ever having a dream where she could smell something, but then, she was having a bit of trouble with her memory, she thought ruefully. I must be home, she thought, but then, when she tried to get a clearer picture of what her home was like, or at least her room, she could not picture either place. Thinking of home caused a huge feeling of loss to overwhelm her, but she did not understand why. As Meryl came more and more awake, she realized that the porridge smell had increased, and her stomach growled in answer.

"Ah, good, good, good, you're awake. I was really beginning to worry, worry, worry. Now, no harm here, no harm here," Finn said as Meryl started. "Won't hurt you, no, won't hurt you. You need to move slowly, slowly. Yes indeed, indeed, with that lump, that bump on your head. Been worried, for you have slept for a whole night and day, a whole night and day!"

Meryl looked at the odd little man who was talking to her. At first she thought it was poor lighting that made him look like he was a dappled moonlit shadow, but then, she realized he was mostly varying shades of grey. His hair was a wispy silver grey and stuck up every which way on his head. His face was covered by a scraggly grey beard and lined with age. His clothing had grey splotches of varying shades across its very wrinkled surface. His boots may have once been black, but they were scuffed and covered with grey dust. Even his deep sunken eyes were grey.

"Take your time sitting up. Slow, slow, slow. You've got a nasty bump, nasty lump. No, don't get up. Just prop yourself on the pillows, and I'll bring food, bring food," he said, as he scurried over to the small fire that was burning in the fireplace.

Meryl sat up, slowly, as instructed, and took the time to look about. She was in a small crudely-built hut, not much more than a shell of a building, holding the bunk bed she was lying on, a small table and two chairs, the fireplace, several trunks, and one very sturdy metal-clad box. The two small windows that flanked the door held no glass, and their shutters were open at the moment, letting in a cool breeze. The odd little man approached, holding a wooden bowl and a spoon.

"Nothing fancy now, but it will stick to your ribs. Yes indeed, stick to your ribs. Eat it slow, slow now. No rush, no, no rush."

Meryl did as the little man had suggested and found the nutty porridge tasty and filling. Surprisingly, after she had eaten about half the contents of the bowl, she realized that her head hurt less than when she had awakened. The odd little man had left the hut right after he had handed her the bowl and returned just as she finished it, carrying two water bags.

"Excuse me, sir, but who are you, and where are we?" Meryl asked. She realized that even without knowing the answers to either of those two questions, she did not feel afraid of the odd little man. Her previous sense of danger had lessened, or at the very least, not increased.

"Beggin' your pardon, young miss, I have been remiss, been remiss. I am Finn. We are in one of the forester's shelters scattered about the forest. Yes indeed, one of the forester's shelters. They build them about the forest to provide shelter for themselves and for those who might get lost, get lost."

Meryl was getting used to Finn's habit of repeating words or phrases. "Are you a forester?" she asked.

"Oh, my no, oh no, not me. A finder, that's what I call meself, yes, a finder."

"A finder?"

"I hunts, I do, I hunts for hidden things, lost things you know, you know. I finds them, I do, I finds them."

Well, he has certainly found one lost thing, Meryl thought to herself. Me. Her thoughts were interrupted by Finn's question.

"You have a name? Yes, yes?"

"Meryl."

"You are not from here, no, no. You come from where, where?"

"I wish I knew," Meryl said fervently. "The bump on my head seems to have knocked most of my memories out. I know my name, and how to care for myself, but little else. I suspect I used to know a lot about birds, but it is all pretty muzzy at the moment."

"Not to worry, not to worry. Old Finn is a finder, a finder. Maybe he can even find memories, memories." The little man giggled, made small snorting sounds, and did a few shuffling steps, while hitting his thigh with his hand. "You stick with me for a while. Alright, alright?"

"Do you live around here?" Meryl asked.

"Why no, no. Just traveling through, just traveling through."

"So, you just happened upon me?"

"Not really, not really. It was the griff falcon you see, you see. Drove me down off the bluffs she did, she did. Never seen the like. No, never did. Herded me here just like I was a sheep, just herded me here. Very insistent, very persistent. Been sittin' just outside, it has. Just sittin'. Snared me a rabbit I did, plump rabbit. Gave the griff falcon some. Ate like she was starving, starving."

"She probably was. Her wing is damaged just enough to make hunting difficult, and she has been with me since I woke up from the fall where I hit my head. At least, that is what I think happened. About the fall I mean, not Tashi's wing. That's what I call the griff falcon, Tashi." Meryl stopped talking, for she realized she was babbling. She was also very, very tired and could not hold back a yawn.

"Now you rest, you rest. Storms coming, yes indeed, a rather nasty storm, nasty storm. I need to get back to my camp and break it down, break it down. Be gone a couple of hours, couple of hours, so you rest. There's water in the bag hung by the door, cool spring water in the bag. You rest now," Finn murmured to himself, for he saw that the lass Meryl was asleep.

Finn worried about the lass as he walked swiftly along. He also was worried about his camp. He had never left it unattended overnight before and hoped the wildlife had not moved in or torn it apart. He hoped Heber, his little donkey, was alright too. That griff falcon sure had been determined to get him to the forester's shelter. He had never seen one act like that before. The griff falcons were very elusive and rarely seen up close, and yet here was one driving him off the bluffs and basically herding him where she wanted him to go. Finn had seen a lot of strange things in his years of wandering, but that had to be one of the strangest.

It took him longer than he thought it would to reach where he had set up camp. He was relieved to find his donkey was right where he had left him, and the rest of the camp looked undisturbed. In fact, he mused to himself, it looked cleaner somehow, or neater, or something. He could not put his finger on it. As he began to gather his gear, he also began to notice little things. The strap on his pack he had been meaning to mend had been mended. The end of Heber's lead rope, which had come unraveled, had been woven back together and neatly wrapped so it would no longer unravel. His meager collection of pots and cups had been cleaned and polished. Finn could only scratch his head in wonder. Had someone been there, used his camp for the night, and done all this as thanks? Standing there with his mouth hanging open, wondering, was not going to get him back to the shelter before the storm broke, and if his aching bones were any indication, it was going to be a doozy of a storm.

Maybe it was his good fortune that the griff falcon had made him go to the forester's shelter. He had to admit he lost all track of time when he was hunting on the bluffs. He might have been out there this day and not paid attention to the weather. He and the donkey would have been caught out in the storm right enough. When Finn had picked this campsite, he had known a forester's shelter was somewhere around here, but really could not recall how far it was from his camp. It had been a couple of years since he had been this way. While some might think that forests and bluffs are always the same, they would be sadly mistaken. Nature rearranged the landscape on a regular basis.

After checking his snares and traps and relieving them of their catches, Finn untied the rope from a nearby tree where he had hung his food pack and lowered it down. He had learned early on in his younger days that wild animals were not polite when it came to food packs and were not above helping themselves. While he liked nuts and berries in season as well as the next man, he also liked his warm honey-drizzled biscuits on occasion. Tightening the straps that held his gear to the donkey, Finn picked up the lead rope and began the walk back to the forester's shelter. He had draped an oilcloth tarp over everything before he had tied it down, for his donkey was not one to hurry along. Finn was concerned they would not make the shelter before the skies opened up. The rumble of thunder was growing closer, and that had quickened Heber's pace a bit.

"Come on, come on, you stubborn beast, 'less you wants to get wet, get wet. There's a storm comin', yes, a storm is comin', and you don't want to be out in it."

Whether it was his urging, or the rolling thunder that felt like it was right on top of them, soon both he and the donkey were moving at a ground covering pace. That also might have been caused by the increased howl of the wind, or the fact that the trees were swaying back and forth in a rather frightening manner. Whatever the reason, Finn was grateful for Heber's cooperation, and they arrived at the shelter just as the first few drops of rain began to fall. Meryl was standing in the doorway when they arrived, and with her help, they made short work of unloading his gear. Fortunately, there was a sturdy lean-to attached to the back of the shelter that had been built as a stall to house several horses. Finn tucked Heber in with some water and grain. By the time he had the donkey settled, he could hear that the storm was gearing up, so he raced through the increasingly heavy downpour and got himself inside the shelter.

"Just made it, we did, just made it. This storm is going to be a gully washer, a gully washer it is," Finn said, as he removed his dripping rain cloak and hung it by the door. "Glad I am of this shelter, yes indeed, yes indeed. Ah, I see you've been up and about, up and about. Busy too."

When Meryl had awakened, she had taken the time to carefully check out where she was staying. The forester's hut was simple, but sturdily built. She discovered the wooden boxes contained bedding and other supplies, and the metal chest contained canned and dried food. Certainly stocked for survival, should one need it. Besides checking out the inside of the shelter, she had also explored the surrounding area. Meryl found that bending over, collecting dry wood, and breaking it up was alright, as long as she did not move her head or stand up too quickly. She had tried splitting a log or two, but the shock of the ax hitting the wood reverberated up her arms and made her head pound, so she had given that up.

In her walk about the shelter, she had located the outhouse and also found the small creek where Finn must have filled the water bags. She half-filled the bucket she had carted from the shelter. Walking downstream a short way, Meryl had stopped and had poured the water over her head. Using a sliver of soap, she had washed the blood and grime out of her hair, off her face and neck, being careful of the still large, very tender lump. Putting more water in the bucket, she had rinsed her hair. Just the simple act of washing up made her feel immensely better.

After the few simple chores were done, she felt tired again, but decided she would wait by the door and watch for Finn instead of lying back down. She had heard the thunder becoming increasingly louder and closer, and had closed the shutters in anticipation of the coming storm, but had left the door open. She had been glad when Finn finally arrived. Being alone in a strange place with two strangers seemed imminently better than sitting with just one stranger. That would be herself.

Once everything had been battened down as well as it could be, Meryl took one more look outside, for she was worried about Tashi. Now, thinking that a wild griff falcon could not take care of herself in a storm might have seemed foolish, but she was worried.

"Looking for Tashi, are you, are you? Not to worry, no, not to worry. She's settled in the lean-to with Heber. Perched up there in the rafters, just as snug as can be, snug as can be. Left her there with a small rabbit I snared, and she was feasting, she was. Just feasting."

Meryl and Finn ate a cold supper. They had lit a lamp, which gave out a soft light, making the hut feel cozy and safe as the storm raged around them. It was the crashing noises coming from outside that had Meryl concerned, especially the particularly loud thud that had shaken the hut and rattled the shutters. Then there was a loud crack and the sound of rock falling on rock.

Chapter Thirty-Four

What with the thunder, the thumping and crashing in the forest, and the occasional sound of large rocks falling from the bluff behind them, plus the continued pounding in her head, Meryl felt like she had not slept at all. The storm eventually blew over, just as dawn was breaking. Too restless to stay in her blanket roll, she got up and cautiously opened the door. Finn was snoring softly, and she decided not to disturb him. After listening to the fury of the storm most of the night, what she saw outside was not as bad as she had imagined. She was expecting to see the trees blown over and huge boulders leaning up against the hut. It would seem the storm had been more sound and fury than might. Mostly, when she looked around, she could see there were a number of branches down. As she looked toward the bluff, she could see where some rocks had fallen and rested at the base, but all in all, the forest and surrounding area looked more messy than damaged.

Meryl walked around to the back of the hut to check on the donkey and Tashi. The donkey was placidly chewing on some hay, and Tashi was perched on a rafter, her head under her wing, preening. Both appeared unharmed, which was more than could be said for the lean-to. A very large tree branch was half on and half off the lean-to's roof. The branch might explain the loud thump they had heard at the beginning of the storm. Meryl had just about gotten the big branch off the roof when Finn appeared around the corner of the hut.

"Now then, now then, let me help you."

Between the two of them, they finished wrestling the big branch off the roof, and then together they cleaned up the area around the hut, stacking the downed branches in a neat pile. Both had worked up quite an appetite, so Finn, once again, cooked up some of the hearty nutty-tasting porridge. After he took his last bite, he turned and asked Meryl what she intended to do now. Where did she intend to head off to?

"I don't know. I can't remember where I came from, so I don't know how to get back there. I don't know how I hit my head, but every once in a while I have a vague memory that I didn't trip and fall, but that I was shoved, but it's only a feeling. I have this strong sense of looming danger, and a feeling that I shouldn't go back the way I came."

"Where does the griff falcon fit in, fit in? Is she yours? Does she belong to you, belong to you?"

"I don't think griff falcons can belong to anyone, and I'm guessing they shouldn't. I don't know where she fits in, or why she has continued to stay close."

Just one more mystery I do not have any answers to, Meryl thought to herself. But then, what do I know about griff falcons? The more she thought about it, the more surprised she became that she did indeed know quite a bit about griff falcons and other birds. She could hear a pine wren over her left shoulder, and when she caught a flash of green, the color of sunlit leaves, she knew that bird for what it was, too. How could she know all that and only know her name? Not where she came from, who her folk were, or what she was doing here. What she was supposed to do next?

Finn, seeing the worried look on Meryl's face, said, "Nothing, no nothing ever gets fixed by worrying, worrying. Mostly things come out right, come out right, in the end."

"It's the meanwhile that has me at loose ends," Meryl quipped.

Finn chuckled and told her that while she might have lost some of her memory, she did not seem to have lost her sense of humor. Between the two of them, they got the breakfast dishes cleaned up and the hut put back to rights.

"We work well together, well together," Finn said. "You are good folk, good folk, indeed."

Meryl wondered about that. She hoped she was good folk, but she did not have enough memories of her life before she awoke from banging her head to know. What if she were some sort of bad or evil folk? What if she had done something terrible? There was no use dwelling on it, so Meryl shoved those disturbing thoughts to the back of her mind and turned her attention to what Finn was saying.

"I need to move on, move on, back to beyond where I was camping. Good pickings, very good pickings up in the bluff. You're welcome to come with me. Plenty to find, yes indeed, plenty to find."

"What are you talking about? What are you looking for, or finding for that matter?"

"You never know, you never know. By the sea, it's things that gets washed up, washed up. In the mountains, there's an occasional nugget of gold, ah yes, nugget of gold in the streams, in the streams, or a gemstone the Günnary missed, yes, missed. And here, it's the tyvfugl birds' stashes, yes, their caches. Never know, no, never know, what you'll find. They like shiny objects, shiny objects, and this is one of their home places. They will fly miles, miles, to stash what they have stolen. Just little thieves, little thieves is what they is. Come here every couple of years, every couple of years to see what they've squirreled away, squirreled away. Most of it's trash, just trash, but I've found a few good baubles, shiny baubles, and some coin, yes, some coin. You come with me, come with me. You can be my apprentice, that's it, my apprentice. A finder, a finder, that's what you'll be, like me, like me."

Meryl gave the offer considerable thought. It would not be fair to this odd, but very kind, little man to say she would be his apprentice, for she hoped she would recover her memory. She hoped she had a home and family somewhere. On the other hand, since she had no clear plan as to what to do next, for now, sticking with Finn seemed sensible.

"I don't want to sign on as an apprentice, for I don't know who I am, or if I'm already apprenticed to someone else, but I would like to travel with you for now," suggested Meryl.

Finn looked disappointed and then grew serious. "If you go with me, with me, you have to promise not to tell, promise not to tell anyone my secret places, secret places, for others would then ruin my findings for me, for me."

The request seemed more than reasonable to Meryl, and she found herself giving her solemn oath to Finn. Unless she was a truly bad folk, she felt she would not betray her promise.

The talk of tyvfugl birds touched a spark of memory in Meryl, which hovered just at the edge of her mind. Something was nagging at her concerning tyvfugl birds, but when she tried too hard to bring the memory forward, it illusively slid away. That seemed to be how her memory was working. She would just catch a glimpse or a snatch of a memory, but when she tried to bring it forward, it slid away back into the fog of her mind. It made no sense to worry too much over something she had no control over, and she was just grateful that her head did not hurt as much at this moment as it had the day before.

Finn went out the door saying he was going to bring the donkey around and pack up his gear. He suggested that she might want to put hers in order. It did not take them long to get everything packed and ready for travel. It did not surprise Meryl that when they left the forester's shelter and started on the trail, Tashi joined them. The griff falcon landed neatly on the top of the donkey's pack and clung there, balancing with ease, as if she rode donkeys all the time. But then, maybe she did, Meryl thought to herself. What did she know anyway?

The walk along the base of the bluffs was pleasant, with the sun shining brightly and sending shafts of sunbeams down through the pine boughs. Birds sang, and there was the constant rustling of small game in the brush. Such a contrast to the storm of the night before. After several hours of walking, Finn called a halt.

"This is where I had set up camp, set up camp, but I have searched here, looked here, and was going to move on, move on. Let's break for the noon meal, and then go look for the next likely site, next good site."

Once they had settled in to eat, Meryl asked how Finn knew a good site. He went on to explain that while tyvfugl birds were great thieves and swift flyers, they were not very good at landing. They could not grip the side of a bluff like some birds. They needed a ledge to land on. Then the tyvfugl bird needed to find a hole or crack in the bluff where they could cache their stash. He had chuckled when he told her this.

Meryl thought over what Finn had told her and then took a long look at the bluff above her. "How do you get up to the ledges?" she asked.

"Very carefully, very cautiously," Finn replied. "Sometimes the climb is easy, easy. Somet imes I lower myself down on a rope, on a rope."

"That sounds pretty risky."

"Used to have a partner, a partner I did, and 'twas easier then, easier then, but . . . ." Finn's words just drifted off, as he looked at the bluffs, but not before Meryl caught a look of sadness in his eyes.

Shaking himself, Finn suggested they get back on the trail. They needed to find a suitable place to set up camp before nightfall. The two walked on in companionable silence, and it was almost dusk before Finn stopped.

"This looks like a good spot, a good spot," he declared. "See that shelf over there?" he asked, directing Meryl's gaze toward the overhang. "Make a good place for you to put your blanket roll and gear, blanket roll and gear. Cut a few pine boughs for a soft bed, comfy bed."

As Meryl walked towards the ledge to inspect it, Tashi flew from the back of the donkey to settle on the ledge. "So, do I have your approval to set up here?" Meryl asked the griff falcon, and could have sworn that the griff falcon nodded her head. The area under the ledge was deep enough to keep rain off, if it came straight down, but Meryl thought she should make the place snugger if they were to stay more than just overnight. She asked Finn if they would be staying just overnight, or longer.

"Be here 'bout a week, 'bout a week," Finn replied. "Use this as a base camp, base camp."

While Finn set up his tent and set about building a fire ring, Meryl cut herself a pine branch and used it to sweep out under the ledge. When that was finished, she cut down some small saplings, stripped the bark, and used it to lash the saplings together to form a lattice. She wedged the lattice into the soft earth and leaned the top of it against the ledge. Into this she wove pine boughs, forming a wall. How she knew to do this she did not know, but she had stopped questioning such things. Once she had the wall up, Meryl tucked her gear inside and went to see what she could do to help Finn.

Finn directed her to fill the kettle and the pot with water from the nearby stream and then to gather firewood. While she was doing that, he had gone off into the woods. A short while later, he returned with an armful of tubers and a net bag that held mushrooms and other bounty from the forest. The soup he produced from the combination of what he found was tasty and filling. After the evening meal, Finn banked the fire and suggested that it was time to get some rest, for they would start at dawn the next day. Meryl had no objections to heading to bed early, for she was tired from the long walk.

Finn had told her they would do the easy searches the first day, and so, after breakfast they set off along the base of the bluff. He called the morning "a reconnoiter." Meryl called it a long walk over uneven ground, trying not to trip while moving forward and looking up at the same time. When Finn saw a likely place to search, he would mark the base of the bluff with a piece of chalk.

"I rubs it out, I do, I do, after I've checked the spot out, checked it out," he had told Meryl. "A few rains, yes, a few rains, and the mark is all gone, it's all gone."

It took most of the morning before Meryl was able to begin to distinguish what caused Finn to place a mark, and most of the time, only after he had pointed out the small ledge or tiny animal path leading upward.

While the morning had been set aside to check out likely places to look, the afternoon was another matter. Finn had explained that the area they had covered in their walk that morning would take two to three days to search. Each day they would walk out to where they had left off the day before and work their way back towards the base camp. Now that they had marked places, it was time to go exploring.

"We'll start with this one, yes indeed, with this one, since it will be an easy climb, easy climb," Finn said, as he began to scramble up and over rocks and boulders.

Easy my foot, Meryl thought to herself, as she tried to keep up, getting bruised knees, elbows, and scraped hands for her effort. When she finally made it to the narrow ledge that Finn had said looked promising, she found him hunkered down, peering into a small opening. Standing up he took off the small pack he was wearing and took out what, at first glance, looked like a bundle of sticks. Meryl watched with fascination as he fitted the pieces together and then attached a hook onto the end.

"Never good to stick your hand in a hole, stick your hand in a hole, no never good. Never know what or who might be inside, no never know."

Cautiously, Finn stuck the rod slowly into the hole, and when nothing growled, rattled, or hissed at him, he stuck it in until it would go no further. Removing the rod, Finn took the hook off and put on a small hoe blade. Keeping the rod elevated near the roof of the hole, he stuck it back in until it hit the back of the hole. He then let it drop down to the floor and, ever so slowly, pulled it forward. Meryl could hear something rolling ahead of the hoe blade.

Chapter Thirty-Five

What rolled out of the opening flashed a brilliant green in the sunlight. For a moment, Meryl thought they had found a gemstone and felt her heart race just a bit. Upon closer inspection, however, the round object turned out to be a large glass bead that had a slight chip out of it. After putting the hoe in the hole several more times, they had an odd collection of small shiny objects including several buttons, a salt spoon, and a very small bell. While interesting, Meryl was disappointed, for these small objects held very little worth to anyone other than the tyvfugl bird who had put them in the hole. She wondered how anyone could make a living being a finder if this is what one found. Finn did not seem at all disappointed. Instead, he seemed quite pleased with his find.

"Oh, this is good, this is good."

"How is this good?" Meryl asked, and realized the disappointment she was feeling showed in her voice.

"Because it suggests that we're in a section of the bluffs that the tyvfugl birds frequent, that they frequent. Even though this hole did not produce great riches or worthy treasure, no, no great riches, it means this area is worth exploring. Yes indeed, worth exploring, yes indeed."

When Meryl looked skeptical, Finn went on to explain that finding was a matter of faith. Most holes were going to be like the one they had just explored, interesting, but of very little value. Think of it as cleaning up the area, he had said, because tyvfugl birds are very forgetful. They cannot remember from one theft to the next where they stashed their "shineys". But remember, he had told Meryl, for every dozen holes that contain worthless trash, there will be that one that contains something of worth.

"You can make a living at this?" Meryl asked.

"Oh yes, oh my yes," Finn answered. "This hunting in the bluffs is more like a holiday for me, a holiday for me, for I only come here every other year, only every other year. I have a little place, just a little place, along the Rumblesea shore. There is a narrows between the shoreline and the great reefs, where ships have to sail. The area is treacherous in heavy seas, very treacherous. Often after a bad storm, much is washed up, much is washed up, onto the shore. Washed off the deck of the ships mostly, deck of the ships. Occasionally a ship wreck. Most sad, most sad. Also, the currents bring many odd things, many strange things, from far distant places. We finds enough, finds enough, and sells enough, to keep Heber and me in comfort, in comfort, it does."

As the day went on, the two checked other holes and crevices. By the end of the day, they had a motley collection of broken glass bits, shiny pebbles, bits of polished wood, glazed crockery, and enough buttons to furnish several coats. In addition, they had found a glass stopper, a very small carving knife, and several crystals. The real prize came late in the day, when among the bits and pieces they pulled out of a particularly small hole, there was a gold nugget that flashed bright and shiny in the late afternoon sunlight.

"Know a goldsmith, know a goldsmith I do, who will give me a nice price, nice price for this. Worth a day of hunting, a day of hunting it is, it is."

Throughout the day, Tashi had kept close to the two who were clambering up and down the rocks, landing nearby each time they stopped to check out a likely place. For some unexplained reason, Meryl found comfort in having the griff falcon close. It was as if Tashi were her anchor in this new and strange world in which she found herself.

After her first disappointment, Meryl found herself caught up in the hunt. Finn held such optimism at each new hole that it was hard not to catch at least some of his enthusiasm. Finn found such joy in finding what to others might seem worthless. He would exclaim over each piece, and even make up stories of where they might have come from. One of the buttons they found was very, very old, and off the uniform of a royal guard.

That night, just when Meryl was drifting off to sleep, her mind kept circling around and around about bright glittering things. Just on the edge of sleep she saw an image of a locket, but when she tried to focus on it, sleep claimed her. The next morning the two set off and worked the next section of bluff. After several more days, they had worked their way back to the campsite.

"Tomorrow, we'll work the other direction, the other direction. We'll reconnoiter again, once again. Oh, I found something I forgot I had, forgot I had."

Finn got up, went into his tent and returned with a small narrow roll of leather. He handed it to Meryl, and she unrolled it. Inside were the pieces to a tool similar to the one Finn had been using to coax objects out of the holes and narrow openings in the rocks.

"Here, you can use this, use this tomorrow, yes, tomorrow. I will help you practice, practice, and then we can both check openings, yes, both check. That way we can cover more ground, cover more ground."

For some unexplained reason, Meryl felt overwhelmed by Finn's simple gesture and had a strong urge to cry. Instead, she thanked him quietly and, keeping her head down, busied herself putting the tool together, familiarizing herself with the attachments. The next day the two walked and marked where they thought there might be likely spots to explore. Finn often asked her what she thought of this hole or that crack, and Meryl realized he was teaching her his trade, even though she had not signed on as his apprentice. She found she was profoundly touched.

The bluff they walked along had more narrow paths running up and down it, which would make their searching easier, with the exception of one area that Finn said they would have to reach by rope. Meryl was not so sure how she felt about dropping over the edge of a cliff and dangling on a rope several hundred feet up. The next day they walked to their farthest mark, which was at the beginning of a long narrow upward path that went all the way to the top of the bluff.

"You want to take the top of the bluff, top of the bluff and work down, down, or the bottom of the bluff, bottom of the bluff, and work up?" Finn asked. "Might suggest the top, yes, the top. Fine view, beautiful view, but first we should practice, practice on a few of the lowest holes, lowest holes."

Once Finn felt confident that Meryl knew how to handle the tool to its best effect, he sent her on her way, wishing her good hunting. Meryl supposed she would have to go to the top of the bluff at some point, and this path looked somewhat easier than some they had climbed. She had almost become convinced that Finn was at the very least half spider the way he scrambled up seemingly impossible places on the bluff wall. Tightening the straps on the small pack Finn had lent her, Meryl started up the narrow path and said she would meet Finn in the middle. Finn had certainly been right about the view. It seemed as if she could see forever. What she saw for sure were a great many trees. Just at the horizon line, she thought she saw what was maybe the top of a building or two, but the sky was too hazy and Meryl could not be sure.

Working her way slowly down the path, she became even more aware that the bluff wall was littered with small openings. After spending a week with Finn searching out treasure and finding mostly trash, Meryl was surprised at how much anticipation she felt when she put her stick tool into the first small opening. That feeling of anticipation began to wane when, after several hours, Meryl had had little success at finding much of anything of worth. Bits and bobs of this and that, but nothing that was going to pay for a meal. Resting on her haunches, Meryl wiped the sweat out of her eyes, for the day had grown warm, and looked way down to see where Finn was. He, she noticed, had made more progress upward than she had made downward on the path. Shifting her weight carefully, Meryl slid her feet down the path and located the next opening.

Easing the rod tool slowly into the opening, Meryl listened for any sound that might indicate somebody had made the hole its home. Discovering that nobody was home, she changed the tip of the tool and put it back into the hole, just as Finn had instructed her. Applying pressure downward so that the hoe's bottom edge held firmly to the floor of the hole, she pulled the tool towards her. When she brought it to the mouth of the hole, she was rewarded with the sight of not one but two coins, both silver. She put her tool back in the hole, but nothing more came forward. Finding the two coins made her eager to move on to the next opening however, and Meryl could understand the lure of being a finder. More often than not, one found nothing, but every once in a while when one did find something, it made one want to keep looking.

Buoyed up by her small success, Meryl moved swiftly on to the next opening only to find it disappointingly empty, and so it went as she worked her way down. Finn was right, there was always more trash than treasure, but the lure of finding that one great treasure kept her searching. By midday Meryl and Finn met and decided to climb back down and get out of the sun. Sitting in the cool shade of a large pine, they compared what they had found. Meryl opened the small pouch she had been putting her findings in and tipped the objects out onto a small kerchief she had spread on a bed of pine needles.

"Most of it's bits and bobs of trash," Meryl pointed out apologetically.

"But it's not, it's not. While it might not put coin in your pouch, coin in your pouch, it can give you the gift of knowledge, the gift of knowledge," Finn replied.

"Knowledge?"

"Yes, oh my yes. Take this bead for example, for example. It is made of glass, made of glass."

Meryl could see the bead was made of glass. It was quite pretty actually, and she had been quite taken with it when it had rolled out of the opening and caught the sunlight. The bead had flashed red in the light, and on closer inspection Meryl had seen thin streaks of yellow and blue swirled within.

"This cut crystal bead comes from Vann Vadested, which is a far distant land, far distant land. It comes to Sommerhjem by way of an overland trade route, and then a long ship voyage along the spice trade route, the spice trade route. Only a few of our ships, a very few of our ships make the very risky journey, very risky journey each year. The sailors bring back small items, small items such as a bead like you found to sell, to sell. So this bead, this bead has come a long way, a very long way, to be snatched by a tyvfugl bird and hidden here, hidden here."

Finn went on to pick other pieces up from the kerchief and told what he knew about them. A piece of china that had probably come from a noble's house, a small buckle from a shoe when buckles on shoes were in style, and several crystals that had most likely been found naturally, but not in the area they were looking in now. Meryl found what Finn had to say about what she had found fascinating. She also appreciated his words when he praised the few things of worth she had found. When Meryl tried to give him the coins, he had insisted that she keep them.

"No, no, you keep them, you keep them. Save the first one you found on your own as a good luck piece, good luck piece. Keep it close, keep it close. Do you remember, remember which one was first, which one was first?"

Meryl reached down and plucked up the first coin she had found. When she had first seen it, she did not know it was a coin until she looked at it closely. It was not round like the coins she was familiar with but rather an uneven shape with the head of some woman on one side and what looked like a griff falcon on the other. She had been intrigued by it. Meryl held it out for Finn to see.

"I didn't think it was even a coin when I first looked at it, or even that it was something of worth. I think it's silver, but it's very tarnished. The markings are very clear on it however, and I think it might have been in the hole I found it in quite a long time."

"Your guess would be right, be right. I've only found a few like it, a few like it, and I think it is several hundred years old, several hundred years old. I wonder how I've missed it, missed it, for I've searched along this path before. Yes, I've searched here before."

"I found it in a small opening that looked like it had come to light because part of the bluff face had fallen away at that spot. Maybe the opening had been covered up until recently."

"That would explain it, yes that would explain it. Now then, where did I put that pouch, that pouch," Finn said, as he rummaged through his small daypack. "Ah, here it is, here it is. This pouch is made of golden pine spider silk and would be a good one, yes a good one, to carry your lucky coin in, your lucky coin."

Meryl thanked Finn for the pouch and placed her lucky coin inside. Closing the pouch, she put the cord the pouch hung on over her head, around her neck, and tucked it in under her clothing.

"Well, my dear, my dear," Finn stated, "there is no time like the present, no, no time like the present to tackle the next part of the bluff. As you can see, you can see, there is a promising ledge, yes, a promising ledge about a quarter of the way down. We will have to get down from the top, from the top. Plenty of handholds, plenty of handholds, but to be safe best to use the ropes too. Yes, best to use the ropes."

Meryl was not so sure she wanted this new adventure, but since she could think of no reason why she should not go with Finn, other than sheer terror, she followed him up the path they had worked. After arriving at the top of the bluff, Meryl followed Finn to a spot over the ledge he had indicated from below. He showed her how to tie the rope to a sturdy tree, and then how to tie the rope about her. Finn explained the rope was just a safety precaution, lest she lost her hold on the rock face. Meryl gathered her courage around her and slowly eased herself over the edge of the bluff. Cautiously, she moved down the side of the bluff, for Finn had been correct in suggesting there were many available hand and foot holds. Once down on the ledge, Meryl was surprised how wide it was and how long, for it had not looked so from below. Finn had instructed that they start in the middle and move towards opposite ends.

The first few openings held little of value, but as Meryl moved on, she found several more coins and what looked to be a green gemstone. As she worked her way farther and farther from Finn, her rope began to get taut which gave her a feeling of security, especially since the wind had begun to pick up.

"We had best head up, head up. The wind is getting too strong, too strong."

"Alright, I have just one more opening to check," Meryl replied.

It was a good thing she had a rope holding her, for when she pulled the tool out, the first item that appeared was a golden locket on a broken chain, and memories came rushing back, causing Meryl to feel dizzy and disoriented.

CHAPTER THIRTY-SIX

Meryl could hear Finn urging her to get a move on, for the wind was beginning to howl through the tops of the pines below, but her feet were rooted on the ledge. Only her white-knuckled grip on the rock face and the rope kept her from being swept off. She was trying even harder to hold onto the images that had swept through her mind when she saw the locket emerge from the opening than she was to hold onto the rock face of the bluff. Finally Finn's now frantic calls broke through the swirl of images rushing through Meryl's mind, and she realized that her situation was becoming perilous.

"Just hold there, hold there," called Finn. "I'll climb up, up I'll climb, and hold your rope and help you get up, help you . . . ." The last of Finn's sentence was blown away in a fierce burst of wind.

Meryl watched Finn slowly and carefully climb to the top of the bluff. She started to breathe again once he was at the top and away from the edge. Finn untied his rope and moved over to where Meryl had tied hers and refastened his rope. Holding tightly to his own rope, he leaned over the edge and called down instructions. Meryl loosened the grip her left hand had on a handhold and stretched up to secure her hand on the next handhold up. Then with her right foot she pushed herself up so she could reach the next handhold. Moving first one hand, then one foot, then the next hand, then the next foot, Meryl slowly made her way up towards the top of the bluff. During the whole upward journey, which she felt probably took hours, but only took minutes, Finn had kept her rope taut and helped her move upward.

Once they both stood at the top of the bluff, they took a moment to catch their collective breaths, for they still had to get down and back to their camp. Only the top portion of the path down proved to be difficult. Once they got into the trees, the effect of the wind lessened, and soon they were at the bottom of the bluff. Not wasting time, they turned and headed back to their camp. They were fearful of what the wind might have done to it, but when they arrived, they were pleasantly surprised to find a minimal amount of damage. Meryl had to replace a few pine boughs on her makeshift wall, and Finn had to pound a stake back in holding a tent rope. He added a few more ropes, crisscrossing the tent with them to make it more secure, and once that was done, met Meryl at the cold fire pit.

"I think it will be a cold supper, yes a cold supper, this night. Don't want to risk a fire in this wind, no not in this wind."

The evening meal was unusually quiet. Meryl chewed slowly on a cold biscuit, thinking all the while on what had flashed through her mind when she had seen the locket emerge from the opening in the bluff. She did not know how she knew, but she knew the locket belonged to her. How a tyvfugl bird had gotten a hold of it was a mystery, but she had caught a bit of a memory of it being dangled above her just out of reach and cruel laughter.

With the finding of the locket also came a rush of feelings that confused her. On the one hand, there was a feeling of warmth and love. The kind face of a woman came to mind, but along with the feeling of love came the feelings of loss and longing. On the other hand, and what had held Meryl's feet to the ledge of the bluff when she should have been moving, was the great sense of fear and danger. When Finn asked if she was alright, Meryl answered honestly that she was not and went on to explain what had transpired on the bluff. Finn suggested that maybe someone kind had given her the locket, and someone cruel had taken it away. That explanation made sense but did not reduce the ever increasing sense of danger that seemed to lurk on the edge of Meryl's mind.

"I've been thinking, yes I've been thinking, that it is time to move on, time to move on. The weather hasn't been cooperating, no not cooperating, and storm season will begin soon, begin soon at home." Seeing the panicked look on Meryl's face, Finn reached out and awkwardly patted her arm, telling her that she was welcome to come with him. "No matter, no matter. I have a small cottage just down from mine that I have been meaning to clean out, meaning to clean out. You could stay there, stay there and help me. That's a fine plan, a fine plan, don't you think?"

The plan was a very fine plan and a generous one, but Meryl was concerned. Finn had asked her to become his apprentice several days earlier, and she had turned him down because she did not know who she had been before he found her. She worried that if or when her memory returned, she would return to the life she was once a part of, and then where would that leave Finn? Like so much else, there did not seem to be a ready answer, and so Meryl told Finn that for now she would like to stick with him. They talked about what area Finn hoped to cover over the next several days, and then what route they would take to get to his home.

It struck Meryl that she had readily accepted Finn's invitation without even considering other choices, both at the forester's shelter and then just now. Neither time had she even considered striking off on her own to find someone who knew her, or knew of her, and could direct her towards finding answers as to who she was. The feeling persisted that danger lurked if she were to pursue trying to find out more about herself.

Instead of dwelling on her predicament, Meryl turned to Finn and said, "I'm glad we're not leaving the area right away, for I would worry about Tashi. Her feathers are almost back to where she can soar and hunt, but I'd like to stick around until she can. From what you have told me, it's most unusual for her to have come this close to us much less to have stuck around all this time."

"Aye, it is unusual, very unusual behavior for a griff falcon. She would probably fly off soon at any rate now that she is flying better, feeling better."

Meryl found herself unexpectedly feeling sad at the thought of the griff falcon not being nearby, even though she instinctively knew that Tashi was not a pet but a wild bird. Meryl had found comfort in Tashi's presence, for the griff falcon and Finn had been the two constants since she had come to in the clearing.

The next few days passed quickly as Meryl and Finn covered the last sections of the bluff that Finn had marked out. It was on the last day that Meryl truly understood the allure of being a finder. After an afternoon of finding mostly worthless shiny items, Meryl was about to quit for the day when she spied a small hole and almost passed it by, but something just drew her to it. After making sure nothing that could bite her was living in the hole, she attached the hoe blade to the end of her rod tool but discovered it was too wide to reach very far into the hole. She called over to Finn to ask what he did in that situation.

"Look in the bundle I gave you, gave you. There's a narrower hoe blade. If that doesn't work, try using the hook sideways, sideways."

Meryl carefully opened the bundle her searching rod was stored in and discovered an inner pocket she had not really taken notice of before.

Inside were several more attachments, and she selected the narrower hoe blade. She would have to ask Finn what the other ones were used for. Meryl inserted the new hoe blade into the opening, and it went further than the wider one, but still met some resistance on one side. Pulling the rod handle back brought only twigs, leaves, and other natural debris. Changing from the narrow hoe blade to the hook, she inserted the rod again and moved it a little to the right. The rod went into the hole farther, and Meryl thought she heard the faint sound of metal hitting metal and hoped whatever she had just touched had not been pushed farther into the hole.

Meryl had been working with the flexible, adaptable rod for days now, but she knew she did not have the deft touch that Finn had. She was about to call him to come help but something held her back. Maybe it was stubbornness, or something else she could not name, but she was determined to get whatever was in the hole out by herself. Strangely enough, instead of feeling frustrated as she worked the rod, she felt remarkably calm. Sitting back, Meryl wiped her forehead with the back of her sleeve and caught movement out of the corner of her eye. Tashi was sitting almost within touching distance of her. She had been concentrating so hard on trying to retrieve what was in the hole that she had not realized Tashi had landed near her.

"Come to supervise have you?" Meryl asked the griff falcon and watched in amazement when Tashi moved just a little closer. Meryl was glad she had not scared the griff falcon off by talking to her.

Now that she had taken a short break, Meryl was more determined than ever to get whatever was in the hole out. Easing the rod back in, she slid it down the right side of the hole, scraping the tip along the wall. It felt like it went in just a bit farther this time, and again when she pulled it back, she heard a metallic clink, but the hook tip slid right by something. Whatever is in there must be wedged in, she thought. It then occurred to Meryl that if she sent the hook into the hole in the up and down position, got it past whatever she was trying to get out, and then turned the hook sideways, she might be able to shift whatever was in there enough to move it.

The first time Meryl tried her idea, the hook end slipped off. The next time, however, the hook held, and Meryl felt something shift. Cautiously and slowly, Meryl alternated between pulling and pushing, trying to dislodge whatever was stuck in the hole. Finally, she felt a major shift as she was pulling. Levering her stick up to the top of the hole and pushing it as far back as she could, Meryl eased the hook down and very carefully and very slowly pulled something forward.

⚬⟋⟋⟍⟍⚬

Fordon was steaming. His stupid uncle was being totally unreasonable. He had delivered the last of the messenger birds and having to do all the work had convinced him once again that he did not want to spend his life working for his uncle. Now that he had a nice little nest egg with the coin he had taken off of Meryl, he knew he would not have to work with messenger birds much longer. No, he had grander ideas of what he wanted out of life. A few more schemes, a little skimming off the top of what customers paid him, and he might be able to set himself up nicely. In the meantime, he needed to get his uncle off his back.

Fordon had arrived back at his uncle's house with what he thought was a rather convincing tale as to why Meryl was not with him. "I don't know what got into her," he had told his uncle. "One minute we were having the noon meal, and the next minute she was screaming at me. She went on and on about how none of us cared about the business or the messenger birds, and she was tired of doing all the work. She just grabbed her things out of the wagon, took the coin we had collected, and told me she was done. I tried to persuade her to reconsider, but she said she would rather take her chances on living as a hermit, or starting over in another town, than return here."

His uncle had looked at him in disgust as if her "walking off" was his fault and had told him that since he had lost her, he could darn well go and find her. However, there was no way that he was going to go traipsing all over hill and dale looking for someone who could accuse him of attacking her, which was what had brought him to this less than reputable pub looking at an old acquaintance. At least he did not have to deal with the messenger birds for a while. His uncle had sent his two cousins off on deliveries and had hired the lass from down the way to care for the home roost. His uncle had given him enough coin to pay for food and lodging while he was searching for Meryl. He intended to use that coin to sit out the search in comfort at a little inn he knew and hire himself a tracker.

Fordon looked at the man seated across from him. Olwydd always seemed full of nervous tension, always looking around, always checking

234

his surroundings. Fordon knew the man was a dreamer and a schemer, but his grand ideas were rarely practical. It was a good thing he was a skilled tracker, for he rarely made any coin off of his plots and plans. Fordon had just endured over an hour of Olwydd telling him about his latest get rich quick venture and finally cut him off.

"Well, until that particular ship comes in, I have a job for you. I need you to find my step-cousin." Fordon went on to give him the same version of the story he had told his uncle. "So," he repeated, "I want you to find her."

"You should've come to me earlier, for the trail will be mighty cold by now."

"You would say that and still call yourself the best tracker in the land," Fordon scoffed, knowing his acquaintance would bristle and then take the bait. Once Olwydd had agreed to take the job, Fordon told him what was going to happen. "Alright, you get half the coin now and half after you find her. I don't want you to grab her or anything. I just want you to locate her. Once you've done that, send a messenger bird to the inn where I'll be staying, and I'll come straight away. Now let's look at the map, and I'll show you where I last saw her."

After the two men had poured over the map, Fordon gave Olwydd an in-depth description of his step-cousin. The two men departed. Fordon hoped Olwydd would be successful and be successful quickly. This little venture was cutting into his nest egg too much as it was. Why could Meryl not just have hit her head and died? He should have checked. Now she was out roaming the countryside, and he was fearful that she would show up any day now and tell his uncle what had really happened. He did not intend to spend time rotting away in some dungeon because of her. No, he needed her found so he could make sure she never had a chance to tell his uncle her side of the story.

CHAPTER THIRTY-SEVEN

Meryl slowly and carefully pulled towards her whatever it was her hook had caught on, only to have it slip off once again. Hoping that she had moved the object far enough towards the opening, she took the hook off and put the narrow hoe blade back on. Moving her rod to the roof of the hole, she gently slid it along the roof of the opening as far as she could and then lowered it down, hoping it would come to rest behind the object. Once she felt the edge of the hoe blade touch the floor of the hole, she eased it forward, only to be disappointed. The bottom of the hoe blade had touched something metal but had slid off of it. Meryl was fairly sure that action had pushed the object farther back rather than bringing it forward. When Finn had called over and asked how she was doing and did she need any help, Meryl had replied with a terse "no thank you". She then changed the tip of the rod back to the hook and began coaxing whatever was in the hole out again.

It would be ironic if after all this effort what came out of the hole was just a scrap of worthless metal, Meryl thought to herself as she reinserted the rod, her tongue sticking slightly out of her mouth in concentration. It took a number of tries, but each time she stuck the rod back in, she made more progress forward than backward, until she had brought the object close enough that she could once again put the hoe blade on and finally bring the object sliding out of the hole. Once the object was out in the open, Meryl was not sure what she was looking at. It looked like a very small shallow box with a lip overlapping the sides on the top and bottom. Whatever it was, it was made of silver, and the top was inlaid with tiny jewels. Meryl just sat back on her haunches and stared.

The tiny box was certainly worth the effort she had gone through to get it out and certainly made up for all the disappointing holes she had searched the last few days. Meryl could not even begin to estimate what the exquisite little box might be worth. With a hand that trembled with excitement, she reached out and picked up the box. The box felt very warm in her hand. For the life of her, Meryl could not figure out how it had gotten so warm in the short time it had been outside the dark of the hole, especially on such a cloudy day. She was holding the box in the palm of her hand, just looking at it, when a shadow fell across her hand. Her first instinct was to close her hand tightly, for fear that a tyvfugl bird was flying over and would snatch it. Something stopped her from closing her hand, and she felt a great calm come over her when Tashi lightly brushed the tip of her wing over the box and then backed away, launching herself off the ledge. The griff falcon soared overhead and gave a loud triumphant cry.

That was strange, Meryl thought, as she placed the tiny box in her pack. As she watched the griff falcon fly higher and higher, it suddenly struck her that Tashi was fully healed. Meryl watched her catch a warm updraft of wind and begin to soar. Meryl sat on the ledge until Tashi was a mere speck in the sky. When she came back to herself, Meryl realized that Tashi had left, and the joy of finding something as valuable and beautiful as the tiny box was quickly replaced by an overwhelming sadness, thinking that Tashi might be gone for good.

Later, after the evening meal, Meryl and Finn spread a light-colored cloth in front of them and each set up a display of what they had found that day, as had become their habit. They first would set out what each of them had determined was trash. Sometimes Finn would spot something among Meryl's trash display that really was a treasure in disguise. Other times he would tell her what the object might have been part of, or tell her a bit about its possible history. Sometimes they would have no idea what a find was and might make up a story about it. That was Meryl's favorite part, for Finn was a born storyteller and could make up outrageous stories.

After sorting through the trash, they would each in turn lay out their good finds of the day, always holding back the one they deemed the most valuable. The value of an item was not always measured in what the item might be worth, as in the case of found coin, or how much an item might bring if sold. No, sometimes an item was valuable because of its beauty or because of its age and the story it told.

Coins were displayed first. From the first day, Finn had insisted that Meryl retain some of the coin, and they had argued, for she felt he should keep all of what she found. After all, she had told him, he was the one supplying food and teaching her a trade. He had told her that if she were either a worker or an apprentice, the split would be the same. He got two-thirds of what she found and she got one-third. No arguments, he had said. The coins were easy to divide. The other valuable bits, not so much. Meryl had found she quite enjoyed the haggling with Finn as to how to divide the valuables.

There was one exception as to how to divide up the day's finds. Meryl could take one of her finds out of the bargaining if she wished. Its value was noted and subtracted from her take, which was only fair, but it was something that Finn could not take as his portion. Finn had explained that every now and then a find just struck one in a certain way and giving it up created more friction between folk working together than it was worth. No sense in pining over something and becoming madder and madder that you had had to give it up. Did not make for a good working together, he had said. Meryl was very thankful for this exception to the rules, for she did not know if she could have given up the small box she had found this day

Finn laid his finds out first, and they went through what he had found. This portion of the sorting was not to divide the profits, because Meryl did not get any of Finn's finds, but so Finn could teach Meryl about what he had found. This way, he had explained, she would become more and more knowledgeable as to what was worth keeping. Then Meryl would lay out her finds, and they would begin the process again.

"I have held one back," Meryl explained, as she began to lay her found items out. "I would like to keep it. I think it is very valuable, and so I will probably owe you when the haggling is done."

"Ah, I can tell, yes I can tell, I have more to teach you about haggling, about haggling. Never, no never give away that you have an item you value or desire, value or desire," Finn said, with mock sternness in his voice but a twinkle in his eye. "Let's look at what you found, what you found, but save the best for last, yes, the best for last."

Meryl laid out the few bits and bobs she had found, and the haggling began. She knew she was at a disadvantage because besides Finn being so much better at haggling than she, she was also anxious about showing him the tiny box. She did not really understand why she had such a strong desire to keep it. Except for the locket, she had not been drawn to any of the other things they had found. Meryl did not think it was the monetary worth of the piece that drew her, nor did she think it was because of its beauty or fine craftsmanship. No, it was something else she just could not put her finger on. All too soon it was time to put the box out on the cloth. It was with great reluctance she reached into her pack and pulled the box out, holding it in her closed hand momentarily. Taking a deep breath, she opened her hand and gently placed the box on the cloth.

Finn just looked at the tiny box for a long moment but did not move to pick it up. Finally he reached out his hand, letting it hover over the tiny box, but then slowly drew it back. It was all Meryl could do not to snatch the tiny box back up and shove it into her pack.

"It draws you, yes it draws you, does it not, does it not?" Finn asked.

"Yes."

Meryl did not tell Finn what had happened when she had brought it out into the light, or what Tashi had done. Tashi had still not returned, and Meryl's feelings were still too raw to bring that up.

"A beautiful piece, a beautiful piece. Very old I think, so very old. I have never seen the like, no never. Have you tried to open it, open it?"

Meryl gave her forehead a slap in disgust, for the idea of opening the box had not occurred to her. She picked it up and began to look for a way to open it, if indeed it did open. She could not see a latch of any kind or any hinges. As Meryl turned the tiny box this way and that way, she thought she could see a very thin line marking where the two sections of the box came apart. Now the only thing I need to do, she thought to herself, is to figure out how to get them to come apart. After fussing with it for quite some time, Meryl asked Finn if he wanted to take a crack at it.

"Just set it down there, down there," he said, pointing with his elbow, for his hands were full at the moment working on a knot that had formed in the drawstring of a small pack. "Ah, got it, got it I did. Now then, now then, let's see what we have here, have here." Once again Finn reached for the small box but did not pick it up. After his hand had hovered over the box for several moments, Finn withdrew his hand. "I think, yes, I think this is not for me, no not for me. Something special, oh my yes, something special. You need to keep this tucked away, oh my yes, keep it tucked away safely in a pouch, tucked away safely."

Meryl fiddled with the box until the light became too dim to see, but she still had not figured a way to open it. She did not want to take any type of tool to it, for she did not want to mar or damage its surface. The box was surprisingly unmarred by all the pushing and pulling it had taken to get it out into the daylight.

While they had been sitting around the cook fire enjoying the mild evening, Finn suggested that they should pack the campsite up the next morning and begin to head west and south. He had found enough on this trip to have made it worthwhile, and there were a few gem fields he wanted to stop at before making the long push home. When Meryl had inquired as to what gem fields were, jokingly asking did he mean there were just precious gems lying about a field just waiting to be plucked up, Finn had answered in the affirmative. Apparently there were fields where the gemstones worked their way to the surface, and some could be found each year, if you knew where to look and what to look for. The gems really did not look like all that much when they were lying in the dirt, Finn had explained, but give one to a fine gem cutter and some of them could be right beautiful.

Early the next morning, Meryl packed up her few belongings. Finn had questioned her lack of gear if she had been traveling about the country. He had asked if she had been traveling by horse or wagon, but she had no answers. She just could not remember. Meryl was leaving with a heavy heart, for Tashi had still not returned, and she found she missed the griff falcon's presence. The griff falcon and Finn had been her two solid anchors in a world that was foggy at best. Now one of her anchors was missing. In addition, Finn had explained that from now on they would be staying in one place only for a day or two before they moved on. Meryl had mixed feelings about leaving the area where Tashi and Finn had found her.

The weather was fair the day they left the campsite by the bluff. Finn regaled Meryl with stories about some of his favorite finds as they walked along. They stuck to the smaller lanes that meandered towards their next destination rather than going by the straighter, more well-traveled royal road.

"We might get there quicker," Finn had told her, but he was in no hurry. "Never know what you might find along the way, never know," he had suggested.

Finn told her about a time he had stopped at an old falling down farmhouse and had been poking around in the cupboards, not really expecting to find anything, when he happened to knock a board loose and found a hidey hole. Inside was a very old cracked leather pouch that almost crumbled in his hands when he picked it up.

"So, what was in it?" Meryl had asked.

Finn paused, making her wait for the answer. "Well," he said, "it contained very old and very beautifully made marbles, very beautiful marbles."

"But marbles aren't worth much," Meryl had protested. "Glassmakers make them all the time from leftover bits of glass. I had a pouch of them when I was young lass."

Finn had gone on to explain that she was right in that most marbles were not worth much, but these marbles were very old and of a design and technique that had been lost. He had sold them for a goodly amount to a journeyman glassmaker, one whose name was Rollag, he thought. It had been a while back, Finn had told her.

"The journeyman had seemed fascinated by them, yes positively fascinated. I later heard he figured out the technique, figured it out he did, and then used that technique in other of his glassworks, other works. Became quite well known for the unique and beautiful glass pieces he makes. Quite well known, and all because of my finding the marbles, finding the marbles."

The stories made the day go by swiftly, and Meryl was surprised when Finn called a halt for the day and began to set up camp. After the evening meal, Meryl once again pulled out the small silver box she had found on the last day they were at the bluffs and tried to figure out how to open it, if indeed it opened. She was concentrating so hard that she did not hear the quiet sound of wings coming ever nearer and was extremely startled when a beak plucked the small silver box from her hand.

CHAPTER THIRTY-EIGHT

In the instant the small silver box was snatched from her hand, Meryl's first thought was of the irony of having taken the box from some tyvfugl bird's cache only to have it snatched back by a tyvfugl bird. Her second thought was that if she did not have bad luck she would not have any luck at all. As she turned, anticipating watching her best find fly away, she was startled, for she found herself looking not at the departing tail feathers of a thieving tyvfugl bird but into the brilliant green eyes of Tashi. Her annoyance at the box being snatched was replaced by her joy in seeing Tashi again. It took several long moments for Meryl to realize that Tashi was now holding the small silver box in her left talon.

Speaking very softly, Meryl addressed the griff falcon. "I'm so very glad to see you again, Tashi. You're welcome to the silver box." And all that I possess, thought Meryl, since she owed the griff falcon her life. If it had not been for Tashi, who knew what would have happened while she had been unconscious in the clearing.

While Meryl was thinking these thoughts, the griff falcon had shifted the small box in her talon and then dipped her head down. Using the very tip of her beak, Tashi began to apply pressure to the top lip of the box while holding the bottom lip of the box with the tip of a claw. With great concentration, Tashi worked each side of the top lid, pulling just a little as she turned the box until the lid lifted off. The last strong ray of sunlight glinted off what could only be something gold nestled inside the box.

Meryl leaned forward just as Tashi held the bottom of the box out towards her. Meryl reached out, and Tashi placed the box bottom in her hand. Inside the box bottom was an irregularly shaped gold ring. She tipped the ring out into her hand and was surprised at how warm it felt. Upon closer inspection, Meryl noted that there were what looked to be deep scratches carved into the ring. A memory of having seen something similar flashed through her mind but was gone before she could make sense of it.

Her fingers closed swiftly over the ring as she caught movement out of the corner of her eye. When she realized it was Finn returning from checking on Heber, she found she was reluctant to show Finn what Tashi had uncovered, and so quickly slipped the ring into her pocket. Meanwhile Tashi had set the box lid next to Meryl.

"Ah, I see you finally figured out how to open the wee box, open the wee box. Good for you, yes indeed, good for you. Filled with gems was it now, was it now? Enough to make your fortune?" Finn asked, and there was a definite flicker of knowing in his eye. "Ah lass, I thinks I best not see what you have found, no best not see. Nice to see Tashi has chosen to join us again, nice to see. Now then, 'tis time to turn in, turn in. Tired I am, yes, tired."

As Meryl lay looking up at the stars, she wondered about Finn's decision not to ask to see what, if anything, Meryl had found in the box once she had gotten it open. By all rights, he could have demanded to see what she had found and put a price on it, but he had not. Strange, Meryl thought, but then her immediate reaction to the ring had been strange also. She had not wanted to show it to Finn. Why was that, she wondered. What was also keeping her awake was the fact that it had been Tashi who had opened the small silver box and not she. That action was the strangest part of the day. She had not really thought about Tashi's actions until now because she had been so overjoyed with the return of the griff falcon. Reflecting back to when she had found the little box, she realized that Tashi had seemed very close to her all the while she had been working to get the box out of the hole. Once the box was out in the open, Tashi had flown off abruptly. Meryl wondered what that had been all about.

Just as Meryl was drifting off to sleep, she abruptly sat up and realized the ring was still in the pocket where she had put it when she had seen Finn return. She realized her pocket was not the safest place for the ring to be. It was all too easy to lose it that way. Reaching into her pocket, she pulled the ring out, and for just a moment it caught the moonlight. Meryl thought she saw a flash of light, but it was so quick she could not be sure. She quickly reached for the leather pouch she had tucked in a hidden pocket under her shirt where she kept her other treasures and dropped in the silver box and the ring. Meryl tucked the leather pouch back in under her shirt. When it touched her skin, she felt a flash of heat. How odd, she thought.

⌁∕⧖∕⌁

Olwydd was, quite frankly, glad that Fordon had looked him up and given him the means to get out of the capital for a while. His latest plan to gain wealth had not gone quite as planned, and there were some folks looking for him he did not want to meet anytime soon. Fortunately, he had not had to sell his horse to cover some of his debts, so he was able to make swift progress towards the site where Fordon had last seen his step-cousin. Olwydd knew he had the reputation of being one of the best trackers in Sommerhjem, but the time delay since Fordon had last seen the lass Meryl and now was a long one in terms of finding any trace of her. Rain, wind, or animal movement could have caused any trace of Meryl's whereabouts to vanish. Olwydd knew he was going to need a great deal of luck.

More than a great deal of luck, Olwydd thought to himself as he stood in the clearing Fordon had pinpointed on the map. There was not much left of the lean-to, due to a strong storm. The fire ring was still there. Olwydd spent some time walking around the glen, but if there had been any clues as to which way Meryl had gone, the storm had certainly obliterated them. Now it was time to use logic. It seemed obvious that the lass had not gone on to Klippedal, or Fordon would have either seen or heard about her. It also seemed obvious that she had not headed back to the capital the way he had ridden to the clearing, for the same reason. No, logic suggested that she may have followed the base of the bluff.

A half day's ride brought Olwydd to the forester's shelter. Here it was obvious that several folk had used the shelter recently, one of them possibly a female with long dark hair, one an older man. There had also been a donkey sheltered in the lean-to attached to the hut and some type of bird who had golden feathers. There had been rumors that a griff falcon had been sighted in the area over the last year. Fordon had not mentioned anything about seeing one. Maybe it had sought shelter from a bad storm in the lean-to. Olwydd had heard they were very smart birds.

Olwydd decided that with no better traces than the ones he had found at the forester's shelter, he would follow the trail left by the two who had sheltered there with the donkey. While he could not be sure he was following Meryl, he could at least talk to the two he was following. If neither of them was Meryl, he could discreetly ask them if they had seen her. With that idea in mind, Olwydd began to follow the trail the three had left behind. While the storm had washed away much of the trace, he found a hoof print here and a footprint there in the rain-softened earth of the trail.

Olwydd found a campsite but concluded it had been used only by one folk and the same donkey he had been following. Maybe this Meryl had planned all along to ditch Fordon and take the coin. She could have had a rendezvous set up with the man with the donkey. That idea made sense to him. She must be a little schemer. Had to admire a good schemer, Olwydd thought. Olwydd continued to follow the tracks and found the second campsite. He noted the folks had stayed there for a while. That struck him as odd, for if he had taken off with someone else's coin, he would not have stuck around in the same area for so long. What had they been doing here anyway? What also struck Olwydd as odd was the fact that besides staying in one spot for such a long time, they had done nothing to obscure their trail leaving this campsite. Maybe he was following the wrong folks.

❦

It took two more days of meandering through the countryside to reach the area where Finn said the gem fields were. Meryl could agree with him that they were indeed standing in fields, but as to seeing gems sparkling in the browning vegetation, well, that was another thing.

Finn responded to her quizzical, disbelieving look. "Easier to find what you're looking for in the spring, yes in the spring, when the grasses are shorter, but still possible, yes still possible to find something now. Have a little faith in old Finn, a little faith. Let's set up camp next to that small grove of trees over there first. Give Heber some shade it will, nice shade."

Once settled in, the two began to walk a pattern slowly back and forth across an area Finn had marked out. Meryl was surprised that on closer inspection, what she had thought of from a distance as a fairly lush field of grasses, turned out to be much rockier than she had imagined. It was no wonder that the field was not used for farming, for there was too much rock and gravel in the earth, which would have made plowing and planting difficult. After several hours of walking back and forth, Meryl began to envy the donkey, for it had grown hot in the open field. Hunting for a particular type of stone on ground covered by rocks and stones was not very easy. It was not as if the elusive gems were just lying on the ground winking up at one when the sunlight hit them. The gems in their uncut state were dull looking and looked very similar at first glance to dozens of the other stones they lay amid. Finn had explained it was a bit easier to notice the gem stones among the other rocks when it was raining, but there was not a cloud in sight.

It was mid-afternoon before Meryl chanced upon her first really good find. Prior to that time, she had found a few very tiny gemstones that were, according to Finn, neither of good quality nor clarity. Not worth much, in other words. It was actually when Meryl had mostly given up in disgust and had sat down to give her aching back a break and have a drink of water that she found the gem. She had been idly scooping up the large gravel that was in a mound next to her left hip, and letting it dribble though her fingers, when she spotted a rather large stone that had a hint of red in it. Picking it up, she poured a little of the water from her water bag on the stone and thought the stone was possibly a gem. Finn had confirmed that it was. The rest of the afternoon flew by, for she now had what Finn described as finder's fever.

The two had just arrived back at their campsite when they heard the sound of a lone horse approaching. Finn motioned to Meryl that she should quickly put anything of value away. They had had several discussions before they left the bluffs concerning what to do if someone approached them, for Finn had two concerns. One was that there were always unscrupulous folk who would not mind relieving one of the treasures one had found. Second, since Meryl did not know who she was or what type of danger she might be in, it was best to be overly cautious. As the sound of the horse's hooves grew closer, Meryl noticed that Tashi had silently flown into a nearby pine, finding a perch deep in the shadows formed by the thick branches. Even though she had seen the where the griff falcon had landed, it was still hard to spot her.

When the rider drew up at their campsite, Meryl had a very uneasy feeling about the fellow. He was friendly enough, dismounting and asking if he could join their fire. As was the custom in Sommerhjem, they did not turn him away, and he contributed to their evening meal.

Introducing himself, the rider said, "My name is Olwydd. I have been retained by a wealthy family to locate their missing daughter, Meryl. They are worried that she has been kidnapped, or worse."

Olwydd had looked at them expectantly, so Finn had introduced himself, and then introduced Meryl as his daughter Beryl. Finn kind of chuckled to himself. "Names are close sounding, Meryl and Beryl, but my daughter is clearly not the one you are looking for. No, not the one you are looking for."

No one was more surprised than Meryl that she had all of a sudden obtained a father.

"Been up visiting relatives, visiting relatives," Finn said. "Big doings, oh yes, big doings. Me brother's oldest lass got married you know, got married. And where would you be heading next, heading next?"

"Probably back the way I came. I have been following your tracks it seems. What were you doing near the bluffs?"

"The bluffs, ah, the bluffs. Why we were looking for berolige pods, looking for berolige pods. Grows near the base of the bluffs you know, right at the base of the bluffs. Alas, for all our looking, we were not successful. No, not successful at all. Must be too late in the season, too late in the season. With the weather changing it seemed time, yes time, to head home."

"And where is home for the two of you?"

"South," Finn answered, and then asked if Olwydd wanted any more food.

When Olwydd said he was full, Meryl removed the kettle of hot water from the fire. Clean-up was quickly accomplished. Then Finn told Olwydd that it had been a long day, his old bones were aching, and if he and his daughter were going to get an early start, they had best turn in. Finn motioned to Meryl that she should follow him into the tent.

Once inside the tent, Finn whispered to Meryl, "I don't trust that man, no, don't trust him at all. Have a bad feeling, a very bad feeling about him."

CHAPTER THIRTY-NINE

Olwydd felt strongly there was something just a little off about the pair he had finally caught up with. The lass certainly fit the description Fordon had given him. He was not convinced the two were related at all, much less father and daughter. He did know that they would not welcome him tagging along the next day, so he needed to pretend to be heading back the way he had come. He would wait a short time, and then turn back and follow them. With a plan in place, Olwydd settled down to sleep.

Several hours after they had entered the tent, Finn gently shook Meryl and whispered to her that she should not talk but remain quiet.

"We're going to try to sneak out of camp, sneak out of camp without waking Olwydd. I don't trust that fellow, no, don't trust him at all. You go get Heber and load the packs, load the packs. I'll bundle the tent up, just bundle it up, and we can pack it proper later. I slipped a sleeping draught in that fellow's tea, but I don't know, I fear I don't know, if I put in the right amount. We'd best be quick and quiet, quick and quiet."

The amount of sleeping draught must have been at least enough, for Olwydd did not stir and Meryl, Finn, and Heber slipped out of the campsite. On silent wings, Tashi glided down out of the trees and landed on Heber's pack-laden back. Fortunately, the half moon was very bright and not obscured by clouds, giving enough light to see by. Meryl knew that leaving in the middle of the night would put them at least a half day ahead of Olwydd, but he could follow them, for they were doing nothing to obscure their tracks.

When Meryl had asked Finn if he had a plan, he had told her not to worry. Easier said than done, Meryl had thought to herself.

Finn had learned over the years how to protect what he had found from those who might want to relieve him of his treasures. He had a number of plans in place on how to elude those who would follow.

It was still dark when the lane they had been following led to a small fishing village situated where the mouth of a river spilled into a very large lake. On a clear day, you could almost see the opposite shore, but only barely. Other than by boat, there were two ways to cross to the other side. One was where they were, at the north end of the lake where the river entered, and a ferry was tethered. The second one was a good day's walk to the south end of the lake to take the ferry there.

Instead of heading down to the ferry, Finn turned down a side lane that ran through the village and on out the other side. The little village's streets were cobblestone, and the three of them left no trail to follow as they headed towards a cottage perched half on the street and half in the water. There Finn halted, handed Heber's lead rope to Meryl, and stepped forward to knock on the door. Just before the door opened, Tashi took flight, winging out over the water.

The door opened and silhouetted against the light spilling out of the cottage was a man of average height, average build and coloring, dressed in the oilcloth pants of a fisher. The pants were held up by bright green suspenders that clashed with the bright orange shirt he wore.

"Finn, you old rascal, what brings you to my door this fine night? And who is the lovely lass standing there with the donkey?"

"It be a long story, a long story it be, and I would most surely like to stand here jawing with you, just jawing, but I've need of a boon, an important boon."

"You name it my friend, for I and mine are in your debt."

"Nay, you were never in my debt, never in my debt, and we can talk of that later. We need to get the three of us on the water and away from here as quickly as possible before the one following us makes it into the village, into the village, and spots us."

This must be serious, Fisk thought to himself, for Finn had hardly repeated himself. "Well, come on then, follow me."

Fisk led them down the gentle ramp along the side of his house to a dock. Tied to the dock was a boat the likes of which Meryl had never seen, for it was much broader a beam than any of the sailing boats she had seen in the capital harbor or on the Addergoogle River. Stacked on deck were what looked to Meryl like open crates with netting inside.

Seeing the confusion on Meryl's face, Fisk informed her that he not only fished but also set traps for the green crabs that the lake and the region were famous for. He had also been known to do some cargo hauling to various islands spotted around the lake. The reason the boat was so broad a beam was so it would draw less draft. The lake, in many places, was not very deep, so the boat needed to be able to traverse the shallower parts.

"Easy to keep the two of you out of sight should we meet anyone on the water, but it'll be harder to hide that donkey of yours. Step lively now, for we have some rearranging to do," Fisk stated, and he nimbly jumped aboard the boat. "Best hurry for we've a good wind a-blowin' at the moment."

Fisk started rearranging his traps, forming an opening in the middle. Finn helped while Meryl stood and held on to Heber, who did not seem at all disturbed by being on the narrow dock. After the crab traps were arranged to Fisk's satisfaction, he opened up a section of the boat's side rail and set a ramp out between the boat and the dock. Heber docilely followed Meryl aboard. Once Heber was within the opening in the center of the stacked traps, Fisk and Finn quickly moved more crates, closing Heber in. Fisk then threw a tarp over the top of the crates and lashed it down. Meryl decided unless someone got really close and knew what and where to look, they probably would not notice the donkey.

What was left of the night passed quickly, and Meryl was surprised upon waking that she had slept as long as she had, or for that matter had slept at all on the boat. Carefully looking out of the window situated above the bunk she was lying on, the water stretched out a very long way and the land was only a smudge on the horizon. Drawing her head away from the view, Meryl looked around the cabin and noticed that Finn was sitting in the shadows near the top of the steps leading to the hatch, conversing quietly with Fisk.

"Did you have a nice nap, a nice nap?" Finn asked.

Meryl nodded her head, not quite able to stifle a huge yawn.

"Been smooth sailin', smooth sailin' it has. Fisk said we should reach our destination by dawn's break, dawn's break."

⚜

Olwydd could not understand why the ground under him should be quaking. As he groggily clawed his way out of sleep, he realized that he was being shaken, and quite roughly. Opening his eyes, he recognized the man shaking him, and when he saw the man looming behind the man shaking him, he closed his eyes, hoping he was dreaming. The stinging slap across his face snapped his eyes open again.

The man slapping and shaking Olwydd turned to the man behind him and said, "Well, Mako, I think I finally have his attention."

"Thank you Pivane, I'll take it from here," and with that said, Mako reached down, gripped Olwydd by the shirt front and hauled him up out of his blanket roll. "Now my friend, you have some explaining to do, and you had best make it quick, for my patience is at a very low ebb at the moment."

Olwydd's thoughts were racing as fast as his heart, and he knew he needed to come up with an explanation the two before him would buy, or his life expectancy was going to be considerably shortened.

"I was just now heading back to the capital with the coin I owe you and stopped here to camp, see, and, and there were these two folks camping here. Where are the others who were camping here? Why am I so groggy? Oh no, they must have given me something to make me sleep. Where is my pack? I need to check my pack." The panic in Olwydd's voice was the only thing that was completely real in his story so far. When Mako released his shirtfront, Olwydd knelt down and started digging frantically in his pack, as if he might find the coin he owed these two. "It's not here! It's gone! My coin pouch is gone. Those two stole all my coins."

"What two? What are you talking about?" Mako asked. What a stupid dunderhead, Mako thought to himself. Anyone with brains would not have left his coin in his pack while he slept.

By the tone of Mako's voice, Olwydd could tell Mako was still not convinced. "It was late, see, and I knew I had to stop for the night, so I sees this campfire, see, and so I stops, you know, likes one does when travelin'. There was this old gent and a lass. Seemed nice enough. Offered fireside, see, so I's joins 'em. They must've slipped somethin' in my tea and, then when I was out, robbed me. Slipped away in the middle of the night, they did."

"It's still the middle of the night you fool," Mako spat out.

While the two had been talking, Pivane had been looking around the campsite. "Looks like he is telling some truth. There were others here recently. Looks like two folks and either a small horse or a donkey," he said.

"See, see, I'm tellin' yer the truth. Theys gots the coin I owe you."

"Good thing I have two of the best trackers in Sommerhjem with me then because you both are going to work together and find me this pair.

Pack your gear and let's mount up. There's no time to lose. We should be able to catch up to them by daybreak, and you had better hope they haven't spent my coin by then."

The three arrived at the small fishing village just as it began to stir. Mako sent Pivane to one end of the village to see if he could find any trace of the three they had followed. Much to Olwydd's dismay, Mako kept him close at hand as they checked out the ferry landing. When they met in the center of the village, Pivane reported he could see no sign that the two folks and the donkey had left the village and headed down the lane leading out of the village. Since the ferry was still docked and had not moved all night according to the ferryman, they had not crossed the river.

"This village is so small that it only boasts about six fishers, and there are five boats tied to docks. One seems to be out," Pivane observed.

"Find out about it," Mako barked, for he was tired and not convinced that he was not being strung along by Olwydd. The man was a slippery one, and he should never have let Olwydd talk him into investing in his schemes.

Pivane scurried off to do Mako's bidding and soon returned, dragging a scruffy dirty man who smelled of fish and things best not mentioned. "This here bloke has some information that he's willing to part with for a few coppers."

"We'll give him a few coppers, and he'd best earn them or he'll be swimming in that lake yonder. From the looks of him, I'd say he has an aversion to water."

"I knows what yer wants to know," the scruffy man insisted, looking longingly at the coin Pivane had taken out. "Yer after knowing where Fisk's boat is and who mightin' be aboard. I knows that answer."

"Well, spit it out man, and be quick about it," Mako forced out between clenched teeth.

"Well, yer see, I was restless last night and couldn't sleep . . ."

"I don't need your life story, just tell me what I want to know," Mako said, and it was clear to everyone there that he had very little patience left.

"Fisk had several visitors, middle of the night. Couldn't see 'em clearly but there was two of 'em, and they had a donkey loaded with packs. Fisk loaded 'em up on his boat and headed west."

"Where do you think they were going?"

"It's a big lake, sir, so's I can't say. Now could I have me coins? I've told ye all I be knowin'."

"Before you get your coin, I have several more questions. Where does this lane lead to?"

"Why it runs along the shore of the lake, it does."

"Anyone here have a map of the area?"

Mako gave the scruffy man such a look that he knew he could not ask for more coin, and he was lucky to get what he had out of the exchange.

"I've got a chart of the lake in me boat. I'll gets it right away, sir."

"No, we'll go with you," Mako directed, and the group headed north of the ferry crossing along the shore.

When they arrived at the boat drawn up onto the narrow sandy beach, it was clear that it was just barely afloat. The man disappeared into the cabin of the boat and returned moments later with a battered and torn chart. Spreading it out on the nearby tall boulder his boat was tied to, and holding it down with rocks, the man showed it to the three looking over his shoulder.

"From the looks of this chart, there are any number of places this Fisk fellow can drop off the ones we are looking for. There's not a boat here that could carry us and the horses, and I don't want to abandon the horses. Looks like we can follow this lane along the shoreline until we reach the very southern end of the lake. If we don't run across the two on this side of the lake, you had better hope we can pick up their trail on the other side," Mako said, looking straight at Olwydd.

CHAPTER FORTY

Fisk had been heading the boat steadily in a westerly direction for several hours before he turned the bow of the boat south. The wind had been brisk, allowing the boat to move along at quite a clip. The break of dawn saw the three near the south end of the lake. The journey would have taken Finn and Meryl almost a day if they had walked, and at least half a day had they had horses. As they drew closer to land, Meryl could see that what she had thought was an irregular shoreline was instead a series of small islands.

"Fisk says he is going to slip in between the islands and the shore, the islands and the shore. He normally sets his traps in the shallow water so the other fishers we have passed, the ones we have passed, will not think anything is unusual, no not unusual. Says there's a natural landing on the shore between one of the islands coming up and the shore, a natural landing. He is going to put us off there, put us off there."

Fisk had explained where he was going to put them off was just up from the southern ferry crossing. From there, there was a good path they could follow that would take them to a well-traveled road that led to the Gatekryss crossroads. They could travel in any direction from there. Finn had nodded that he was familiar with the crossroads, and a route from there could get them well east of the capital. Even though it was a roundabout route to get them to his home, it would do. His worry was that they were not all that far ahead of the man who might be following, and he was on horseback. They had put some time and distance between them and the man called Olwydd, but not enough, he was afraid.

Getting Heber off the boat was not as difficult as Meryl thought it might be, and they were soon on their way, after thanking Fisk. Once they had cleared the shoreline, the land sloped upward and the trees grew thick around them. Meryl could hear the birds singing in the trees and quiet rustlings in the underbrush as small animals went about their daily lives.

It was the sudden lack of sound that alerted them that something had changed in the woods. Meryl looked up just in time to see Tashi glide in on silent wings and land on the top pack on Heber's back.

"I see your feathered friend, your fine feathered friend, has come back to join us, yes indeed, join us again. Maybe she'll bring us luck, bring us luck."

"I think we may have to bring our own luck. I have a bad feeling about that Olwydd fellow who camped with us. I think we have not seen the last of him," commented Meryl.

"You could be right, could be right. We had best think about whether we want to take to the more traveled roads or not, take them or not. Traveling the back byways might leave us open to an ambush, an ambush, but may keep others from seeing us and telling the one who follows where we have been. Traveling the main roads gives us some protection, for there are more folks on the roads, more folks. That is also a disadvantage, a disadvantage for more folks could tell the one who follows us where we are or have been. We have a way to travel before we have to decide, before we need to decide. On foot, our progress is going to be slower, much slower than the one traveling by horse. We will need to be vigilant whatever way we go, very vigilant."

<hr />

Olwydd felt like he was between a rock and a hard place. On the one hand, was the immediate danger from the two he now traveled with. On the other hand, was the precarious situation he would be in if he failed Fordon, for though the lad was young, he was a dangerous enemy. Olwydd needed either to get away from the two who were now watching him like hawks, or get a messenger bird off to Fordon, suggesting he head for the Gatekryss crossroads. Olwydd had taken a look at his map, and his best guess was the two he was trying to catch up with would probably choose the back byways and that would lead them to Gatekryss crossroads. There was really no other way around it. All roads in this area converged there, and from there led off in eight different directions.

After a long hard half day's ride, the three arrived at the ferry crossing, only to find the ferry was on the other side of the broad river that flowed out of the lake. Having to wait for the ferry's return did nothing to improve the mood of the two Olwydd traveled with. All too soon, in Olwydd's thinking, the ferry would return, and he still did not have a plan as to how to get away. It was probably too much to hope for that Mako and Pivane would just happen to fall overboard.

While they waited for the ferry to return, Olwydd was dragged off to a nearby tavern for a meal. When the three exited, they found that a small group had gathered, cueing up to board the ferry. Heading the line was a rover homewagon. Mako and Pivane started arguing with each other as to whose fault it was that they were now at the end of the line.

"You just had to have a meal. Just had to fill that fat belly of yours, and now look what happened," Mako said quite forcefully, in a low voice.

"I didn't sees yer draggin' yer feet any on the way to food," Pivane shot back, his voice less restrained and a little louder.

"Yah, well, I wasn't the one who had to have a second helpin' of everything," Mako said, raising his voice.

"'Twas the first decent meal I've had in weeks cause you can't cook, and you won't let me."

"I wouldn't feed what you cook to my dog . . . ."

Mako's last sentence was interrupted when the smaller Pivane charged Mako and, with head down, plowed into Mako's midsection, causing the big man to fall like a timbered tree. The ground actually shook. While the altercation between the two men was taking place, the rover homewagon loaded onto the ferry. Olwydd, taking advantage of the two men now scuffling in the dirt of the lane, calmly gathered the reins of his horse and led it aboard the ferry. He knew he would have been safer if he had taken Mako's and Pivane's horses, but they would have cried thief, and then he would have had more than just the two of them after him. Horse thieving was a serious crime in Sommerhjem.

Not willing to wait until Mako and Pivane settled their dispute, the ferry keeper cast off and, with the help of both passengers and crew, began poling and pulling the ferry across the river. Olwydd knew he had garnered himself only a small breathing space and did not doubt the two would be after him. Going now might just give him enough time to get a messenger bird off, and then get off the road and make his way towards Gatekryss crossroads on a less traveled byway.

Once across the river, Olwydd scribbled a hasty note to Fordon and sent a messenger bird. He then took off at a fast trot, heading towards the Gatekryss crossroads, knowing that it offered a myriad of choices of where to head next. He knew that Fordon would be a threat later, but Mako and

Pivane presented an immediate threat. Since Olwydd had become fond of his hide over the years, he thought taking off away from any threat was the best choice. He had bought himself a bit of time, but not much. Mako and Pivane would be delayed by having to wait for the ferry and further delayed for they would have to go just a bit slower trying to find his trail, even though at this point he was not doing much to disguise it.

As Olwydd traveled, he began to have second thoughts about just taking off. There might be some profit to be had yet. If he did it right, he thought, he could follow Mako and Pivane instead of the other way around, and they would never know they were being followed. If they caught up with the lass he thought was Fordon's cousin Meryl, he would know and could decide what to do next.

Meanwhile across the river, another altercation had broken out between Mako and Pivane, each accusing the other of losing Olwydd, their chance to cross the river, and their chance to recover their coin. Mako's mood could be best described as thunderous.

"When I get my hands on that little weasel, I am going to demand double payback," Mako remarked over his shoulder, as he led his horse onto the ferry that had finally returned.

In the end, Finn and Meryl decided that following the more well-traveled roads would be safer than continuing on the back roads. Besides, Finn had remarked, all roads in this area led to the Gatekryss crossroads, which they would probably make by evening if they picked up their pace. He had always intended to go that way, for there was someone he wanted to see there, and it would give them a number of options as to where to travel next.

Meryl had heard of the Gatekryss crossroads but had never had the occasion to travel there herself. Finn spent part of the walk telling her about it.

"'Tis a pretty unique place, very unique. No one knows just why all of the roads ended up converging on that spot, but the crossroads has been there since time out of mind, time out of mind. Some say the crossroads was there before our folk came to settle here, before we settled in Sommerhjem, so it was just natural that it remain, that it remain. Built up some over the years 'cause of the traffic, lots of travelers. Almost like a small village it is, a small village. Has a good inn, a blacksmith, and some shops. Nothing fancy mind you, nothing fancy. We can pick up supplies. Short on supplies we are, very short. Has good camping it does, good camping. There'd be safety in numbers there, yes, safety in numbers. Maybe we can find some folk to travel on with, travel on with."

Even traveling a bit cross country, and stopping only briefly for the noon meal, it was close to late afternoon before Meryl and Finn drew close to the Gatekryss crossroads. While traffic on the road they traveled was not heavy, it had certainly increased, for they had linked up with the road that ran from the ferry to the crossroads. Once they had come onto the main road, Tashi had taken wing, but Meryl did not feel so fearful this time that the griff falcon was leaving for good. She had the feeling that Tashi was never that far away when she flew off.

Really small villages in Sommerhjem usually consisted either of one long lane with buildings on both sides of it, or a central square with buildings around the edge. At most, there would be four streets leading off the square. Gatekryss crossroads was very different, for eight major roads led into a wide circle. Each road aligned along a compass point: north, northeast, east, southeast, south, southwest, west, and northwest. In the center of the circle was a series of shallow terraces that rose up until they leveled off, forming a flat paved area, the center of which held a fountain. Eight stairways climbed up the small terraced mound, each stairway aligned with a road. Each terrace was covered with some type of low growing evergreen so it would remain green even in the cold season. Most of the plants bloomed at different times, so a touch of color could be seen on various terraces throughout the year.

Besides the center area being a surprising place of beauty, Meryl was also surprised to note that no buildings fronted the circle but rather were placed well back, so the outside of the circle was like a park with tall trees and bushes. As wagons, riders, and walkers entered the circle, their pace slowed, and folks made their leisurely way around the circle. Some pulled over and took the time to walk up to the fountain. Finn stopped and tied Heber to a hitching post and suggested they do the same.

"Aren't you worried about Heber and our packs?" Meryl asked.

"Not here, no never here," Finn replied. "This crossroads is under the same rules as the royal road. No harm here, no harm here. For this day we are safe, we are safe. It will give us time to find some allies, yes find some friends."

Meryl climbed the steps leading up to the fountain and with each step felt some of the tension of the last few days draining away. When she reached the top however, she felt as if someone were watching her, judging her. It was a very odd sensation. When she looked around, she could see no one who was paying particular attention to her or Finn. Must be my imagination, she thought to herself, but even after they made their way down to Heber, she could not shake the feeling.

It took about an hour for Finn to make his purchases, and then the pair followed the northeast road to a camping area. Because it looked like it might rain later in the evening, Meryl set about rigging up a lean-to out of a tarp she had purchased that afternoon. She was grateful she had found some coin when they had been searching at the bluffs so she could purchase some things she needed and contribute to the supplies. She did not like being beholden to Finn.

A number of rovers had chosen to camp in the same area. Meryl thought that besides being beautiful, their homewagons were such a practical way to travel. Finn wandered over to their cook fire and made their acquaintance. After cleaning up from the evening meal, Meryl found herself sitting by their fire too and listening to some fine fiddle music. Others who were camped nearby also drifted in to enjoy the entertainment, but Meryl was having trouble trying to relax into the music, due to that prickly feeling on the back of her neck. Someone was paying more attention to her than she felt comfortable with.

Chapter Forty-One

Not wanting to draw attention to herself, Meryl pretended to scratch a bug bite on her left shoulder so she could look behind her. There were two rough-looking men standing just on the edge of the group, partially hidden in shadow, and they quickly glanced away when she spotted them. Meryl wondered what that was all about. Did they know her? Should she ask? When she looked back a second time, they were gone. As the evening wore on, folks came and went. Finally the two fiddlers put their instruments down, and those remaining began to stand up to depart. Just as Meryl was about to get up off the log she had been sitting on, a very small rover man sat down next to her.

"Your pardon, lass, but would you mind sitting with an old man for a moment? The fire is warm, and the night sky too full of stars for the evening to end so soon. Besides, your friend Finn is over there haggling with my young friend Tannar, and it will be awhile. My name's Shueller by the way."

"You're welcome to share my log. I'm called Meryl."

"Do you know the two men who watched you, and the one who watches the watchers? No, don't look around," Shueller told Meryl. "The two men who have been watching you all evening are now to your right just at the edge of the light. The one who has been watching them is even more hidden. He is under the grain merchant's wagon and has been mostly hidden all evening. He has been watching both the two men and you. Do you know why you've attracted their attention?"

Meryl did not know what to do. Get up, move away from this man sitting next to her and try to get back to the campsite she shared with Finn, or remain sitting with the one called Shueller? She did not like the looks of the two she had noticed watching her, and yet she did not know Shueller either. At the moment, he seemed to pose the lesser threat. Meryl did not know why the two rough-looking men had been watching her, but she had certainly been aware of them. Why were three men watching her? What Shueller said next stopped that train of thought.

"You are carrying something of great value, but it is not shielded well. You really need to take care of that."

What was this man talking about, Meryl wondered. Sure, she had found some pretty baubles and a few coins, but nothing that Finn had told her was of great value. The only thing of great value she carried was the golden locket, which had given her feelings of both comfort and loss. Was it the silver box? She knew it was the most valuable thing she had found besides her the locket. The small box had worth because of its age, design, and the fact that it was made of silver. Other than that, what would make it of great value? Meryl gave Shueller a questioning look.

"When your friend Finn is done haggling with my young friend Tannar, I would like a chance to talk to Finn and you in a less open place. I have known the likes of those two who watch you, and I don't think they have a want to become your friends. There are troubling rumblings in the land again, now that the third part of the oppgave ringe has been placed in the Well of Speaking. Those who oppose the current rule and those who are still loyal to the Regent are on the move, trying to prevent the challenge from happening."

Meryl did not understand a word of what Shueller was talking about. Third part of what? What challenge? When he mentioned the Well of Speaking, a memory flashed through her mind of a lad in a column of light, but it was swiftly gone.

"I'm sorry, I really don't know what you're talking about."

Shueller looked at the lass he was sitting next to and could read the utter confusion in her eyes. Her manner of dress, her manner of speech, suggested to him that she had grown up in the capital. Yet if that were true, how could she not know about the Gylden Sirklene challenge, all that had happened during the time of the great fair at the capital this summer, or all that had happened more recently? The news had spread far and wide throughout Sommerhjem, even to the smaller hamlets in the back of the beyond. There was something very odd about the lass sitting next to him. Before he could ask his next question, Tannar and Finn approached.

"He drives a hard bargain, this Tannar. Yes, a hard bargain, but I think I gots what I wanted, gots what I wanted," stated Finn.

Meryl could believe that, since she had been on the receiving end of Finn's bargaining herself. She noticed that Tannar was not looking as confident as he had when he had walked up with Finn.

"Don't let Finn's boasting get to you. While he has been known to squeeze a copper coin until you can hear it squeal, he can be out-bargained."

"Now, Meryl, you shouldn't be givin' away me secrets, givin' away me secrets," Finn said with mock seriousness. "'Tis time we turn in so we can get an early start, get an early start."

"Excuse me, I wonder if you might indulge me with a bit more of your and Meryl's time," Shueller stated in a soft voice. "We need to talk, but not here. Would you both join Tannar and me in our homewagon?"

Tannar reached down to give Shueller a hand up off the log, and then reached for Meryl, but she had already risen. The four walked to the rover's homewagon and proceeded inside. Tannar turned a lamp on low so that it gave off a soft light, and then invited Meryl and Finn to have seats around the table. Shueller settled himself on the cushioned bench with a sigh.

"These old bones don't take well to sitting on logs anymore," Shueller said, shifting himself on the bench pillow to get a little more comfortable. "Now then, perhaps we can continue our discussion from before, Meryl. But first, I have a question for you. Have you been out of the country or out of touch with most everyone in Sommerhjem for the summer and fall?"

Finn looked at Meryl just as Meryl turned to look at him, and chuckling said, "Go ahead, lass, his is a good explanation, yes, a very good explanation, but not the right one, no, not the right one. I know of this rover and you can trust him, oh yes indeed, you can trust him."

It was Shueller's turn to give the man who named himself as Finn a closer look, and there was something familiar about him that he just could not put his finger on.

"I haven't been out of the country, nor do I think I've been lurking beyond the fringes of human contact for the summer and fall. Rather, I've had an accident in which I hit my head and seem to have knocked most of the memories of who I am right out of me. I don't remember much before several weeks ago, other than my name and some flashes of memory that really don't make much sense to me," answered Meryl.

"Ah, that would explain it then," Shueller said. "Well then, let me catch you up a bit so you can understand what I am talking about, and my concerns. When the old queen died a number of years ago, our former royal princess, now Lady Esmeralda, was not of age to rule, and so a regent was appointed, one Lord Cedric Klingflug. As time went on, he became more and more powerful by fair means and foul, and as the time approached for the then Princess to come of age and take over the rule, the Regent and his followers tried to prevent that. To make a long story short, he was thwarted in the end because the Gylden Sirklene challenge was called by the Lady Esmeralda. It seems that rulers in Sommerhjem, up until the last couple hundred years, were chosen by the challenge. Are you following this so far?"

"Yes," Meryl replied.

"The challenge has to do with something called the oppgave ringe, which is made up of nine parts. Three of those parts have been returned to their proper place in the Well of Speaking in the capital. I won't go into all the details of how that came about, or we would be here until morning. Needless to say, the other six parts of the oppgave ringe are being sought after by both those who would have them returned to their proper place so the challenge can proceed and by those who would prevent that from happening," Shueller explained. "Those two who were watching you this night are the type of hired thugs that will do anybody's bidding for a price and are the type that the Regent and his followers are likely to hire. Why they are paying such close attention to you is the mystery."

"We had another odd encounter just last night, just last night," Finn remarked. "We were camped on the other side of the lake and a lone rider, named Olwydd, chanced by. Asked to camp with us, camp with us. Told us he was looking for a lost lass, but something about him or his story did not feel right, just did not feel right. Gots us away from him I did, gots us away." Finn went on to explain what he had done.

"Meryl here couldn't have been the one he was looking for, could she?" Tannar asked, entering the conversation for the first time.

"Bein' a finder I've had to learn to trust my instincts about folks over the years, and I felt like that Olwydd was lying through his teeth, through his teeth. Oh, our Meryl here might have been the Meryl he was looking for alright, but not because she was the daughter of a wealthy family who might have been kidnapped. No, he was makin' that part up, just purely makin' that part up."

"You mean that you don't think I could come from a wealthy family?" Meryl inquired.

"No, lass, sorry to burst your dreams, but no. Can't really explain why, but no," Finn said, shaking his head.

"Describe this Olwydd fellow for me," Shueller requested, and Finn did so with Meryl adding details. "How curious. The man you just described sounds rather like the man who was watching both you and the two men watching you. He was hiding out of sight most of the evening, but I caught enough of a glimpse of him to think your Olwydd is here nearby. Hum-m-m."

The rover homewagon was silent then except for the muffled sounds of the wind blowing against the closed windows. After a brief time, Shueller seemed to pull himself out of his reverie and addressed Meryl. "Do you remember earlier when I suggested that you might be carrying something of great value?"

"Yes, but I can't imagine what that could be."

"You have something on you that is emanating, I guess you might call it a signal for lack of a better word, that some of us can recognize. Should the wrong sort become aware you are in possession of something old and possibly containing some gift or power, they would not hesitate a second to relieve you of it any way they could," Shueller stated.

"I don't recall either of us finding anything that might fit what you are talking about, though granted, I wouldn't know from emanating, wouldn't know from emanating," Finn suggested, "but I have heard of such, heard of such. The only thing Meryl found that I didn't know much about was a small silver box, small silver box. Would you show that to Shueller, please Meryl, show it to him please?"

Meryl excused herself, got up from her seat, and went to stand at the front of the homewagon with her back to the three who remained seated around the table. She reached under her shirt and opened the leather pouch she stored her valuables in. After straightening up her clothing, she returned to the table. She was a little worried for the box was now empty, and she had not told Finn about the ring she had found inside as she should have.

Meryl quickly covered up her worry by saying, "I had quite a time getting this little box out of its hidey hole in the bluff, I can tell you that much. It was jammed in there pretty tight and just didn't want to come out. Pretty little thing, don't you think?"

Meryl then held out the box in the soft glow of the lamp. The light glinted off the silver, and the tiny gems winked with sparks of fire deep within them.

"Would you allow me to look at it more closely?" Shueller asked.

Meryl glanced at Finn questioningly. He nodded to let Meryl know that it would be alright to let the rover have the silver box for closer inspection. Meryl handed the box to Shueller, and then sat back and watched as he moved the lamp closer to him to put more light on the box he held. Shueller turned the box this way and that. The rover homewagon was so quiet it was as if everyone were holding their breaths.

"A very interesting piece, and one of great age I suspect," Shueller remarked as he handed the box back to Meryl, "but not what I sensed. Were you able to get the box open?"

"Yes," answered Meryl and hoped he would not ask her if the box had contained anything. Finn had been so good and kind to her, not to mention fair, and she had not been truthful with him. Not exactly untruthful really, Meryl thought, for Finn had not pushed her at the time to tell him what was in the box. Meryl did not know why she had not said anything to Finn about the ring when she had first opened the box. At the time, it had just seemed to be the right thing to do, but now, she was not so sure. Should she tell him now when among the two rovers who were, after all, strangers, or tell him later?

To cover her circling thoughts and stall for time, Meryl cleared her throat several times and felt all of the folks in the homewagon looking at her intently. Realizing that holding back about the ring and telling Finn later, or telling him now, was going to have the same result, Meryl decided that she had best just tell the truth.

"I'm sorry, Finn, I should have told you when I first opened the box that there was something in it. I won't blame you if you don't want me to travel with you anymore."

Getting up once again, Meryl walked to the front of the homewagon feeling a great weight of sadness resting heavily on her shoulders. Reluctantly, she pulled out the leather pouch and removed the ring. As she closed her hand around the ring, a feeling of calm came over her. Meryl came back to the table, sat down, held out her hand, and opened it. In the stillness, all she heard at that moment were three simultaneous sharp intakes of breath.

Chapter Forty-Two

Shueller was the first one to speak. "Ah, that explains much."

Meryl looked at him, hoping he would explain, and was surprised to notice that Finn was beaming at her rather than looking disappointed or angry.

"I knew it, I just knew it. She's a natural finder she is, a natural finder," Finn remarked, looking for all the world like he had just been given a second helping of his favorite dessert. "It was my lucky day when that griff falcon led me to her, my lucky day."

"I thought I had caught a glimpse of a griff falcon while riding here from the ferry landing, but dismissed it as either my imagination or wishful thinking, since Tannar hadn't seen it," stated Shueller. "This ring explains much that I have wondered about this day."

"What a find, oh my yes, a great find. This is a good thing, but dangerous, yes, dangerous."

"It might explain why she is being watched, but then, how would the two watching her know of the ring?" Shueller questioned.

"How indeed, how indeed? No one was around when she opened the box, no, no one was around. If she didn't show it to me, then I don't think she showed it to anyone else, not to anyone else."

Meryl, still holding the ring out, was growing impatient. "Hello, you two, I'm still here."

"Begging you pardon, Meryl," Shueller said and had the good grace to look mildly uncomfortable. "What I suspect you hold in your hand is one of the pieces of the oppgave ringe. If only it could talk and tell us how it ended up in a hidey hole in the side of a bluff. What an amazing tale that might be, but I digress. The important question is not how the ring ended up inside of a bluff, but rather, how do we get you and it to the capital safely? First things first, however. You need to get the ring inside something that will shield it. The silver box would probably work, but if you had a small pouch made of golden pine spider silk, that would work better."

Meryl reached into the neckline of her shirt and pulled on the cord that was attached to the golden pine spider silk pouch Finn had given her to hold her lucky coin. Pulling it out, she lifted the cord over her head and held it and the pouch out for Shueller to see. "Will this do?"

"Yes, that should do quite nicely, with a little modification. The pouch is of golden pine spider silk, but the cord is not. Tannar, could you go out to the cart and grab a spool of golden pine spider silk for me please? Better yet, bring several spools that you think might match her coloring."

When both Finn and Meryl gave Shueller a questioning look concerning the color, he went on to explain that the closer the color of the cord was to Meryl's coloring, the less likely someone might notice she wore a cord around her neck. That made sense to both Meryl and Finn. Tannar returned quickly with a number of spools of golden pine spider silk, and all of them realized that it would be foolish to try to match color to coloring by the light of a dim lamp.

"I must be more tired than I thought," shrugged Shueller, "for not thinking of that sooner. So that we might all get some sleep this night, let's make tentative plans for tomorrow. Had you intended to leave early, and where might you have intended to head?"

"I had hoped to meet an old friend here who once had a small shop, but the shop was closed. Boarded up it was, all boarded up. Woman in the neighboring shop said the high taxes the Regent imposed put him right out of business, right out of business. Sad I was, very sad indeed. He often bought my findings, but with him gone there's nothing to delay our leaving, no, nothing to delay us. As to where we're heading, well, that seems to have changed with Meryl's discovery, with Meryl's discovery."

Meryl had been only half listening to the two men while she thought about what Shueller had said, and what he had not said. How had he known she carried something of value? What had he meant when he said the ring explained much concerning Tashi? When she brought her focus back to the conversation, she heard Finn say something about where they were heading next.

"I'm sorry, I wasn't paying attention. Where did you say we were heading next?"

"Why, the capital, of course, the capital. The ring needs to get to the Well of Speaking, the Well of Speaking," Finn exclaimed.

Meryl addressed her next remark to Shueller. "Am I correct in thinking that if anyone knew I had the ring, I would be in danger?"

"You mean more than you are now with two thugs and one other obviously interested in you?" Shueller asked.

"Yes."

"If anyone knew you had a piece of the oppgave ringe, you would be in a great deal of danger from those who want the challenge never to happen," Shueller replied honestly.

"So, if I found a royal guard for instance, or a whole patrol of royal guards, couldn't I just give them the ring and be done with it?"

"'Fraid not."

"No?"

"I'm sorry, my dear. I know this must be doubly confusing, since you have really no recall of the past and have not heard anything about the oppgave ringe or the challenge. From what I have observed and what I know, only a very few can handle the rings. I had occasion to talk to a few folks who know about the rings, and they suggested that only those folks whose families had been charged with keeping the rings safe, and a few rare others, can handle the rings. You are either descended from one of the families charged with keeping the rings safe, or you are one of those rare folk. Without knowing who you are, it is hard to tell which category you fit into."

Shueller did not mention that he felt strongly that she fit into the second category. She was definitely Neebing blessed, but he did not want to get into an explanation of just what that meant at the moment.

"I know it's late, but could I ask one more question?"

"Of course, my dear," Shueller replied gently, for he could see the confusion and worry in Meryl's face.

"Why does the ring explain the griff falcon?"

"That's an excellent question and one I would be happy to explain, but it will take some time and it's late. What I would suggest is that we travel together tomorrow, for there is safety in numbers, and as we travel, I will try to explain why I think the griff falcon travels with you. Would that be acceptable to you both?"

"I was going to ask, yes, going to ask, if we might travel with you, so yes it would be acceptable, most acceptable, the traveling together that is. The waiting for tomorrow to get an explanation about Tashi, about Tashi the griff falcon, well, that's Meryl's decision, Meryl's decision alone."

"Tomorrow would be fine," Meryl said graciously, as she stood, for she had seen how fatigued Shueller was.

She and Finn left the rover's homewagon and walked the short distance to their campsite. Their cook fire had burned down to just a few embers, so Finn threw on a few more logs.

"I'll take first watch and you sleep, you sleep. I'll wake you half way through what is left of the night, half way through," said Finn.

"Do you think that's necessary?"

"This night I do, this night I do. Those three watching you have made me want to be very cautious, very cautious. No telling what they're up to or what they want, no telling."

Meryl felt like her head had just hit her pack that she used as a pillow when she was being shaken awake by Finn. Once he had gone into his tent, she threw a few more logs on the fire, pulled her cloak around herself and tried not to fall asleep. This second night with very little sleep was making staying awake very difficult. She was very glad to see sky begin to lighten, which signaled that her watch was almost over. As the campground began to stir, Finn emerged from his tent. He did not look any more rested than Meryl felt. This day is going to be a very long day, Meryl thought.

Once Heber was loaded up, the two walked the short distance to Shueller's homewagon. Shueller and Tannar were ready to leave, but before doing so, Shueller held up different spools of the golden pine spider silk and made a choice of the one that most closely matched Meryl's coloring. Once he had braided a cord, Meryl threaded it through her pouch and placed the pouch over her head. After that was accomplished, the four started off and headed back into Gatekryss crossroads. Meryl expected they would circle around the fountain and head immediately off, but Shueller pulled his homewagon over and got down. Finn tied Heber to a hitching post and walked with Meryl to where Shueller was standing.

"I want to climb to the top and fetch some water from the fountain. This is an old and somewhat mysterious place where the fountain runs all year long no matter how cold it becomes. No one really knows who built it or exactly how it works, but the water is crystal clear and cold as a mountain stream. It will also put us higher than those who are driving, riding, or walking around the circle, and we may have a chance to spot our watchers," Shueller suggested.

Tannar and Finn chose to stay down with the homewagon and the donkey, so Meryl and Shueller made their way up the stairs to the top of the mound. Meryl was once again filled with a sense of peace and calm.

"You feel it too, don't you?" Shueller asked. "That sense of peace. Not everyone does. I would dare say those who are following you would not. Come, let me fill my small bottles with water, and we will be on our way. While I'm doing that, see if you can spot our lurkers. Just take a casual walk around the fountain."

Meryl did as she was asked and was disturbed to note that the two men who had been following her were indeed still watching, but from the shadows of a large tree opposite where they had stopped. If she had not been looking really hard, she would have missed them. She did not spot the man called Olwydd, but that did not mean he was not out there, too. Meryl casually stepped back up to Shueller and reported what she had seen.

"Nothing to be done about it but to wait and see if there are others heading our direction. I figured if we can hook up with others and form a caravan of sorts, the two or three following you might be less inclined to try to confront us on the road. Let's enjoy the view a few moments longer and watch to see if there is anyone else heading southwest," Shueller suggested.

The two stood by the fountain filling small bottles with water, and for all that were watching, seeming not to have a care in the world and to be in no hurry to go anywhere.

⁂

Olwydd had spent a miserable night trying not to fall out of the tree he had hidden himself in trying to keep a watch on the one he thought was Fordon's Meryl, despite the older man saying her name was Beryl. He did not want them sneaking out in the middle of the night on him again. Olwydd had a few tricks up his sleeve, and early morning when the two he had been watching set about fixing breakfast, he had taken himself off to find a man he knew who owed him a favor or two. When he reached the man's shop, he was disappointed to find it was boarded up, but that did not stop him. Looking both ways to see if he were being watched, he checked twice before he slipped down a very narrow gap between two buildings and made his way to the back of the shop. After checking once again to make sure he was alone, Olwydd approached a small shed behind the shop, made quick work of the lock on its door, and hastily slipped inside. The shed held very little, but the contents of the shed was not why Olwydd was inside.

During the time of the Regent's rule, when times had become tough for everybody, Olwydd's friend had made a little extra cash by buying goods that had come into the seller's possession by fair means or foul. Because of the nature of his business, he had built an escape route, should things become dicey. Olwydd was about to use the escape route as an entrance. The other thing his friend had been good at was helping folks disappear when hunted by the Regent's agents or others. For a stiff fee, this man had items that would allow one to change one's identity and that was what Olwydd was counting on. Olwydd had discreetly traded his horse and tack the night before, and now he needed to change his appearance so that even his own mother would not know him.

⚜

"Are you looking for anybody in particular?" Meryl asked.

"I sent Tannar off to casually stroll through the campground this morning to see if he could get a sense of where others were heading. Ah, I think it is time to head down, for there is the grain merchant's wagon that I think is heading our way, according to Tannar."

The two reached the bottom of the steps just as the grain merchant's wagon approached. Tannar stepped out from alongside the homewagon and hailed the driver. After a brief conversation, he walked back to Shueller and informed him that the grain merchant was indeed heading their way and would welcome company along the road. This had been his first venture out since the Regent had been ousted, but he still did not feel very safe this far out from his home, which was several villages down.

Just as Shueller and Tannar had settled themselves in the homewagon and were about to snap the reins to start their horses, a lone rider pulled alongside. The man was of middle years, with a neatly trimmed beard and mustache. He was a very well-dressed man astride a fine horse. He appeared to be a man of means and certainly did not look like he had spent the night camping. His clothes were clean and pressed and his boots polished. On closer inspection, however, Meryl could see that the clothes, while clean, were worn and patched in places. The same was true about the horse's tack which was old, but well cared for.

"Which way would you kind folks be heading?" the man asked.

"By the southwest road," Shueller replied, since he could see no reason to lie.

"Would you mind if I rode with you? Heard tell there has been some trouble with bandits around here and would feel safer if I traveled with others. Name's Thayne."

Meryl had drawn up next to the homewagon and overheard Thayne asking to join their group. There was something about the man that seemed familiar, but she just could not put her finger on it. Shueller told the man he was welcome to join the group, and it would have been rude to have refused. She noticed the man had a small cage on the top of the pack that was tied to the back of his saddle. It contained small birds. A memory teased at Meryl's mind but was soon gone.

CHAPTER FORTY-THREE

Mako and Pivane watched from the edge of the trees as the two they had followed stopped in the circle that formed the Gatekryss crossroads. The two were now apparently traveling with the rover homewagon, which complicated things. The two of them against four, one a short old man, were not too bad odds, but then they saw the four join up with a grain merchant's wagon, and then a single rider. It was getting to be a crowd, and the odds were swinging away from their favor.

"This whole trip has been a bust from beginning to end," stated Mako, as he threw his hat in the dust in disgust. "That weasel Olwydd has slipped through our fingers once again, and there is no guarantee that that lass even has Olwydd's coin pouch. The more I observe them, the more it seems unlikely. I suggest we move on. Just cut our losses for now. We'll likely run into Olwydd another time, and when we do, he won't get away from us again. Now then, there was that job tracking down that Høyttaier lad. Rumor has it he's supposed to be arriving at the port of Marinel, and then is heading towards the ol' homestead. If we hurry, we can get there before him and set up a nice surprise. Good pay, if we do our job right." The evil gleam in Mako's eye made even Pivane shiver.

Having reached agreement that either following the lass in hopes of recovering their lost investment, if she even had it, or trying to pick up Olwydd's trail were both less than profitable, the two walked back to where they had left their horses and headed off.

Once Finn and Meryl left Gatekryss crossroads, they made frequent checks behind them, but there was no sign that the two who had shown interest in Meryl were following them. The morning passed by swiftly, and for a time, Finn rode with Shueller and Meryl walked with Tannar, and for a time, Meryl rode with Shueller.

As she rode with Shueller, he talked to her about what had led up to Lady Esmeralda calling the Gylden Sirklene challenge and the present search for the remaining six parts of the oppgave ringe. Shueller told Meryl that Lady Esmeralda had formerly been called Princess Esmeralda and had been the heir to the throne. She had stepped down after she had called the challenge in hopes of maintaining peace in Sommerhjem. At the point that she called the challenge, many folks wanted neither the Regent to continue to rule nor did they have much faith in Lady Esmeralda. Shueller explained about the present interim ruling council and the fact that even though the Regent had been ousted, he and his followers were still a threat to Sommerhjem. There were many who were scrambling to find the remaining six parts of the oppgave ringe, and not all of them had the country's best interests at heart.

The two rode in silence for a while, and then Meryl remembered to ask what he had meant when he had said that her being in possession of the ring explained the griff falcon.

"Well now, griff falcons are a very, very old type of bird, and many suspect they flew the skies of Sommerhjem long before our kind settled here."

"Our folk haven't always lived here in Sommerhjem?" Meryl asked.

"No, lass. What little has been handed down through time suggests we came here a long time ago from far across the western seas. No one seems to know what caused us to leave our land there. What the historians can tell us is that this land was once occupied, but again, no one seems to know what happened to those who came before us. That fountain we took water from this morning is just one example of what those who came before us left behind. At any rate, there is certainly more to this land than we know, and griff falcons are a part of that not knowing. Though their normal habitats are the high hills and mountains, they are also found in quirrelit groves. There are accounts in our history of them partnering on very rare occasions with one of us. I could make a guess that you, the ring, and the griff falcon are all connected somehow. Ah, here's Tannar looking for a chance to ride. We'll talk more later."

In addition to talking to her, Meryl discovered Shueller had also been a very good listener. He had asked her very insightful questions concerning what she knew about herself and then made some observations. It certainly gave her a great deal to think about when she was back walking with Finn.

The group stopped for the noon meal and, as was the custom, shared what they had with those they were traveling with. The two traveling in the grain merchant's wagon were going on only as far as the next village, where they had some business. The man who had introduced himself as Thayne said he would be glad to continue on with them down the road they were traveling, but wanted to know where they were heading when they reached the next crossroad.

There had really been no time during the morning's walk for Meryl and her companions to all discuss together just what route they were going to take, other than to know that they needed to get to the capital. The longer Meryl was in possession of the piece of the oppgave ringe, the more opportunity there was for something or someone to interfere with her placing the ring in its proper place in the Well of Speaking. Meryl and Finn could set off on their own, but that would reduce the safety in numbers factor. On the other hand, Shueller had a route he took this time of year and regular customers. If he deviated too much from it, it might be noticeable. Sticking with Shueller and Tannar would mean a longer time on the road, but they would eventually get to the capital.

Shueller answered the man's question by suggesting they were headed towards Garving, for he was low on hides of fine leather. Both Shueller and Finn indicated they had business there and might stay a day or so, so if Thayne were heading on, he might want to find another group to travel with.

"Well, you just happen to be heading my direction," Thayne suggested, "so I will travel as far as Garving with you. My trip out from the capital was quite fast, so a slower pace on the way back would be welcome."

"What is it that brought you this far east?" Shueller asked.

"Oh, a little of this and a little of that," Thayne answered, and then stood up, brushed himself off, and said, "It looks like the grain wagon is about ready to head out. I'd best check my horse and mount up."

When Meryl glanced back after they had started walking once again, she noted that Thayne had still not mounted up. She watched him take a bird out of the small cage on the back of his horse. After doing something with the bird, he released it. The man's action niggled at a memory in Meryl's mind, but she could not quite catch it. There was something important she should know about what Thayne had just done, but what?

She turned to ask Finn, and then realized she was no longer walking next to him but was walking next to Tannar. She did not feel like she knew Tannar well enough to ask him, so she tucked her question away for later.

Thinking of birds, Meryl turned her attention to Tashi who, now that they were traveling with others, no longer rode on Heber's pack nor flew in sight of them. Meryl had worried that the griff falcon had gone away once they had arrived at Gatekryss crossroads. This morning when Meryl was packing up to get ready to leave the campsite, a small golden feather had drifted down in front of her. When she looked up into the branches of the thick pine tree she had camped under, she saw Tashi concealed in its boughs. As she walked, Meryl had a feeling that Tashi was not far away. That set her thinking about what Shueller had told her about griff falcons. Could it be that she and the griff falcon were somehow paired?

The rest of the day passed by very uneventfully. They had bid the grain merchants adieu mid-afternoon and made good time, arriving at the next village early evening. Shueller knew of a farm just outside of the village where they could camp. Thayne said he would be staying at the small inn in the village and asked what time they anticipated leaving in the morning. Thayne and Shueller made arrangements for the five of them to travel on together the next day.

When they arrived at the farmstead, Shueller directed them to a small grove where they could set up camp. He then invited both Finn and Meryl to accompany Tannar and him to the farmer's cottage. On their short walk to the cottage, Shueller explained it was rover custom to offer to do chores in exchange for a place to camp. When they arrived, they found the farmer, his wife, and their children all scurrying about trying to round up the laying hens. Someone had not latched the gate properly that morning, and the hens had all wandered out.

Without even thinking twice, Meryl stepped forward and asked the farmer's wife what she did when she fed the hens.

"Why, I put grain in a small bucket, and . . ." The farmer's wife looked a little embarrassed at this point but went on ". . . I make clucking noises and rattle the grain in the bucket."

"Rather than chasing the hens, who don't seem to have gone all that far but are being difficult to catch, why don't we fill several small buckets, and you and I and maybe several of your children all make like we are going to feed the hens? I think they might be eager to follow us into the enclosure for a bit of grain," Meryl suggested.

Since chasing the chickens had not been all that successful, the farmer's wife was more than willing to try Meryl's suggestion, and with the exception of a few hens, the trick was successful. No one was more surprised than Meryl that the trick worked, and she wondered how she knew to suggest that. A very grateful farmer and his wife asked the four if they wanted to share a meal with them, and so the evening passed by quickly.

⚬⟫⟩⟨⟪⚬

Fordon was sitting quite comfortably, leaning back in his chair by the fire in the main room of the inn where he had been staying, when the innkeeper's son cleared his throat to get his attention.

"Herr-m-m. Your pardon, sir, but a messenger bird arrived late this afternoon for you." The lad held out a small capsule, and it was all Fordon could do not to snatch it out of the lad's hand. With great control, Fordon graciously accepted the capsule and gave the lad a copper coin. Fordon then got up and leisurely stretched, as if he had all the time in the world and the message was of no great urgency or importance. Once he got to his room however, he swiftly opened the capsule and read the message inside. A wide grin spread across his face. Had anyone been in the room with Fordon at the time, they would have shaken in their boots at the evil that was within that grin.

Fordon made quick work of packing his belongings, descending the stairs, and walking swiftly to the inn's stable, where he ordered the groom to prepare his horse. Finally, Fordon thought to himself. He could finally take care of Meryl once and for all and then get on with his life. He had almost lost faith that Olwydd would be able to track Meryl down, but the man had come through. The first messenger bird had arrived the day before with information that Olwydd had found Meryl, and he was heading to the Gatekryss crossroads. This last message said Meryl was to be in Garving by the next evening, and it looked like she would be there several days. Even if Meryl left Garving before he arrived, at least now her trail would no longer be cold.

It took several days of hard riding for Fordon to come within a short ride of Garving. Olwydd had set up a rendezvous for noon the next day at a spot to the east of Garving, and Fordon was looking forward to meeting him and finishing what needed to be done. Fordon was familiar with the area and took care to avoid the main roads while making the last leg of his journey. The next day when he reached the rendezvous spot, a covered bridge that spanned a slow moving deep river, he was surprised to find no one there. That fool Olwydd cannot even make his own meeting, Fordon thought angrily to himself. He got off his horse and was looking for something to throw or pound when he heard the sound of a horse approaching. Looking up, Fordon saw a man of middle years with a neatly trimmed beard and mustache. A very well-dressed man astride a fine horse. If I were a thief, this rider would be pretty easy pickings. While tempted, I do not want to draw attention to myself, Fordon thought as the rider came closer. He was surprised when the rider pulled to a halt next to him and addressed him by name.

"Sorry I'm late, Fordon, but I have good news," Olwydd stated.

"Olwydd?" Fordon questioned, for had he not recognized the voice, he would not have guessed the man astride the horse next to him was the tracker he had hired to find Meryl.

"Pretty good disguise, don't you think? I definitely fooled the lass Meryl, and you too, it would seem," Olwydd said smugly.

Not liking to be made a fool of, Fordon asked Olwydd to report. Olwydd went on to say that he had found Fordon's step-cousin. She was traveling with an odd little man named Finn, and the pair had hooked up with two rovers.

"When I first caught up with them, that Finn fellow told me your step-cousin's name was Beryl." Olwydd did not fill Fordon in on how Finn and Meryl had sneaked out in the middle of the night, or about Mako and Pivane. "Anyway, I changed appearance and caught up with them again. They are to spend several days in Garving, seemin' in little hurry to move on. I got the distinct impression that Meryl intended to continue travelin' on with both the fellow Finn and the rovers. However, here's the good news part. I overheard a part of a conversation between her and the older rover fellow, a one Shueller, and I think she doesn't have any clear memory of who she is." Olwydd looked pleased that he could deliver this information. "She seems to have had her memories knocked right out of her."

"Are you saying you don't think she knows who she is?"

"That's what I'm sayin'."

Fordon thought about that for a moment, and then decided he could use that knowledge to his advantage.

"I left Garving yesterday because I really didn't have a good excuse to stay, and while my disguise is a good one, somethin' might have given me away at any moment. I didn't want to risk that. My impression was that the lass Meryl intended to stick with the rover shoemaker's party. Seems to have gotten real chummy real fast with him."

"You said she's traveling with some older man?"

"Yah. An odd little man. Not quite sure what he's all about. He and Meryl are either friends or workin' together, but I don't really know at what."

"So there's four of them you say?"

"Yes, just the four."

"And you think Meryl has lost her memory?" Fordon asked again.

"From what I was able to overhear, she had a knock on the head, and it knocked the memory of who she is and where she is from clean out of her mind."

"Hum-mm, I'm going to have to think about this. In the meantime, we had best see if they are still in Garving, or try to pick up their trail. The sooner we locate them, the sooner this is done, and you can get paid the rest of your coin."

When Olwydd saw the look that crossed Fordon's face, he was glad he was not the lass Meryl.

Chapter Forty-Four

Meryl, Finn, Shueller, and Tannar stayed in Garving for two days. While Shueller and Tannar spent time at the leather works picking out much needed hides for their craft, Finn and Meryl took advantage of the time to take care of those common chores that need to be done while on the road. They did laundry, fixed some of their equipment, replenished supplies, and even had some time to poke around some old abandoned buildings, seeing if anything of large or small value had been left behind.

On the third day, the four broke camp in the early dawn's light and headed out. The road they traveled was a winding one that followed a small creek and was nicely shaded due to the large trees that grew on either side. While the shade was welcome, it did make it difficult to tell if anyone were following, or if anyone were ahead of them on the road. All of them were attentive, however, for the possibility that they might be followed was on everyone's mind. The day passed by quietly enough, and the four met few on the road. That evening, as they gathered around the dying fire, they began a serious discussion as to what would be best for all of them.

"After tomorrow's stop, where I only have a delivery, my way is pretty much open for the next week. Tannar and I had made arrangements to meet up with his family midweek, about a two day's ride out from the capital. A number of rover families will be gathering, and some of them would be more than willing to change their plans and travel into the capital with us. I think even the most dangerous of those loyal to the Regent, if they knew of the ring, would think twice about trying to get at you amid a determined group of rovers," Shueller said with a smile.

"It will be good to see my family," Tannar said shyly, for he was not one to carry on long conversations.

"Hush, did you hear something?" said Finn quietly.

All four stilled to listen, as did Olwydd, who had crept up to the edge of the clearing where Meryl and her traveling companions were camped.

Finn stood up and motioned to Tannar. "Let's check on your horses and Heber."

Meryl took a long stick and stirred up the fire, adding a few small logs. The logs caught, and the flame put more light out into the clearing.

Olwydd was silently berating himself for stepping on the very dry branch that had snapped underfoot, alerting those gathered around the fire to his presence. He prided himself on his ability to move silently and undetected both in the country and in town. Such a stupid mistake he thought, as he slipped away deeper into the shadows and headed back down the road to where Fordon was waiting.

"Well?" Fordon asked when Olwydd slipped into their camp, which was dark, for Fordon did not want to be noticed by either the flicker of firelight or the smell of wood smoke.

"I only overheard a little bit before they began to check the outskirts of their site," Olwydd replied. He did not want to admit that he had been the one to alert them to his presence.

"Well?" Fordon's patience was never long and having to sleep outside rather than sleeping in a soft down feather bed in some fine inn had not improved it.

"The group we've been followin' sounds like they's headin' toward the capital. Seems the rover lad is meetin' up with his family midweek, but I don't know just where. Here's the interestin' part however . . ." Olwydd paused for effect.

"Get on with it," Fordon all but growled.

"They was talkin' about a ring. Seems this step-cousin of yours found some ring, and there must be some secret about it or somethin'."

"What do you mean?"

"I overheard the rover Shueller say, and I quote, 'I think even the most dangerous of those loyal to the Regent, if they knew of the ring, would think twice about trying to get at you amid a determined group of rovers'. Must've found a ring with a really big gemstone in it ifin' others would want to relieve her of it. Might'n be a bonus for us to relieve her of it ourselves."

While Olwydd had been talking, Fordon had been thinking. So, alright, a ring with a rare or large gemstone would be attractive to thieves or scoundrels, but would it attract the notice of the Regent's followers? Sure, he might need treasures such as a valuable ring to convert into coin. Fordon had heard rumors that the Regent's fortune was considerably reduced, as were his holdings. The current interim ruling council had set up a court where claims against the Regent and his cronies were heard. The court, in most cases, had ruled against them, making them give up much of what they had acquired through less than honest means. The more Fordon thought about it, the more unreasonable it seemed to him. Even if the ring Meryl supposedly had was a valuable ring with a large rare stone, it did not make sense that the Regent's agents would go after it, if they knew about it. What kind of ring would the Regent want that the rover Shueller felt that he needed to surround Meryl with many rovers for protection?

Fordon continued to sit in the dark long after Olwydd had rolled up in his blanket roll and was snoring softly. The night was quite bright, with the light of the full moon shining down into the clearing in which they were camped. What kind of ring was it that Shueller felt needed to be kept safe and out of the reach of the Regent or his followers? That thought kept going around and around in Fordon's head when suddenly he sat up abruptly from his slouched position against a tree. Of course, he thought. Of course. Now he was more determined than ever to get his hands on Meryl and especially on what she had. Besides saving his hide, there could be a fortune in this for him, also.

There was an almost feverish excitement in Fordon as he stood up and moved quickly over to the sleeping Olwydd. Prodding him with the toe of his boot, Fordon whispered forcefully, "Get up and make it quick. Here's what we're going to do. We're going to sneak into my step-cousin's campsite and snatch her right out from under the noses of those she's traveling with."

"I think they may have someone keepin' watch."

"Then we will have to make the watcher end his or her watch sooner than expected, won't we? Now pack up."

Fordon and Olwydd moved closer to where Meryl's group was camped and tied their horses to nearby trees. Walking silently down the road, keeping to the shadows, Fordon indicated they should halt, and the two men slipped into the woods ringing the campsite. Fordon could not believe their luck, for it was Meryl's turn to watch. The rover homewagon was dark and silent as was the tent occupied by the man Olwydd said was called Finn. Meryl was sitting with her back to a tree, and unless one was very alert and looking for her, one would not have seen her there in the shadows. Fordon gave Olwydd a hand signal that he was to follow him. The two crept with great stealth to circle around behind Meryl.

Meryl had been on watch for several hours and was having trouble keeping her eyes open. When she pushed herself up a little straighter from the slouch her body had slid into, she though she heard a noise and went on the alert. Not soon enough, for suddenly she found her mouth covered, and she was being yanked sideways.

"Not a word, not a sound if you value anyone else who is camped here. Do you understand? Nod your head if you do," said a voice that sounded vaguely familiar to Meryl.

Meryl nodded her head that she understood, all the while trying to think of a way to get out of the situation she was in. What could she do? That choice was taken away from her when suddenly she felt a sharp blow to her head, and then nothing.

When Meryl went limp in his arms, Fordon stifled an oath. He grabbed a better hold on the now unconscious body of his step-cousin, dragging her a few feet before he hoisted her over his shoulder. Once he had her away from her campsite and back at their horses, he lit into Olwydd.

"Why in the world did you hit her? You just made her dead weight. I need her conscious. Did you manage to grab her pack?"

"You didn't tell me you wanted her pack," Olwydd whined.

It is so hard to get good help these days. To think that I entrusted this nitwit with some of my coin, Fordon thought to himself. Well, I will not be burdened with either of these two after tomorrow.

"We don't have time to go back for it. We don't know when Meryl's watch was up, and her being gone could be discovered any moment. Also, she could come to at any moment. You had better hope she has the ring on her. I'll mount up, and then you can boost her up to me."

Olwydd did as Fordon asked, and soon Meryl was slung across the saddle in front of Fordon. Even though they would have to pass by the campsite they had snatched Meryl from, Fordon chose to head that direction, for he had a place in mind about a day's ride down the road. There he could have the privacy he needed to question Meryl, and then dispose of both her and Olwydd. Once that was done, if the ring Olwydd had talked about was what he thought it was, he would plot out his next moves. By the time Meryl's traveling companions made it as far down the road as where he intended to stop, there would be nothing there to indicate what had happened to either Meryl or Olwydd. It would just remain a mystery. Maybe even a double mystery, Fordon thought to himself. They would not know what happened to her, and they would never even know who she really had been. Ah, life was looking up.

⁂

Finn was awakened by the sound of horse's hooves thundering past the campsite and leapt up, worried that the rover's horses and Heber had somehow gotten loose and were running off. He emerged out of his tent at the same time Tannar clambered down the steps of the homewagon, tucking his shirt in. Both ran to where they had left the animals only to discover, much to their relief, that they were still tied where they had left them.

"Seems some folks must have been in a real hurry to go by so quickly in the dark, so quickly," stated Finn. The words were no sooner out of his mouth when it suddenly occurred to him that Meryl had not come rushing up with them to check on the horses. He turned around, searching the campsite, peering into the shadows of the surrounding trees, but he could not see hide nor hair of her. "Do you see Meryl anywhere, see her anywhere?" Finn asked Tannar.

It had also occurred to Tannar that Meryl was not anywhere to be seen, and he was just about to comment, when Shueller emerged from the homewagon. He quickly crossed the clearing to where the two others were standing.

"What is going on?" Shueller inquired.

"We heard several horses passing on the lane. They were traveling fast, and both Tannar and I got up, thinking maybe our animals got loose, got spooked. They are fine, but Meryl seems to be missing, just missing."

"We had best spread out and see if we can locate her," Shueller suggested gently, hearing the worry in Finn's voice.

The three moved to the outer edges of the campsite and began working their way into the surrounding trees, calling for Meryl. After quite some time, they returned to the campsite. Tannar built the fire up, and the three gathered around it seeking both the warmth and light. None had found Meryl.

"I know you are as worried as am I," stated Shueller, addressing Finn. "There's really not much we can do before daylight. I would suggest we try to get some sleep, or at the very least, rest until dawn. We'll be able to see more once the sun comes up. I think it's my watch. Go on you two. At least lie down for a while."

After Finn and Tannar reluctantly went back to their respective beds, Shueller settled himself on a camp chair near the fire, for the night had grown cooler, and there was a dampness in the air. Pulling his wool cloak closer around him, Shueller tried to keep his impatience down, since dawn was taking its sweet old time in coming. They needed light in order to continue to look for Meryl. Lantern light just did not show enough. Shueller was worried for Meryl. What if she had, for some reason, left the campsite and had become injured? What if she was even now lying in the woods, and they had missed her in the dark? If they did not find her, that would be tragic in its own right, and also the ring she carried would be lost again.

The other option concerning Meryl's disappearance was also not a good one. What if somehow, someway, someone had discovered she has one of the pieces of the oppgave ringe and had kidnapped her? Her life could be in extreme danger, and Shueller did not even want to think of what might happen if the ring fell into the wrong hands.

CHAPTER FORTY-FIVE

Meryl's head was pounding, and it was also hanging upside down. It was so hard to gather her thoughts and hold onto them. When she opened her eyes a slit, she quickly closed them because she could see the ground moving by at a fast pace, which did not help the dizziness she already felt. Then it all came rushing back. She had been standing watch when someone had put a hand over her mouth to silence her, and then she had felt something strike her head. She remembered nothing after that until now.

Meryl decided that she would continue to remain quiet until she had a chance to figure out just what was going on, besides being draped over a horse and having a huge headache. That voice she had heard when she had been snatched was teasing her memory. She knew that voice, but how did she know that voice? Fordon, it was Fordon's voice. But wait, she thought to herself, she had been standing watch. Was that just a dream? Fordon had shoved her when she had caused him to miss his shot at the griff falcon, and then what?

Meryl's confusion grew, as did her aches and pains from being draped over a horse. Fordon had pushed her. She had hit her head. Had he come back for her and was even now trying to get her somewhere to get her help? No, that did not make sense. If he were concerned for her health, he surely would not have flung her over the front of his saddle, would he? Had she just dreamed of her time with the little grey man named Finn? What was real?

The horse beneath Meryl began to slow, soon turned off the main road onto a side lane, traveled a short way, and came to a stop. Meryl felt the rider behind her shift and dismount. She decided to continue to pretend she was still unconscious.

"Olwydd, tie your horse up and then come over here and give me a hand with Meryl."

Meryl felt herself being none too gently pulled off the horse and dumped on the ground. She opened her eyes just enough to see the horse being led off. Moments later, she could see two sets of boots approaching her.

"You take her feet, and we'll move her up onto the porch," Fordon told Olwydd. "This would have been so much easier if you hadn't hit her. At least not so hard. I have some questions I want answered by her before she is no longer useful. Put her down here," Fordon indicated.

"What is this place?" Olwydd asked, looking around at the small farm cottage and surrounding outbuildings. Both the land and the buildings looked abandoned and worn.

"This is the hardscrabble little piece of land that my parents thought of as home and hearth. They were content here, but I couldn't stand the place. It was my good fortune when, after they died, the farm was so in debt that I couldn't stay. I was getting ready to leave anyway. But enough idle chatter, go get some rope. I don't want her getting away when we're not looking, and we have a few things to do."

Once Fordon had secured Meryl to the railing, he led Olwydd into the cottage. The thatch had blown away in places in the roof, allowing rain to enter. The cottage smelled musty and dusty. Several somethings scurried in the shadows. The cottage consisted of a large open room with two doors off the back wall. Olwydd thought they probably led to bedrooms. Fordon walked directly into the kitchen area and kicked back a moldering rag rug. He squatted down, grabbed hold of a metal ring, and pulled up the trapdoor. Light poured into the opening from a hole in the roof, and a cold damp smell rose from below.

"If I stand back, there should be enough light for you to see. I want you to climb down and check in that barrel to the left there. Do you see it? I want you to bring up what is stored inside," Fordon directed.

Without even questioning what was in the barrel, or why he was going down rather than Fordon, Olwydd did as he was asked and climbed down into the root cellar. Once his feet touched the dirt floor, Fordon slammed the trapdoor closed and slid the latches home, trapping Olwydd in the root cellar. He thanked his mother in his mind for always fearing animals might somehow be able to open the trapdoor and insisting that his father put sturdy latches on it. Fordon paid no attention to Olwydd's yelling or pounding. He turned and headed back out to the porch and Meryl.

⚜

Finn, Shueller, and Tannar had no better luck finding Meryl in the light of day than they had during the dark of night. They did, however, find signs of there having been several folks in their campsite and some drag marks. Tannar had backtracked along the lane and returned to report that there had been someone camping not too far from them, but they had not built a fire. It looked from the tracks that they might have been the ones who had been at the campsite last night.

"They tied their horses up fairly close to camp. The horses were there for only a little while, and then they headed past us," Tannar suggested.

"While I hate to leave here when Meryl might be nearby and we just haven't found her, I strongly suspect someone has taken her, taken her," Finn said sadly.

"I think you're right," replied Shueller. "Those on horseback have a good head start on us but don't seem to be doing anything to disguise their tracks. I suggest we follow them."

All were in agreement and so tied Heber, Finn's donkey, to the back of the homewagon, climbed aboard, and headed down the road, hoping against hope that Meryl was alright.

⚜

When Fordon came back out onto the porch, he toed Meryl's prone form roughly with his boot. It jarred Meryl, causing her head to hit the porch rail, and she had let out a moan.

"I know you're back with me, so open your eyes and quit faking that you're still out. I'm certainly willing to kick you harder," Fordon said.

Meryl was more than convinced that he meant every word. She slowly opened her eyes and struggled to sit up, which was difficult because both her hands and feet were tied. While Meryl had been bouncing around on the horse and while she had lain on the porch, she had had time to think. The second hit on the head seemed to have jarred her memories loose, and she now knew who she was and what had happened to her. Fordon was not anyone she wanted to anger, so she struggled to sit up.

The muffled pounding and yelling coming from inside the cottage seemed to disturb Fordon, so he hauled Meryl up and told her he had had a change of plans. He reached for his knife and brought it down towards Meryl's ankle, slitting the rope that bound her. Grabbing her elbow, Fordon dragged her off the porch and towards what once had been the barn. Shoving her through the gaping opening, where the door to the barn had once hung, Fordon sat her down on an old crate.

"Now then, if I remember right, you used to keep your valuables in a leather pouch under your shirt in a hidden pocket. That's where I found them the last time," Fordon told Meryl, as he reached in and plucked Meryl's leather pouch out with nimble fingers that would make a pick-pocket envious. Fordon set his knife down on the lid of an upside down barrel. He then unknotted the drawstring on Meryl's leather pouch and tipped the contents into his hand. As he looked over the meager collection of odd objects, his look of greedy anticipation turned to anger.

"Besides the silver box, there's nothing here but a few paltry coins and some rocks. While the silver box might fetch some coin, it isn't what I'm looking for. Where's the ring?" Fordon demanded.

Meryl tried not to look surprised and said, "What ring?" How had he known about the ring, Meryl wondered.

"Look, I don't have time to fool around. Olwydd overheard you talking about a valuable ring, and I have a good idea that it's not valuable because it has a large gemstone set in it. Here, I'll even give you back the little silver box for the ring."

Fordon flipped the silver box towards Meryl, who snatched it out of the air. She knew Fordon had no intention of letting her keep it.

"Now give me the ring."

Fordon snatched up his knife and began advancing on Meryl, who had stood and moved around to the other side of the bench. Fordon having to skirt the bench might slow him down a bit, but even if Meryl bolted out the barn opening, she did not think she had much chance of escaping. Just as Fordon reached for her, there came a loud scream and the sound of beating wings. Meryl only caught a flash of gold and red before she turned and fled. She ran as hard as she ever had, straight towards the horses. Untying the reins quickly with her hands tied was difficult, but fear made her fingers nimble. Keeping hold of the reins of one of the horses, she vaulted into the saddle of the other and urged them to turn and head down the lane. Glancing over her shoulder, Meryl could hear the scream of the griff falcon echoing out of the barn and a scream from Fordon. She hoped the griff falcon would be alright. She did not care very much about the fate of Fordon.

Fordon, and Olwydd for that matter, could declare her a horse thief, but at the moment and under the circumstances, Meryl was not worried about it. Not being held captive and not giving up the ring were all that mattered. She urged the horse she was riding to greater speed to put as much distance between Fordon, Olwydd, and herself. She had just given the horse his head and did not know where he was taking her. She just knew she wanted to be as far away from Fordon as she could get. Meryl only slowed the horses when Tashi flew in low over her head and landed on a low-hanging tree branch several hundred yards beyond her.

⟐

Fordon picked himself up off the barn's filthy dirt floor and wiped his sleeve across his face, wincing as the dirt-covered cloth of his sleeve scraped the deep grooves scoring both cheeks where the griff falcon had raked him with her talons. What in the world had just happened? One minute he was poised on the brink of securing himself a fortune, and the next minute he was being attacked by a griff falcon. He shook his head. If he told anyone that he had been attacked by a griff falcon, they would think he was just blowing smoke. No one would believe him.

It had taken Fordon just a few short moments to recover from the attack, and he quickly ran out of the barn, only to discover both of the horses were gone. He would never catch up to Meryl on foot, but he knew where she was heading. Now all he had to do was find some transportation other than being on foot and get to the capital before her. While he might not have gotten the ring, knowing she had it would be worth something to the right folks. Brushing himself off, Fordon jammed his hat down lower on his head and headed out, ignoring the faint pounding and yelling that was still coming from the inside of the cottage.

Fordon walked away from his family's homestead as fast as his legs could carry him. At least he had eliminated one threat to his continued wellbeing. Olwydd could rot in that root cellar, and no one would be the wiser. As for Meryl, he had plans. Whomever he found to give the information he now had to, he was going to want the guarantee that, in the end, he got to decide what was to happen to Meryl. After walking half a day, Fordon's luck changed, and he was overtaken by a long haul merchant's wagon heading for the capital. He had contacts there who would know just exactly to whom he should sell his information. They would have the resources to find and stop Meryl from ever reaching the capital.

⌘

Meryl slowed her horse to a walk and rode up to where the griff falcon was perched.

"I thank you for your timely rescue, Tashi." Meryl no longer felt foolish talking to the bird. "You wouldn't happen to know where Finn and the rovers are, would you?"

Tashi dipped her head and then took flight heading down the road in the direction Meryl had been traveling. The horse she was riding began following the griff falcon with very little urging from Meryl. After several hours of riding at a steady pace, Meryl stopped the horses just before a short bridge and slid down out of the saddle, hoping her knees would hold her up. She walked the horses for several minutes to cool them down before letting them drink. Just as she was about to mount up, she heard the sound of a wagon approaching. She did not notice that Tashi did not immediately take flight, which had been her normal response when others besides Meryl and Finn were around. Meryl held herself at the ready and let out a huge sigh of relief when she recognized the rover homewagon approaching the bridge. She felt even more relieved when she saw Finn riding up front with Tannar. Shueller, she concluded, must be riding inside.

When the rover's homewagon had crossed the bridge and come to a full stop, Finn immediately jumped down and rushed towards where Meryl was standing next to the two horses.

"Ah lass, you are a sight for sore eyes, a sight for sore eyes. What happened? We were so worried, so very worried. Here let me cut the rope tying your hands, tying your hands."

"Thanks," Meryl said. "As to what happened, it's a long story, and I'm famished. Do you think we could take a break for a meal? Then I'll tell you all I know."

As the four sat and ate, Meryl filled the others in on not just what had happened since she was snatched from their camp the night before, but also on what she now knew about herself and what had happened just before Finn had found her in the forester's shelter.

"That knock on the head that Olwydd gave me must have jarred my memories loose. It's nice to know who I really am, and I can tell you, I'm not all that anxious to see Fordon ever again," stated Meryl emphatically.

"You may not be anxious to see Fordon again, but I don't think he is done with you," said Shueller. "He knows where you're heading and, from what you've told us, he may have guessed what you're carrying. Getting away from him solved your immediate problem, but has, I am afraid, created more problems that will be equally dangerous."

CHAPTER FORTY-SIX

"Well, what has happened, has happened. Spending time worrying will only use up more time. Our time would be better spent figuring out how to avoid Fordon or any he might enlist to help him. Do you know how he discovered you had the ring?" asked Shueller.

"I honestly don't know," replied Meryl.

"I think I might," said Tannar shyly. The others looked at him expectantly. "You said you recognized the other voice of the folk with Fordon as that of Olwydd. It would seem he was the owner of one of the horses you, ah, borrowed."

"Yes, Fordon called the other man Olwydd, and his voice sounded like the voice of the man who camped with us before we met you," Meryl stated.

"Well, one of the horses you borrowed is the one who was being ridden just a day back by Thayne."

"Are you sure? How did Olwydd come to be riding Thayne's horse?" Meryl asked.

"Maybe because they are one and the same, one and the same," Finn replied. "There was something familiar about that Thayne fellow, something familiar, but I just couldn't figure it out. The voice was different, but . . . ."

"You're right," Meryl exclaimed. "Now that I think about it, there was always something off and yet at the same time familiar about Thayne. He was following us, and maybe . . . ."

"And maybe he followed more closely than we knew and overheard us discussing the ring when we were camped last night," suggested Shueller. "I wonder how he's connected with Fordon, and where he is now."

"As to how he's connected, I remember him releasing a messenger bird when he was traveling with us as Thayne. I suspect he might've been sending it to Fordon. It would be like Fordon to hire someone to do the hard work like finding me rather than doing it himself. As to where Olwydd is now, when I was tied up on the porch, I heard pounding and what sounded like muffled yelling coming from inside the farm cottage. That seemed to disturb Fordon for some reason, and he moved me to the barn. I wonder if he locked Olwydd up somewhere in the cottage?"

"While it might be risky, I think we should return to the farmstead you just came from. We might be able to get some idea of what's going on. It will be four against two if they're both there, which makes it better odds. I suspect Fordon probably has cut his losses and headed out," suggested Shueller.

The four agreed that it would be worth the risk to head back to the farmstead where Meryl had been briefly held captive. It was not much out of their way. Finn mounted up on the spare horse, and much to everyone's surprise, Tashi landed on Heber's pack load and settled in for the ride. When they arrived at the farmstead, it looked abandoned and deserted, but the travelers approached it with great caution. A check of the barn and the other outbuilding revealed nothing of great interest. When they entered the cottage however, the scene changed.

Upon hearing footfalls on the floor above, Olwydd began yelling and pounding on the trapdoor to the root cellar. "Let me out you churlish rough-hewn varlet, you bootless beetle-headed cutpurse, you half-faced clay-brained mold-warp! Let me out!"

"Ah, I think we may have found out what happened to that fellow Olwydd. Yes indeed, we may have found him. Quite creative in his hollering he is too, quite creative," chuckled Finn.

Following the sound of Olwydd's voice, the four found the trapdoor. Deciding that being prepared was more important than rescuing Olwydd right away, Shueller sent Tannar out to fetch some rope. Once they released Olwydd from the root cellar, they did not intend to turn him loose. They certainly were not going to trust him, and it made no sense to just let him go on his merry way so he could contact others with the information about the ring Meryl carried.

Once Tannar returned with the rope, Shueller cautiously opened the trap door, telling Olwydd to climb up slowly. Tannar stood on the side of the trap door opposite from where Olwydd would climb up. Olwydd was so busy telling Shueller how grateful he was to be rescued, how he had been duped by Fordon, he did not notice Tannar until it was too late. Tannar very quickly slipped the rope over Olwydd's head and tightened it, locking Olwydd's arms to his side. Olwydd protested mightily and loudly, but that did not stop Tannar from tying him up tightly. Once they had Olwydd safely contained, they asked him what he might know about Fordon's plans.

"Well, I certainly didn't know he was going to double-cross me," Olwydd spat out in disgust, "and I don't know what his plans are. Now let me go."

"We think not," Shueller answered. "We will make you comfortable but not let you go. You really didn't expect we would after you tried to kidnap Meryl here, now did you?"

Olwydd tried again unsuccessfully to convince his captors that he was innocent, that he had been forced by Fordon to kidnap Meryl, but by then no one was listening. He had been unceremoniously dumped onto the floor of the rover's homewagon. Tannar tied his feet up and settled in to watch him. Once Olwydd was secure, Meryl and Finn mounted up on the two horses, and the group set off. Shueller had suggested that they travel the back byways and head towards their meeting with Tannar's family. He thought Fordon, if he had acquired faster transportation, would probably head towards the capital, unless Olwydd had also discovered that they were heading to meet up with Tannar's family.

The group's luck began to change mid-afternoon when they came upon several more rover families, who had pulled over to rest and water their horses. Shueller knew them and went to talk with them. When he returned, he told them that the rover families had agreed to join them and travel with them to the place where Tannar was to meet up with his family. The addition of three more rover homewagons and families added considerably to their numbers and gave Meryl and the others a measured feeling of safety.

"Did you tell them about the ring?" Meryl asked Shueller when they had a moment of privacy.

"No, lass, I did not," Shueller replied. "I just called in a few old favors. No explanation was needed."

Very few folk knew the part Shueller had played in helping the Lady Esmeralda escape the clutches of the Regent, or the price he had paid. The rovers did, and they knew what Sommerhjem owed him.

After several days, the rover caravan came to the encampment where not only Tannar's family was gathered, but a number of other rover homewagons as well. Shueller explained to Meryl and Finn that gatherings like these took place a number of times a year, so rover clans could get together and exchange information, do repair work, make music, and tell tales. As rover children grew old enough to travel on their own, or travel on with another rover such as Tannar had done in order to learn a trade, there needed to be gatherings like this one so folks could reconnect.

Meryl was riding in the homewagon with Shueller when they pulled in, and she noticed a smile grow on his face as he pulled past a green homewagon decorated with beautiful and intricate designs. She was surprised to see a hunting cat asleep in the shade under the homewagon.

"Someone you know?" Meryl asked.

"Ah yes, and it would seem our good fortune continues to hold," Shueller answered but did not explain.

Shueller drove the homewagon to the far side of the encampment and pulled in next to Tannar's family and their homewagon. Tannar had beat them there and was presently caught up in a bear hug by his father Bertram, as his mother stood patiently by, waiting for her chance to greet their son. Bertram's brother Oscar waved at Shueller and headed his direction.

"So good to see you, and thank you for bringing my nephew here. I hope he's been a help," stated Oscar.

"The lad has been a great help and a good traveling companion. More importantly, he has become very skilled in the crafting of leather goods. I'm hoping he will continue on with me rather than going off on his own," replied Shueller.

"I'm sure that'll be part of the family discussion this night. It's hard to see the children grow and leave the family, even if it's just for a little while. Bertram's youngest, Shyla, has been mounting a campaign to be allowed to travel over the next few months with our friend Nissa. Of course, she hasn't even had the opportunity to ask Nissa if that would be alright."

"I saw that Nissa is here. Do you think that once the family reunion is over we could all get together? It's a matter of some urgency. We have some travelers with us that I think you all should meet and hear their story."

Oscar understood that the group Shueller wanted to get together included him and his wife, Bertram and his wife, Nissa, and Tannar plus the travelers. "Will a couple of hours be too long to wait?"

"No. We intend to spend at least the night, but like I said, there are urgent matters we need to discuss, and we need to be really discreet about it."

Oscar could see the look of grave concern on Shueller's face and assured the Günnary shoemaker that what he wanted would be done. "Now then, introduce me to your traveling companions, and let's see if we can get everyone situated."

"Ah, one more thing," Shueller stated somewhat reluctantly. "We have a reluctant passenger who happens to be tied up at the moment in my homewagon. We will need to discuss what to do about him also."

It was decided that the gathering of all the parties would need to wait until after the evening meal, when the others in the encampment gathered around the community fire to listen to the fiddlers and drummers. The music would make it more difficult for anyone to listen in on their conversation. The group gathered in Oscar's homewagon. Olwydd was being guarded by Oscar's oldest daughter, and she had strict instructions that she was not to untie him under any circumstances, unless Shueller's homewagon was in imminent danger of burning down.

Even though the prospect of danger had not been eliminated, Meryl found that she was feeling more relaxed and safer than she had in several days. The camaraderie and simple joy of the folk in the encampment at just being together did much to ease the tension Meryl had been feeling. That momentary feeling of calm was quickly squashed once the discussion began in Oscar's homewagon. Having to retell all that had happened to her since she had left home was difficult. The next request was even harder.

"While I'm sure Shueller and Finn are right in their guess that the ring you carry is one of the pieces to the oppgave ringe, would you mind if I took a look at it?" asked the rover who had been introduced as Nissa.

Meryl looked questioningly at Shueller, and he assured her that it was alright to let Nissa take a look. "She's probably the only one here, other than you, who could handle the thing, since she once carried not one but two of them for quite some time. That, however, is a story for another time."

Meryl found herself feeling quite reluctant and somewhat protective of the ring she carried, but she had grown to trust Shueller over the last few days, so she reached in to pull out the golden pine spider silk pouch and opened it. Taking the ring out of the pouch, she placed it in the palm of her hand and held it out. When Nissa reached for it, it was all Meryl could do not to close her hand over the ring and pull her hand back.

Sensing her inner struggle, Shueller spoke up. "Most folks would not be able to even touch the ring, lass. You may have noticed that both Finn and I never have. Nissa, however, will be quite alright, and you can trust her."

"It would really help if I could have a chance to hold the ring," Nissa said. "From here I can see that the ring certainly looks like the ones I carried, but I could really tell if I could hold it."

Meryl felt a sense of calm spread from her hand up towards her heart and, trusting that feeling, she dropped the ring into Nissa's outstretched hand. Nissa closed her hand over the ring and closed her eyes. She was silent for several long moments before she opened her eyes and spoke.

"It is one of the pieces of the oppgave ringe." When some in the homewagon gave her questioning looks, she said, "I wish I had a way to explain other than it feels right, but I don't. I just know that what Finn and Shueller suspected is true. Now all we have to do is figure out how to keep Meryl safe and get her to the capital without any more trouble."

CHAPTER FORTY-SEVEN

"The problem that I see is we have several choices," Nissa stated. "We could get all those here to travel with us and gather more rovers along the way, but that puts a lot of folks at risk and makes our movements really obvious. At the other extreme, we could just send Meryl and one other on very swift horses and have them head straight to the capital, but that's really risky. I would like to propose a different alternative."

Everyone gathered in the homewagon looked at Nissa expectantly.

"I would suggest Shueller, Tannar, and Finn, when the time comes to move out, head towards the capital without Meryl. Don't take the horses you 'borrowed' with you. If you are stopped for any reason, you can tell those stopping you that Meryl took the horses and left you. You can explain you don't know where she is. How good an actor are you Finn?"

"Well now, I might not be a candidate for the royal players, but I can tell a pretty good tale if needed, a pretty good tale. Why?"

"If push comes to shove, you need to be convincing that you are disgusted with Meryl. After all you've done for her, all you taught her, and she just up and left you, the ungrateful, no good . . . . Well, you get the idea."

"But where will Meryl be, where will she be?" asked Finn.

"It will be best that you don't know, but trust me, she'll be as safe as we can possibly make her," answered Nissa. "But we are making plans without asking Meryl what she wants to do. After all, the burden of getting the ring to the capital rests solely on her shoulders."

"Since you obviously can handle the rings, could you carry this one to the capital instead of me?" Meryl asked hopefully.

"While it is true that I can handle the ring, this ring is connected to you and, I think, your griff falcon friend. You might be willing to give up the burden, but do you think Tashi is?"

"Ah," whispered Shueller so quietly that it was almost inaudible, but Meryl heard him.

"Ah, what?" Meryl asked.

"I think Nissa is right. While the griff falcon is important to you, she may be even more important to this journey you are taking. I've had the opportunity to spend some time with the royal historian. We know so little about the Gylden Sirklene challenge, and I was curious. One small piece of information I picked up concerned a flag flown by the early rulers of Sommerhjem. The main figure featured on the flag was a griff falcon. Would seem griff falcons were quite a symbol of importance at one time. I think we need symbols right now," suggested Shueller.

"There's also a statue of a griff falcon near the southern market place in the capital, if I remember right," mused Nissa.

"This is all very well and good, but have you noticed that each time we gather with others, Tashi disappears?"

"You might want to revise what you're saying," Oscar spoke up, and his voice was filled with laughter.

At first, Meryl did not know what he found so humorous, until she followed his gaze. Sitting on the driver's seat peering into the homewagon was Tashi, looking for all the world like she was attending the meeting. Meryl caught movement out of the corner of her eye and saw Nissa's hunting cat Carz slowly rise. She had forgotten he was there. A sudden fear gripped her, and she was about to quickly stand and try to block Carz when Nissa's voice stopped her.

"No harm will come to Tashi from Carz. Watch."

Carz took a long look at the griff falcon, and Tashi stared back. Then both of them dipped their heads, and both settled back into more relaxed positions.

Under normal circumstances, a bird at rest would be a potential dinner for a hunting cat, and yet these two nodded at each other as if they were old acquaintances, thought Meryl to herself. As she glanced at the others, she noticed that none of them looked surprised at what had just transpired, not even Finn. With all that had happened in the last few days, Meryl did not know why she found the non-reaction of the others to two wild creatures nodding at each other strange, but she did. She did not take much time to dwell on it, however, since Nissa had begun the discussion once again. Meryl found it interesting that the others gathered in the homewagon all seemed to defer to Nissa, even though she was younger than most gathered there. Meryl wondered what Nissa's story was.

"This encampment is due to break up in two days, and it would look strange if Shueller and Tannar did not stay the whole time. While I trust all of the rovers here, we are not exactly hiding away, and you do somewhat stick out. Give me a few hours to make some arrangements, and then you are going to 'run off with the horses'. I would suggest that you pack up your belongings and be ready to move at any moment. Just pack a light pack, all you will need for the next few days. Oscar will stow the rest of your belongings in his homewagon and will bring them to the capital. It would be best if neither Finn nor Shueller had anything of yours."

The group talked a few minutes more, for they needed to decide what to do with Olwydd. Oscar suggested that Olwydd travel on with them, for they were heading to Glendalen before going to the capital and could turn him over to Lord Hadrack for safekeeping. When the discussion ended, Oscar and his wife, Bertram and his wife, and Tannar left the homewagon and went to join the other rovers around the community fire. Tashi had left just prior to Nissa and Carz, who slipped out the front of Oscar's homewagon leaving just Shueller, Finn, and Meryl alone.

Finn suggested that Meryl go and pack up what she needed to travel lightly. He would meet her at his tent in a few minutes. A short while later, Finn and Meryl were settled in Finn's tent. They could hear the music and laughter coming from around the community fire.

"This plan, does it make sense to you, Finn?" Meryl asked, and Finn could hear the worry in her voice.

"What you're really asking is, do we trust these folk, do we trust them? I know of this Nissa, and while she is young like you, being the keeper of not one but two parts of the oppgave ringe can only change one and make one stronger. She is both lucky and smart, very lucky and smart. If she has a plan that she says will keep you safe, I would trust her, trust her."

Meryl then asked the question she was not quite sure she wanted to know the answer to. "Will you stay with Shueller and Tannar and travel on to the capital?"

"Of course, lass, of course. Our journey together is not at an end, no, not at an end. I will meet you at the Well of Speaking. That's why I stayed behind to talk to Shueller. He has assured me we will know when you arrive, when you arrive, and will be able reconnect with you. Not to worry, no, don't worry."

Meryl did not have much time to feel relieved because a soft voice, barely heard over the sound of the music, asked for entrance.

"Come," Finn answered softly back.

Nissa slipped inside. "Are you ready to go?" she asked Meryl.

"I'm packed, but I'm not sure I will ever be ready to go on this next leg of the journey."

"Trust me, I know just how you feel," stated Nissa ruefully. "Best say a quick farewell and then not look back. Slip out the back when you are done, and I will meet you there."

"Finn . . . ." Meryl started, but Finn cut her off.

"Now, now, lass. Go quickly now, and I'll see you in a few days, in a few days. Not to worry. I have a good feeling about this, like I get just before finding just the best hole, yes just the best hole on the bluffs. Yes, I've got a good feeling. Go now and be safe, be safe," Finn said, as he made shooing motions with his hands.

Meryl slipped quietly out the back of the tent, not looking back, so she did not see Finn wipe away a single tear that slid down his weathered face.

❧❧❧

Fordon's string of bad luck began to change a day after he had fled the old family homestead. The long haul trader he had hitched a ride with had bought his story that he had been thrown from his horse into a thorn patch. Just his bad luck he had gone headfirst, he had complained. The trader had stopped for the night at a small inn where Fordon had then chanced across someone he knew. Not exactly the folk he needed to find eventually to sell or bargain his news to, but someone who knew those folk and could get him to them.

His acquaintance fortunately had several horses, and so the two took off the next morning, heading for the capital. While this "favor" his acquaintance was giving him was not free, Fordon felt that in the end, the coin would be well spent. During the ride, he had two thoughts going over and over in his head. One concerned the riches he was going to receive because of the information he carried, and the other was about what he was going to do to Meryl when he had her in his sights once again.

While Fordon was concerned about someone recognizing him once he arrived at the capital, he felt the beard and mustache he had grown while

302

he had been away would be a good disguise. Besides, the folks Fordon wanted to make contact with did not reside in the same part of town as his uncle. After they settled into a small inexpensive inn and stabled their horses, Fordon's acquaintance left for several hours. When he returned, he told Fordon someone would meet him at the statue of the griff falcon near the southern market. There was some irony in that, Fordon thought.

Fordon passed the time between getting his instructions and the time of the meeting swinging between elation and fear. He knew the folks he was likely to be dealing with were supporters of the Regent to the point of being obsessed with returning him to power. That made them both dangerous and sometimes not very rational. He had information that could turn the tide, but he did not want to give it away for free, nor did he want to be harmed in any way. He spent time thinking about a plan that would keep him in one piece. He for sure did not want to give the information away to some lackey. No, he needed to meet with someone who had some power and authority.

At the appointed time, Fordon left the inn, but left his horse and meager belongings behind. Since he did not know what was going to happen next, he wanted his things where he could easily retrieve them. It was always important to have an escape plan. He had been told to look for a man wearing an eye patch and not be late. Fordon had arrived early because he wanted to be really familiar with the ins and outs of the small square where the griff falcon statue was located. He sat on the low wall surrounding the statue, and to the casual observer, looked like a man just relaxing after a long day's work.

Just as the bells tolled from a nearby clock tower sounding the appointed hour, a tall thin man of middle years wearing an eye patch strolled into the square. He walked up to Fordon.

"Fordon?" he inquired.

"Yes, and you are?"

"No need for names. Just follow me."

Fordon followed the man out of the square, and for quite some time, they took a very meandering route, often doubling back not once but several times. In the end, they arrived at a short dark alley that ended at a low wooden door. Due to the route they had taken, Fordon was not sure he would be able to find that alley ever again. Maybe that was the point, rather than to make sure they had not been followed. The man with the eye patch knocked out a rhythm on the door, and the door creaked open. No light shown out of the opening.

"It's me, and I brought the man the boss wants to talk to."

The door swung open just wide enough for them to enter, and Fordon was told he was to walk straight forward about ten paces. He was to turn to the left and walk ten more paces. The man who had answered the door would be there to meet him. With that said, the man with the eye patch slipped back out the door and was gone. Fordon did as directed, and when he had walked the twenty paces, he came upon an open door lit by a very dim light. He walked through the doorway, looking for the man who had met them at the alley door, but saw no one ahead of him. Suddenly a sack descended over his head, and he was warned not to take it off. He was told to put his hands behind his back, and they were swiftly tied. Something sharp prodded his ribs to make his captor's point.

Fordon's captor spun him around and around until he was dizzy and thoroughly disoriented. He then was prodded forward but had no idea in what direction. The route consisted of so many twists and turns that Fordon knew he was hopelessly lost, and for the first time, felt very, very scared.

Chapter Forty-Eight

Meryl reluctantly left Finn and quietly slipped out of the back of his tent. Nissa was waiting there in the dark shadows with Carz.

"Follow me. Keep to the shadows," Nissa whispered. "I have moved the horses farther into the woods."

A few moments later, the two arrived at the edge of the large woods next to the encampment. Because there was very little light, they moved through the thick woods slowly and cautiously, emerging suddenly into a small meadow. Meryl's eyes had become accustomed to the dark, so she could see the outlines of the horses. When the two arrived at the horses, a woman stepped out from the deeper shadows and addressed Nissa.

"You called, clan friend?" the woman asked. "I am Seda, at your service."

Even in the dim starlight Meryl could see the shining white of the woman's hair peeking out from under her forester's cap. Just who was this Nissa, who was called a clan friend by someone who was obviously an elder of one of the forester clans, Meryl wondered.

"This is Meryl, who needs to get to the capital as quickly and as safely as possible. She carries one of the parts of the oppgave ringe. I believe she is also Neebing blessed. We suspect that those we would not wish to have the knowledge of what she carries now do, or will soon. There could be much danger ahead for you and her."

Nissa had barely finished speaking when a whisper of wings sounded in the clearing. Meryl did not know what caused her to extend her arm, but she did. Tashi landed on it, walked up to her shoulder, and settled in. Meryl could feel the slight prick of Tashi's talons through her shirt.

"Ah, so that's the way the wind blows," remarked Seda, showing little or no surprise that Meryl was now standing facing her with a griff falcon perched on her shoulder. "Neebing blessed indeed." Turning to address Nissa once again, Seda asked if the horses were hers.

"No, and turning them loose somewhere away from here would be a good idea. They are what you might call 'borrowed due to necessity'."

Meryl did not see Seda do anything to signal anyone, but suddenly a shadow detached itself from the surroundings. Another forester stepped forward, nodded to Seda, and led the horses off.

"I need to get back before it is noticed that Carz and I have been gone longer than it should take just to check on the horses. Also, I intend to head out shortly and need to pack up. Meryl, know that the foresters have no love for the Regent and his followers. You can trust Seda and her clan to get you safely to the capital. I will get a coded message to Master Rollag at the Glassmakers Guild to expect several visitors, and he will know what to do when you arrive. Take care, Meryl, and we will see you in the capital."

Meryl was beginning to feel like a hot tuber being passed from hand to hand just after it has been taken out of the glowing coals of a cook fire. She had no time to think about it, however, because Seda had told her to follow and was quickly disappearing down a narrow animal path that was hardly distinguishable in the dim starlight. It was either stand there and lose sight of her or follow. Meryl set off and followed.

⁓⁓⁓

After walking what seemed like an hour or two, but was probably more like half an hour, Fordon was halted and told to stand still. He did as he was told. He could hear what sounded like a heavy door being opened, and then he was pushed from behind. He stumbled forward and then was brought up short. He heard a scraping sound from behind him, something hard hit the back of his legs, and he sat down abruptly. He felt the tug on the ropes that bound him, his arms were freed for a few seconds when they were grabbed, placed on the armrest of the chair, and quickly bound again. Once he was secure, the hood was removed.

Fordon found himself in a small, dimly lit, musty-smelling chamber. He was sitting in a chair that faced a large table. Someone sat in the shadows behind the table. Fordon could not make out whether it was a man or a woman, for the one behind the table was wearing a cloak with the hood up. Fordon was also aware of movement behind him and knew there was at least one other folk in the room.

"I will give you a chance to tell me in a few brief sentences just why I should not think you are a spy sent by that sham of a ruling council to worm your way into my organization. If you are successful in convincing me, I may yet let you live."

Fordon could feel sweat beading up on his upper lip and a trickle of it running down his spine. What had seemed like a grand idea that would bring him fame and fortune did not feel so grand at this moment. He had not thought things through. If he told this folk in front of him what he knew, there was nothing to prevent an order to be given for him to be quickly and quietly disposed of. It struck Fordon at that moment that if he were dead, there would be no one to even mourn his passing. How had he come to this sorry state?

"Well?" the cloaked figure asked impatiently.

"I'm not a spy. I couldn't give anyone any information as to where I am, or who you are, and I wouldn't. I was told you might be interested in some information I have."

"Go on, I'm listening, and you're not dead yet."

"I have some information concerning a p-p-piece of the oppgave ringe, but I, I need some guarantees," Fordon stammered.

"Guarantees, you say. Not a huge purse filled with gold coins?"

"Well, there is the matter of payment, yes," Fordon stated, beginning to feel more confident. "After I tell you what I know, you will be happy to pay me plenty of coin. What I know is worth it."

"And just what is to prevent me from just beating the information out of you?"

Fordon gulped down his growing fear and stammered, "I, I, I have let others know that I was going to seek a meeting with your group and that I have valuable information. If word gets back to them that you reward loyalty to the Regent with betrayal, then who will trust your group? And who is to say you're the one I should be giving my important information to? I want to talk to someone who has the authority to give me what I want, and who has the resources to use what I tell him or her." Fordon had decided that bluster might get him further than just sitting there like a victim.

"Watch him," the cloaked figure snapped, stood, and with the swirl of cloak exited the room through an archway that Fordon had not noticed before.

Time passed slowly. Fordon grew more and more uncomfortable. He could hear the one behind him breathing, and somewhere nearby he could hear the drip, drip, drip of water. The longer he sat, the more chilled he became, and the more worried. Had he overplayed his hand? His thoughts had begun to go in circles when he was pulled abruptly out of his thoughts with the return of the cloaked figure. The cloaked figure was accompanied by another cloaked figure, a very tall and imposing figure, who took the seat behind the table.

"So, what is it you have to tell me, young man?" This cloaked figure was definitely a man and had a deep commanding voice.

Maybe I would have been better off negotiating with the first one, Fordon thought to himself. Knowing that looking nervous or weak would not help his cause, he said, "I have some information that I am willing to sell concerning the location of a piece of the oppgave ringe, but I need some guarantees first."

"And what might those be?"

"That once I have given you the information I receive my payment right away and am allowed to leave here unharmed. I need your promise on that, on your honor."

"That seems reasonable. You have my promise, on my honor, that you will receive your payment right away and will leave here unharmed. Anything else?"

"Yes. Once you have taken possession of the one who has the piece of the oppgave ringe, you let me know where that one is, so I might extract my own personal revenge. That folk has caused me a great deal of trouble."

"Is that it?"

"That should be it," stated Fordon. He was beginning to feel a whole lot better about this negotiation. The new fellow seemed quite accommodating and reasonable.

"Then the only thing left is to come to an agreement on the worth of your information. Remember, if your information proves to be false, there will be nowhere in Sommerhjem that you can go that we will not find you."

Fordon's confidence slipped a little. Determinedly, he forged ahead. Fordon named a price for his information. While he had been waiting for what he hoped was someone who had the power to make deals, he had thought of what he would ask for. He put the price particularly high, thinking he would have to dicker. He was surprised when the man who seemed to be the leader agreed. Maybe he had put the price too low. Feeling even more confident now, Fordon also asked for some supplies. Since the one he had been negotiating with seemed like a reasonable man, Fordon asked if he might be untied while they waited for the one the leader had sent for the coin.

"My apologies, how thoughtless of me." The leader had Fordon untied and sent another of the folk in the room for tea and something to eat. "Gathering up the amount of coin you asked for in addition to finding the other items you wanted will take some time. I ask you to wait here while I see how the arrangements are coming."

After the leader left, refreshments were brought in, and Fordon discovered how very hungry he was. At this point he did not know if he was eating a breakfast or an evening meal. No one had thought to turn up the light, and the room held no windows. More time passed, and finally several folk entered the room, including the tall leader.

The leader placed a heavy satchel on the table and set a tall lit candle next to it. The leader had been careful to stay well out of the light. He then invited Fordon to check out the contents of the satchel. Fordon eagerly drew open the draw string, and the glitter of gold, silver, and copper caught the light. He plunged his hands into the satchel, and lifted some of the coins out, letting them tumble through his fingers back into the bag. There is nothing like the sound of coins on coins, he thought to himself.

"Are you satisfied?" the leader asked.

"Quite."

"Then I suggest you earn that small fortune there with your information."

"My step-cousin Meryl took off with the hard-earned coin from our family business awhile back. My uncle sent me after her." Fordon felt he should stick to the story he had concocted for his uncle. It was partially true at any rate. "When I finally caught up to her, I overheard her speaking with a rover named Shueller about this ring she had found. He said that he did not think even the most dangerous of those loyal to the Regent, if they knew of the ring, would think twice about trying to get at Meryl amid a determined group of rovers. Now what ring do you think the Regent's followers would want, and what ring do you think the rovers would risk their lives protecting? Certainly not a ring whose only worth would be a large and valuable gemstone. No, the ring or rings in which the Regent is interested are those still missing pieces of the oppgave ringe. I am convinced that my step-cousin possesses one of these pieces."

"She was with the rover Shueller you say?" asked the leader.

"Yes. Shueller and another rover named Tannar and a man called Finn. Funny little man. I never did figure out quite what his story was, but it seems that Meryl hooked up with him after she ran off."

"Where are they now?"

"All I know is that they are heading towards the capital." Fordon went on to state where he had last seen them and what roads he suspected they might be traveling on. He described Shueller, Tannar, Finn, and Meryl. He described Shueller's homewagon and the horses Meryl had stolen from him. He told them about Finn's donkey. He did not tell them about Olwydd. "I figured with your resources, you could find them before they entered the capital, and a few rovers wouldn't stop a number of armed and determined men."

"You are right about that. Now then, your information seems worth the fee you have charged. If you will follow my man here, he will escort you out."

"You made an honor oath that I would not be harmed."

"As you can see, I kept the first part of our bargain by meeting your price, and I promise you will be neither harmed nor robbed. To keep our secrets, we need to put the hood over your head once again. Please grab hold of your satchel."

Fordon hefted the heavy satchel, looping the strap over his head, and settling it on his shoulder. The hood was placed over his head. He was spun around and around once again and then told to begin to move forward. The journey out was much like the journey in. Finally, his guide brought him to a halt, and Fordon could hear the creak of metal hinges as a door swung open. A slight push on his back sent him over the threshold, and he heard the door clang behind him. He was told he could remove his hood, and when he did so, he realized he was not outside but in a small barred cell. Still in shadow was the tall leader he had given the information to.

"You promised on your honor you would give me my coin and not harm me."

"And I have kept my promise. You have your satchel of coin and you have not been harmed. When you make bargains, you need to be more careful what you ask for. Fear not, you will be treated well. The clothes and most of the supplies you asked for are on your bunk. You should be quite comfortable here. It will give you time to think about your choice of friends. The one who directed you to me will sell any information wherever he thinks he will get the highest price." With that said, the tall man turned and walked away after assigning a guard. "Come, there is much to be done now, and finding Shueller and this Meryl is top priority."

CHAPTER FORTY-NINE

Meryl was very thankful when the sky began to lighten, and she could begin to avoid pieces of forest left out by mistake, as she had begun to think of the roots and downed tree limbs she had been tripping over most of the night. Seda did not seem to have that problem, or perhaps she was just a very quiet stumbler.

"Why don't you take a seat on that log over there?" Seda suggested when they stopped, pointing to the remains of a downed tree just off the narrow path they were standing on. "We will most likely have a wait."

That was fine by Meryl, for she was tired, having been up since early the day before. She sat herself down on a log wedged against a tree, leaned back, and was immediately asleep. Tashi settled herself on an overhanging branch.

The sound of quiet voices woke her later. As she opened her eyes, Meryl saw by the sun's position that it was near midmorning. Seda had been joined by at least four other foresters, and she could hear the sounds of horses behind her.

"Ah, good, you're awake. Come join us," Seda said.

Meryl stood up, brushed tree bark and moss off her pants, and walked over to join the group. Seda introduced Meryl to four other foresters and told her that there were two more holding the horses. The group gathered was a mixed one, including both men and women and covering a wide range of ages.

"As you know, with age comes some authority sometimes, and in my instance, I am an elder of our clan. The interim ruling council has been requesting that the forester clans send representatives to talk with them to make sure all is well with the forests we live in and monitor, and to make sure we are now fairly content. You may or may not know that under the Regent's rule forester clans were essentially ripped from their home forests and scattered across the land. That was very hard on us, and there is a great deal of resentment still festering because of his actions. The interim ruling council has allowed us to return to our homes, and that has gone a long way towards bringing peace back to the forested lands."

"I remember hearing something about that, and I was as surprised as were many others, that you and yours had been harmed in such a way. We common folk were so unaware of what the Regent was doing. So many folk were just trying to stay one step ahead of the increasing taxes and more demanding rules that they did not have much time to worry about what was happening to others."

"The Regent has a lot to answer for, that's for sure. Now then, here is what I propose. We are about a two to four day ride from the capital, depending on the weather and the conditions of the roads. Folks along the way are used to the comings and goings of delegations heading to and from the capital. You are about to become a forester. Since you are a youngster and traveling with a woman of great age and importance, not to mention wisdom," Seda said with a wink, "few should pay you any mind. After all, if Fordon has made a connection with those who follow the Regent still, they are going to be looking for you to be traveling with Finn at the very least and very likely with Finn, Shueller, and Tannar. Those three will be well-protected by the other rovers, fear not. Even if the Regent's followers get close to your friends, it is going to be obvious that you are not with them. They are, then, going to be looking for a lone female entering the capital gates. I imagine they will have the resources to watch all the gates and then try to get a hold of you once you enter the capital."

"What is to prevent them from recognizing me while I travel with you folk?"

"Folks tend to believe what they see. When we enter the capital, they will see a delegation of foresters. We have clothes like ours that you can change into. In addition, you can tuck your hair up under a forester's cap, which will add to your disguise. It is only while we are on the road that I see any real danger. That would come from someone recognizing you, since I understand you have traveled a great deal. Once we enter the capital, we will head right to the Glassmakers Guildhall and connect back up with your friends and Master Rollag. He has been alerted, and I am sure he will have things in place to get you safely to the Well of Speaking."

Seda handed Meryl a change of clothes, saying she hoped they would fit. She had had to guess as to Meryl's sizes. Meryl ducked behind a thick bush to change. The clothes fit fairly well, as did the boots. She took a few tentative steps in the boots and quickly came to the conclusion that she would not want to give them back, for they were certainly more comfortable than those she had been wearing. Once changed, Meryl rejoined the group, and they mounted up. She had been given one of the horses favored by the foresters to ride. They were not the tall horses or swift, but they were very agile and surefooted, well able to travel the deer and animal paths that crisscrossed the forests. Seda had informed Meryl that they would be traveling the royal road only for part of the journey. Otherwise they would stick to the lesser known lanes, paths, and trails.

After about an hour's ride, rain began to fall and visibility was reduced due to the heavy fog that had risen in the valley Meryl and the foresters were traveling in. Meryl was thankful for the rain cloak she was wearing. It had kept most of the heavy downpour off of her, but she could feel a cold runnel of water trickling down her back. This was the type of rain that, under normal circumstances, she would have pulled off the road and tried to find shelter. Seda felt they needed to press on.

Time and distance blurred as the group continued on through the rain and fog. Even the surefooted horses they rode were having trouble maintaining their footing on the slippery pine needle covered path they were following. Tashi, keeping under the canopy of the trees, was staying dryer than those on horseback. Finally they broke through onto a main road, and while the rain did not let up, at least the road was easier to travel. Seda called a halt after about half an hour of travel on the better road.

"We are going to lose what little light we have soon and need to seek shelter for the night. If I remember right, there is an inn about another hour down this road. Hopefully we can find shelter and warm food there."

With everyone in agreement that the inn was their best choice, the group set off again. Meryl thought she had never seen anything so beautiful as the glow of lamplight coming from the windows of the inn. Other travelers had had the same idea, and the inn was quite full. All of the rooms were taken but one. Seda claimed it for her own, along with Meryl and the two other female foresters. The male foresters were going to grab a night's sleep in the stable hayloft. It would be warm and dry.

The crowded inn's main room was packed with folk trying to get warm and eat a warm meal. Seda's group grabbed a table in the far back corner. Sitting jammed together created more heat in a room that was already overheated due to the number of folks crowded inside. Meryl thought if it got any hotter, she would be able to see steam rising from her damp clothes.

The harried serving lass arrived at their table and set down bowls of soup and spoons. "I'll be right back with bread and cheese. That and soup is what Cook be serving this night, due to the large crowd."

True to her word, the serving lass was back with the rest of their food quickly. It might not have been the best soup Meryl had ever tasted, but it warmed her insides and was filling.

The night was as uneventful as it was noisy. The walls of the inn were thin, and Meryl lay awake late into the night listening to a cacophony of snores and mutterings jumbled in with the howl of the wind and the slash of rain on the windows. When she finally did fall asleep, it was a troubled one, filled with frightening dreams of being chased by hooded men in dark cloaks. She did not feel very refreshed in the morning.

A fine drizzle was falling when Meryl's group left the inn, but the fog had dissipated. By mid-afternoon they had reached the royal road and travel became easier. No one paid them any attention, even as they drew closer to the capital, and the road became more crowded. Tashi no longer traveled with them, but Meryl had the feeling that she was always close by.

In the late afternoon of the next day, they came within sight of the capital gates. Meryl thought that when she saw the capital, where she had been born and grown up, she would feel a sense of homecoming, but strangely she did not. Meryl realized that she really had had no sense of home since her mother had died. She wondered what kind of welcome she would find when she finally did go home. Would her stepfather and stepbrothers believe her tale of what had happened, or had Fordon convinced them that she was to blame for not returning sooner?

For all the fret and worry about getting her to the capital safely, arriving there unharmed and unnoticed was somewhat anticlimactic. The group traveled unimpeded through the streets of the capital and entered the gate to the fairground without incident. As they pulled up to the Glassmakers Guildhall, a very tall man of impressive size came out of the guildhall to greet them.

"Welcome to the Glassmakers Guildhall. I am Master Rollag, and I presume you are the group of foresters Nissa sent the message about. Won't you come in? Journeyman Evan will make sure your horses are well looked after, if that's alright with you. There's plenty of room here for all of you to stay."

"We would welcome your journeyman's kind attention to our horses, but we will not be staying, thank you anyway. Once we have had a chance to make sure Meryl is safely in your hands and to plan with you what is to happen next, we will go on to the royal woods and visit with friends and relatives," Seda answered back.

"Well enough," Master Rollag said, as he motioned them to enter the guildhall.

Meryl was torn concerning the foresters leaving. She also wondered if her friends had arrived or were expected. "Pardon me, Master Rollag, but have my friends Finn, Shueller, and Tannar arrived? A rover named Nissa said they were to come here."

"I'm sorry, lass, no one has arrived this day besides you. We have been expecting your friends, but so far they have not shown up. In addition, we have not seen or heard from Nissa since the first messenger bird arrived. I'm a bit concerned. I'm thankful you have arrived safely, but let's not stand in the entry hall. Please follow me."

Master Rollag led the group down several corridors, up a flight of stairs, and finally motioned that they should enter a room that was filled with a long table surrounded by comfortable chairs. The walls were covered with maps, some overlapping others, some large, and some small. A few were just outlines, and others held incredible detail. At any other time, Meryl would have found herself fascinated by them, but this day she just found herself very weary and afraid for her friends.

❧

Finn was feeling fortunate that Heber seemed content to be hitched to the back end of Shueller's homewagon and was not being stubborn about following along. He had thought of Meryl often during the day and hoped she was alright. Upon reflection of the past few weeks, Finn realized he had grown quite fond of the lass and would be sad to see their partnership end. Finn had hoped that Meryl might want to continue traveling with him and become a finder to carry on his business. He had little hope of that now that she had discovered who she was. After all, she had a family and a family business to return to.

Traveling was fairly easy over the next few days. Finn was especially grateful for Shueller's homewagon when the rain began to fall. Fortunately, they had begun to travel on the royal road, which was paved, so they

316

were not slogging through mud, puddles, and bouncing over deep ruts. It was near noon when they saw a large group of riders traveling rapidly towards them. The large group came to a stop and surrounded the rover homewagons. It was hard to distinguish just who had chanced upon them due to the rain, the rising fog, and their cloak hoods being pulled up. One of the riders detached from the group and rode up to Shueller's homewagon.

"I'm looking for a lass named Meryl, a fellow named Finn, and a donkey named Heber, I believe. They were last known to be traveling with a group of rovers heading for the capital. You are a group of rovers, and I can see you have a donkey tied to this homewagon, so logically you must be the group we are looking for. Now, where is the lass Meryl?" asked the rider who seemed to be in charge.

Chapter Fifty

"You want to know where that lass Meryl is do you, do you? Well so do I, why yes indeed, so do I," sputtered Finn, his face growing red. "That lass you're looking so hard for isn't here, no not here. She left, just up and left, and after all that I've done for her, all I've done for her. You're welcome to her, just welcome to her if you can find her, the ungrateful, unappreciative, no good, weasely, stealer of all my secrets. Oh my yes, you're welcome to her, that, that . . . ."

"Steady on, Finn," suggested Shueller. "It was a fine performance to be sure, and worthy of a round of applause, but there is no need. I know this woman. Hardly recognized you out of uniform, Captain. I take it Lady Esmeralda sent you."

"She did indeed. Nice to see you again, Shueller," said the captain of the royal guard. Turning to face Finn she said, "I take it you are Finn. Now that we have established that I am a friend and not a foe, could you tell me where Meryl might be, or has she really run off with your disapproval winging out behind her?"

"Oh no, Captain, oh my, no. The lass Meryl is a fine lass, a very fine lass. Didn't mean a word of what I said about her, not a word," Finn said, looking horrified that the captain would think badly of Meryl.

Shueller came to the rescue and explained to the captain that they had been prepared to be confronted by folk who were not on the side of the interim ruling council.

"So, now that we have established that I am not on the side of those with evil intent, perhaps you could introduce me to Meryl," quipped the captain.

"That will be a little difficult, Captain, for she's not with us," stated Shueller. "And just out of curiosity, how did you know about us? I know Nissa sent a messenger bird off to Master Rollag, but it only said to expect

Tannar and me, plus a few more guests. I know she didn't name Meryl or Finn specifically."

"Ah, therein lies a tale of intrigue and mystery, and here is not the place to discuss it. We were sent to escort you and your guests back to the capital and make sure no harm befalls you. If the lass, Meryl, is not with you, is she safe?"

"We sincerely hope she's safe and closer to the capital than we are," commented Shueller.

"Then we will continue to be a diversion, shall we? I'm sure there are folks who are watching our movements even if we aren't traveling in uniform. We also can't discount that the Regent probably has spies among us who have reported that the head of the royal guard left with a patrol. When we head back escorting a group of rovers, they will suspect something is up. That's what we will want them to think."

Now that Finn, Shueller, and Tannar had a royal guard escort, those rover families who accompanied them at Shueller's request needed to decide if they would continue on to the capital. They had disrupted their routes and routines because Shueller had asked. They had not asked why, nor did they know why they had been needed. Shueller had not shared the information about Meryl having part of the oppgave ringe. Now that things had changed, a discussion was held among the rover families, and most of them decided to head off to where they had previously planned to go after the encampment was over. Bertram and his family chose to continue on with Shueller's group, since they had intended to meet up with Oscar's homewagon at the capital anyway.

It was full dark by the time the rover homewagons with their royal guard escort arrived at the gates of the capital. A heavy fog had rolled in from the sea, making it difficult to see more than a wagon's length ahead. The eerie glow of lamplight broke the unrelenting gray of the fog at regular intervals. The main thoroughfare across the capital was wide enough that the royal guards could ride on both sides of the homewagons. With the captain at the lead, the group moved without incident at a steady pace across the capital, until they finally reached the main entrance to the fairgrounds where the major guildhalls were located.

As they pulled up to the Glassmakers Guildhall, a journeyman, who was greeted by the captain as Journeyman Evan, directed the rovers to pull their homewagons behind the guildhall. Once the homewagons were parked and leveled, Journeyman Evan offered to take care of the horses, so the travelers could go inside sooner and get out of the damp. The rovers and Finn took him up on his offer, and they followed the captain into the guildhall where they were met by Master Rollag.

"Welcome. There is a lass named Meryl who will be very relieved that you have arrived. Seems she has a fondness for some donkey named Heber and was really worried about him," Master Rollag stated with good humor. "Please follow me." Turning to Finn, Master Rollag said, "It's been a long time since our paths have crossed. Good to see you again."

Master Rollag led the group down a corridor and then up a flight of stairs to a room filled with a large table surrounded by well-upholstered chairs. Curled up in one of the chairs fast asleep was Meryl and perched in the window was Tashi.

"Almost hate to wake her, but we had best sit down, do some introductions, and do some planning so all of us can get some sleep yet this night. Captain, can I prevail upon you to send runners to the others and let them know Shueller and his party have arrived?" asked Master Rollag.

The captain nodded and swiftly left the room, pausing briefly just inside the doorway to let Journeyman Evan enter before she exited. While she was gone, Master Rollag gently woke Meryl, who found herself feeling much refreshed after her nap and very relieved that Finn, Shueller, Tannar, and Bertram with his family had made it safely to the capital. Bertram had left his family with his wife at their homewagon. He, however, had come along to see for himself that Meryl was alright. An hour passed during which the group gathered had a chance to catch up. Soon others began to arrive.

"It would seem we are all here," stated Master Rollag. "I think introductions are in order."

Master Rollag then proceeded to introduce Lady Esmeralda, Lady Celik, Master Clarisse, and several others who were on the interim ruling council to Meryl, Tashi, Finn, and the rovers. Just as Master Rollag was about to close the door, Nissa slipped in accompanied by Carz, apologizing for being late. Once they were settled, Master Rollag turned the discussion over to Lady Esmeralda. No one seemed surprised that a hunting cat and a griff falcon were attending the meeting.

"On behalf of the interim ruling council, I am most happy to assemble this group to discuss what needs to happen next concerning the great news that another piece of the oppgave ringe has arrived safely. The first three pieces did not seem to make easy journeys here. Was this one any exception?" asked Lady Esmeralda.

Meryl was too tongue-tied to answer the question. Even though Tashi had moved and perched on the back of Meryl's chair giving Meryl a feeling of safety, she was having difficulty trying to convince herself that she was not still asleep and dreaming. She was in a room with some of the most well-known and powerful folk in Sommerhjem, including the woman who had once been destined to be the next queen. Desperately she looked to Finn and Shueller for help.

"Would you like me to summarize the tale of this piece of the oppgave ringe for you, Meryl?" Shueller asked.

Meryl nodded her head yes.

"The correct answer would be yes and no," Shueller continued. "Meryl's journey here held much adventure and danger, but in the beginning that was not connected to the piece of the oppgave ringe. Finn, perhaps you could give a short version of what happened to Meryl, and then to the two of you, before we hooked up."

Finn gave a brief summary, with an amazingly small number of repeats for him, concerning his finding Meryl and her finding the ring. He brought the group up to when they had met Shueller and Tannar.

Shueller then took over the tale. He told of meeting up with Meryl and Finn at Gatekryss crossroads and his suspicion about her having one of the pieces of the oppgave ringe. He told of Meryl being kidnapped and her subsequent escape, of rescuing Olwydd, and of Fordon's continuing involvement in causing Meryl injury and trouble. He told them of meeting up with the other rovers at the encampment and of their help in getting him, Tannar, and Finn safely to the capital.

"You will be happy to know that the man Olwydd has been safely delivered to Lord Hadrack, and we have sent a patrol of royal guards to escort him back to the capital to answer for crimes against the Crown. My information is he is so frightened of what might happen to him that he is singing sweeter than a teakettle on a freezing winter's night," the woman who had been introduced as Lady Celik said. Turning to Meryl, she gently suggested that Meryl was the only one who could tell of her journey with the foresters, since their representative had been delayed.

After hearing others tell of what had happened to her, Meryl decided she was being downright silly being tongue-tied, so she sat up straighter and told of her unimpeded journey with the foresters to the capital.

When Meryl was through speaking, Shueller spoke up. "I do have one question that has remained unanswered through this whole recitation. How did the captain here know to look for Meryl, Finn, Tannar, and me?"

"It was a matter of not having any honor among would be thieves," answered Lady Celik. "Meryl's step-cousin trusted the wrong folk. The man Fordon trusted sold Fordon out to the highest bidder, who happened to be one of our agents and not one of the Regent's. So the information about you and your traveling companions came to my ears, and that set everything else in motion. Fordon protested his incarceration for several days, wanting us to believe he was an innocent dupe of others. That tune changed when he was given word that Olwydd was not dead. Charges of attempted murder, kidnapping, and treason are making his future look a bit dim."

"Does my step-father know anything at all? You know, about Fordon or me?" asked Meryl.

"Your family has not been informed as to Fordon's capture or misdeeds or your whereabouts," answered Lady Celik. "Would you like me to send word to your step-father?"

Meryl really had to stop and think about the question Lady Celik had posed. "No, not this night. After I have put the ring where it belongs will be soon enough to meet with my family. I need to do some serious thinking about what I want to do next with my life."

During the next hour, a very simple plan was put in place as to what would happen late the following morning. It had been determined that Meryl was certainly safe in the guildhall, especially since it was now guarded by the royal guard. A later morning hour was chosen to leave for the Well of Speaking, so the weary travelers could get some sleep and have time in the morning for a long hot soak in the guildhall's bathhouse.

"The late morning hour will give us some time to get you a fresh change of clothes," the woman who had been introduced as Master Clarisse had stated.

Meryl, for one, was thankful that someone had thought about that, since what little she had left in clothing was really the worse for wear. Meryl noticed that Nissa drew Shueller and Master Clarisse aside when the gathering broke up, but she was too tired to pay much mind to what they were talking about. In the morning, when she had awakened, she then understood what that discussion had been about. Laid out for her on the chair, in the room she had been assigned, was a beautiful outfit. Meryl noted that the sleeves and shoulders of the over jacket were of a sturdy leather. It took her a moment to figure out why the jacket had leather on it. Tashi, of course. Her boots, which she had been given by the foresters, had been cleaned. Now that she had had some sleep and was feeling sharper, it occurred to her that she had not seen Tashi since the night before. Meryl wondered where she had spent the night.

Chapter Fifty-One

"Are you ready my dear?" Master Rollag asked kindly.

Meryl nodded, for she was worried her voice would crack if she tried to speak. She stood in the main entrance hall of the Glassmakers Guildhall, surrounded by a group of folks all dressed in their finest clothing. A number of members of the interim ruling council were there, along with Lady Esmeralda. Heads of a number of guildhalls were also present. There were rovers and foresters, and Meryl knew other folk waited outside. Most importantly, her friend Finn stood beside her, and Shueller and Tannar flanked the two of them.

Nissa had taken the time that morning to draw Meryl aside for a walk in the guildhall gardens under the watchful eye of the royal guard.

"I know if you are anything like me, you would have preferred to slip out last night and place the ring in the vessteboks, the box that is secured in the wall at the Well of Speaking. Bunch of fuss and bother, not to mention downright intimidating, to have all these important folk watching your every move," Nissa had said.

She had been right about that, Meryl thought to herself. All these folks were looking at her. She just hoped she had not spilled any of her morning porridge down the front of her new clothes. She worried she would do something foolish or stupid. She just worried. Nissa had tried to lessen her worries by telling her what had happened to her and a lad named Greer, both of whom had placed the rings they carried in the vessteboks. That had helped some, but now it was time for her to begin the walk to the Well of Speaking. When Master Rollag signaled that they should head out, Finn gave her hand a little squeeze for support.

When the procession arrived at the entrance to the Well of Speaking, Meryl almost turned around to go anywhere but there. She had not been prepared for the number of folks who were crowded into every seat and space from the top of the amphitheater down to its bottom at the seawall.

"Steady on, lass," Shueller told Meryl. "Just take my arm and Finn's, and we'll make sure you don't tumble down those stairs."

Much as Meryl would have liked to have taken Shueller up on his offer, she somehow got the feeling that this was a journey she needed to make on her own. She looked at Finn and Shueller and thanked them for their support but told them that she was alright. Straightening her shoulders, Meryl stepped forward and started down the steps. She had only taken about ten steps when a collective gasp came from the gathered crowd. Meryl almost faltered, but a sense of great peace and calm came over her. Wondering what had caused the crowd to gasp, Meryl took a quick look up from the steps she had been negotiating to see Tashi circling the Well of Speaking.

As Meryl continued down the steps, she could catch snatches of the conversations that were swirling around her.

"Do you see that? It's a griff falcon."

"Can't be. Trick of the sun off the water."

"What can it mean?"

"Unheard of . . . ."

"What would cause a griff falcon to fly so close to this many folks?"

"So rare. Almost never see one in a lifetime . . . ."

Feeling a steadying hand on her arm when she stumbled on the next step, Meryl tore her eyes away from the sight of Tashi circling overhead, the sunlight shining off her golden feathers and making the red feathers glint like fire. Continuing down the long flight of steps, Meryl kept thinking to herself that all was well again now that Tashi was near.

When she reached the bottom of the steps, the royal guard parted, and Meryl slowly made her way towards the seawall. Set into the wall was a small box, gleaming of gold and decorated with cut gems on the lid. Nissa had told Meryl that she just needed to open the lid and place the ring inside. Nissa had also told Meryl that normally Master Clarisse would have been there to explain everything, but she had been called away on a family emergency late the night before. Nissa did mention that she could not tell Meryl what exactly would happen once the ring had been placed, for it had been a little different for each of the ring bearers.

Meryl could have been the only one in the Well of Speaking, it had become so quiet. All conversation had ended, and all that Meryl could hear was the crash of the waves below the wall and the sound of the wind. Even the noisy sea birds had stopped their raucous calling. Meryl stepped forward and lifted the lid of the beautiful golden box. Reaching beneath her shirt, she drew out the golden pine spider silk pouch, opened it, and tipped the ring into her hand. She felt a comforting warmth flow from the ring and fill her. With gentle care, she placed the ring in the vessteboks.

Nothing happened for a moment, and then a spiral of light filled with ribbons of color shot upward from the box. As the spiral of light reached higher and higher, it began to expand outward, and the ribbons of color began to separate from each other. Tashi, who had been circling the Well of Speaking flew into the spiral of light and began a slow circle down the golden ribbon until she had almost reached the golden box. She pulled up just at the last minute, flapped her wings once to gain a few feet, and settled on Meryl's arm, which Meryl had instinctively held out.

Meryl was unaware of the swirl of talk that eddied around her. She was only aware of Tashi, who moved to her shoulder and brushed her beak against Meryl's cheek in greeting. Meryl was pulled out of her reverie when Nissa suggested it was time to follow the procession up the steps. Even Meryl was surprised when rather than taking off, Tashi remained on her shoulder, even when the crowd began cheering.

It was not until several days later, once the receptions and meetings had ended, that Meryl headed off to the house that had once been her home. Finn had volunteered to accompany her, but she had declined. She felt that this was another journey she needed to take on her own. She had asked him to please be at the Glassmakers Guildhall later that day. Upon reaching the house, Meryl paused on the steps in front of the front door, not sure what waited inside. Before she could reach to open the door, it swung open, and her step-father stood in the doorway.

"So you finally decided to honor us with your presence, did you?" Meryl's step-father stated, in a voice that was less than welcoming.

"Perhaps we could get in off the street and away from the nosy eyes and ears of our neighbors before talking," Meryl suggested.

Meryl's step-father grudgingly stepped aside and allowed Meryl entrance to what had been her home and business. Her step-father directed her into the parlor, which was normally reserved for guests. Here she found her two step-brothers and Theary, the lass from across the street. Theary and her youngest step-brother were seated close together. So that is the way the wind blows, Meryl thought to herself. While she had been away,

Theary had not only been brought in to take over Meryl's chores, but it would seem that she would soon be a member of the family. Just as well, Meryl thought.

"Let me say first that I never intended to be away this long or to cause any trouble with the business," Meryl began and proceeded to tell her family what had happened since she had left home.

"Well, that's some story, and I'm left quite speechless concerning Fordon's role in all of it. So, I suppose you plan to return here and take up with the family business," her step-father said.

"Actually, no." Up until the words came out of Meryl's mouth, she really had not voiced what she was going to do. Seeing her family and Theary ranged in the chairs across from her, a solid front, Meryl knew she would never be comfortable here again.

"Are you thinking of starting up your own messenger bird business then?" her step-father inquired, and Meryl could see he would not be pleased if her answer were yes.

"No, I will leave that to all of you. I am really just here to gather my things, come to some agreement about the value of my share of the business, and move on in life."

"Well, if that's what you want," Meryl's step-father said, and Meryl could hear the relief in his voice. "I think we can see our way clear to give you a reasonable price,"

Meryl could have stayed and dickered about just what her portion of the business was worth. The amount finally agreed on was certainly less than its true value, but she was anxious to be gone. In addition to what she got from her step-father, it turned out that several of the ancient coins she had found and the silver box that had contained the piece of the oppgave ringe were declared to be of historical significance. She had been offered a nice amount for them. She would not be hurting for coin for a while.

Meryl left the home she had grown up in with nary a backward glance and walked back to the Glassmakers Guildhall. She hoped Finn had waited for her. When she arrived, she walked around back and found Shueller sitting on the steps of his homewagon. Finn was nowhere to be seen. Meryl's heart sank.

"Have you seen Finn?" Meryl asked Shueller.

"He's in the barn with Journeyman Evan. They've been having a lively discussion about whether donkeys or pack horses are best for carrying packs. Have you told him yet?"

"Told me what, told me what?" asked Finn, who had come up behind them.

Before Meryl could speak, a very small homewagon pulled by just one horse driven by Tannar, came around the corner of the guildhall. The designs on the homewagon's exterior were difficult to distinguish due to the dust, bits of straw and hay, not to mention bird droppings.

"Ah, you are right on time," commented Shueller.

"Is Tannar striking off on his own, on his own?" Finn asked Shueller. "Won't you miss him?"

Finn's assumption that because Tannar was driving a small homewagon that he was about to take off on his own and become an independent leatherworker was a reasonable one. However, in this case, it was wrong, for Tannar pulled the homewagon to a halt, jumped down, and told Meryl the homewagon rode very nicely.

"Journeyman Evan made sure that the horse was an outstanding one, without putting you in debt for the rest of your natural born days," Tannar told Meryl.

Now Finn was really confused. Had Meryl decided to become a rover, and could someone even do that? Tashi did not seem to have any questions, for she took that moment to glide down out of the nearby tree she had been perched in and land on driver's seat. Finn looked at Meryl.

"I decided that the rovers have the right of it. If one is going to be wandering all over Sommerhjem, what better way than to take your home with you? I really hate sleeping on the hard ground, especially when it's raining. Also, I needed some shelter for a cage or two of messenger birds," Meryl said. "Besides, Shueller made me a good deal on his old homewagon."

"And a hard bargain she drove too," Shueller stated.

"So, you're going to be doing some traveling, some traveling? You're going to continue in the messenger bird business, going to continue?" Finn tried not to look crestfallen, for he had hoped Meryl might want to continue on with him.

"No, messenger birds don't hold my interest the way they used to, and I think I have already been replaced."

"What are you going to do instead, do instead?" Finn asked.

"I was thinking I might just take you up on that apprenticeship, if the offer still stands."

"Be delighted, oh my yes, be most delighted," Finn exclaimed and could hardly contain himself.

"Well then, give me a few days. This was Shueller's first homewagon, and it has been in storage for a great many years. It's going to take a great deal of elbow grease to clean it up, and some persuasion to invite the spiders and other critters that have been living in it to find other homes. I'll also need to paint it a lot plainer than it was. Shueller and Tannar and the other rovers said they would help me make sure it is sound and ready to travel. They already made sure the undercarriage was solid and the wheels freshly greased. Once all is ready, then I will just need to stow my belongings, gather and pack in some supplies, and I'll be ready to be off."

"Take your time, lass, take your time," Finn replied.

Several days later, the rovers said their goodbyes and wished Meryl and Finn good hunting. Meryl was sad to see them go, for she had grown fond of them, especially Shueller. He had assured her that they would meet again. Good to her word, when all was packed and ready, Meryl climbed up onto the driver's seat of her new home. Finn had tied Heber to the back and was settled in beside her. Tashi launched herself off the roof of the homewagon and flew upward to lazily circle above them.

"Well, lass, are you ready, are you ready?" Finn asked. "No regrets, no looking back?"

No, no looking back, Meryl thought to herself. Only forward, to see what she could find in the next unlikely place.